SCHOOL
TRIP

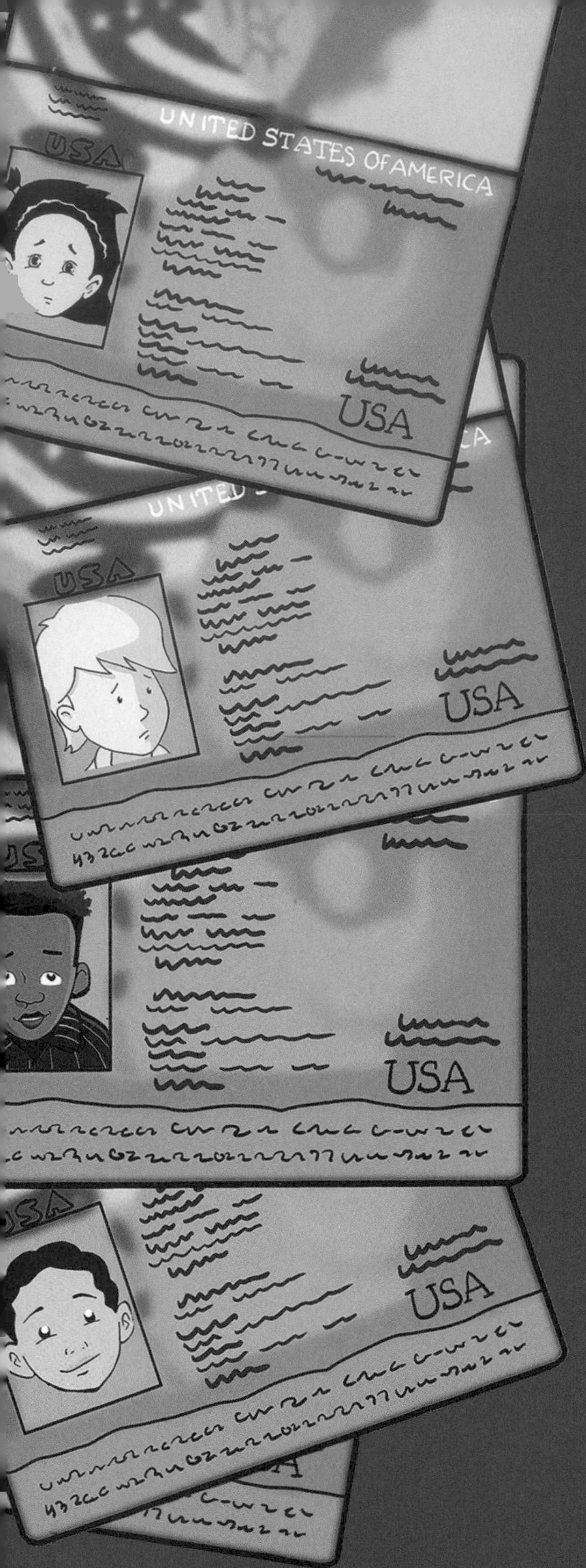
UNITED STATES OF AMERICA
USA
USA
UNITED
USA
USA
USA
USA

JERRY CRAFT

SCHOOL TRIP

Quill Tree Books
Imprints of HarperCollinsPublishers

HARPER
alley

Quill Tree Books and HarperAlley are imprints
of HarperCollins Publishers.

School Trip
Copyright © 2023 by Jerry Craft
For information address HarperCollins Children's Books,
a division of HarperCollins Publishers,
195 Broadway, New York, NY 10007.
www.harperalley.com

Library of Congress Control Number: 2022946437
ISBN 978-0-06-288553-1 (paperback) - ISBN 978-0-06-288554-8
(hardcover)

22 23 24 25 26   GPS   10 9 8 7 6 5 4 3 2 1
❖
First Edition

Don't be a thumbs-downer!

1

I Really Hope . . . But Then Again . . .

As the final chapter of my junior high school life comes to an end, there's so much that I'm hoping for . . . or *AM* I?

For example: I really hope that I get into art school. But I'd miss all my friends at RAD.

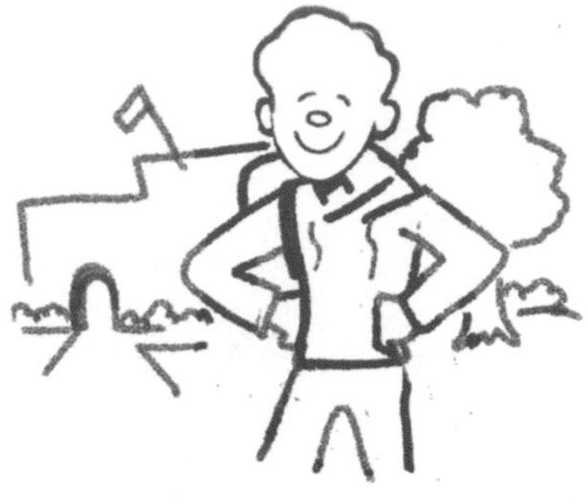

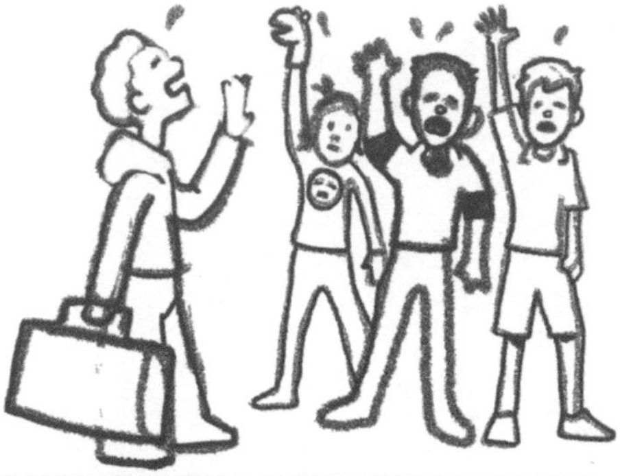

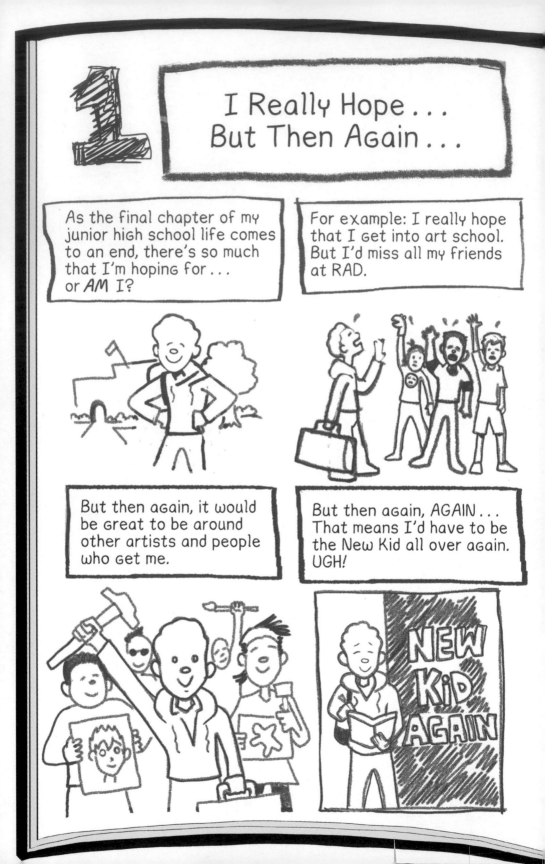

But then again, it would be great to be around other artists and people who get me.

But then again, AGAIN . . . That means I'd have to be the New Kid all over again. UGH!

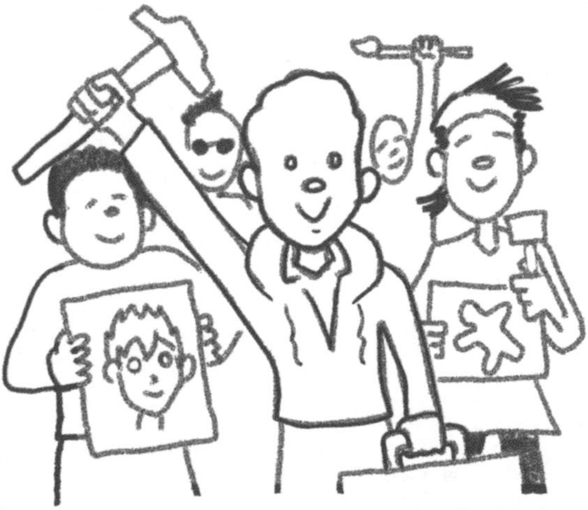

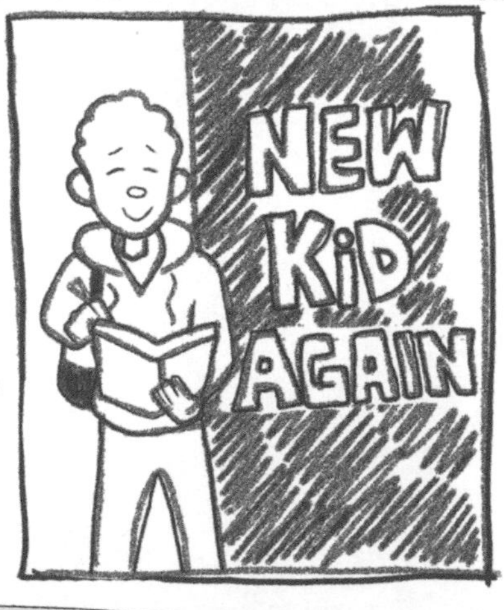
NEW
KiD
AGAIN

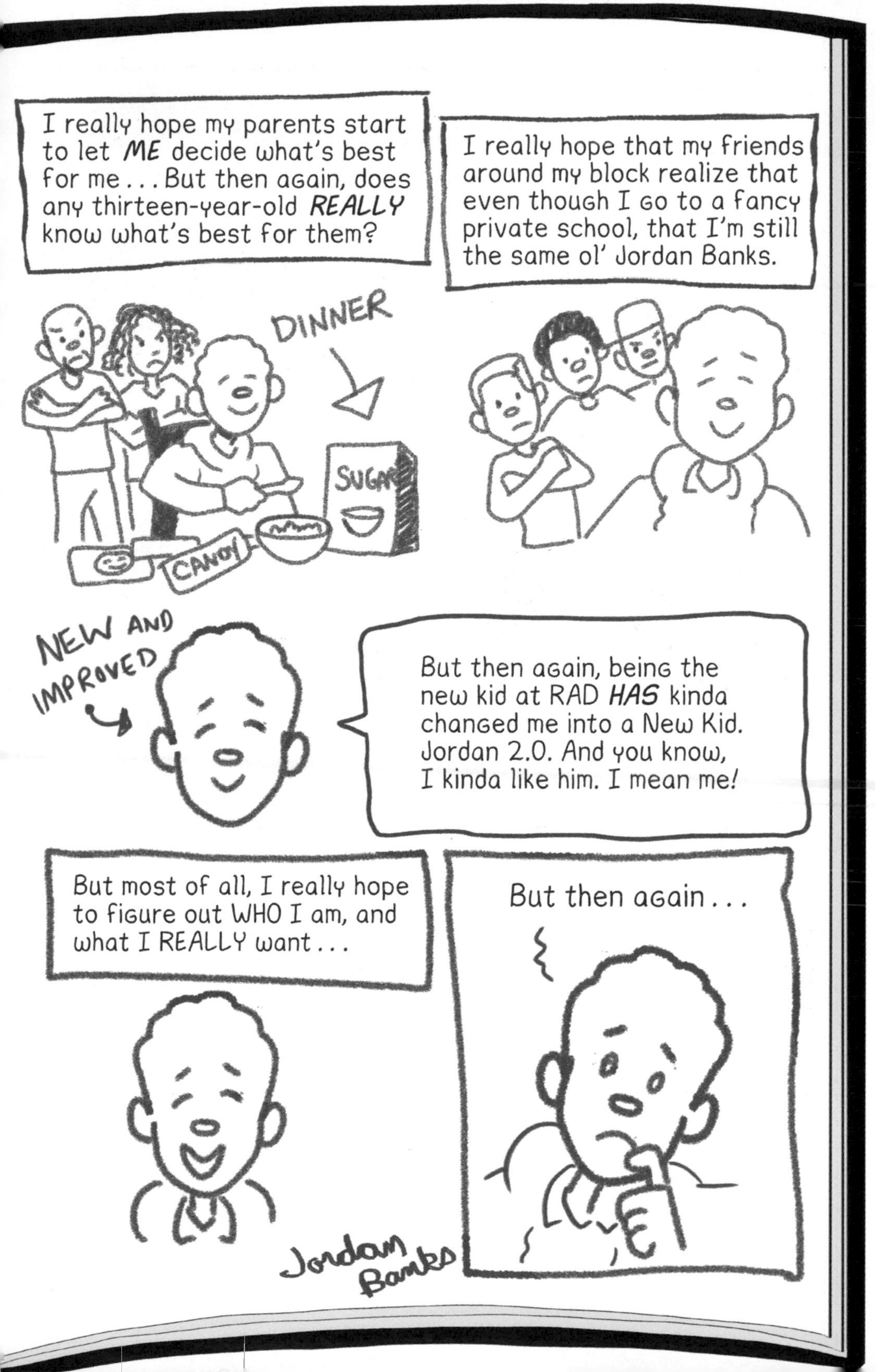
I really hope my parents start to let *ME* decide what's best for me . . . But then again, does any thirteen-year-old *REALLY* know what's best for them?
I really hope that my friends around my block realize that even though I go to a fancy private school, that I'm still the same ol' Jordan Banks.
DINNER
SUGAR
CANDY
NEW AND IMPROVED
But then again, being the new kid at RAD *HAS* kinda changed me into a New Kid. Jordan 2.0. And you know, I kinda like him. I mean me!
But most of all, I really hope to figure out WHO I am, and what I REALLY want . . .
But then again . . .
Jordan Banks

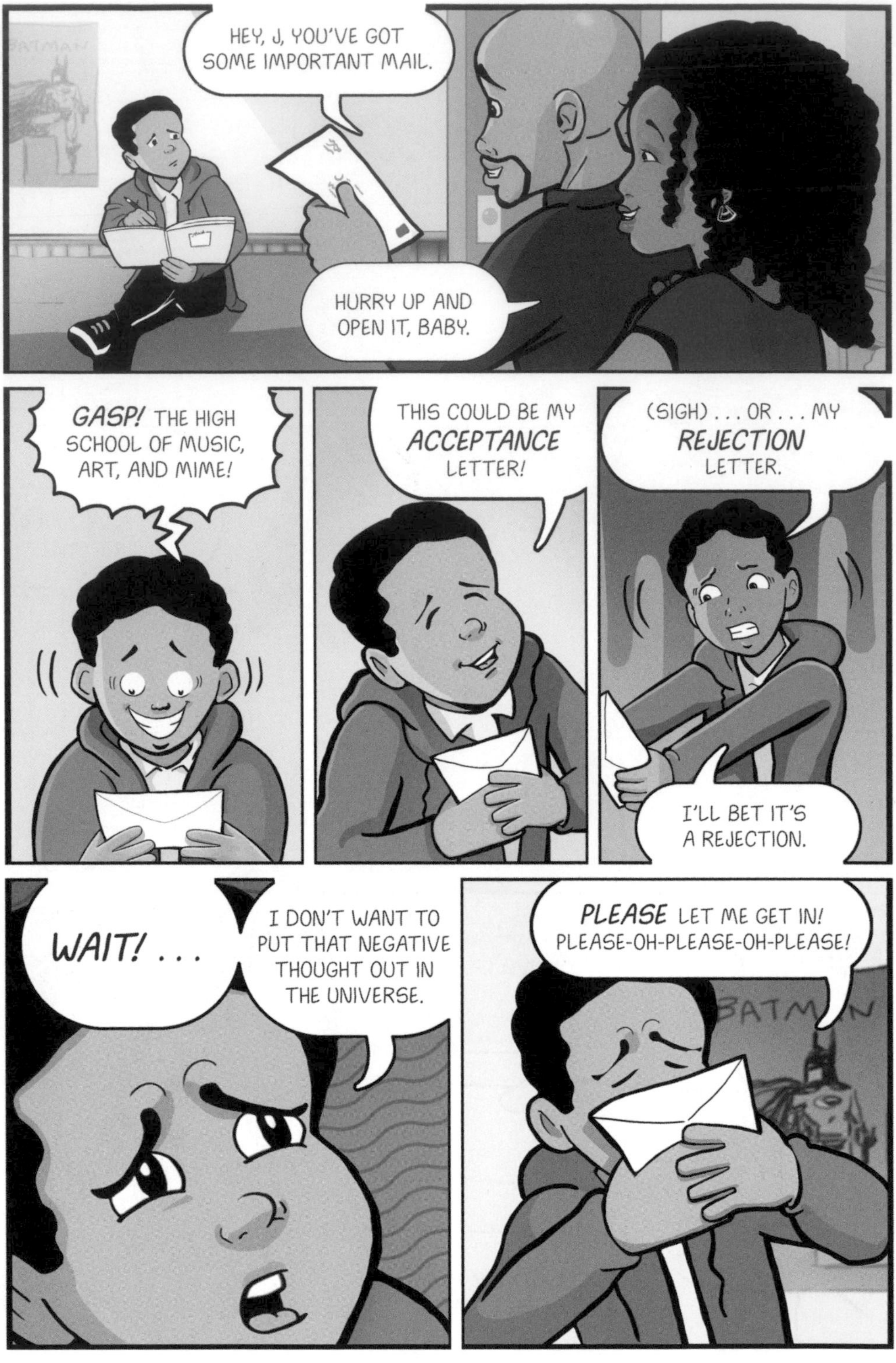
HEY, J, YOU'VE GOT SOME IMPORTANT MAIL.
HURRY UP AND OPEN IT, BABY.
GASP! THE HIGH SCHOOL OF MUSIC, ART, AND MIME!
THIS COULD BE MY *ACCEPTANCE* LETTER!
(SIGH) . . . OR . . . MY *REJECTION* LETTER.
I'LL BET IT'S A REJECTION.
WAIT! . . .
I DON'T WANT TO PUT THAT NEGATIVE THOUGHT OUT IN THE UNIVERSE.
PLEASE LET ME GET IN! PLEASE-OH-PLEASE-OH-PLEASE!

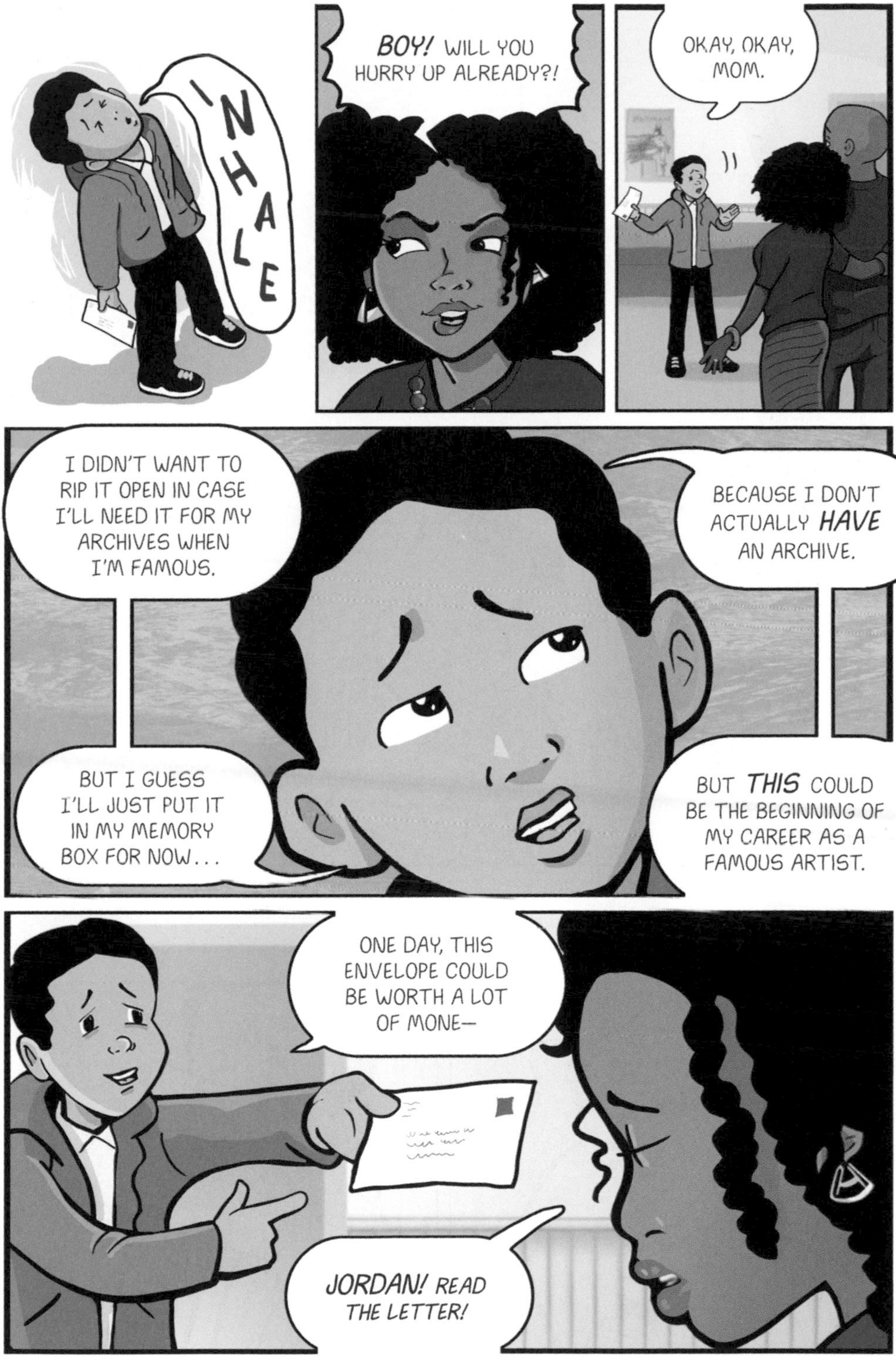
INHALE
BOY! WILL YOU HURRY UP ALREADY?!
OKAY, OKAY, MOM.
I DIDN'T WANT TO RIP IT OPEN IN CASE I'LL NEED IT FOR MY ARCHIVES WHEN I'M FAMOUS.
BECAUSE I DON'T ACTUALLY HAVE AN ARCHIVE.
BUT I GUESS I'LL JUST PUT IT IN MY MEMORY BOX FOR NOW...
BUT THIS COULD BE THE BEGINNING OF MY CAREER AS A FAMOUS ARTIST.
ONE DAY, THIS ENVELOPE COULD BE WORTH A LOT OF MONE—
JORDAN! READ THE LETTER!

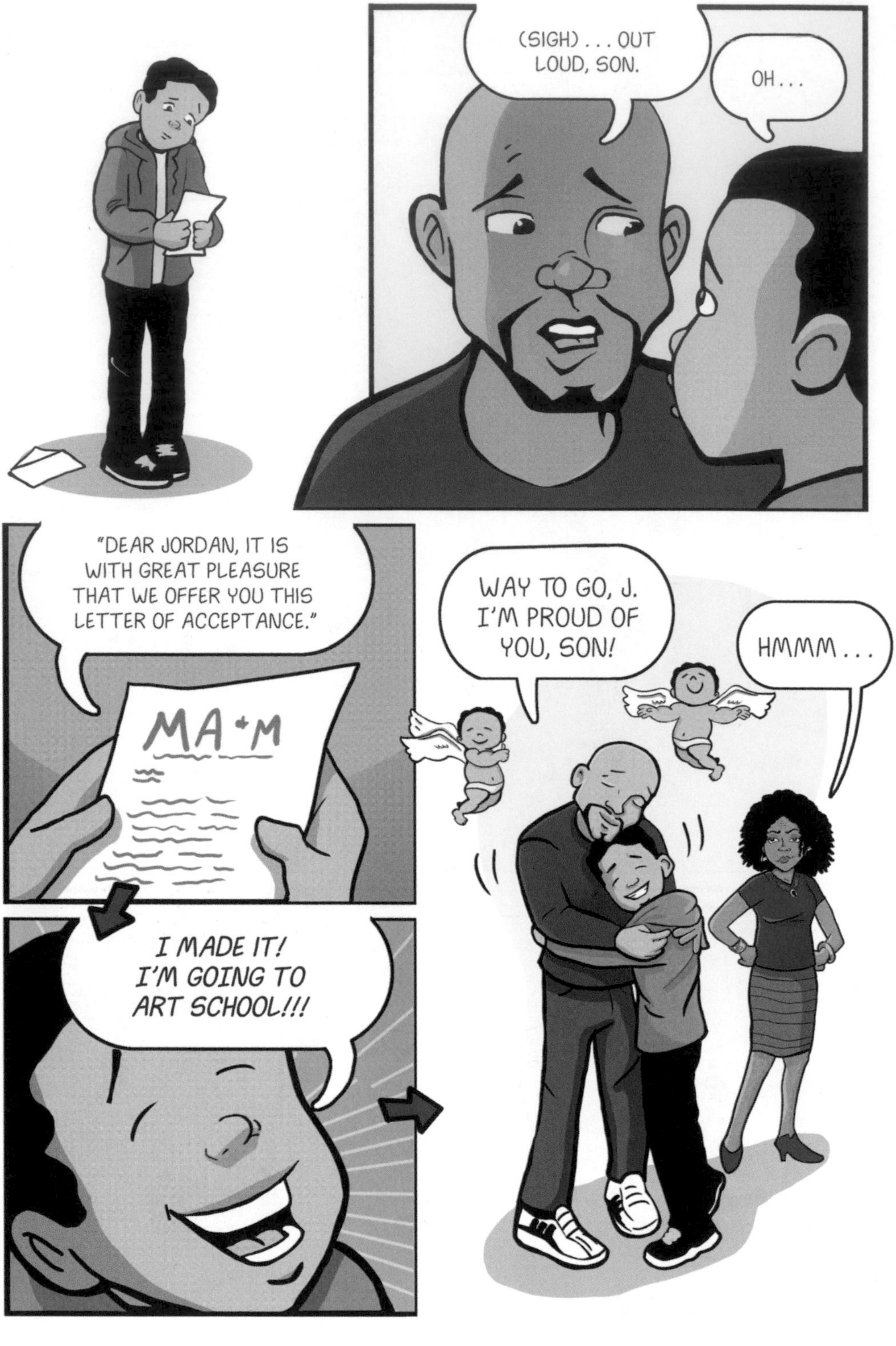
(SIGH) . . . OUT LOUD, SON.
OH . . .
"DEAR JORDAN, IT IS WITH GREAT PLEASURE THAT WE OFFER YOU THIS LETTER OF ACCEPTANCE."
MA+M
I MADE IT! I'M GOING TO ART SCHOOL!!!
WAY TO GO, J. I'M PROUD OF YOU, SON!
HMMM . . .

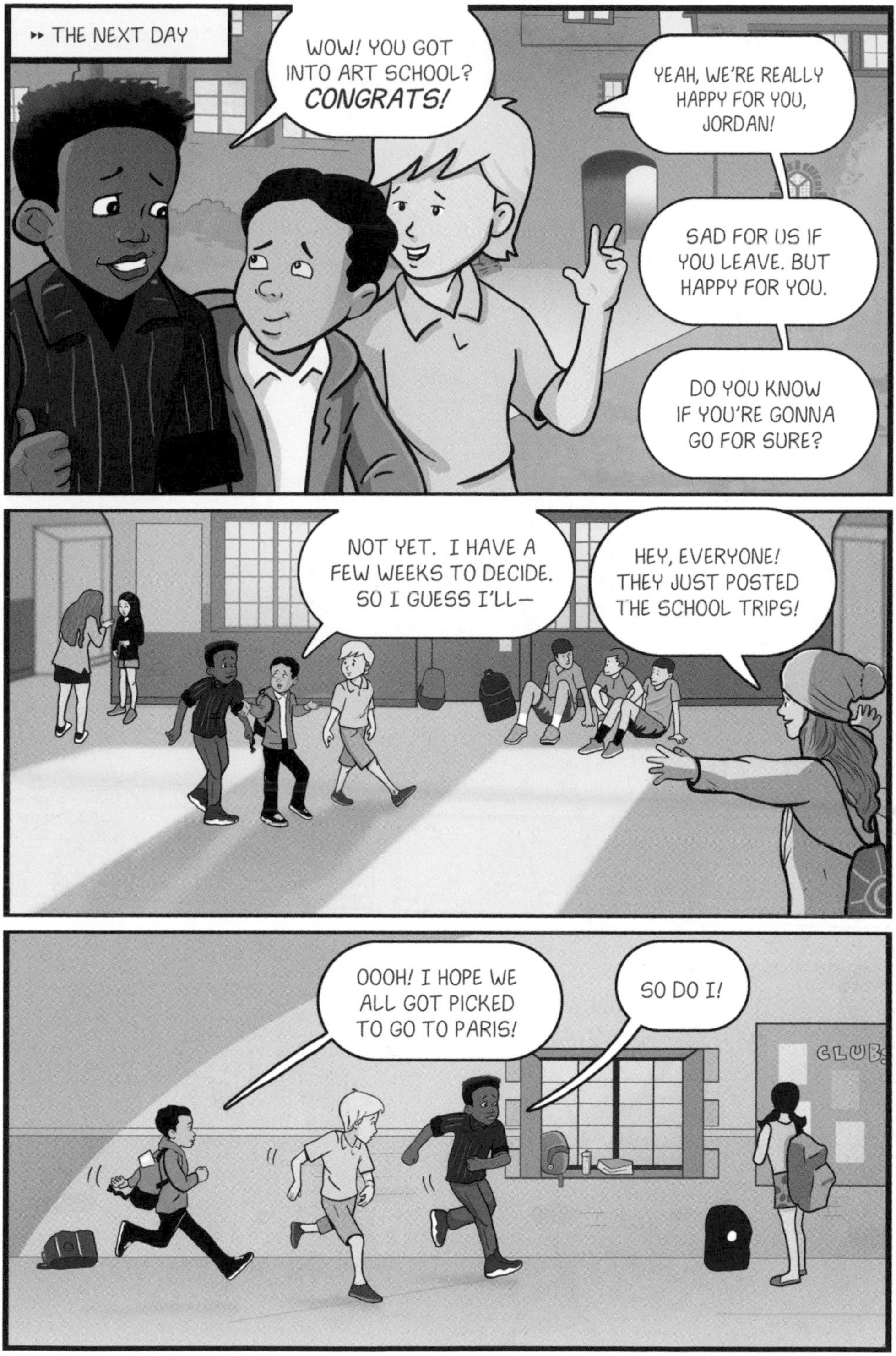
▸▸ THE NEXT DAY
WOW! YOU GOT INTO ART SCHOOL? CONGRATS!
YEAH, WE'RE REALLY HAPPY FOR YOU, JORDAN!
SAD FOR US IF YOU LEAVE. BUT HAPPY FOR YOU.
DO YOU KNOW IF YOU'RE GONNA GO FOR SURE?
NOT YET. I HAVE A FEW WEEKS TO DECIDE. SO I GUESS I'LL—
HEY, EVERYONE! THEY JUST POSTED THE SCHOOL TRIPS!
OOOH! I HOPE WE ALL GOT PICKED TO GO TO PARIS!
SO DO I!

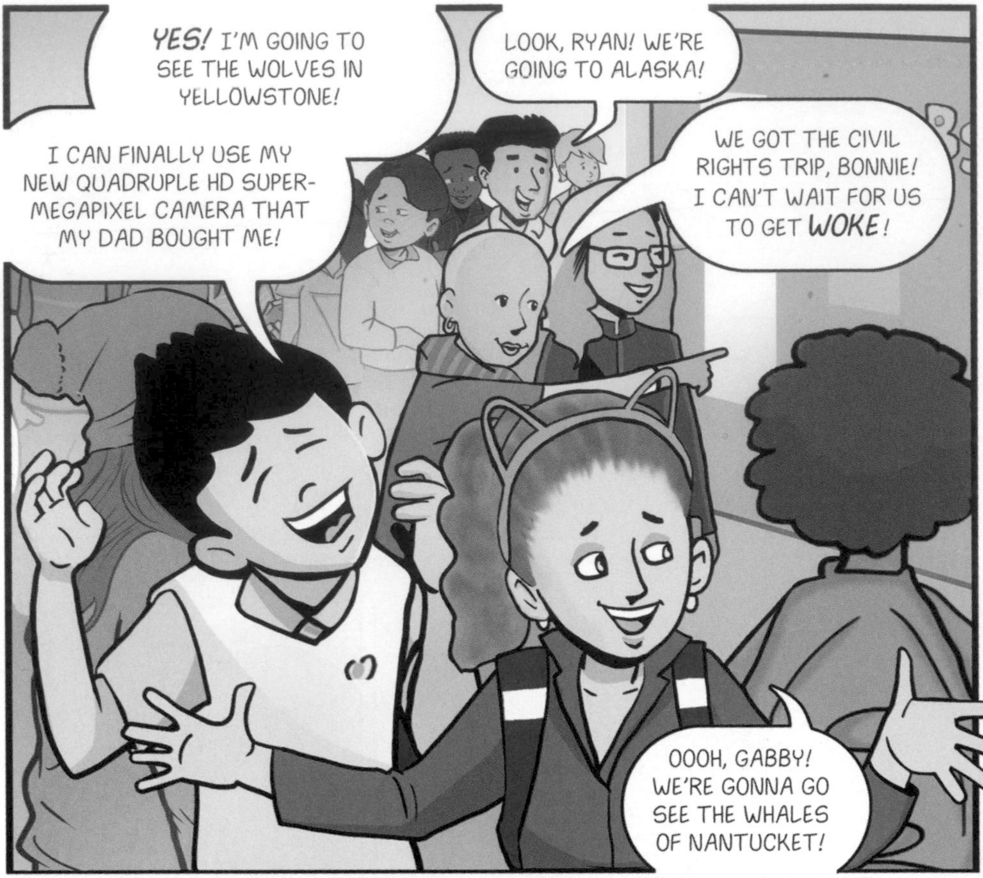
YES! I'M GOING TO SEE THE WOLVES IN YELLOWSTONE!
LOOK, RYAN! WE'RE GOING TO ALASKA!
I CAN FINALLY USE MY NEW QUADRUPLE HD SUPER-MEGAPIXEL CAMERA THAT MY DAD BOUGHT ME!
WE GOT THE CIVIL RIGHTS TRIP, BONNIE! I CAN'T WAIT FOR US TO GET WOKE!
OOOH, GABBY! WE'RE GONNA GO SEE THE WHALES OF NANTUCKET!

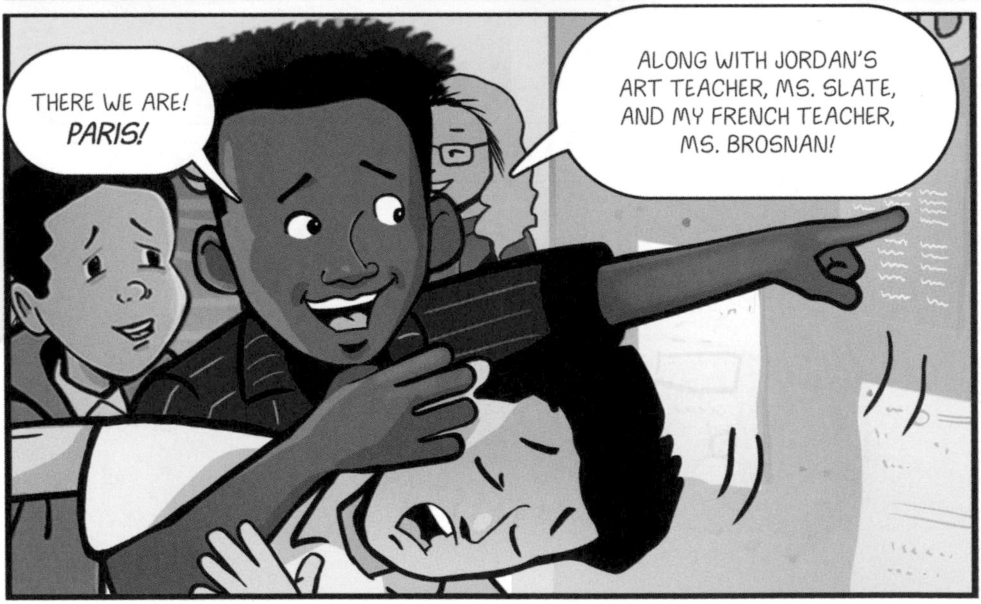
THERE WE ARE! PARIS!
ALONG WITH JORDAN'S ART TEACHER, MS. SLATE, AND MY FRENCH TEACHER, MS. BROSNAN!

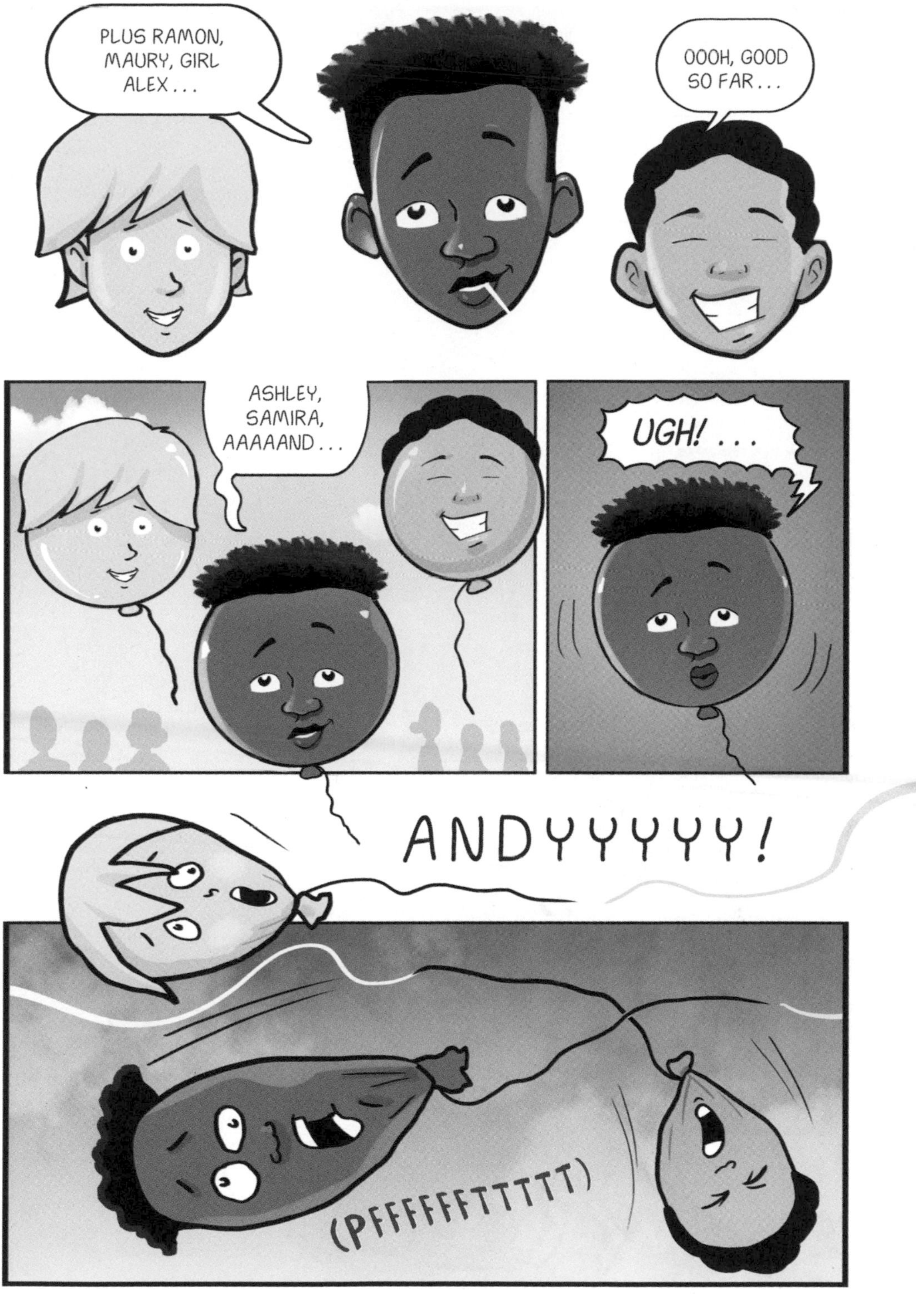
PLUS RAMON, MAURY, GIRL ALEX . . .
OOOH, GOOD SO FAR . . .
ASHLEY, SAMIRA, AAAAAND . . .
UGH! . . .
ANDYYYYYY!
(PFFFFFFTTTTTT)

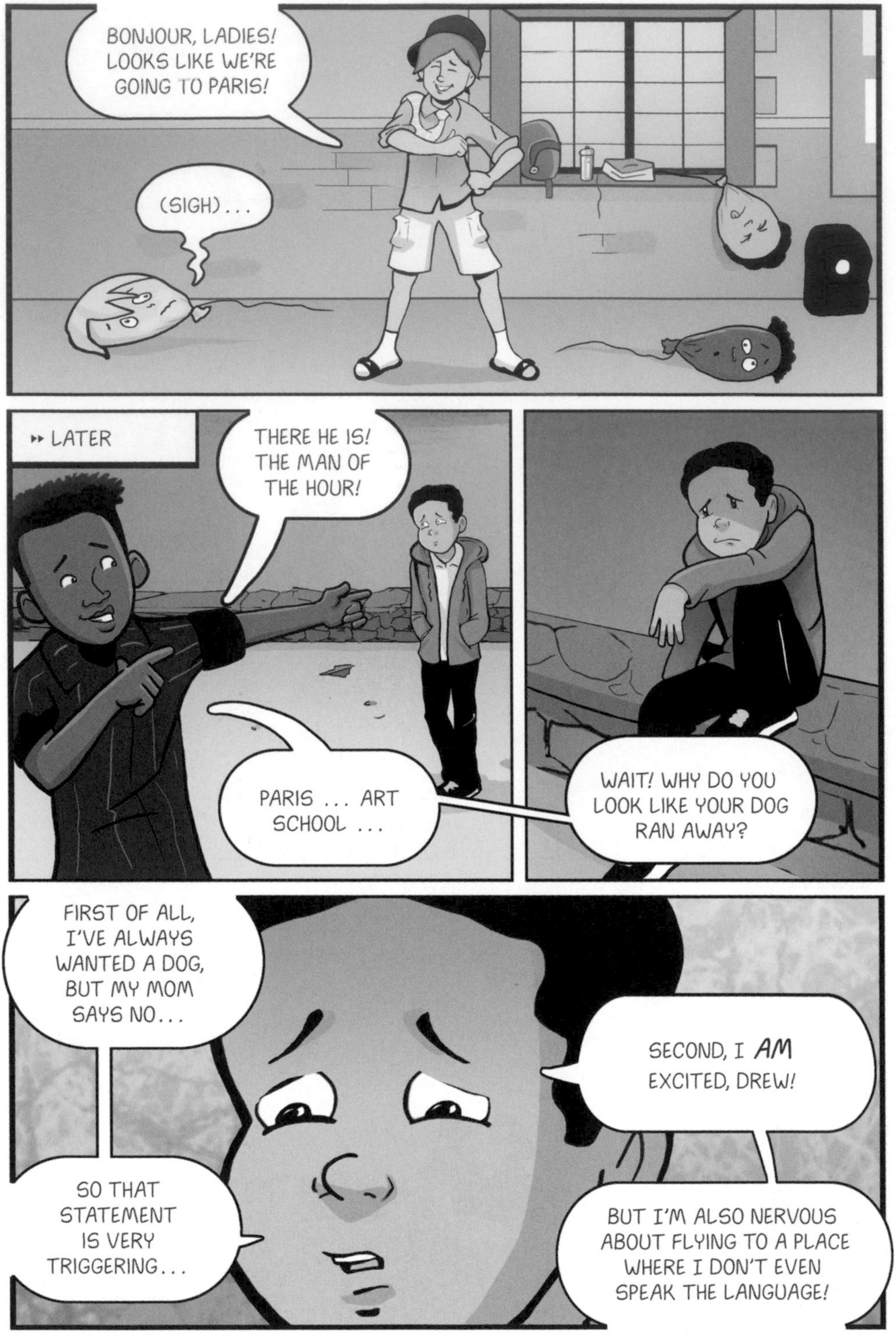
BONJOUR, LADIES! LOOKS LIKE WE'RE GOING TO PARIS!
(SIGH)...
LATER
THERE HE IS! THE MAN OF THE HOUR!
PARIS ... ART SCHOOL ...
WAIT! WHY DO YOU LOOK LIKE YOUR DOG RAN AWAY?
FIRST OF ALL, I'VE ALWAYS WANTED A DOG, BUT MY MOM SAYS NO...
SO THAT STATEMENT IS VERY TRIGGERING...
SECOND, I AM EXCITED, DREW!
BUT I'M ALSO NERVOUS ABOUT FLYING TO A PLACE WHERE I DON'T EVEN SPEAK THE LANGUAGE!

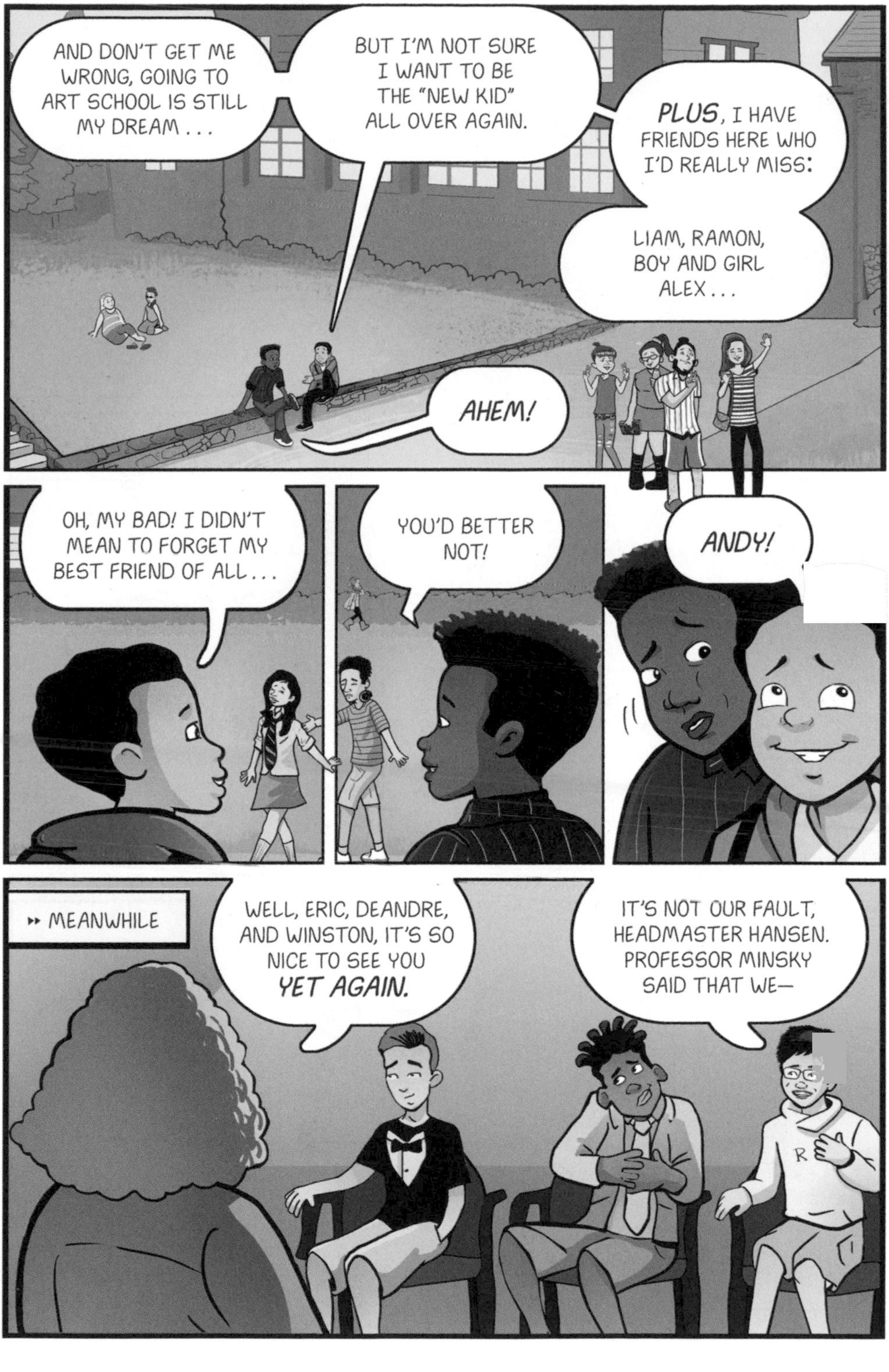
AND DON'T GET ME WRONG, GOING TO ART SCHOOL IS STILL MY DREAM . . .
BUT I'M NOT SURE I WANT TO BE THE "NEW KID" ALL OVER AGAIN.
PLUS, I HAVE FRIENDS HERE WHO I'D REALLY MISS:
LIAM, RAMON, BOY AND GIRL ALEX . . .
AHEM!
OH, MY BAD! I DIDN'T MEAN TO FORGET MY BEST FRIEND OF ALL . . .
YOU'D BETTER NOT!
ANDY!
MEANWHILE
WELL, ERIC, DEANDRE, AND WINSTON, IT'S SO NICE TO SEE YOU YET AGAIN.
IT'S NOT OUR FAULT, HEADMASTER HANSEN. PROFESSOR MINSKY SAID THAT WE—

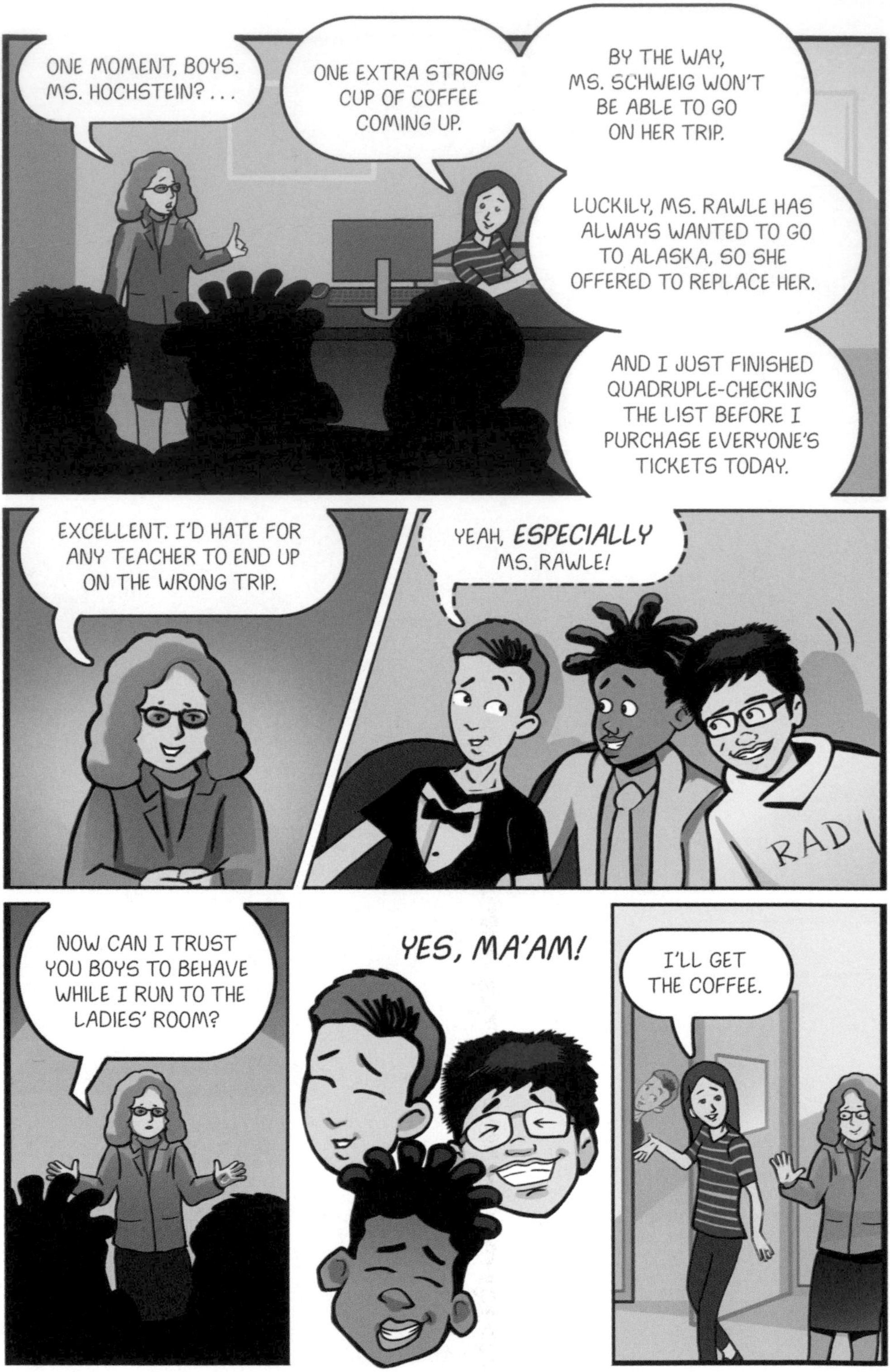
ONE MOMENT, BOYS. MS. HOCHSTEIN? . . .
ONE EXTRA STRONG CUP OF COFFEE COMING UP.
BY THE WAY, MS. SCHWEIG WON'T BE ABLE TO GO ON HER TRIP.
LUCKILY, MS. RAWLE HAS ALWAYS WANTED TO GO TO ALASKA, SO SHE OFFERED TO REPLACE HER.
AND I JUST FINISHED QUADRUPLE-CHECKING THE LIST BEFORE I PURCHASE EVERYONE'S TICKETS TODAY.
EXCELLENT. I'D HATE FOR ANY TEACHER TO END UP ON THE WRONG TRIP.
YEAH, *ESPECIALLY* MS. RAWLE!
RAD
NOW CAN I TRUST YOU BOYS TO BEHAVE WHILE I RUN TO THE LADIES' ROOM?
YES, MA'AM!
I'LL GET THE COFFEE.

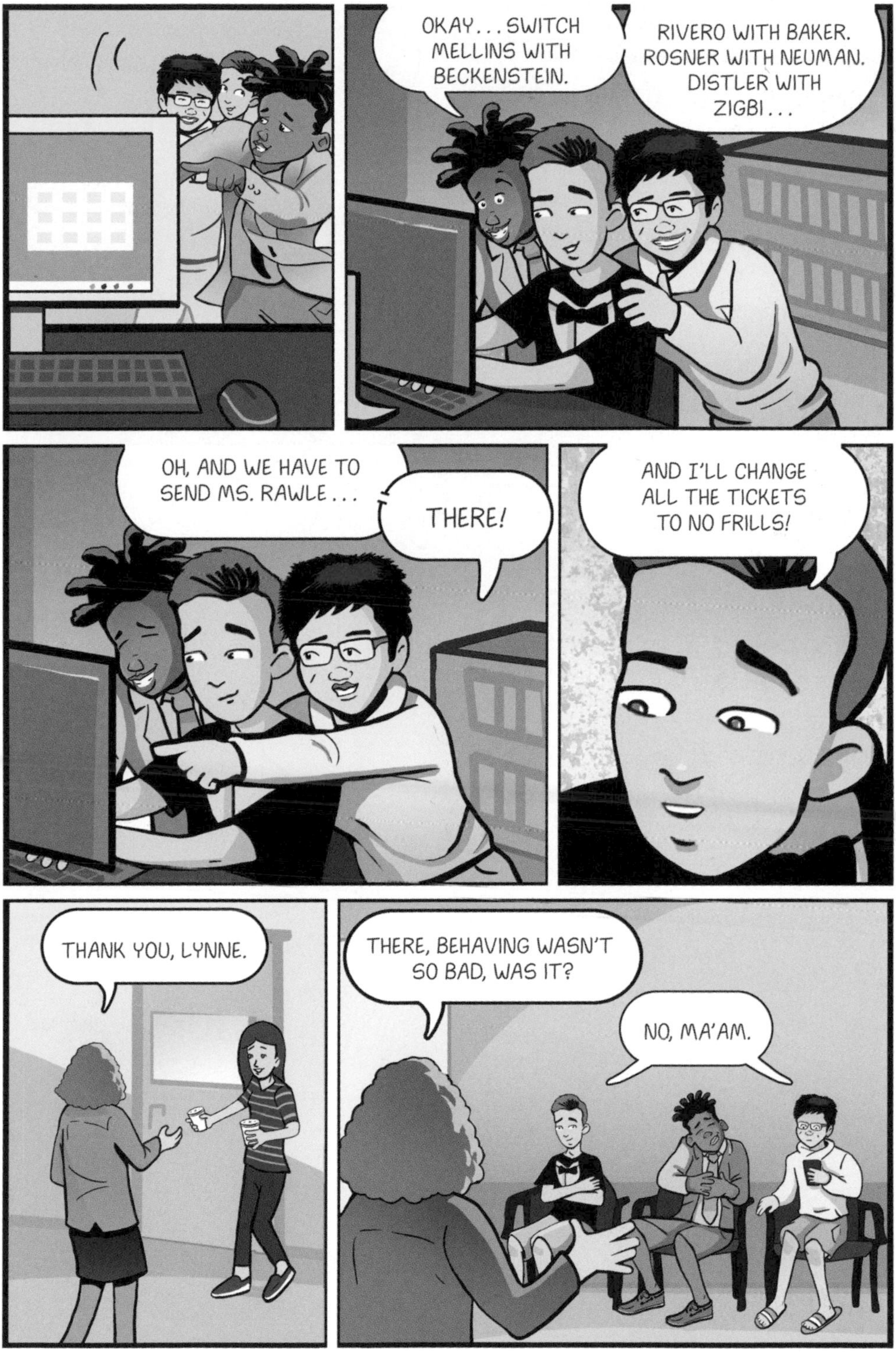
OKAY . . . SWITCH MELLINS WITH BECKENSTEIN.
RIVERO WITH BAKER. ROSNER WITH NEUMAN. DISTLER WITH ZIGBI . . .
OH, AND WE HAVE TO SEND MS. RAWLE . . .
THERE!
AND I'LL CHANGE ALL THE TICKETS TO NO FRILLS!
THANK YOU, LYNNE.
THERE, BEHAVING WASN'T SO BAD, WAS IT?
NO, MA'AM.

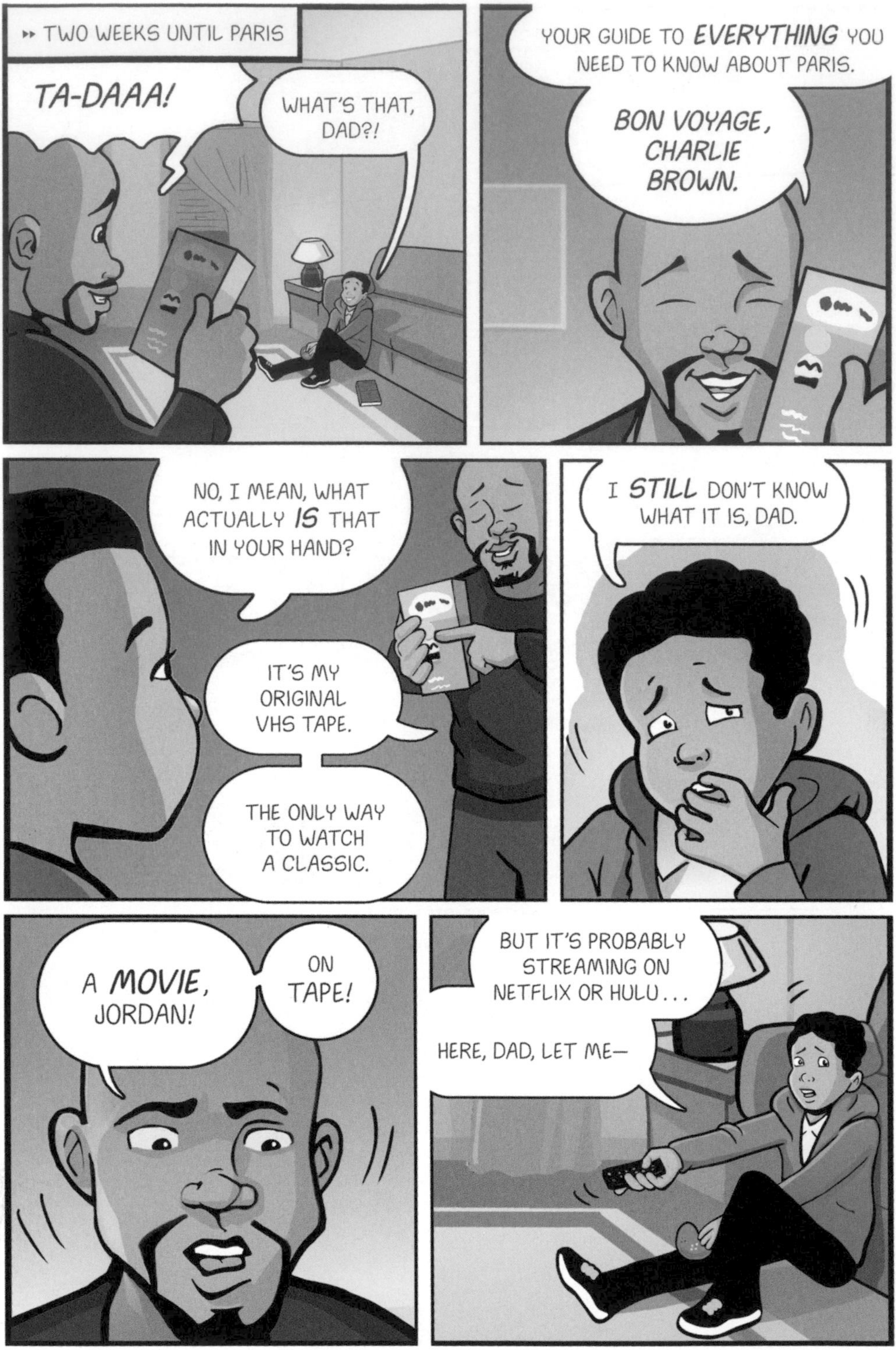

TWO WEEKS UNTIL PARIS
TA-DAAA!
WHAT'S THAT, DAD?!
YOUR GUIDE TO EVERYTHING YOU NEED TO KNOW ABOUT PARIS.
BON VOYAGE, CHARLIE BROWN.
NO, I MEAN, WHAT ACTUALLY IS THAT IN YOUR HAND?
IT'S MY ORIGINAL VHS TAPE.
THE ONLY WAY TO WATCH A CLASSIC.
I STILL DON'T KNOW WHAT IT IS, DAD.
A MOVIE, JORDAN!
ON TAPE!
BUT IT'S PROBABLY STREAMING ON NETFLIX OR HULU . . .
HERE, DAD, LET ME—

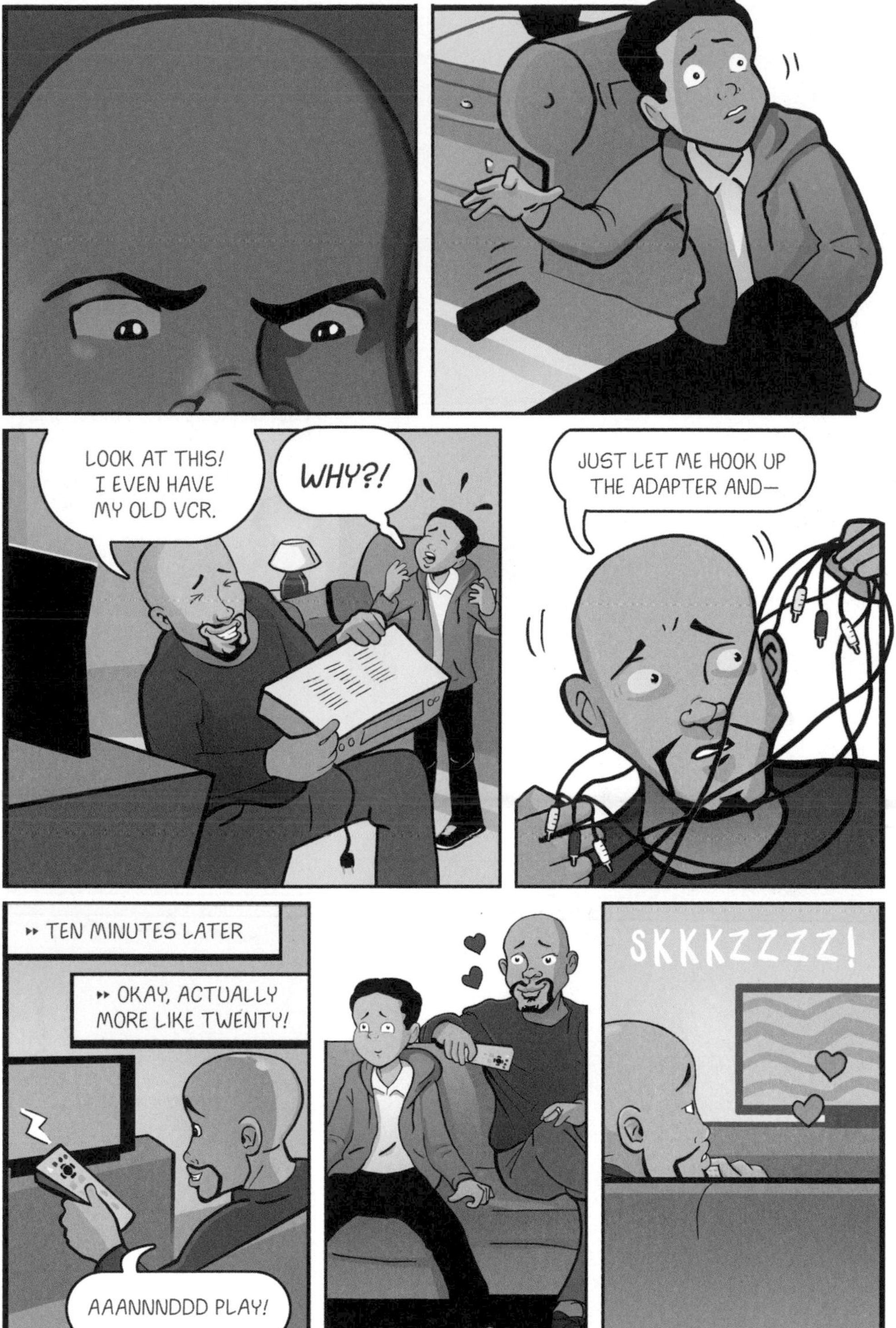
LOOK AT THIS! I EVEN HAVE MY OLD VCR.
WHY?!
JUST LET ME HOOK UP THE ADAPTER AND—
▸▸ TEN MINUTES LATER
▸▸ OKAY, ACTUALLY MORE LIKE TWENTY!
AAANNNDDD PLAY!
SKKKZZZZ!

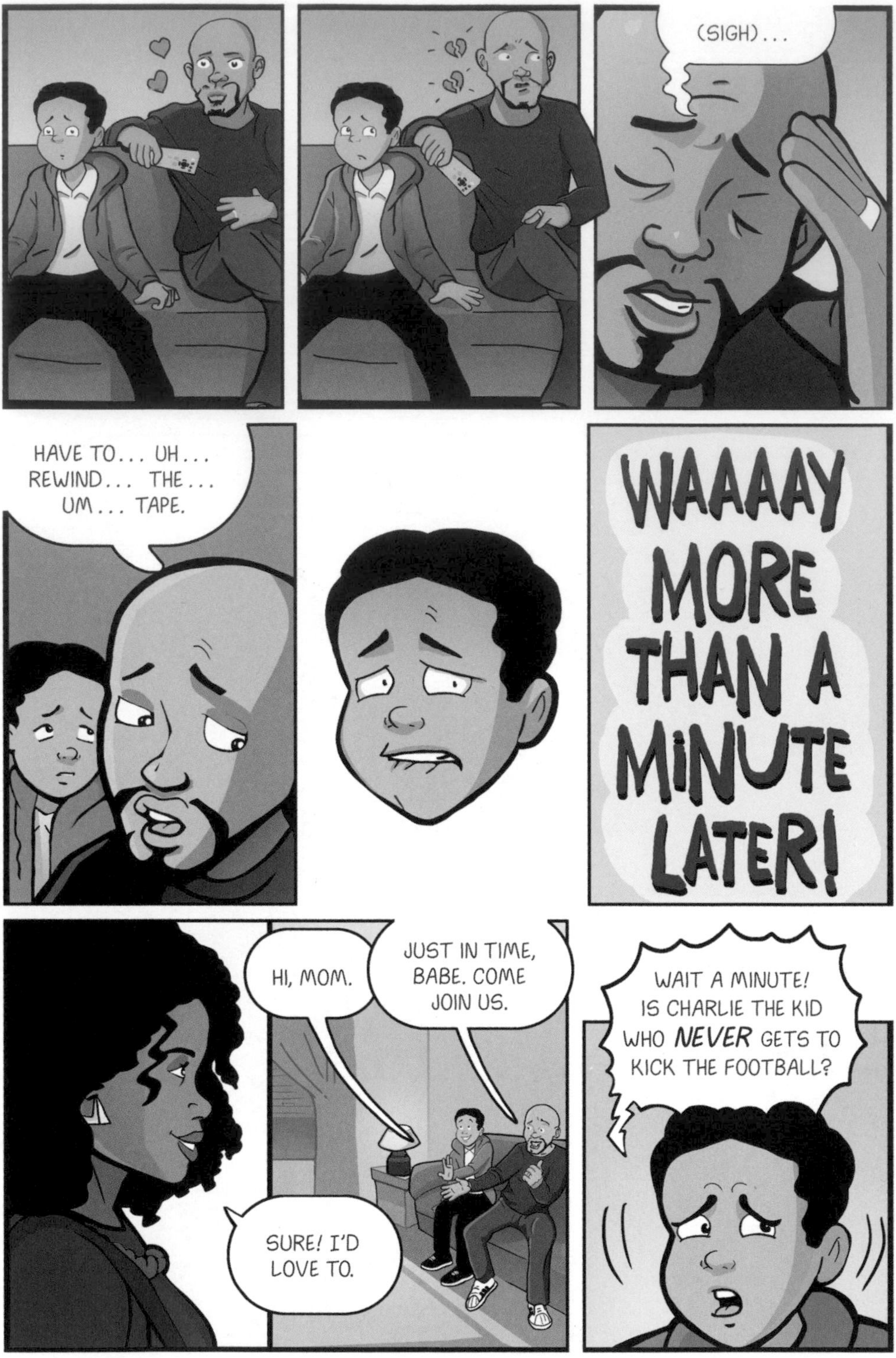
(SIGH)...
HAVE TO... UH... REWIND... THE... UM... TAPE.
WAAAAY MORE THAN A MINUTE LATER!
HI, MOM.
JUST IN TIME, BABE. COME JOIN US.
SURE! I'D LOVE TO.
WAIT A MINUTE! IS CHARLIE THE KID WHO NEVER GETS TO KICK THE FOOTBALL?

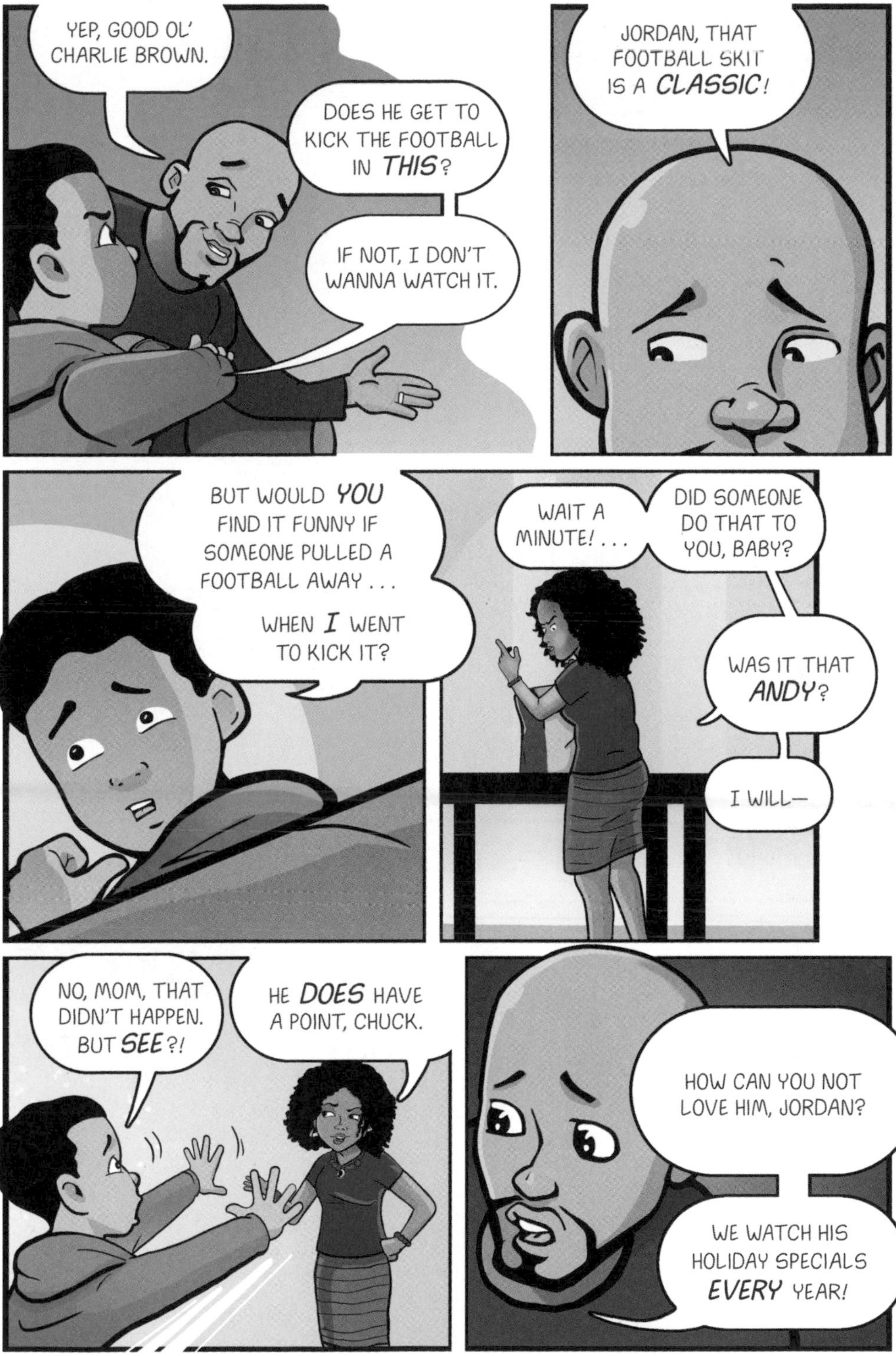
YEP, GOOD OL' CHARLIE BROWN.
DOES HE GET TO KICK THE FOOTBALL IN *THIS*?
IF NOT, I DON'T WANNA WATCH IT.
JORDAN, THAT FOOTBALL SKIT IS A *CLASSIC*!
BUT WOULD *YOU* FIND IT FUNNY IF SOMEONE PULLED A FOOTBALL AWAY . . .
WHEN *I* WENT TO KICK IT?
WAIT A MINUTE! . . .
DID SOMEONE DO THAT TO YOU, BABY?
WAS IT THAT *ANDY*?
I WILL—
NO, MOM, THAT DIDN'T HAPPEN. BUT *SEE*?!
HE *DOES* HAVE A POINT, CHUCK.
HOW CAN YOU NOT LOVE HIM, JORDAN?
WE WATCH HIS HOLIDAY SPECIALS *EVERY* YEAR!

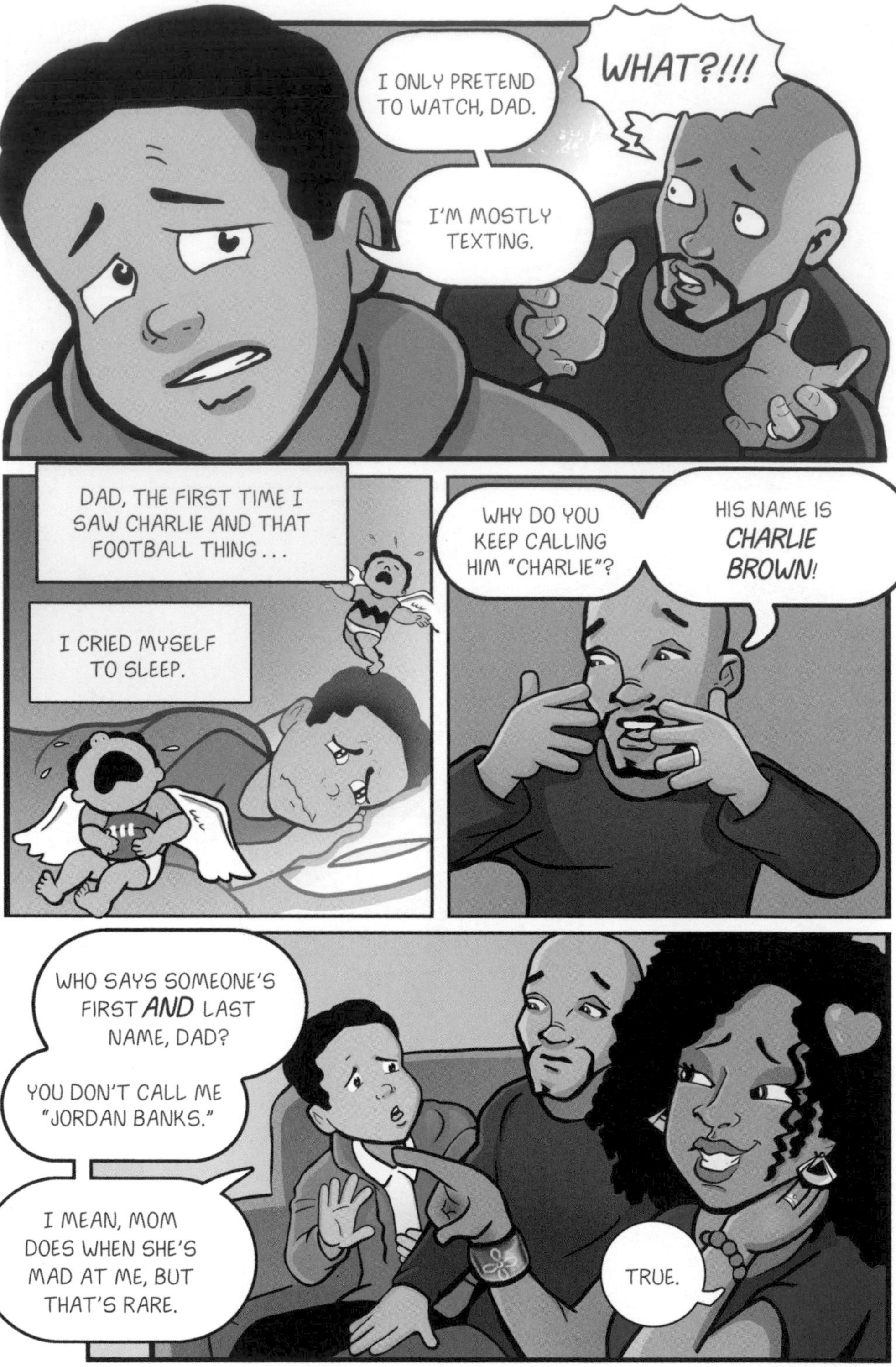
I ONLY PRETEND TO WATCH, DAD.
I'M MOSTLY TEXTING.
WHAT?!!!
DAD, THE FIRST TIME I SAW CHARLIE AND THAT FOOTBALL THING . . .
I CRIED MYSELF TO SLEEP.
WHY DO YOU KEEP CALLING HIM "CHARLIE"?
HIS NAME IS CHARLIE BROWN!
WHO SAYS SOMEONE'S FIRST AND LAST NAME, DAD?
YOU DON'T CALL ME "JORDAN BANKS."
I MEAN, MOM DOES WHEN SHE'S MAD AT ME, BUT THAT'S RARE.
TRUE.

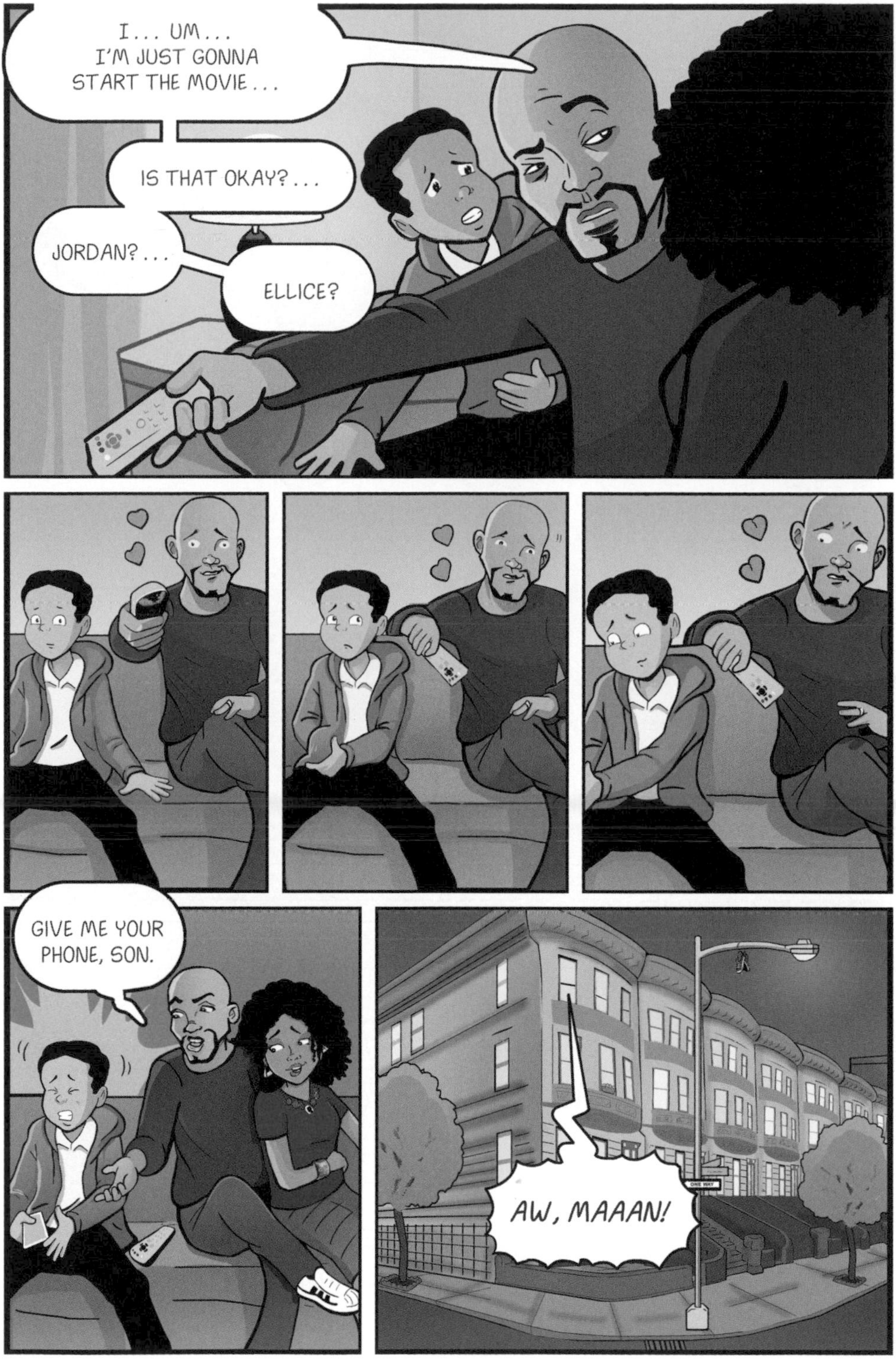
I... UM...
I'M JUST GONNA
START THE MOVIE...
IS THAT OKAY?...
JORDAN?...
ELLICE?
GIVE ME YOUR
PHONE, SON.
AW, MAAAN!

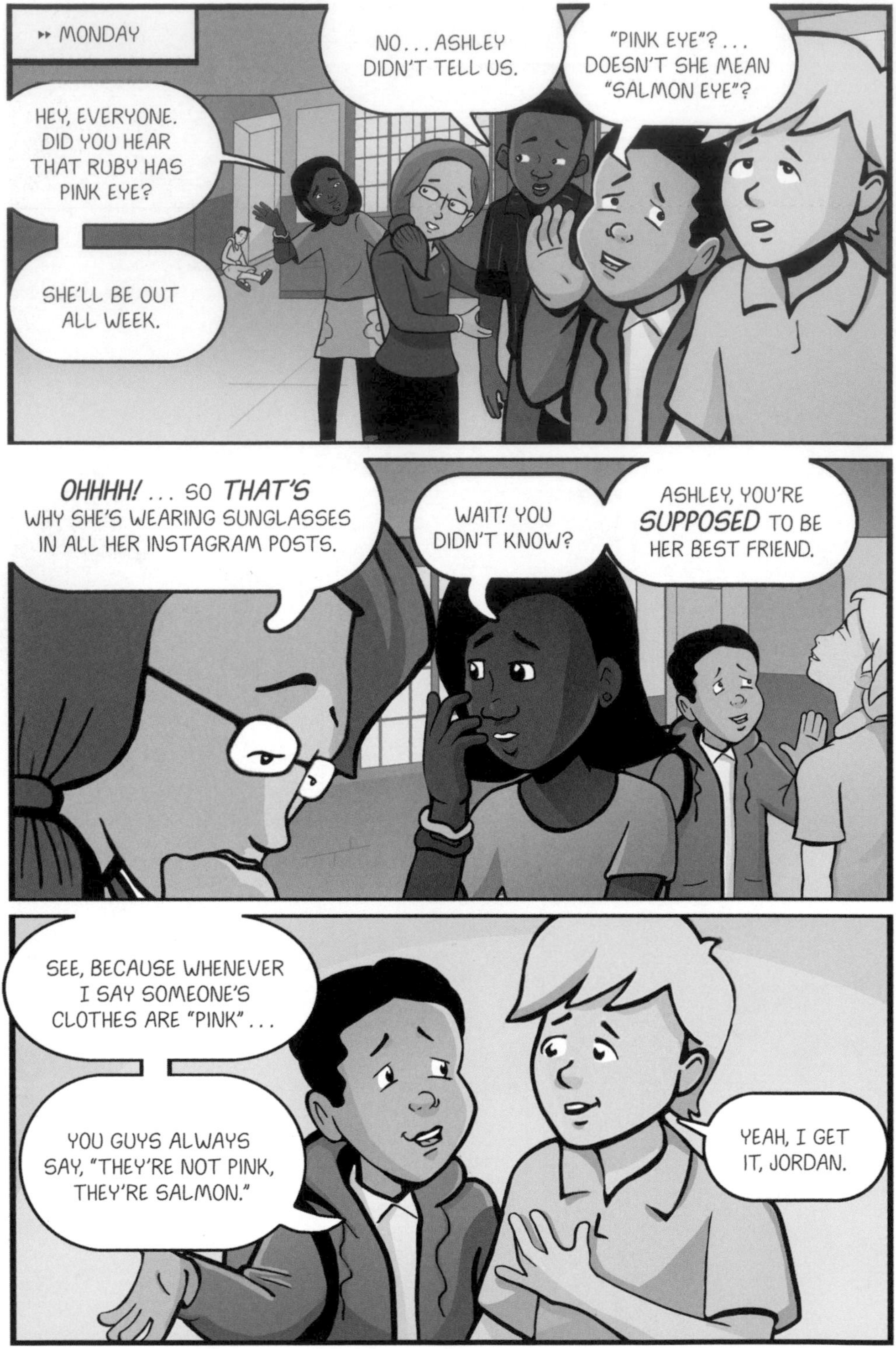
MONDAY
HEY, EVERYONE. DID YOU HEAR THAT RUBY HAS PINK EYE?
SHE'LL BE OUT ALL WEEK.
NO... ASHLEY DIDN'T TELL US.
"PINK EYE"?... DOESN'T SHE MEAN "SALMON EYE"?
OHHHH! ... SO THAT'S WHY SHE'S WEARING SUNGLASSES IN ALL HER INSTAGRAM POSTS.
WAIT! YOU DIDN'T KNOW?
ASHLEY, YOU'RE SUPPOSED TO BE HER BEST FRIEND.
SEE, BECAUSE WHENEVER I SAY SOMEONE'S CLOTHES ARE "PINK"...
YOU GUYS ALWAYS SAY, "THEY'RE NOT PINK, THEY'RE SALMON."
YEAH, I GET IT, JORDAN.

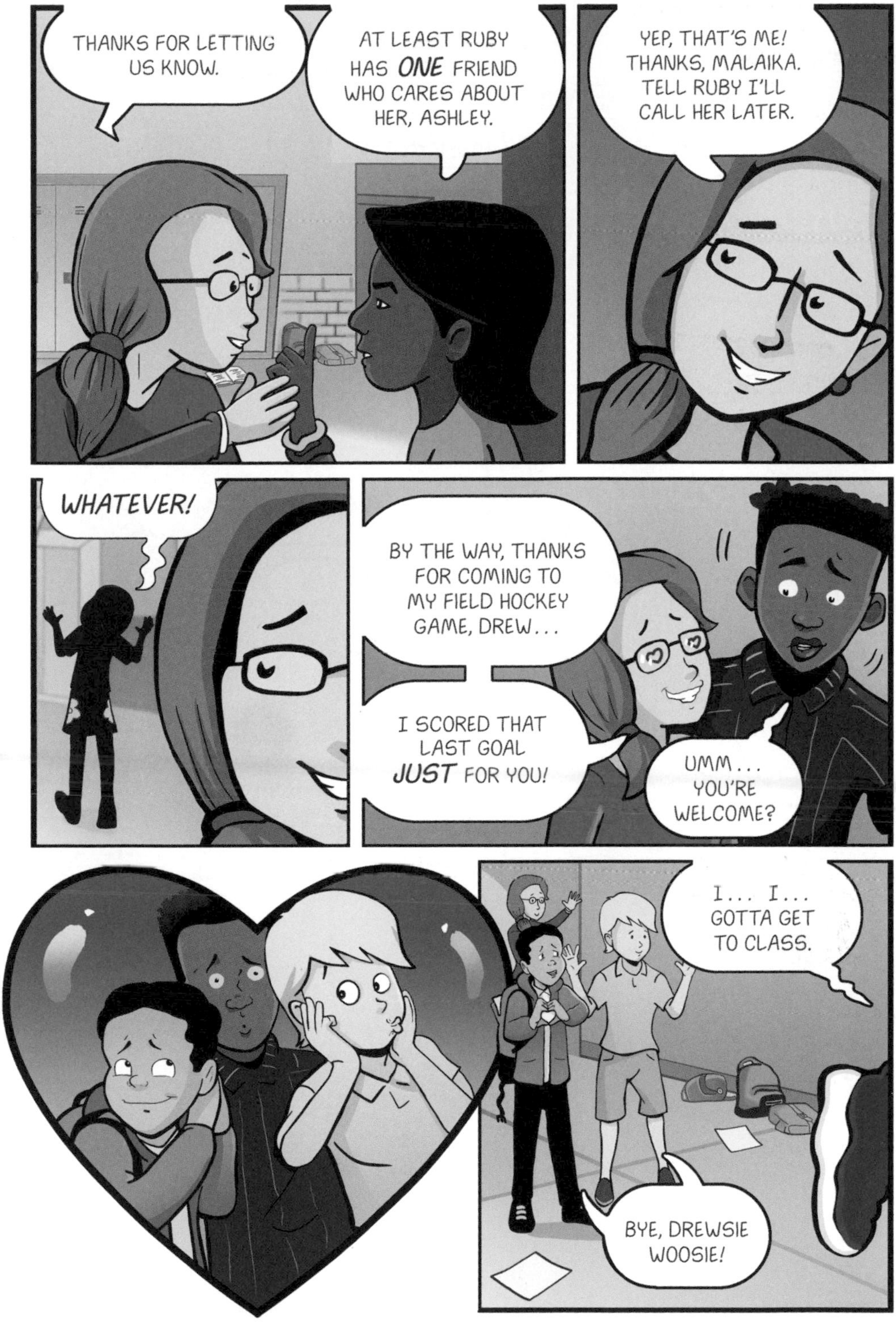
THANKS FOR LETTING US KNOW.
AT LEAST RUBY HAS ONE FRIEND WHO CARES ABOUT HER, ASHLEY.
YEP, THAT'S ME! THANKS, MALAIKA. TELL RUBY I'LL CALL HER LATER.
WHATEVER!
BY THE WAY, THANKS FOR COMING TO MY FIELD HOCKEY GAME, DREW...
I SCORED THAT LAST GOAL JUST FOR YOU!
UMM... YOU'RE WELCOME?
I... I... GOTTA GET TO CLASS.
BYE, DREWSIE WOOSIE!

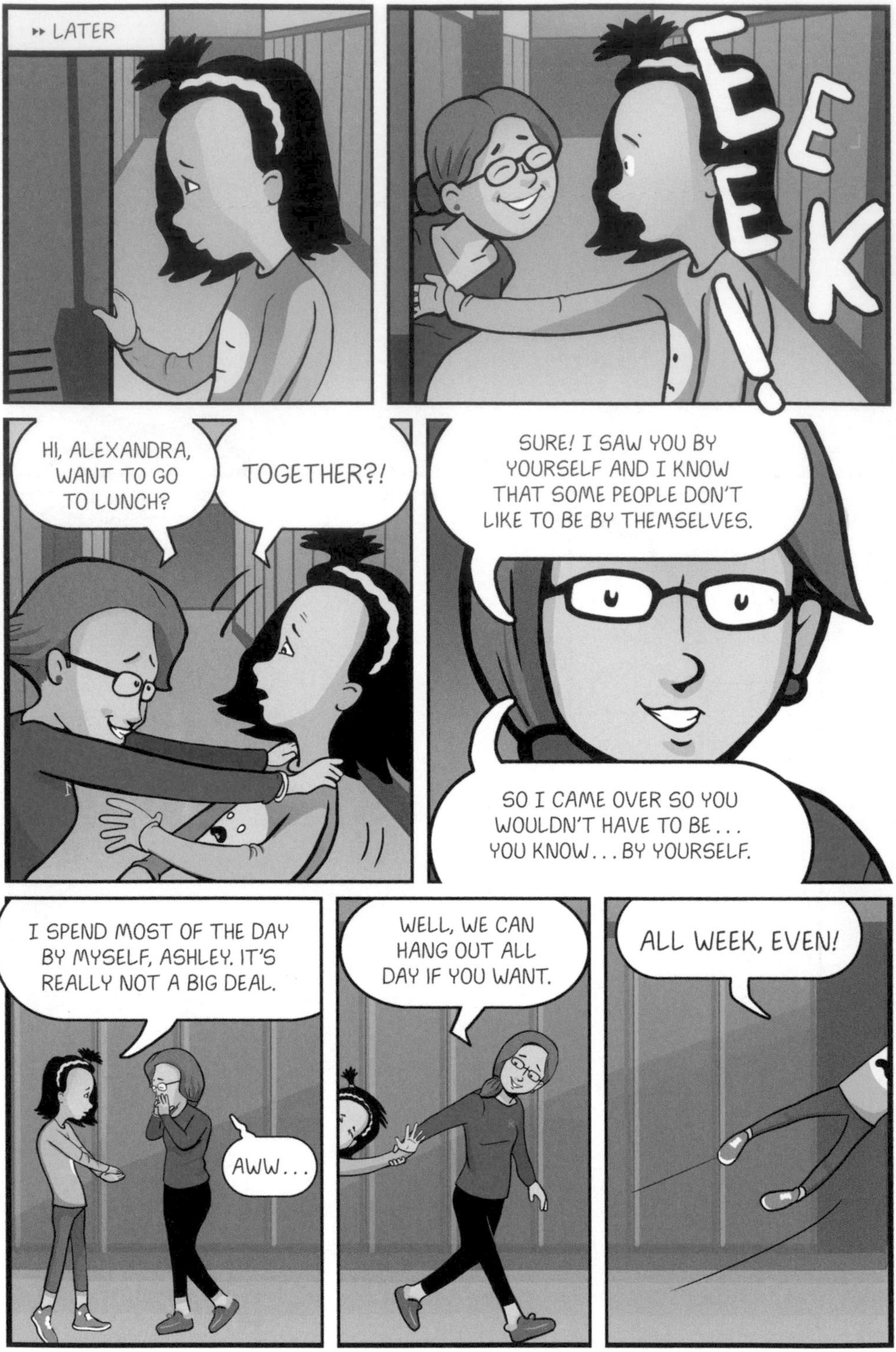
LATER
EEEK!
HI, ALEXANDRA, WANT TO GO TO LUNCH?
TOGETHER?!
SURE! I SAW YOU BY YOURSELF AND I KNOW THAT SOME PEOPLE DON'T LIKE TO BE BY THEMSELVES.
SO I CAME OVER SO YOU WOULDN'T HAVE TO BE . . . YOU KNOW . . . BY YOURSELF.
I SPEND MOST OF THE DAY BY MYSELF, ASHLEY. IT'S REALLY NOT A BIG DEAL.
AWW . . .
WELL, WE CAN HANG OUT ALL DAY IF YOU WANT.
ALL WEEK, EVEN!

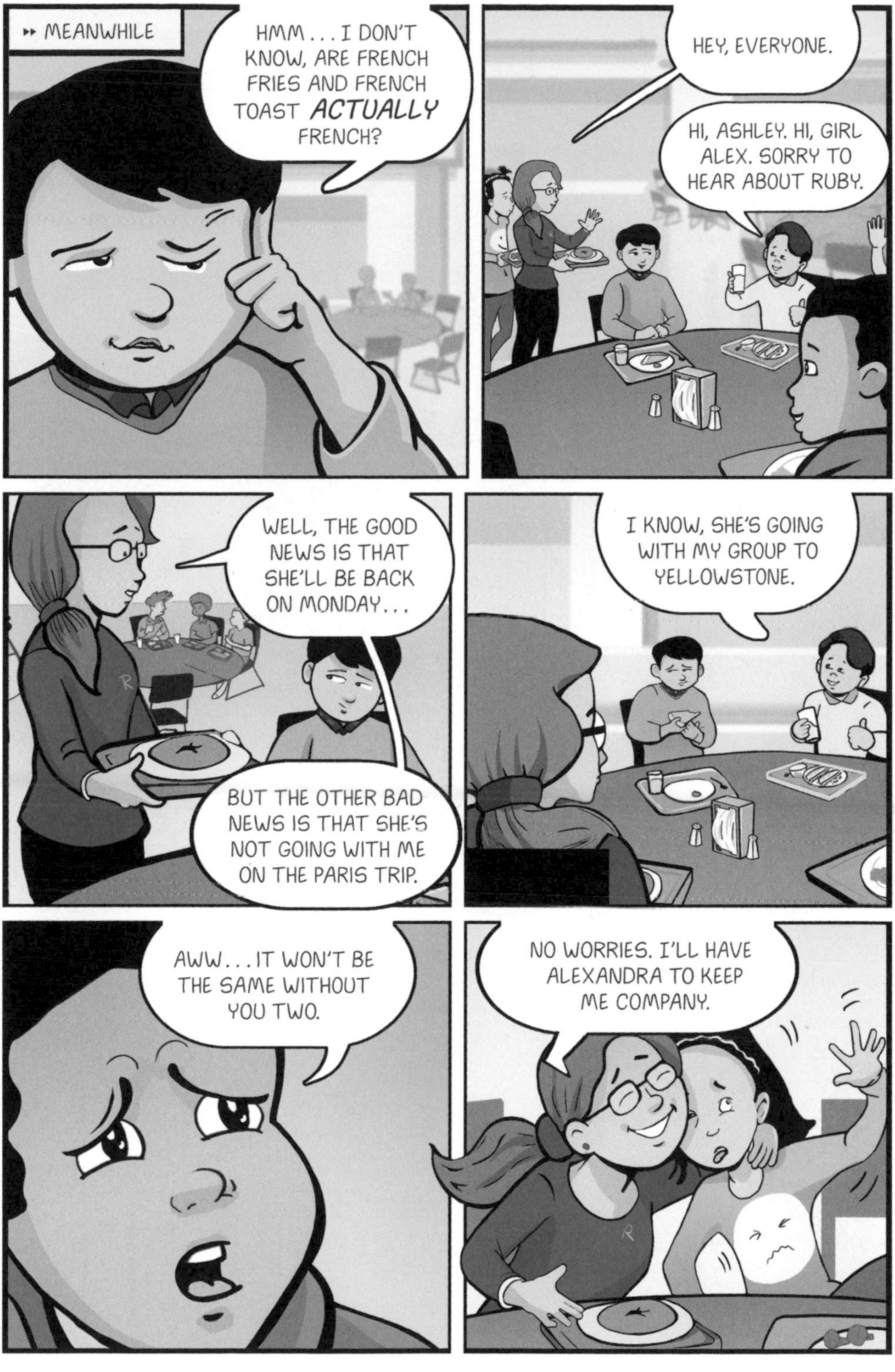
MEANWHILE
HMM . . . I DON'T KNOW, ARE FRENCH FRIES AND FRENCH TOAST ACTUALLY FRENCH?
HEY, EVERYONE.
HI, ASHLEY. HI, GIRL ALEX. SORRY TO HEAR ABOUT RUBY.
WELL, THE GOOD NEWS IS THAT SHE'LL BE BACK ON MONDAY . . .
BUT THE OTHER BAD NEWS IS THAT SHE'S NOT GOING WITH ME ON THE PARIS TRIP.
I KNOW, SHE'S GOING WITH MY GROUP TO YELLOWSTONE.
AWW . . . IT WON'T BE THE SAME WITHOUT YOU TWO.
NO WORRIES. I'LL HAVE ALEXANDRA TO KEEP ME COMPANY.

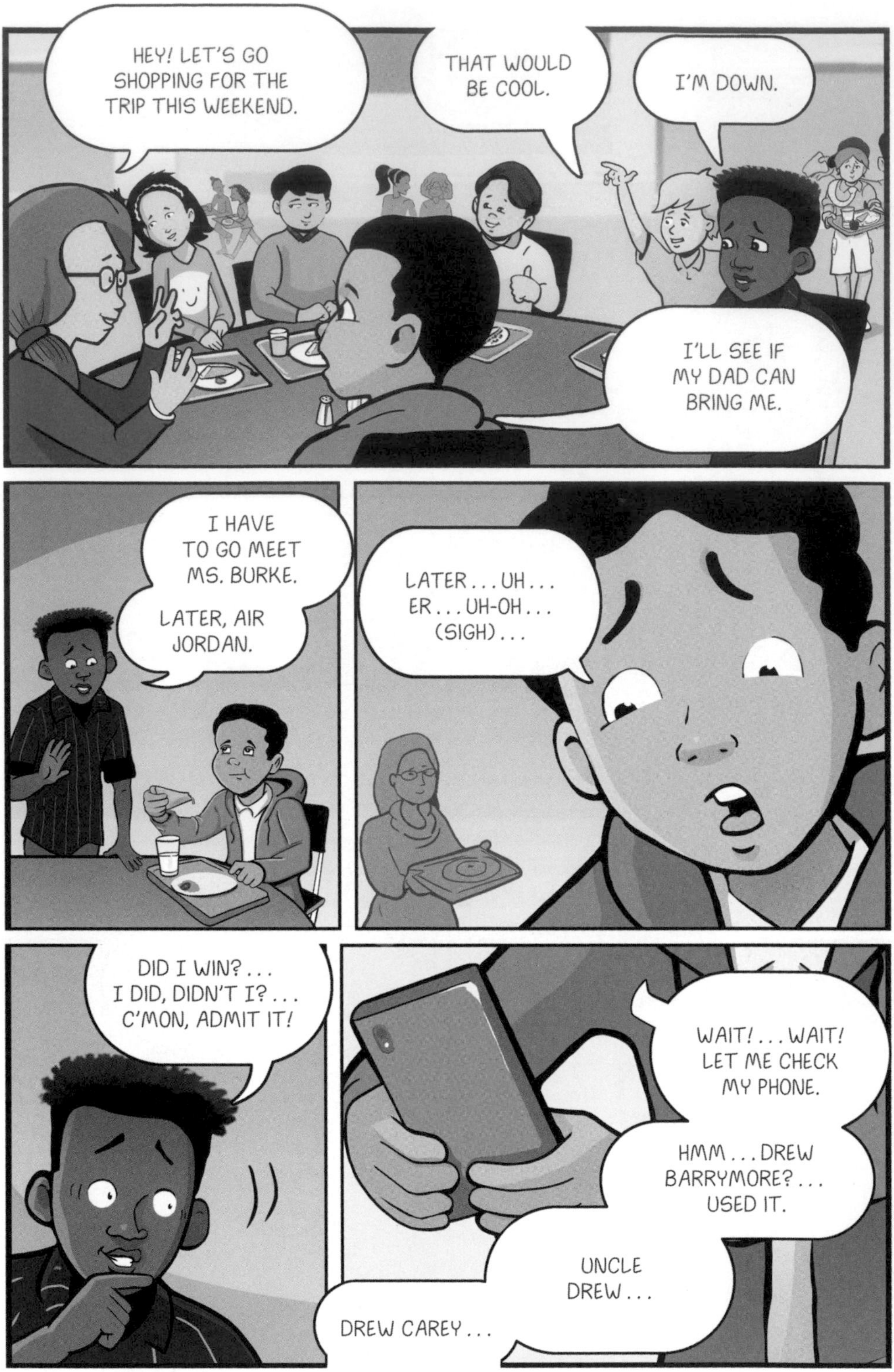
HEY! LET'S GO SHOPPING FOR THE TRIP THIS WEEKEND.
THAT WOULD BE COOL.
I'M DOWN.
I'LL SEE IF MY DAD CAN BRING ME.
I HAVE TO GO MEET MS. BURKE.
LATER, AIR JORDAN.
LATER . . . UH . . . ER . . . UH-OH . . . (SIGH) . . .
DID I WIN? . . . I DID, DIDN'T I? . . . C'MON, ADMIT IT!
WAIT! . . . WAIT! LET ME CHECK MY PHONE.
HMM . . . DREW BARRYMORE? . . . USED IT.
UNCLE DREW . . .
DREW CAREY . . .

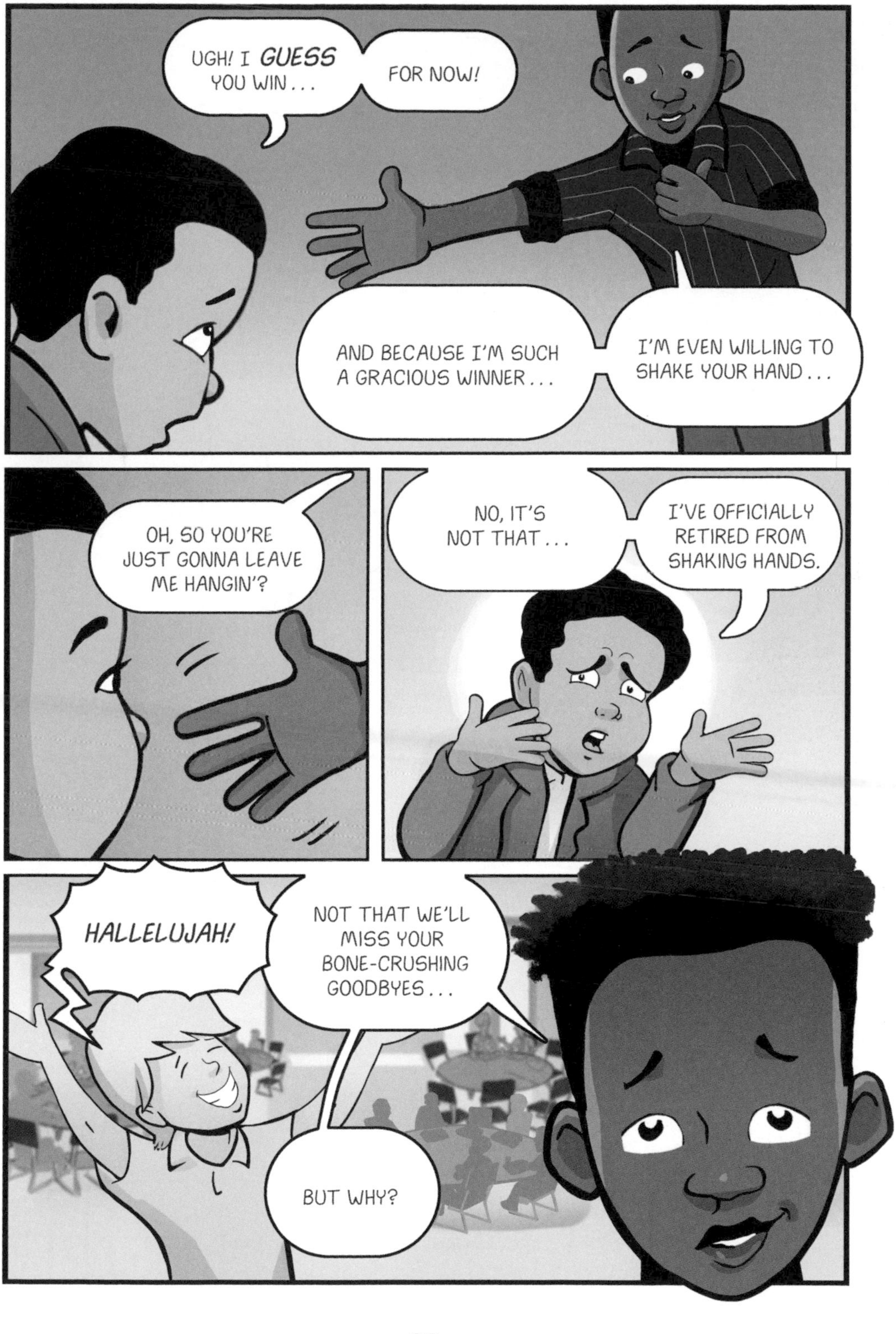
UGH! I GUESS YOU WIN . . .
FOR NOW!
AND BECAUSE I'M SUCH A GRACIOUS WINNER . . .
I'M EVEN WILLING TO SHAKE YOUR HAND . . .
OH, SO YOU'RE JUST GONNA LEAVE ME HANGIN'?
NO, IT'S NOT THAT . . .
I'VE OFFICIALLY RETIRED FROM SHAKING HANDS.
HALLELUJAH!
NOT THAT WE'LL MISS YOUR BONE-CRUSHING GOODBYES . . .
BUT WHY?

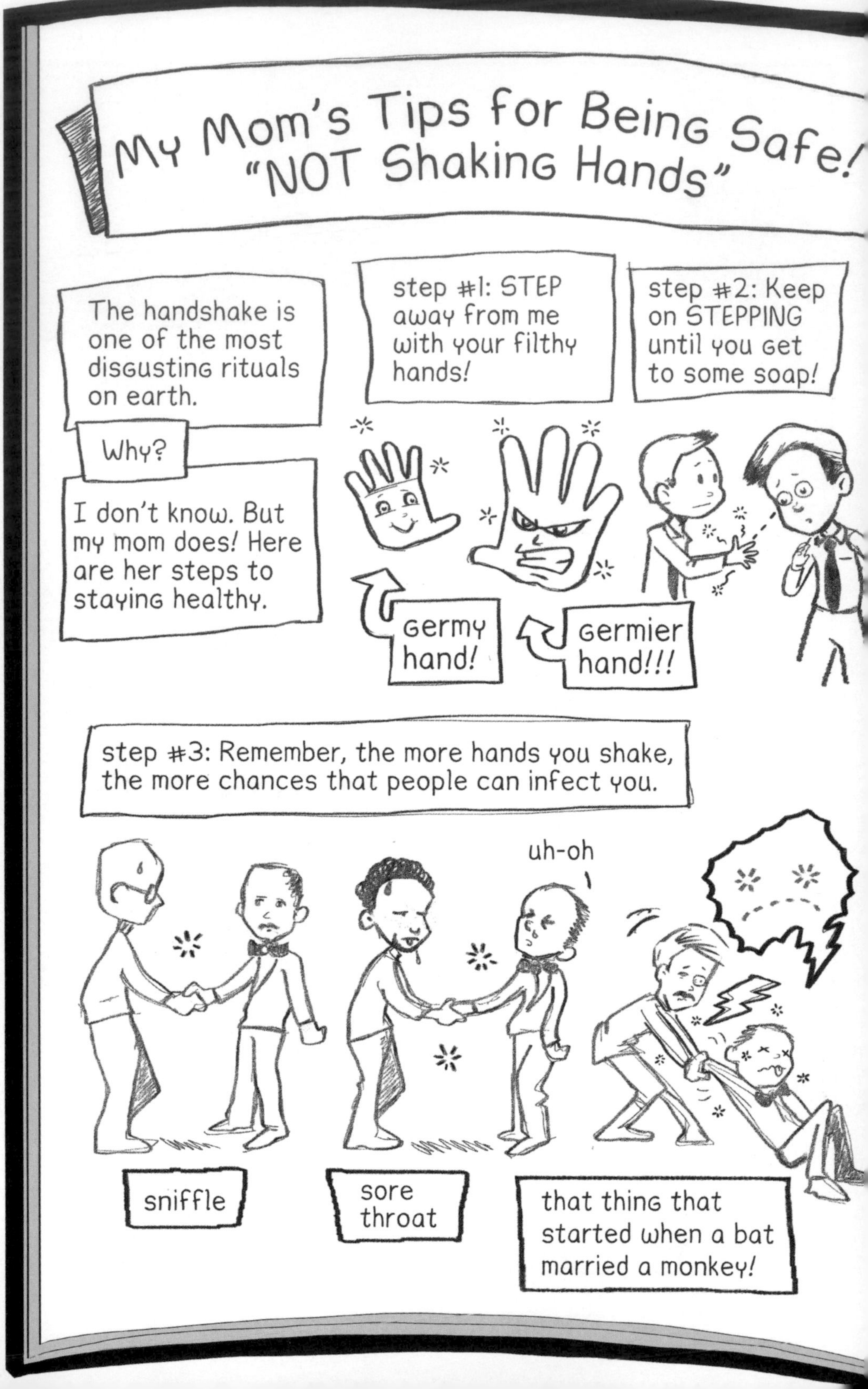
My Mom's Tips for Being Safe!
"NOT Shaking Hands"
The handshake is one of the most disgusting rituals on earth.
Why?
I don't know. But my mom does! Here are her steps to staying healthy.
step #1: STEP away from me with your filthy hands!
germy hand!
germier hand!!!
step #2: Keep on STEPPING until you get to some soap!
step #3: Remember, the more hands you shake, the more chances that people can infect you.
uh-oh
sniffle
sore throat
that thing that started when a bat married a monkey!

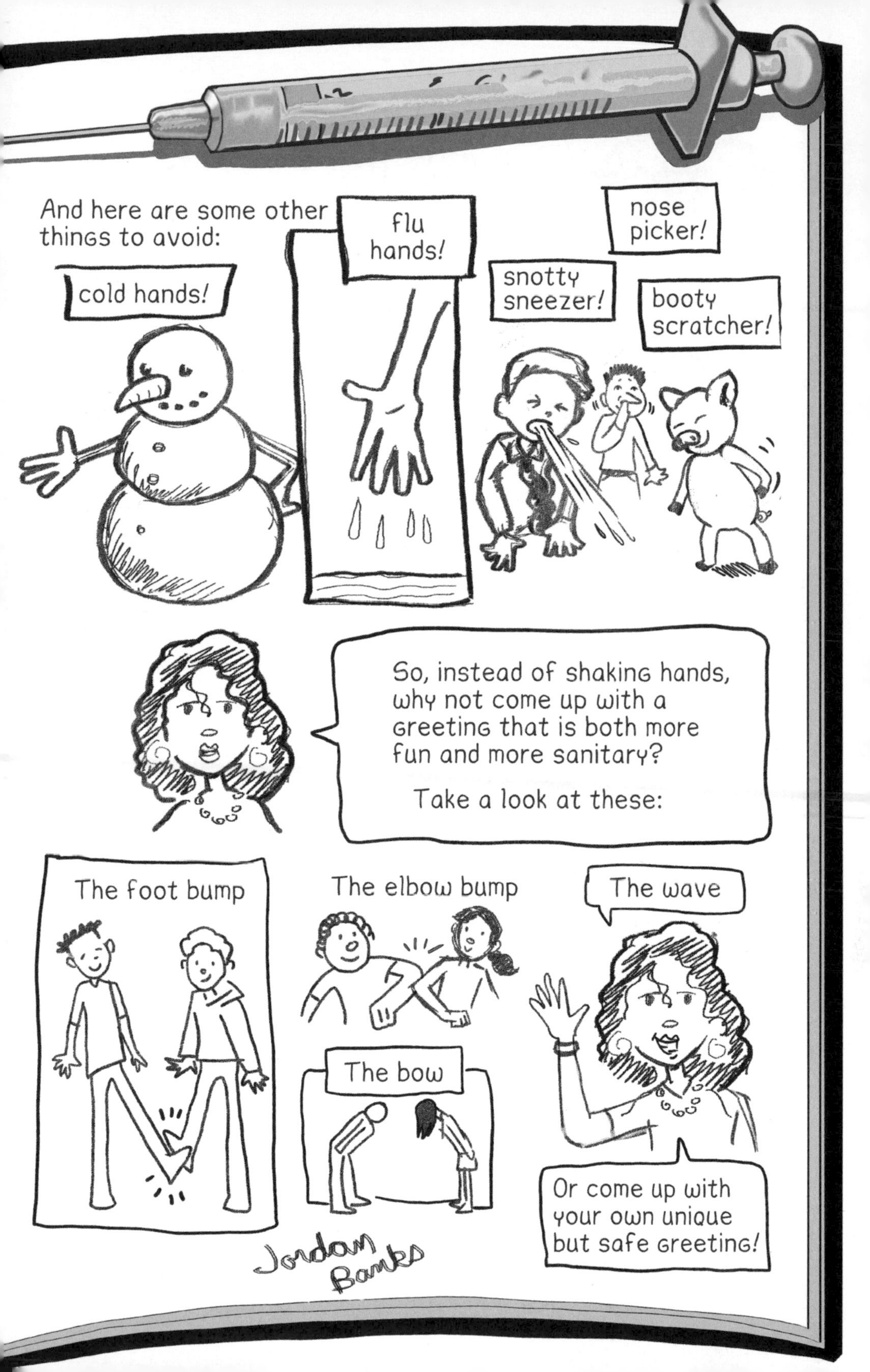
And here are some other things to avoid:
cold hands!
flu hands!
snotty sneezer!
nose picker!
booty scratcher!
So, instead of shaking hands, why not come up with a greeting that is both more fun and more sanitary?
Take a look at these:
The foot bump
The elbow bump
The bow
The wave
Or come up with your own unique but safe greeting!
Jordan Banks

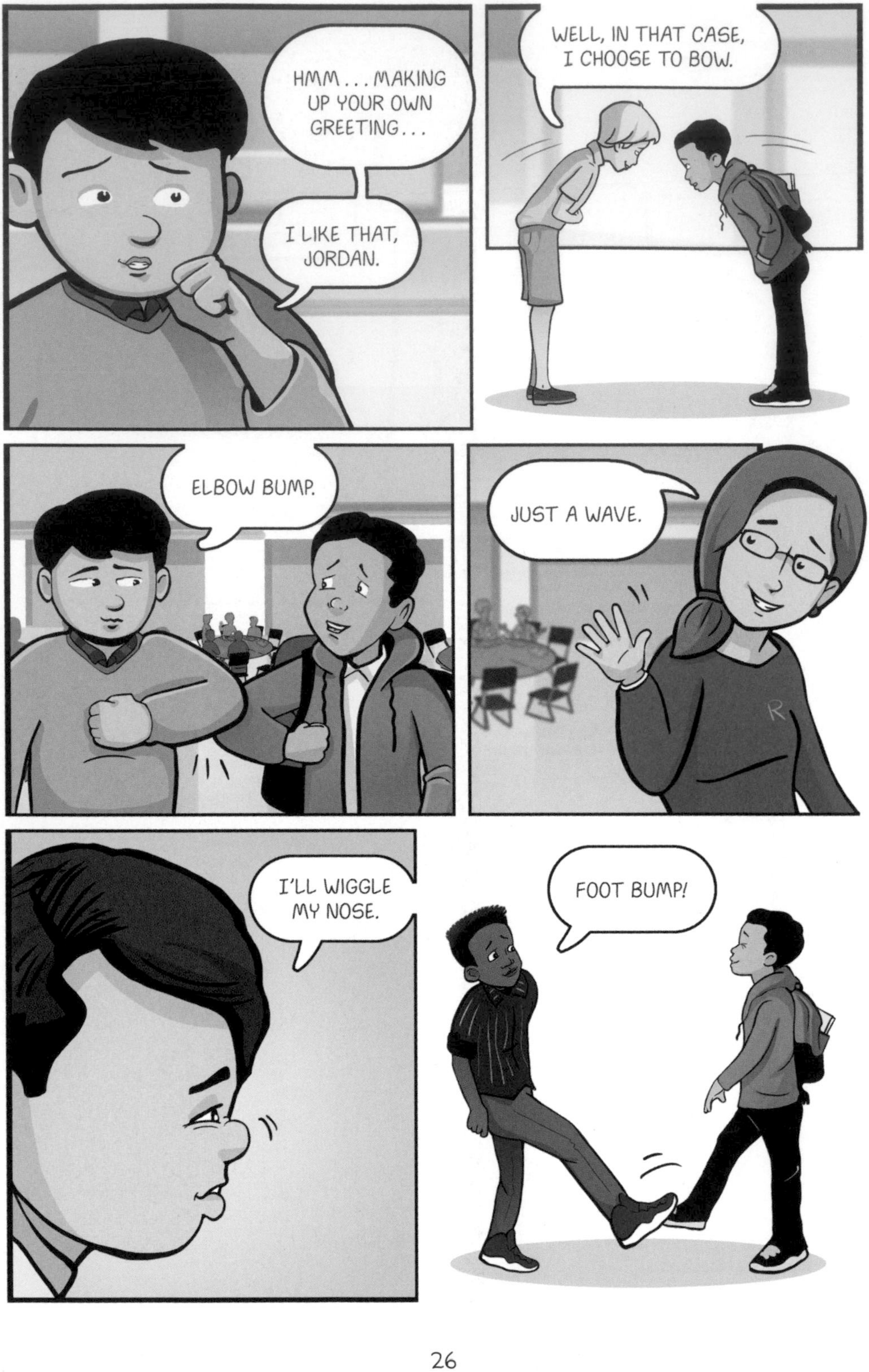
HMM . . . MAKING UP YOUR OWN GREETING . . .
I LIKE THAT, JORDAN.
WELL, IN THAT CASE, I CHOOSE TO BOW.
ELBOW BUMP.
JUST A WAVE.
I'LL WIGGLE MY NOSE.
FOOT BUMP!

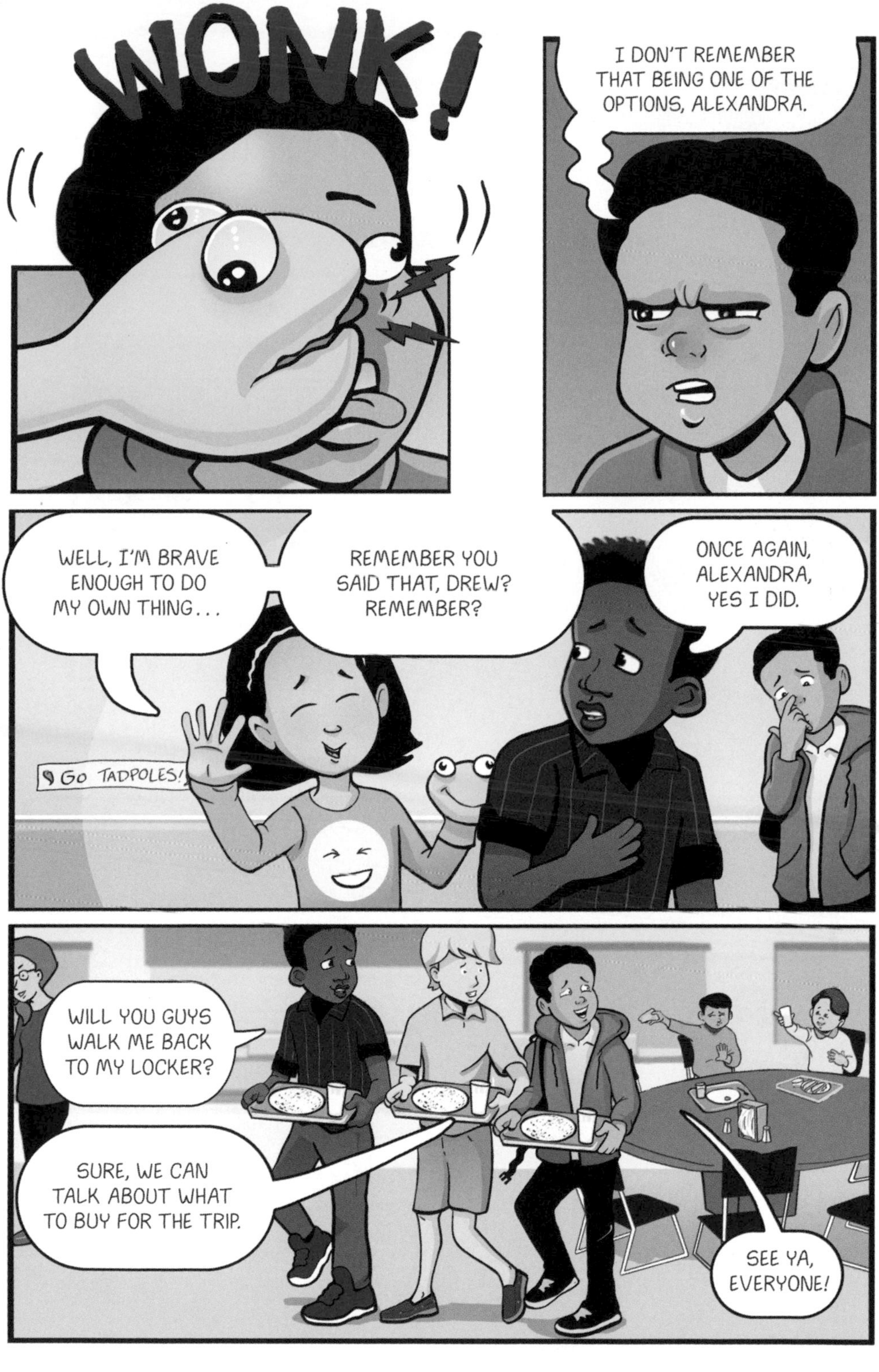
WONK!
I DON'T REMEMBER THAT BEING ONE OF THE OPTIONS, ALEXANDRA.
WELL, I'M BRAVE ENOUGH TO DO MY OWN THING...
REMEMBER YOU SAID THAT, DREW? REMEMBER?
ONCE AGAIN, ALEXANDRA, YES I DID.
GO TADPOLES!
WILL YOU GUYS WALK ME BACK TO MY LOCKER?
SURE, WE CAN TALK ABOUT WHAT TO BUY FOR THE TRIP.
SEE YA, EVERYONE!

2 Where's Mall-do?

(Now You Don't See Us . . . Now You DO!)

Now You Don't See Us:

When my dad tries to get a salesperson's attention while we shop.

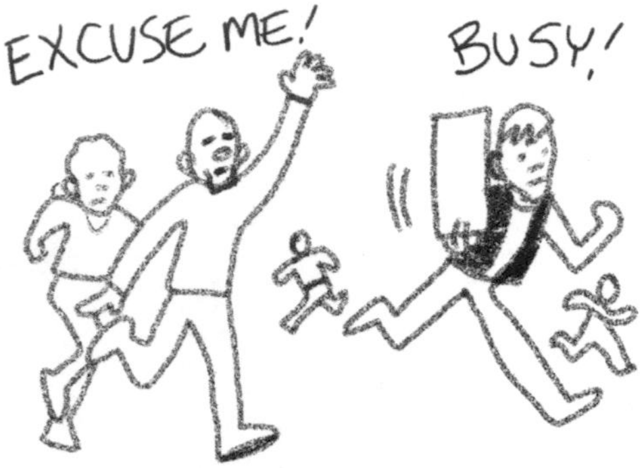
EXCUSE ME!
BUSY!

Now You Don't See Us:

When my mom goes shopping and she says all the clothes are three sizes too small.

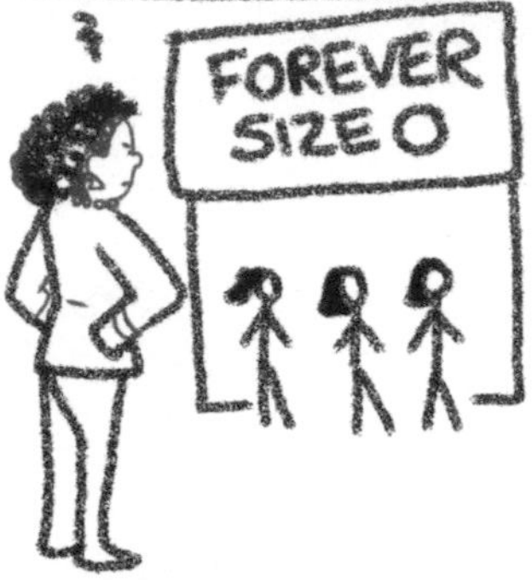
FOREVER SIZE 0

Now You Don't See Us:

When we finally get a salesperson . . .

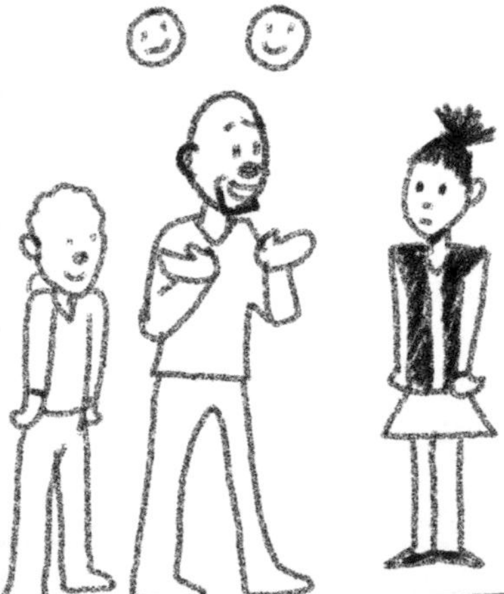

Only to lose them to someone else. AGAIN!

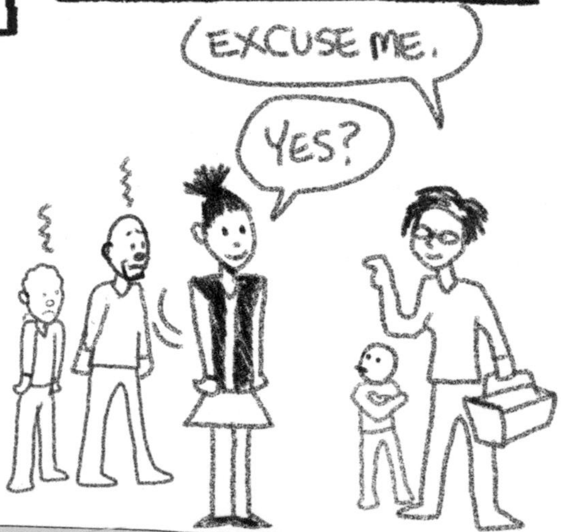
EXCUSE ME.
YES?

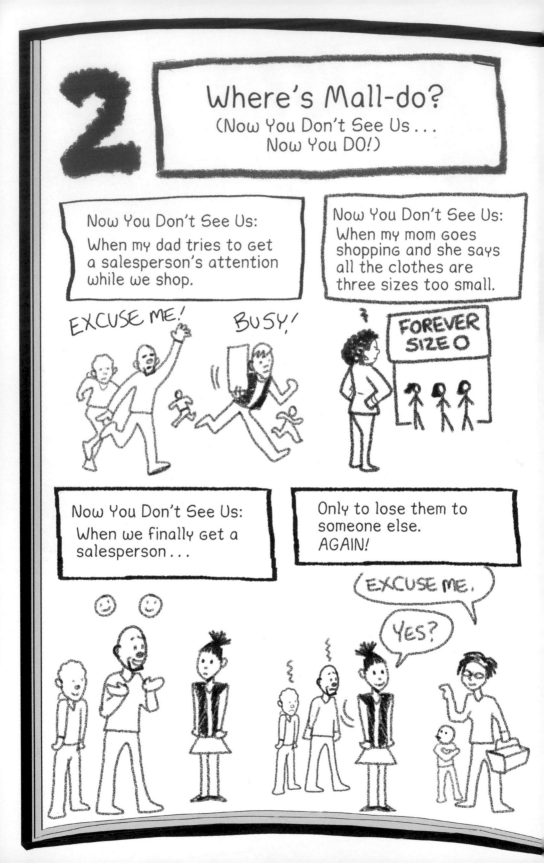

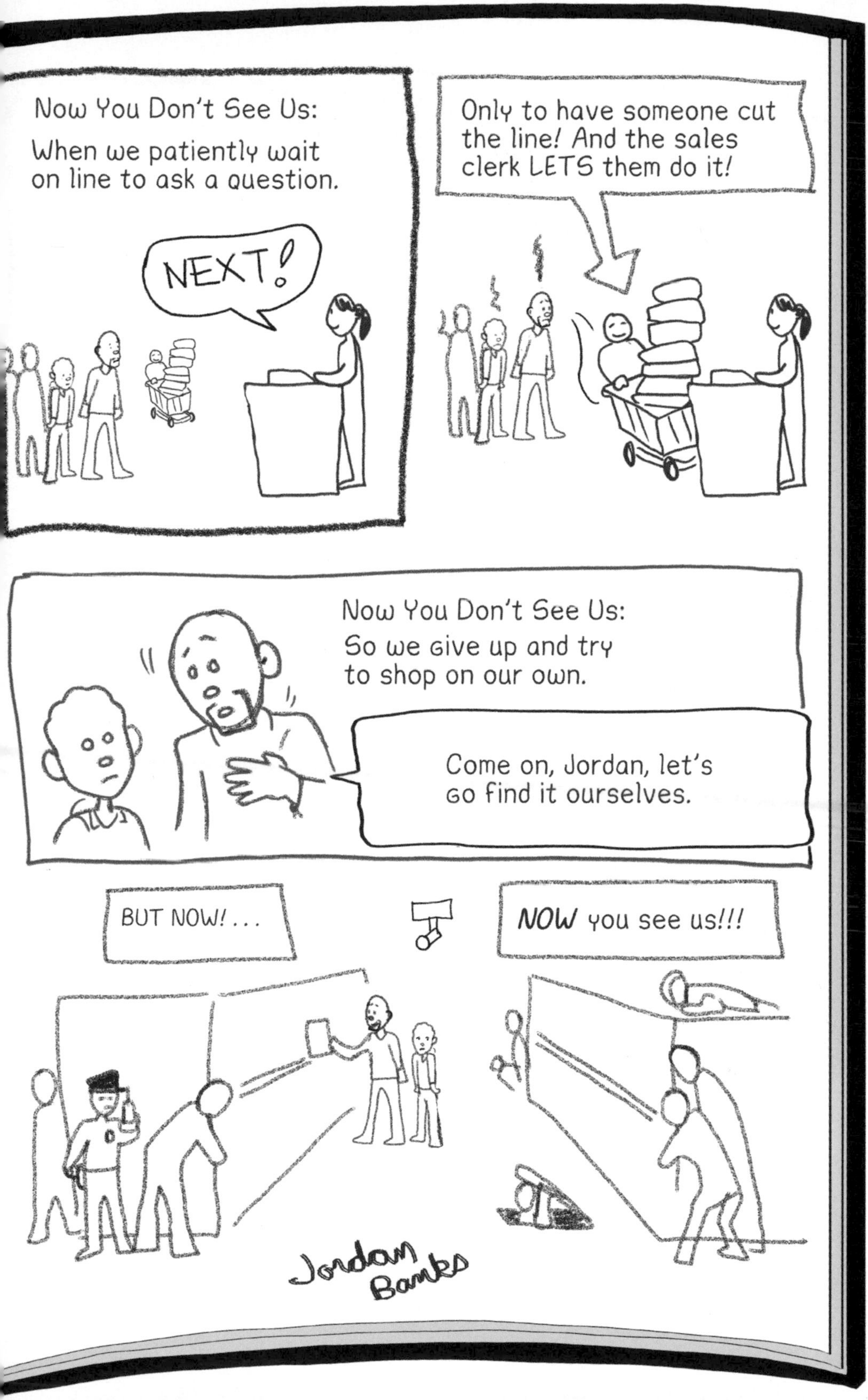
Now You Don't See Us:
When we patiently wait on line to ask a question.
NEXT!
Only to have someone cut the line! And the sales clerk LETS them do it!
Now You Don't See Us:
So we give up and try to shop on our own.
Come on, Jordan, let's go find it ourselves.
BUT NOW! . . .
NOW you see us!!!
Jordan Banks

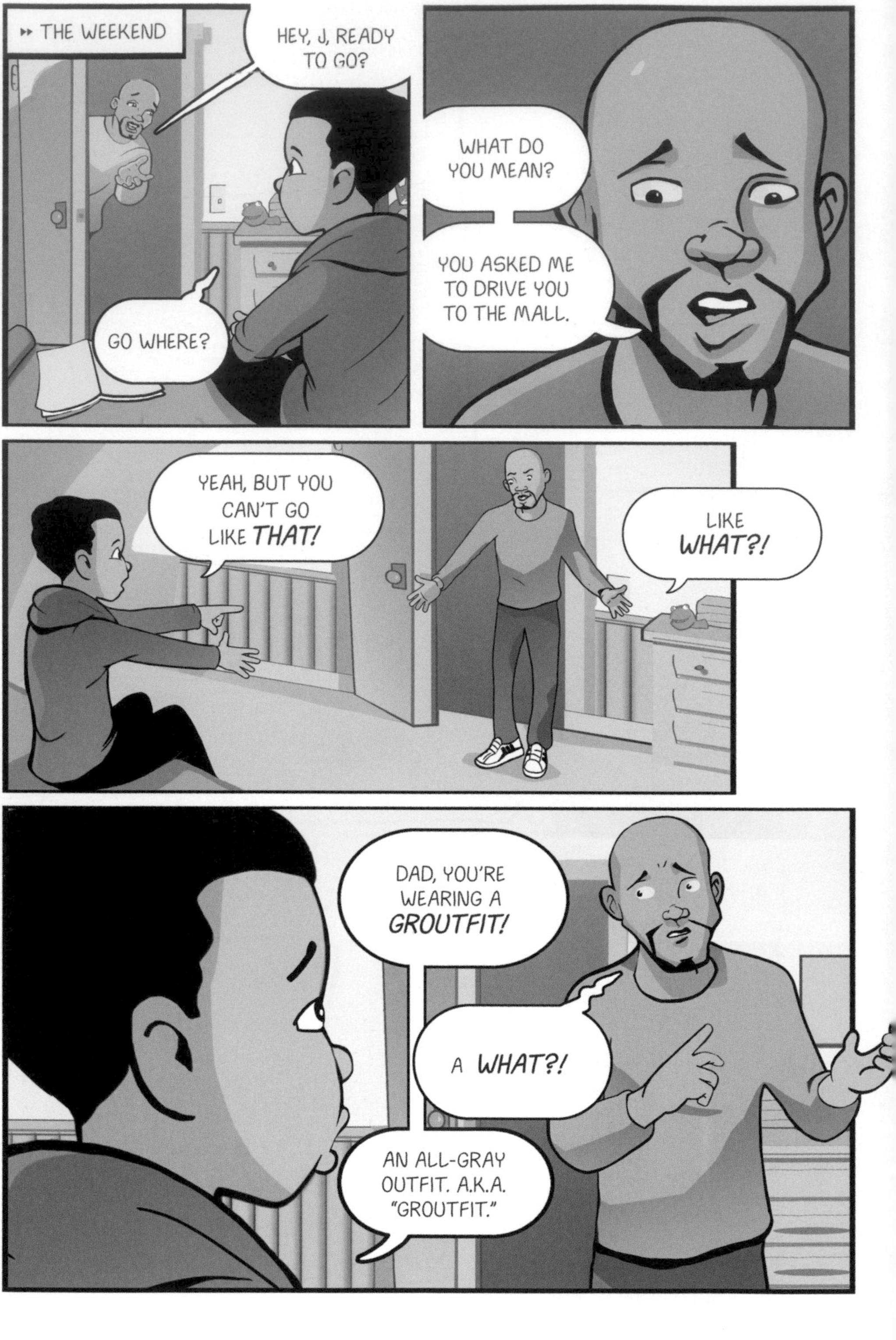
THE WEEKEND
HEY, J, READY TO GO?
GO WHERE?
WHAT DO YOU MEAN?
YOU ASKED ME TO DRIVE YOU TO THE MALL.
YEAH, BUT YOU CAN'T GO LIKE THAT!
LIKE WHAT?!
DAD, YOU'RE WEARING A GROUTFIT!
A WHAT?!
AN ALL-GRAY OUTFIT. A.K.A. "GROUTFIT."

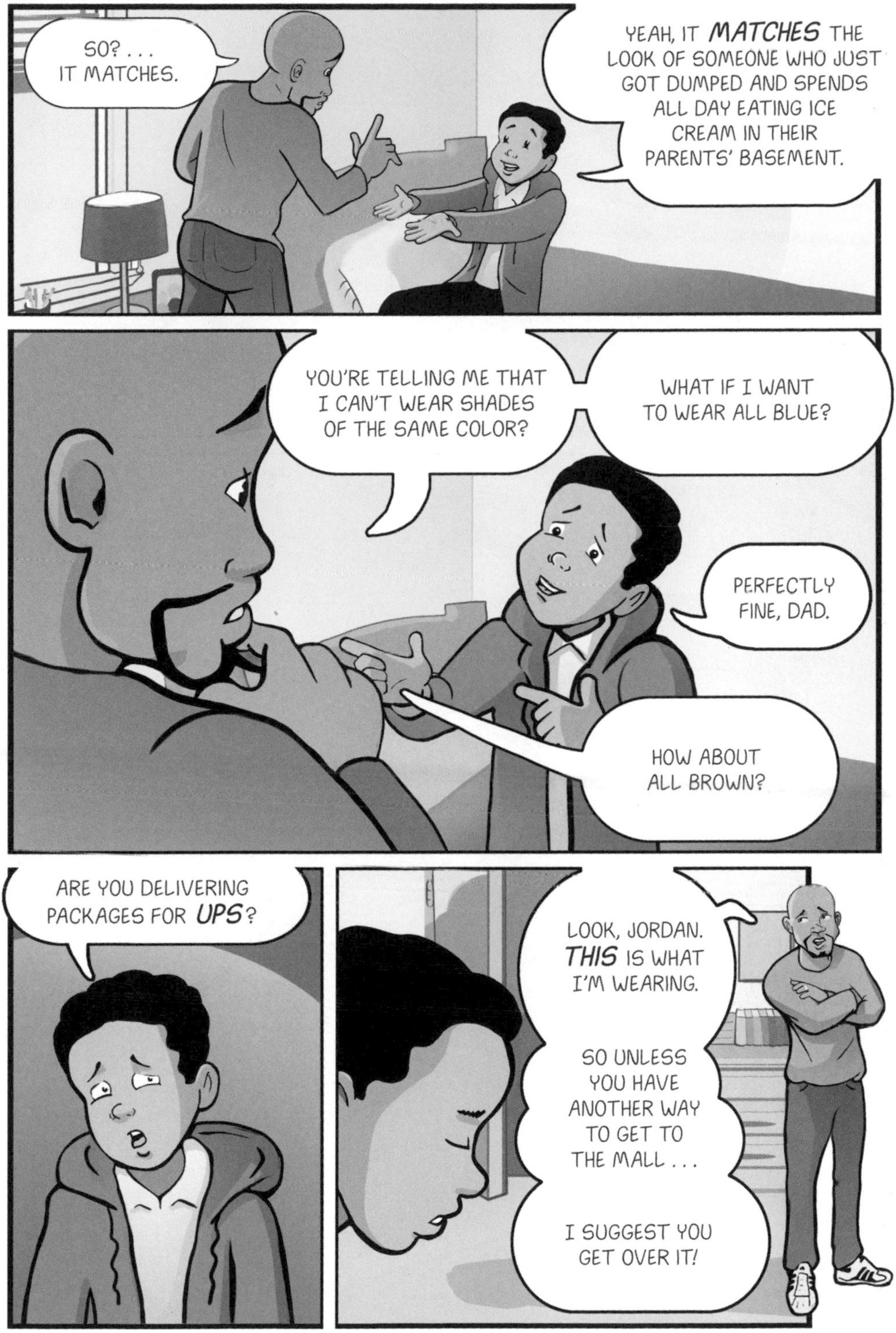
SO? . . .
IT MATCHES.
YEAH, IT MATCHES THE LOOK OF SOMEONE WHO JUST GOT DUMPED AND SPENDS ALL DAY EATING ICE CREAM IN THEIR PARENTS' BASEMENT.
YOU'RE TELLING ME THAT I CAN'T WEAR SHADES OF THE SAME COLOR?
WHAT IF I WANT TO WEAR ALL BLUE?
PERFECTLY FINE, DAD.
HOW ABOUT ALL BROWN?
ARE YOU DELIVERING PACKAGES FOR UPS?
LOOK, JORDAN. THIS IS WHAT I'M WEARING.
SO UNLESS YOU HAVE ANOTHER WAY TO GET TO THE MALL . . .
I SUGGEST YOU GET OVER IT!

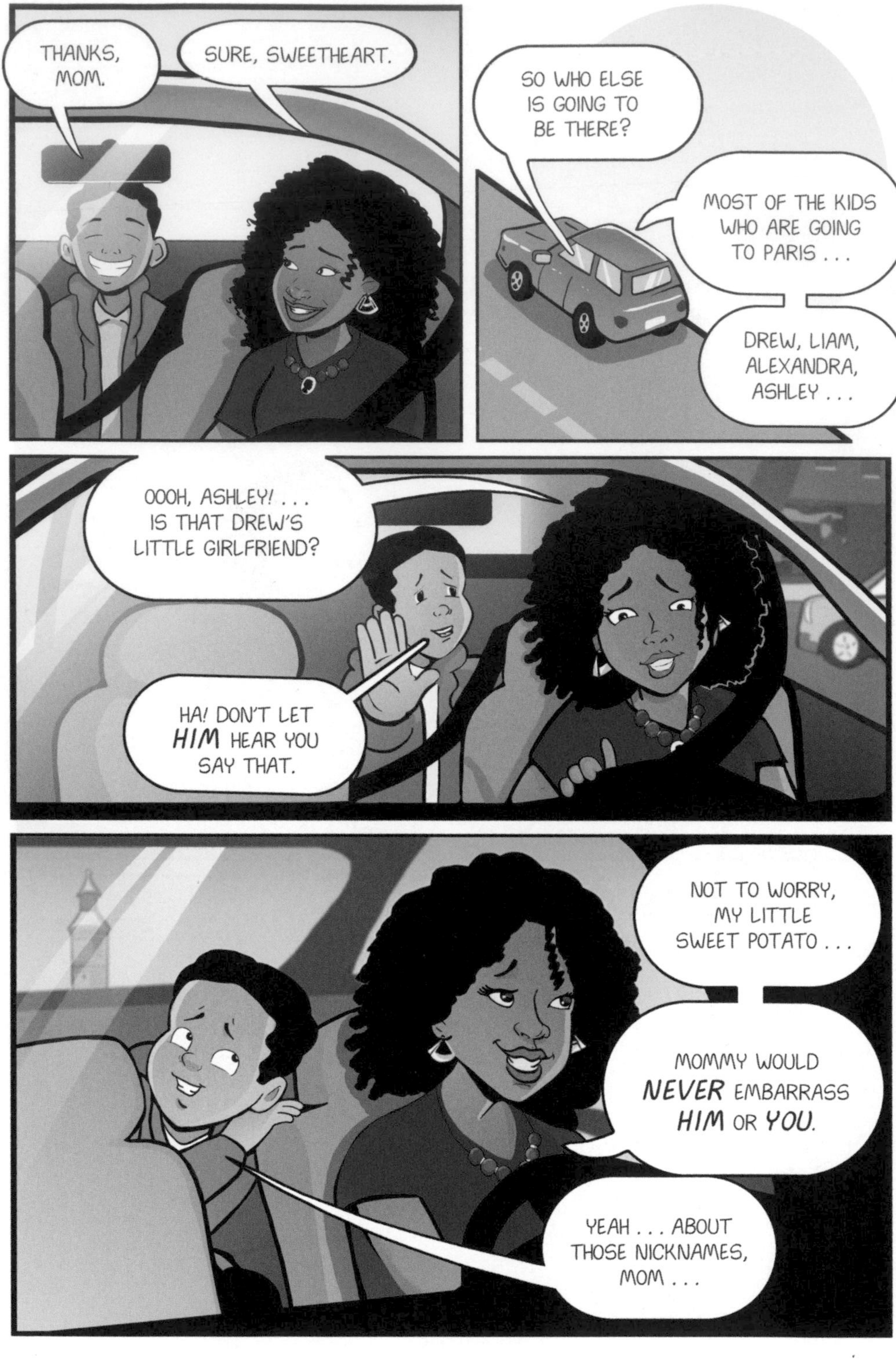
THANKS, MOM.
SURE, SWEETHEART.
SO WHO ELSE IS GOING TO BE THERE?
MOST OF THE KIDS WHO ARE GOING TO PARIS . . .
DREW, LIAM, ALEXANDRA, ASHLEY . . .
OOOH, ASHLEY! . . . IS THAT DREW'S LITTLE GIRLFRIEND?
HA! DON'T LET HIM HEAR YOU SAY THAT.
NOT TO WORRY, MY LITTLE SWEET POTATO . . .
MOMMY WOULD NEVER EMBARRASS HIM OR YOU.
YEAH . . . ABOUT THOSE NICKNAMES, MOM . . .

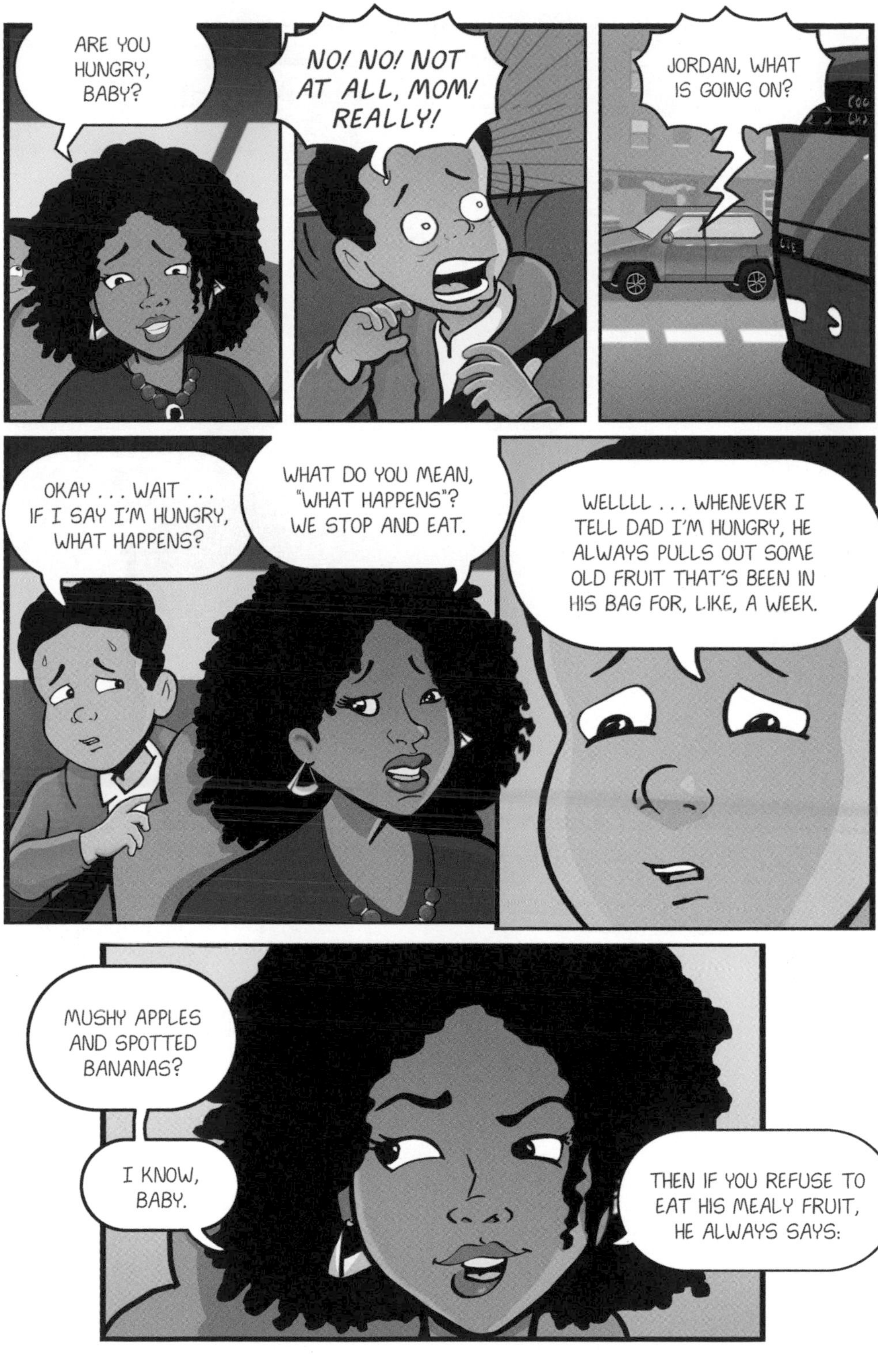
ARE YOU HUNGRY, BABY?
NO! NO! NOT AT ALL, MOM! REALLY!
JORDAN, WHAT IS GOING ON?
OKAY . . . WAIT . . . IF I SAY I'M HUNGRY, WHAT HAPPENS?
WHAT DO YOU MEAN, "WHAT HAPPENS"? WE STOP AND EAT.
WELLLL . . . WHENEVER I TELL DAD I'M HUNGRY, HE ALWAYS PULLS OUT SOME OLD FRUIT THAT'S BEEN IN HIS BAG FOR, LIKE, A WEEK.
MUSHY APPLES AND SPOTTED BANANAS?
I KNOW, BABY.
THEN IF YOU REFUSE TO EAT HIS MEALY FRUIT, HE ALWAYS SAYS:

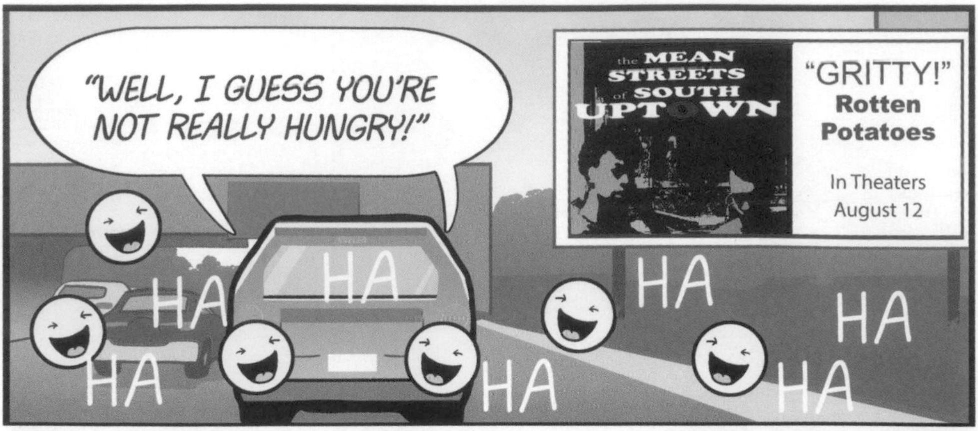
"WELL, I GUESS YOU'RE NOT REALLY HUNGRY!"
the MEAN STREETS of SOUTH UPTOWN
"GRITTY!" Rotten Potatoes
In Theaters August 12
HA HA HA HA HA HA HA

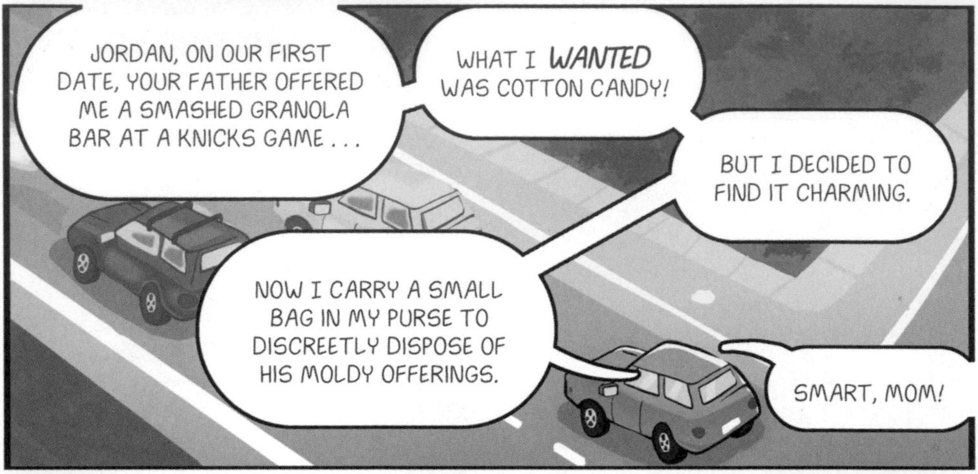
JORDAN, ON OUR FIRST DATE, YOUR FATHER OFFERED ME A SMASHED GRANOLA BAR AT A KNICKS GAME . . .
WHAT I *WANTED* WAS COTTON CANDY!
BUT I DECIDED TO FIND IT CHARMING.
NOW I CARRY A SMALL BAG IN MY PURSE TO DISCREETLY DISPOSE OF HIS MOLDY OFFERINGS.
SMART, MOM!

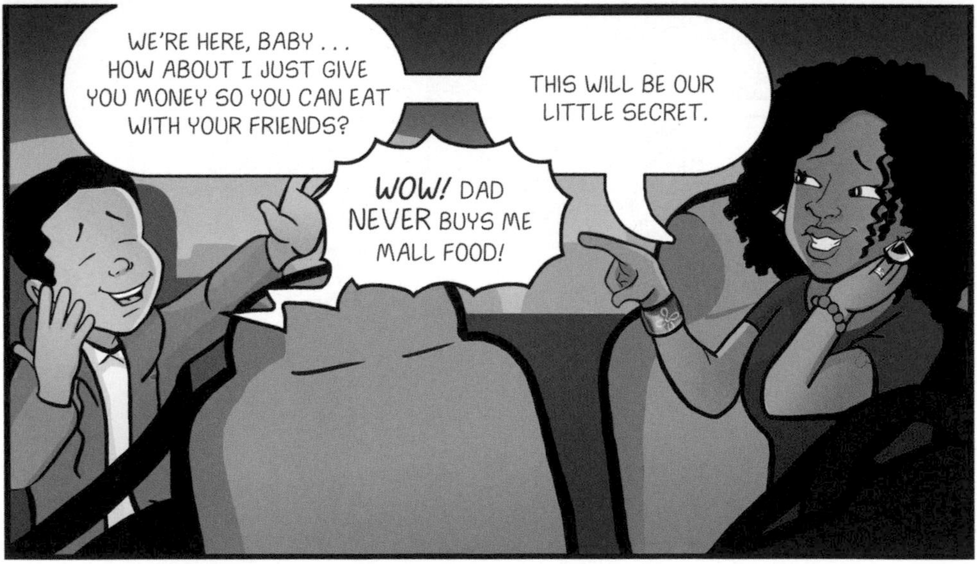
WE'RE HERE, BABY . . . HOW ABOUT I JUST GIVE YOU MONEY SO YOU CAN EAT WITH YOUR FRIENDS?
THIS WILL BE OUR LITTLE SECRET.
WOW! DAD NEVER BUYS ME MALL FOOD!

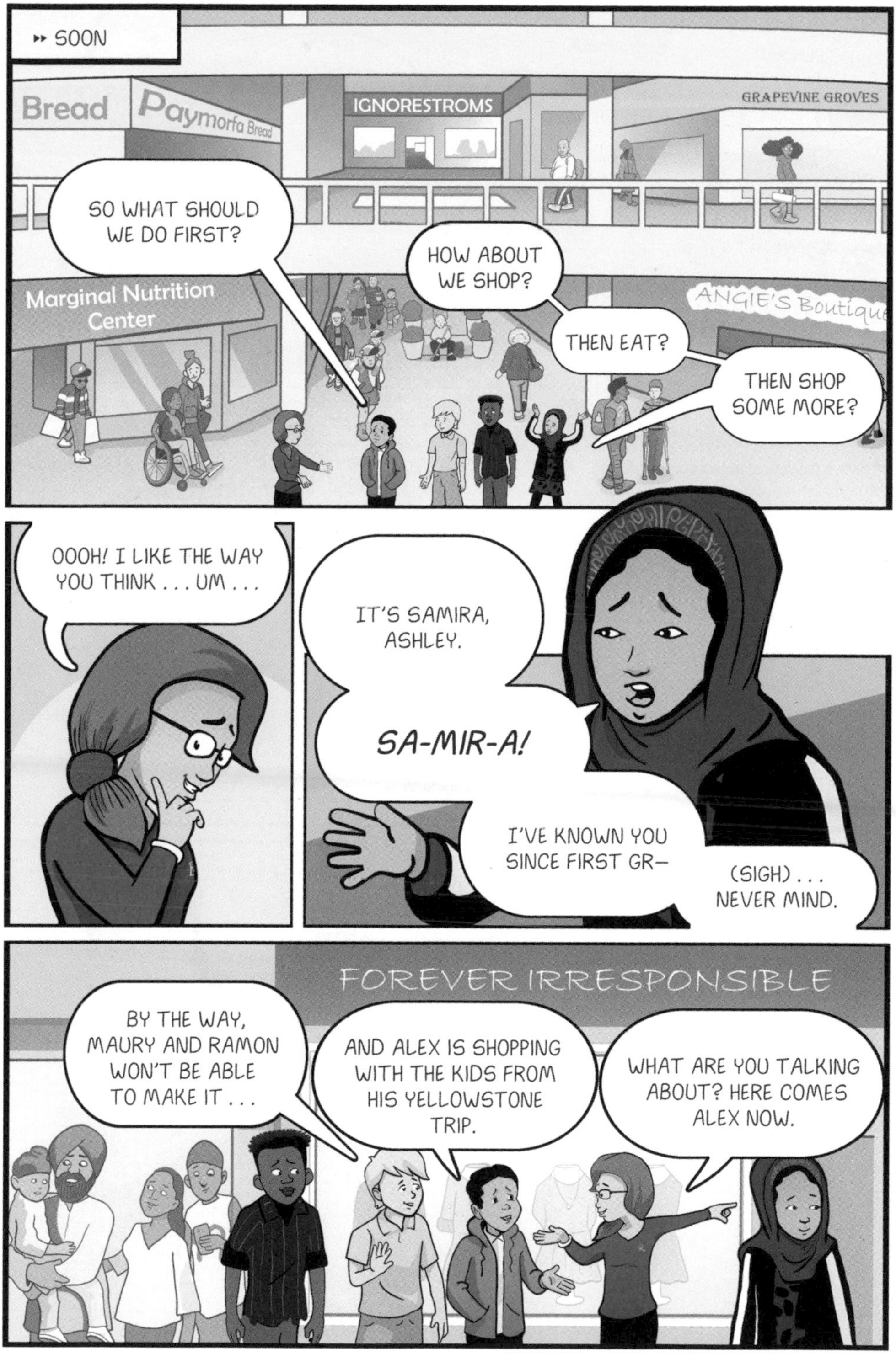
▸▸ SOON
Bread
Paymorfa Bread
IGNORESTROMS
GRAPEVINE GROVES
SO WHAT SHOULD WE DO FIRST?
HOW ABOUT WE SHOP?
Marginal Nutrition Center
ANGIE'S Boutique
THEN EAT?
THEN SHOP SOME MORE?
OOOH! I LIKE THE WAY YOU THINK . . . UM . . .
IT'S SAMIRA, ASHLEY.
SA-MIR-A!
I'VE KNOWN YOU SINCE FIRST GR—
(SIGH) . . . NEVER MIND.
FOREVER IRRESPONSIBLE
BY THE WAY, MAURY AND RAMON WON'T BE ABLE TO MAKE IT . . .
AND ALEX IS SHOPPING WITH THE KIDS FROM HIS YELLOWSTONE TRIP.
WHAT ARE YOU TALKING ABOUT? HERE COMES ALEX NOW.

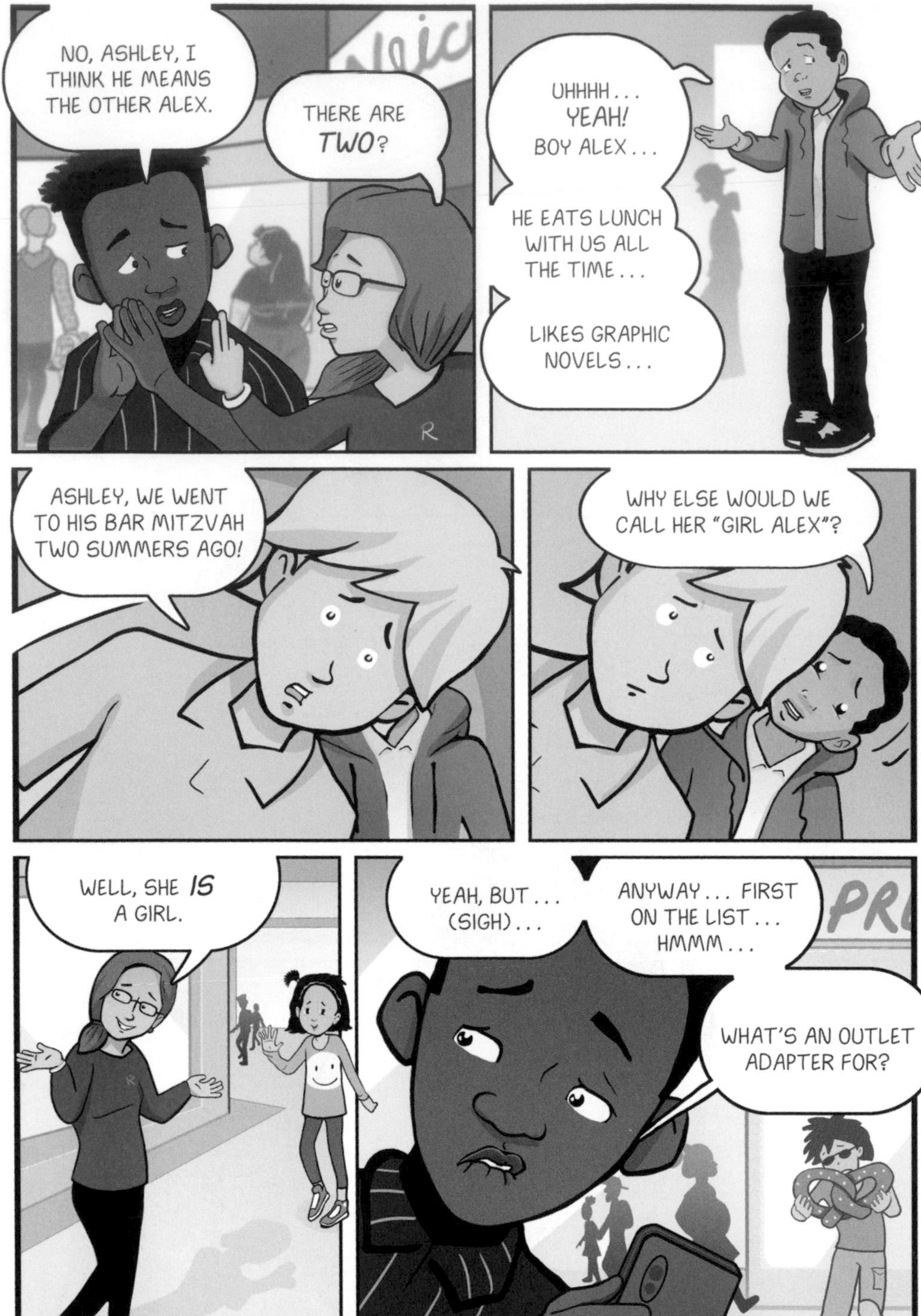
NO, ASHLEY, I THINK HE MEANS THE OTHER ALEX.
THERE ARE *TWO*?
UHHHH... YEAH! BOY ALEX...
HE EATS LUNCH WITH US ALL THE TIME...
LIKES GRAPHIC NOVELS...
ASHLEY, WE WENT TO HIS BAR MITZVAH TWO SUMMERS AGO!
WHY ELSE WOULD WE CALL HER "GIRL ALEX"?
WELL, SHE *IS* A GIRL.
YEAH, BUT... (SIGH)...
ANYWAY... FIRST ON THE LIST... HMMM...
WHAT'S AN OUTLET ADAPTER FOR?

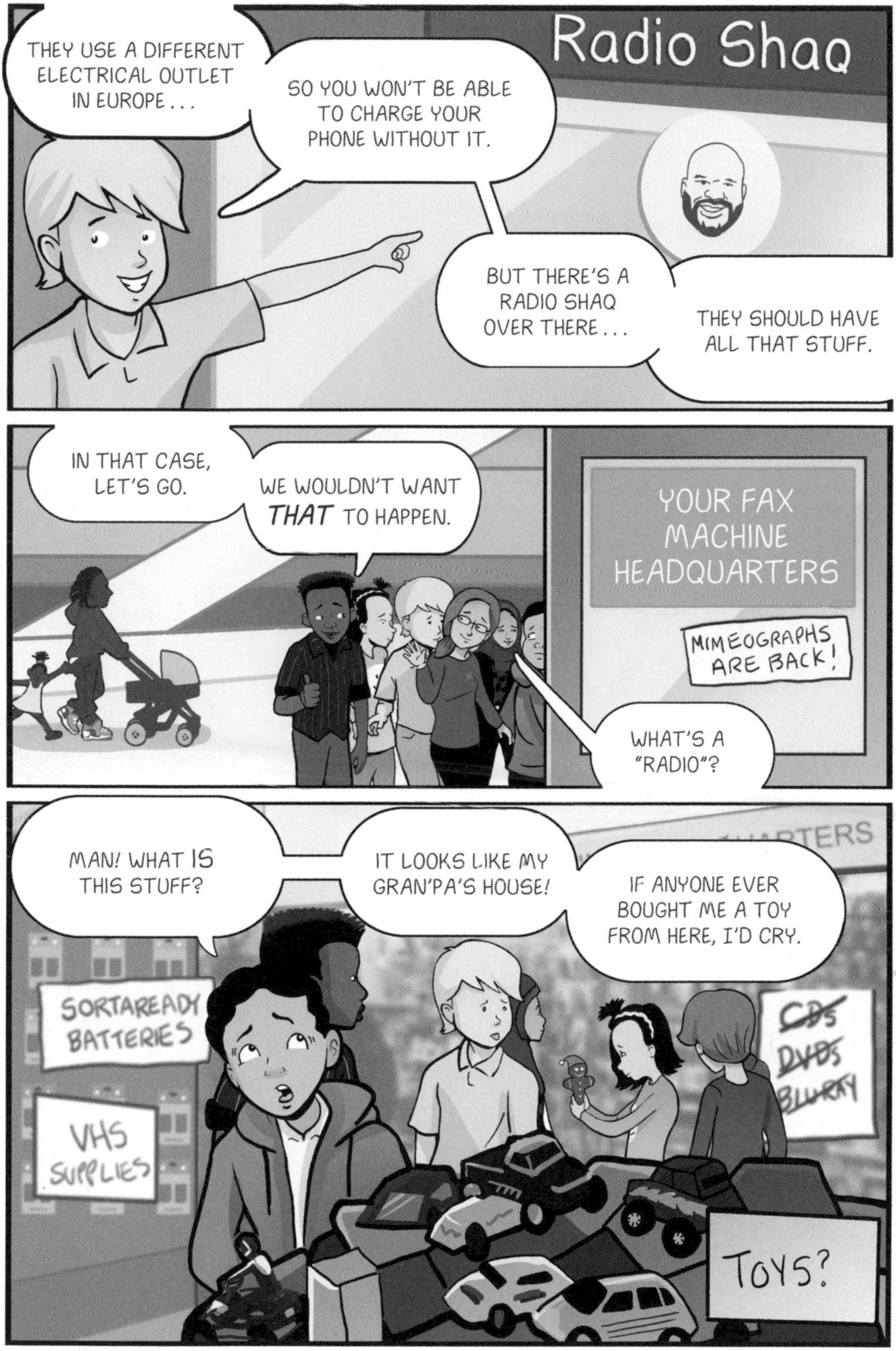

THEY USE A DIFFERENT ELECTRICAL OUTLET IN EUROPE . . .
SO YOU WON'T BE ABLE TO CHARGE YOUR PHONE WITHOUT IT.
Radio Shaq
BUT THERE'S A RADIO SHAQ OVER THERE . . .
THEY SHOULD HAVE ALL THAT STUFF.
IN THAT CASE, LET'S GO.
WE WOULDN'T WANT *THAT* TO HAPPEN.
YOUR FAX MACHINE HEADQUARTERS
MIMEOGRAPHS ARE BACK!
WHAT'S A "RADIO"?
MAN! WHAT IS THIS STUFF?
IT LOOKS LIKE MY GRAN'PA'S HOUSE!
IF ANYONE EVER BOUGHT ME A TOY FROM HERE, I'D CRY.
SORTAREADY BATTERIES
VHS SUPPLIES
~~CDs~~ ~~DVDs~~ ~~BLURAY~~
TOYS?

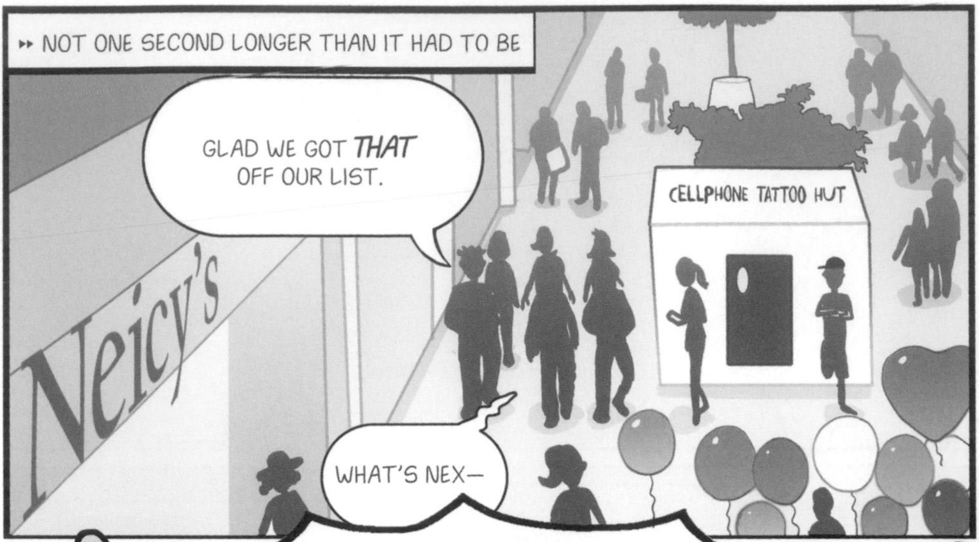
▸▸ NOT ONE SECOND LONGER THAN IT HAD TO BE
GLAD WE GOT *THAT* OFF OUR LIST.
Neicy's
CELLPHONE TATTOO HUT
WHAT'S NEX—

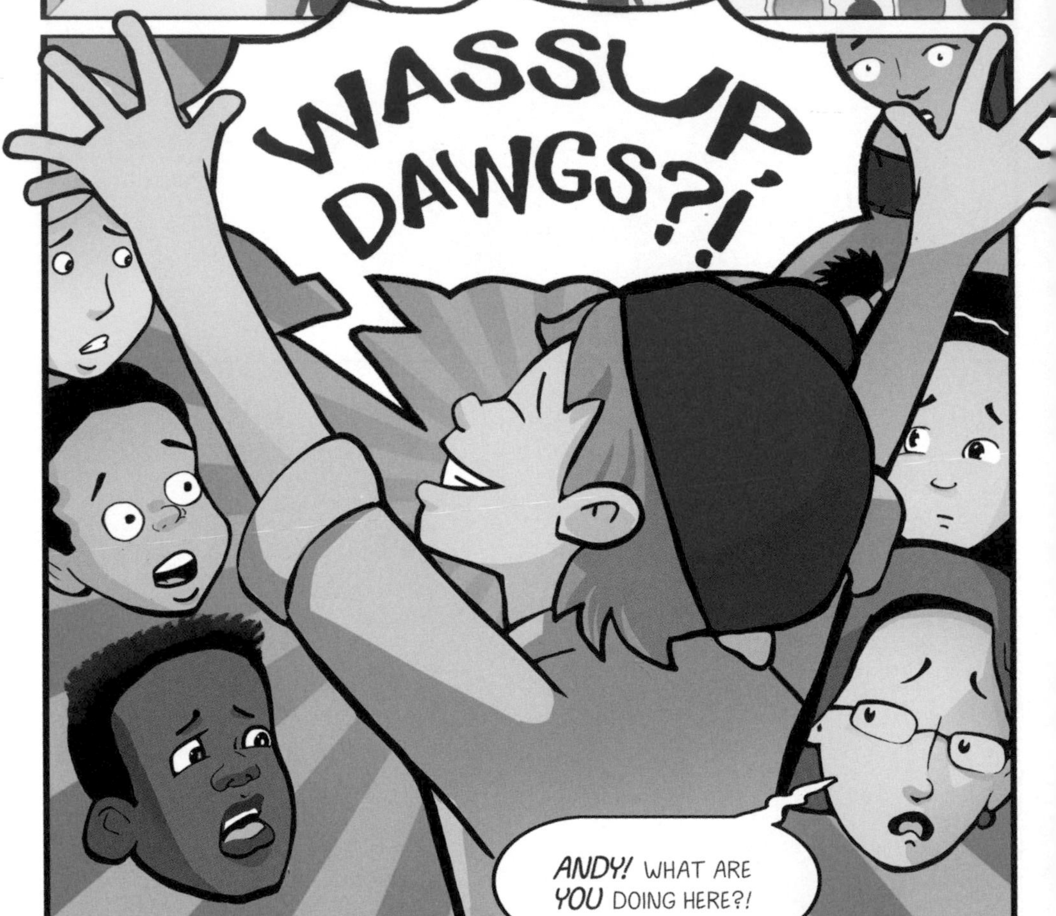
WASSUP DAWGS?!
ANDY! WHAT ARE *YOU* DOING HERE?!

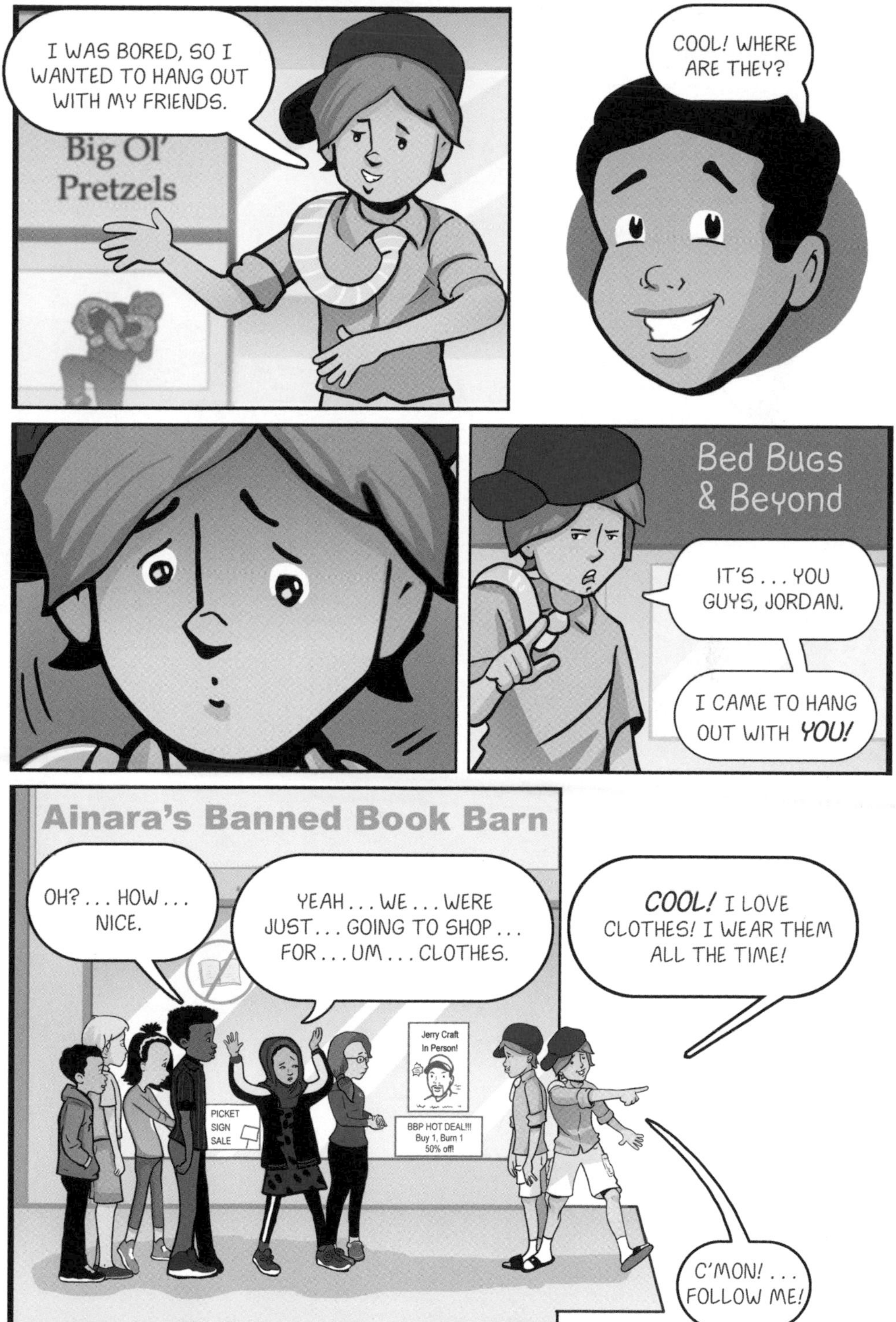

I WAS BORED, SO I WANTED TO HANG OUT WITH MY FRIENDS.
Big Ol' Pretzels
COOL! WHERE ARE THEY?
Bed Bugs & Beyond
IT'S . . . YOU GUYS, JORDAN.
I CAME TO HANG OUT WITH ***YOU!***
Ainara's Banned Book Barn
OH? . . . HOW . . . NICE.
YEAH . . . WE . . . WERE JUST . . . GOING TO SHOP . . . FOR . . . UM . . . CLOTHES.
PICKET SIGN SALE
Jerry Craft In Person!
BBP HOT DEAL!!! Buy 1, Burn 1 50% off!
COOL! I LOVE CLOTHES! I WEAR THEM ALL THE TIME!
C'MON! . . . FOLLOW ME!

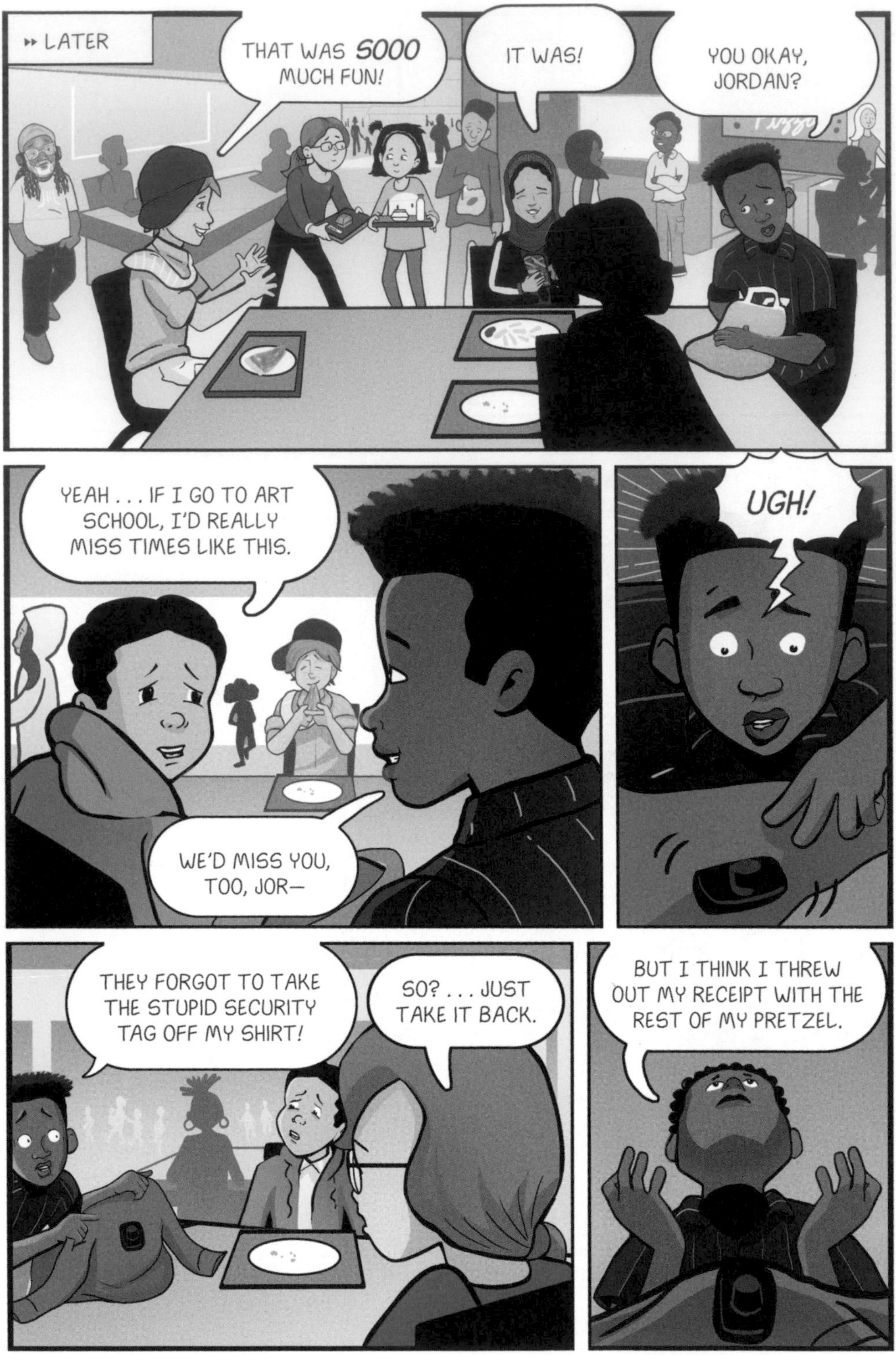
LATER
THAT WAS SOOO MUCH FUN!
IT WAS!
YOU OKAY, JORDAN?
YEAH . . . IF I GO TO ART SCHOOL, I'D REALLY MISS TIMES LIKE THIS.
WE'D MISS YOU, TOO, JOR—
UGH!
THEY FORGOT TO TAKE THE STUPID SECURITY TAG OFF MY SHIRT!
SO? . . . JUST TAKE IT BACK.
BUT I THINK I THREW OUT MY RECEIPT WITH THE REST OF MY PRETZEL.

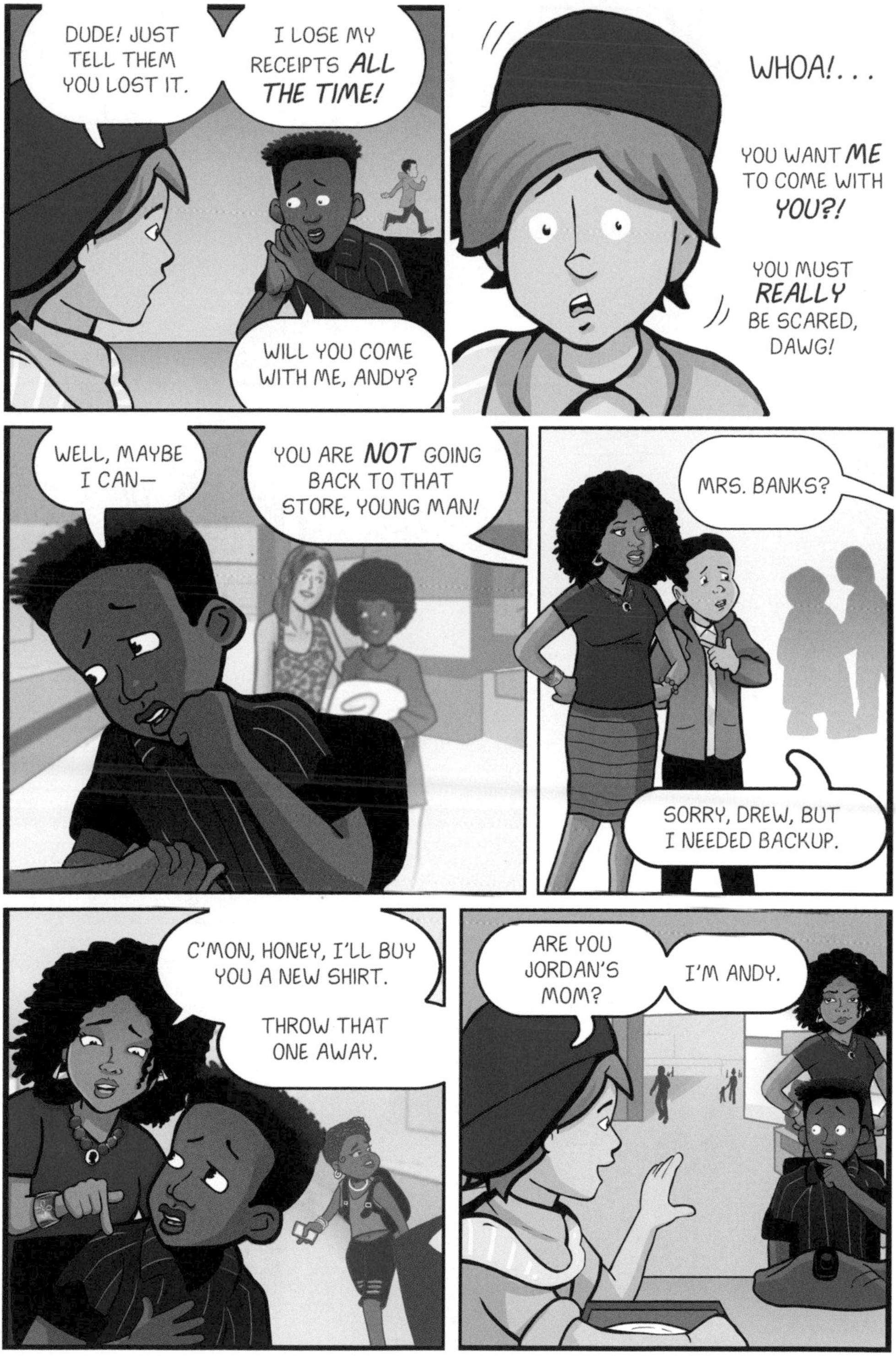
DUDE! JUST TELL THEM YOU LOST IT.
I LOSE MY RECEIPTS ALL THE TIME!
WILL YOU COME WITH ME, ANDY?
WHOA!. . .
YOU WANT ME TO COME WITH YOU?!
YOU MUST REALLY BE SCARED, DAWG!
WELL, MAYBE I CAN—
YOU ARE NOT GOING BACK TO THAT STORE, YOUNG MAN!
MRS. BANKS?
SORRY, DREW, BUT I NEEDED BACKUP.
C'MON, HONEY, I'LL BUY YOU A NEW SHIRT.
THROW THAT ONE AWAY.
ARE YOU JORDAN'S MOM?
I'M ANDY.

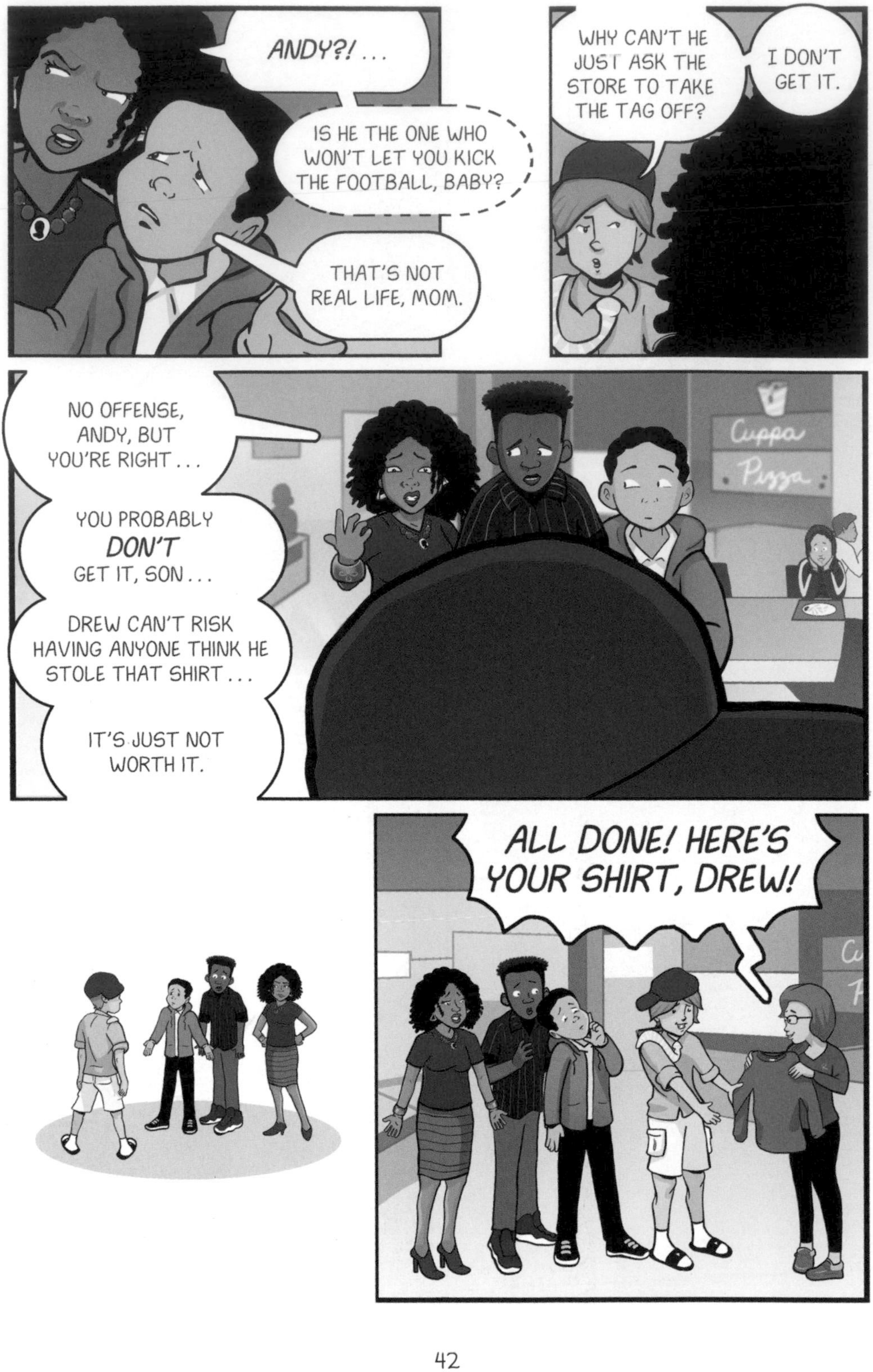
ANDY?! . . .
IS HE THE ONE WHO WON'T LET YOU KICK THE FOOTBALL, BABY?
THAT'S NOT REAL LIFE, MOM.
WHY CAN'T HE JUST ASK THE STORE TO TAKE THE TAG OFF?
I DON'T GET IT.
NO OFFENSE, ANDY, BUT YOU'RE RIGHT . . .
YOU PROBABLY DON'T GET IT, SON . . .
DREW CAN'T RISK HAVING ANYONE THINK HE STOLE THAT SHIRT . . .
IT'S JUST NOT WORTH IT.
Cuppa Pizza
ALL DONE! HERE'S YOUR SHIRT, DREW!

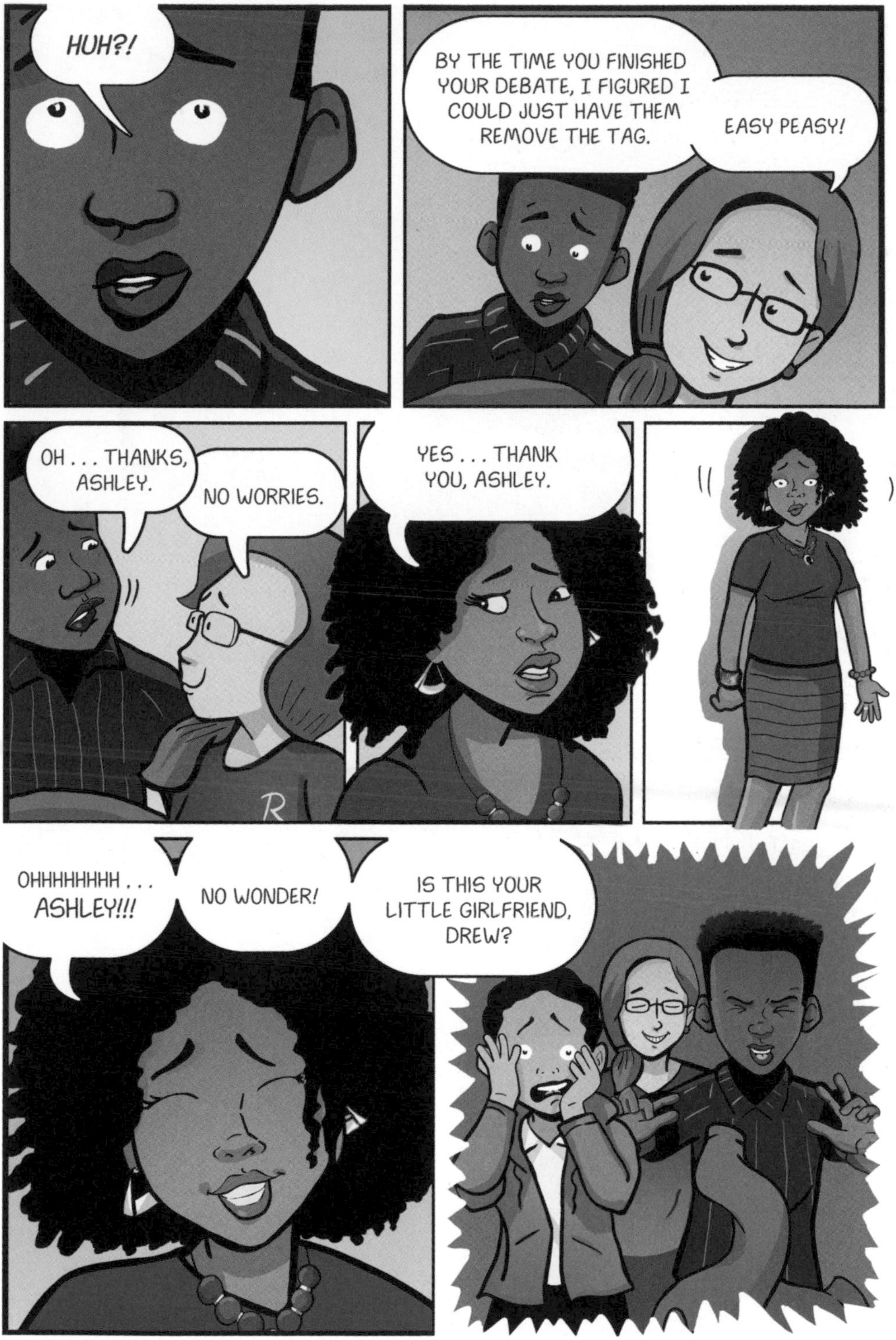
HUH?!
BY THE TIME YOU FINISHED YOUR DEBATE, I FIGURED I COULD JUST HAVE THEM REMOVE THE TAG.
EASY PEASY!
OH . . . THANKS, ASHLEY.
NO WORRIES.
YES . . . THANK YOU, ASHLEY.
OHHHHHHHH . . . ASHLEY!!!
NO WONDER!
IS THIS YOUR LITTLE GIRLFRIEND, DREW?

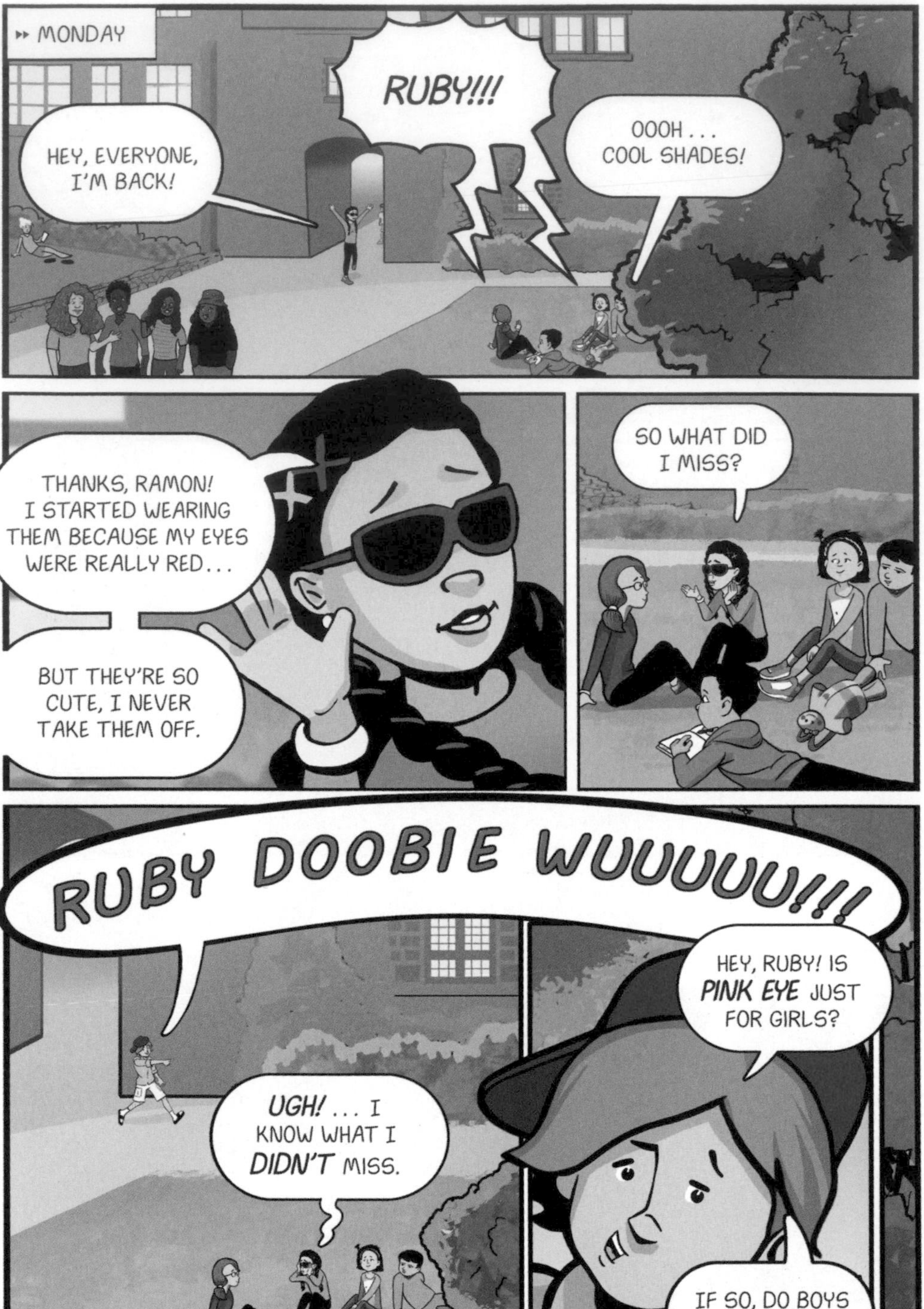

▸▸ MONDAY
HEY, EVERYONE, I'M BACK!
RUBY!!!
OOOH . . . COOL SHADES!
THANKS, RAMON! I STARTED WEARING THEM BECAUSE MY EYES WERE REALLY RED . . .
BUT THEY'RE SO CUTE, I NEVER TAKE THEM OFF.
SO WHAT DID I MISS?
RUBY DOOBIE WUUUUUU!!!
HEY, RUBY! IS PINK EYE JUST FOR GIRLS?
UGH! . . . I KNOW WHAT I DIDN'T MISS.
IF SO, DO BOYS GET BLUE EYE?

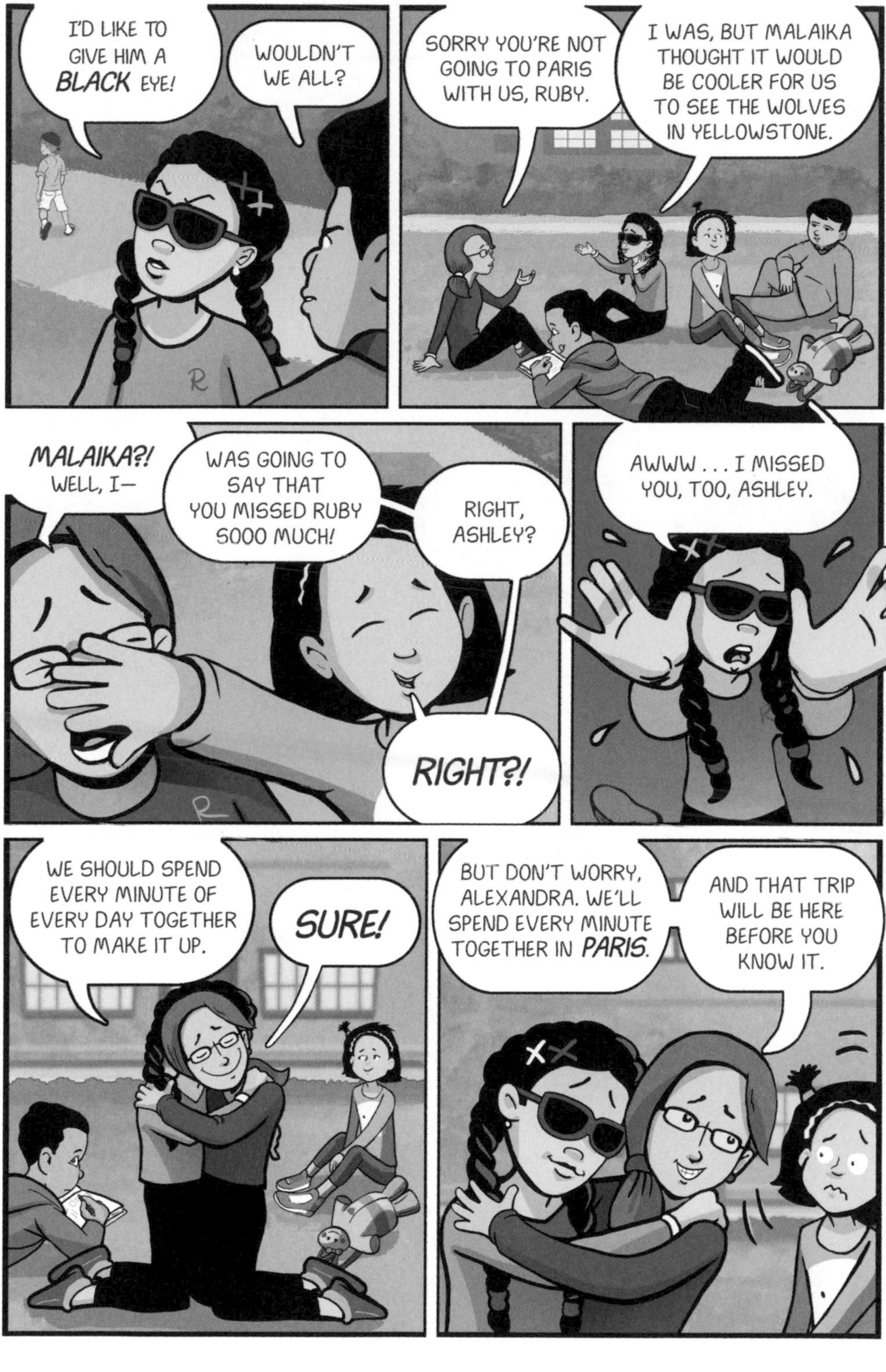

I'D LIKE TO GIVE HIM A BLACK EYE!
WOULDN'T WE ALL?
SORRY YOU'RE NOT GOING TO PARIS WITH US, RUBY.
I WAS, BUT MALAIKA THOUGHT IT WOULD BE COOLER FOR US TO SEE THE WOLVES IN YELLOWSTONE.
MALAIKA?! WELL, I—
WAS GOING TO SAY THAT YOU MISSED RUBY SOOO MUCH!
RIGHT, ASHLEY?
RIGHT?!
AWWW . . . I MISSED YOU, TOO, ASHLEY.
WE SHOULD SPEND EVERY MINUTE OF EVERY DAY TOGETHER TO MAKE IT UP.
SURE!
BUT DON'T WORRY, ALEXANDRA. WE'LL SPEND EVERY MINUTE TOGETHER IN PARIS.
AND THAT TRIP WILL BE HERE BEFORE YOU KNOW IT.

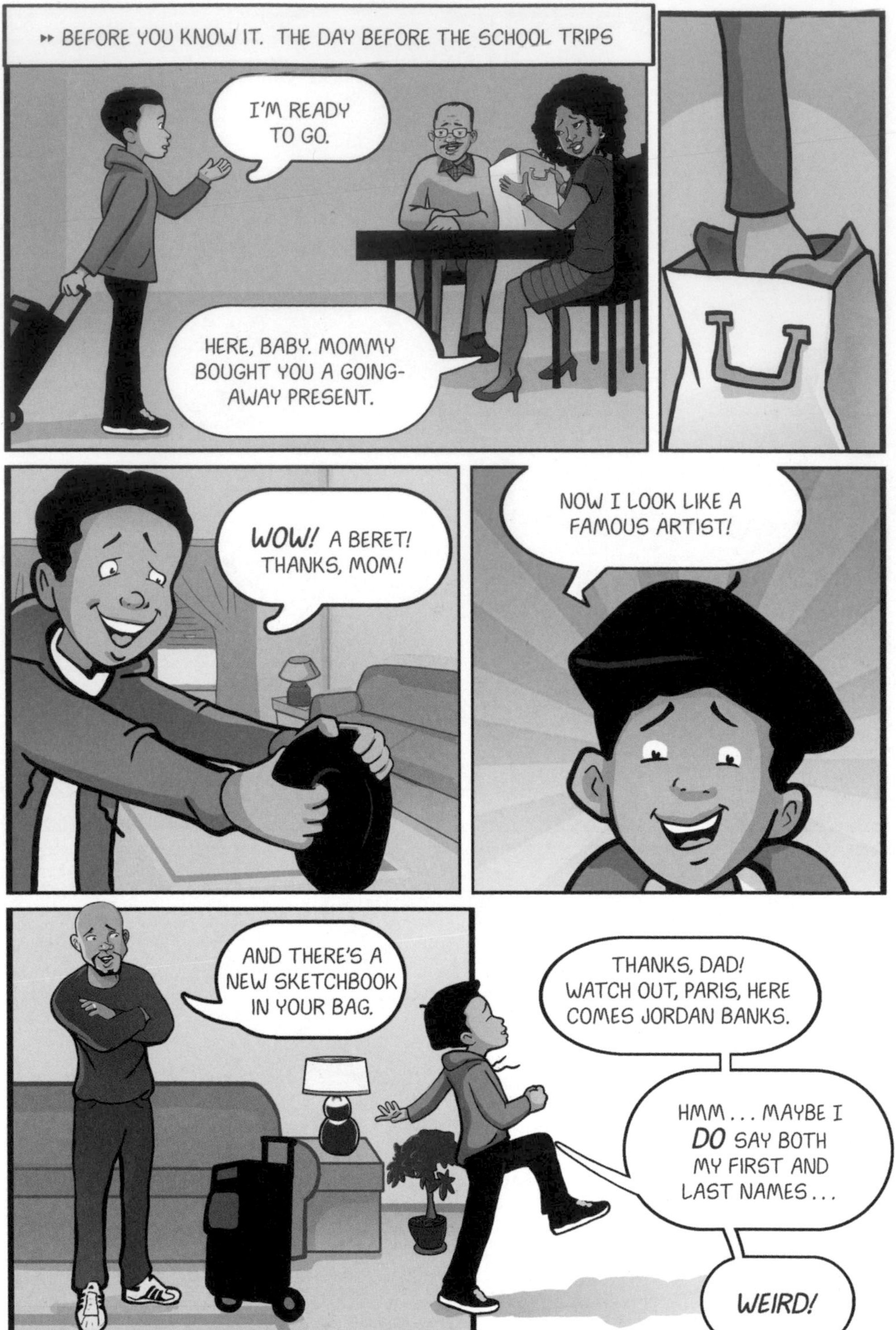
BEFORE YOU KNOW IT. THE DAY BEFORE THE SCHOOL TRIPS
I'M READY TO GO.
HERE, BABY. MOMMY BOUGHT YOU A GOING-AWAY PRESENT.
WOW! A BERET! THANKS, MOM!
NOW I LOOK LIKE A FAMOUS ARTIST!
AND THERE'S A NEW SKETCHBOOK IN YOUR BAG.
THANKS, DAD! WATCH OUT, PARIS, HERE COMES JORDAN BANKS.
HMM . . . MAYBE I DO SAY BOTH MY FIRST AND LAST NAMES . . .
WEIRD!

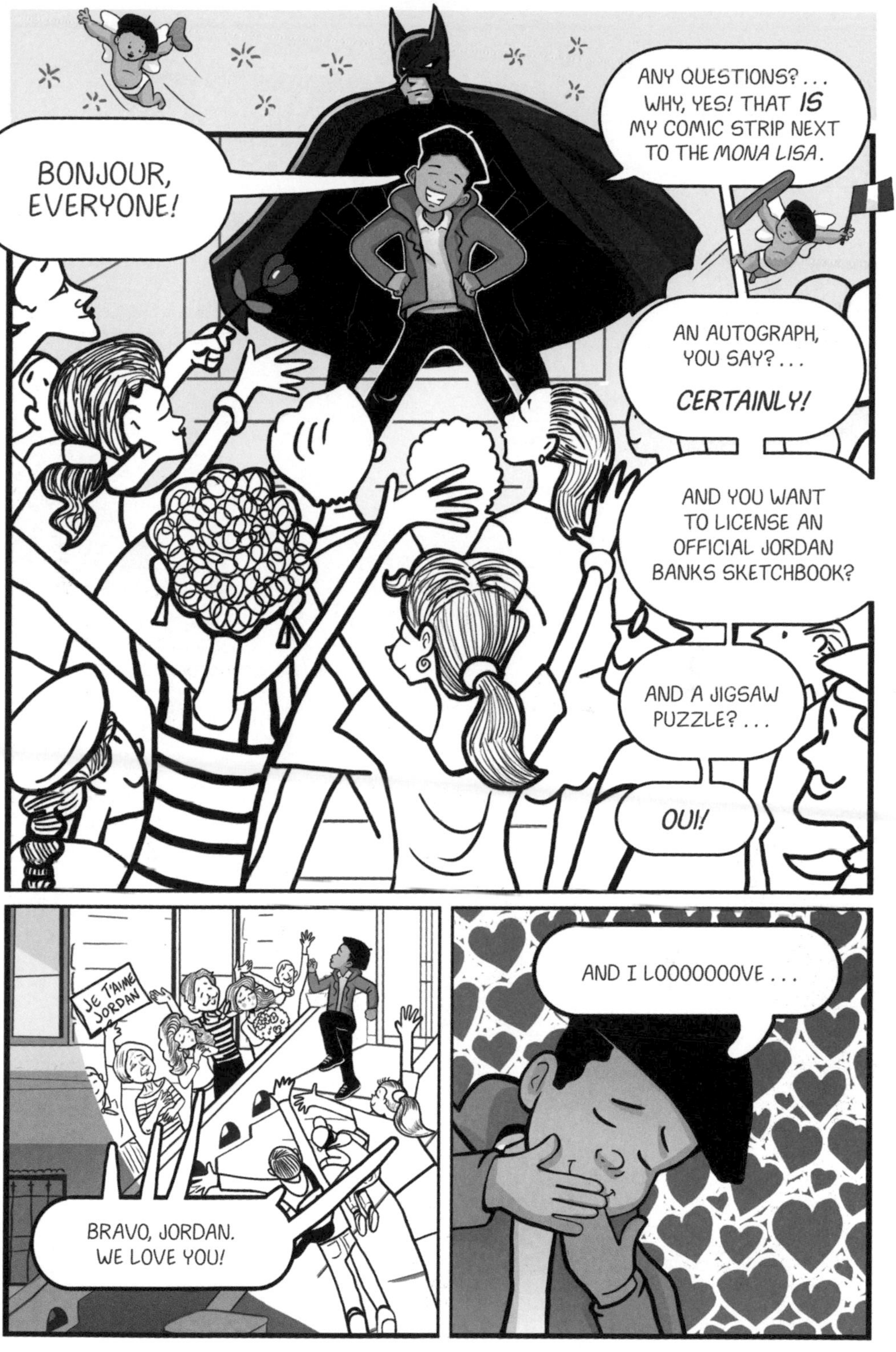
BONJOUR, EVERYONE!
ANY QUESTIONS? . . . WHY, YES! THAT *IS* MY COMIC STRIP NEXT TO THE *MONA LISA*.
AN AUTOGRAPH, YOU SAY? . . . CERTAINLY!
AND YOU WANT TO LICENSE AN OFFICIAL JORDAN BANKS SKETCHBOOK?
AND A JIGSAW PUZZLE? . . .
OUI!
JE T'AIME JORDAN
BRAVO, JORDAN. WE LOVE YOU!
AND I LOOOOOOOVE . . .

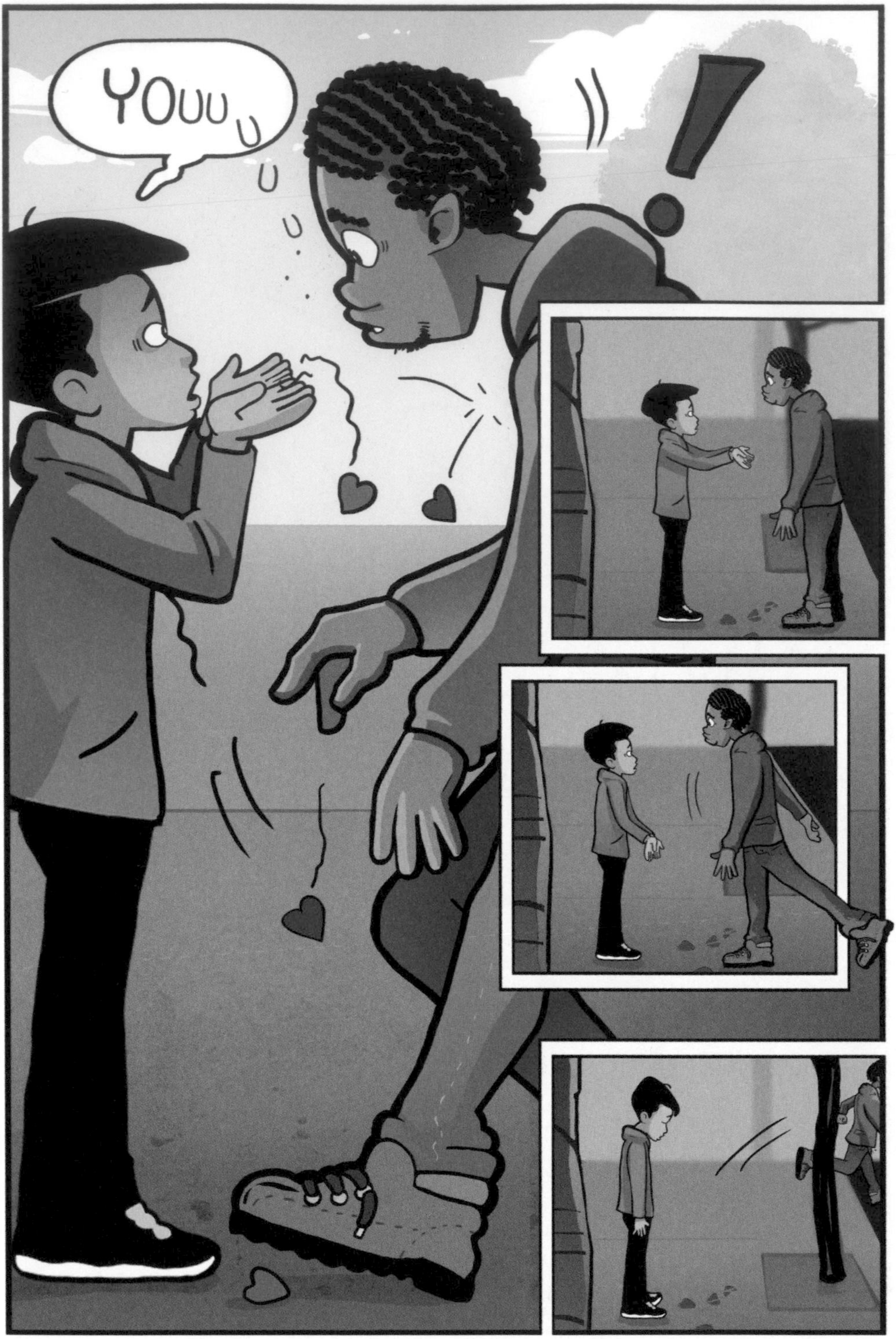
YOUUU
!

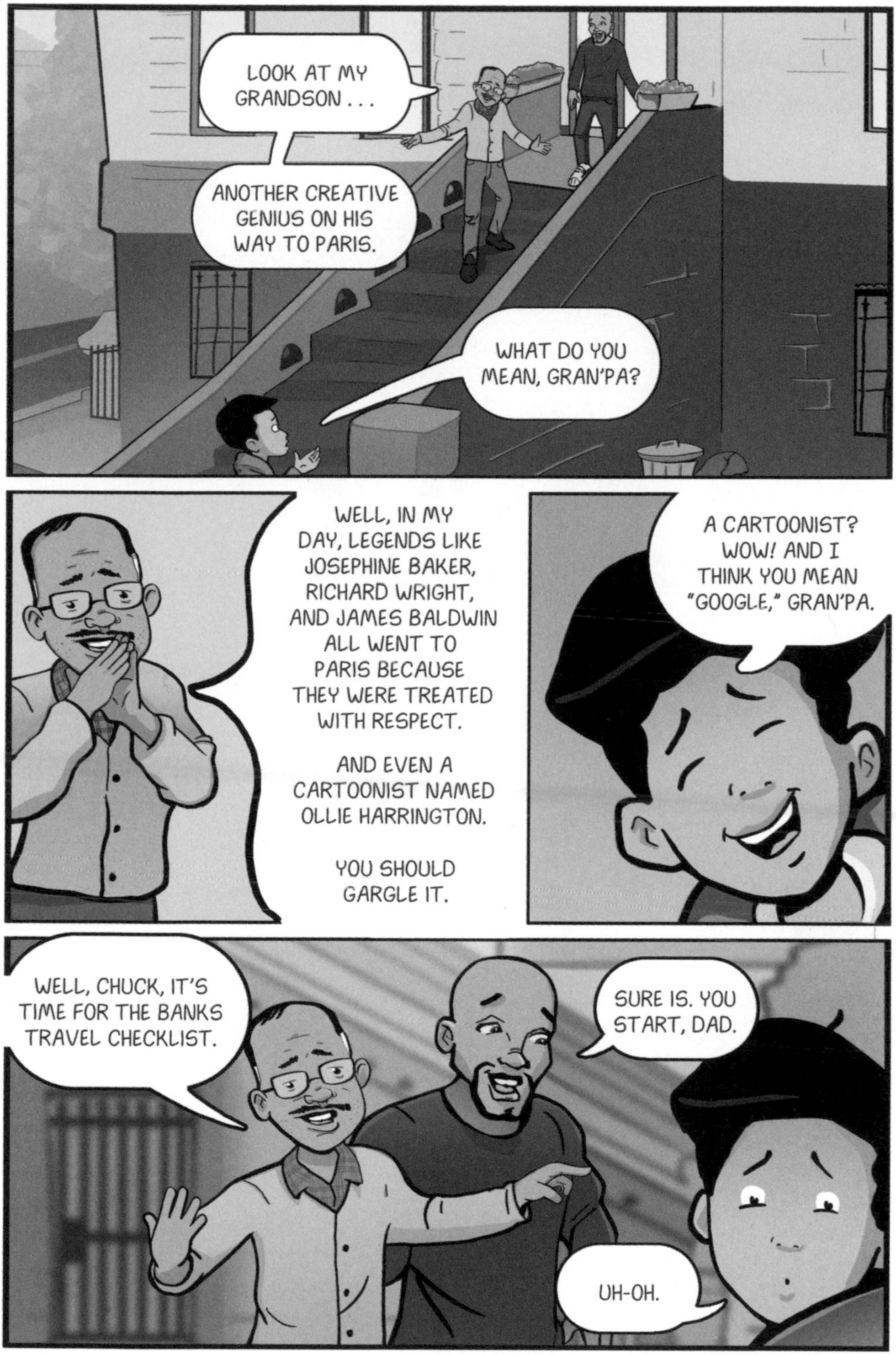
LOOK AT MY GRANDSON . . .
ANOTHER CREATIVE GENIUS ON HIS WAY TO PARIS.
WHAT DO YOU MEAN, GRAN'PA?
WELL, IN MY DAY, LEGENDS LIKE JOSEPHINE BAKER, RICHARD WRIGHT, AND JAMES BALDWIN ALL WENT TO PARIS BECAUSE THEY WERE TREATED WITH RESPECT.
AND EVEN A CARTOONIST NAMED OLLIE HARRINGTON.
YOU SHOULD GARGLE IT.
A CARTOONIST? WOW! AND I THINK YOU MEAN "GOOGLE," GRAN'PA.
WELL, CHUCK, IT'S TIME FOR THE BANKS TRAVEL CHECKLIST.
SURE IS. YOU START, DAD.
UH-OH.

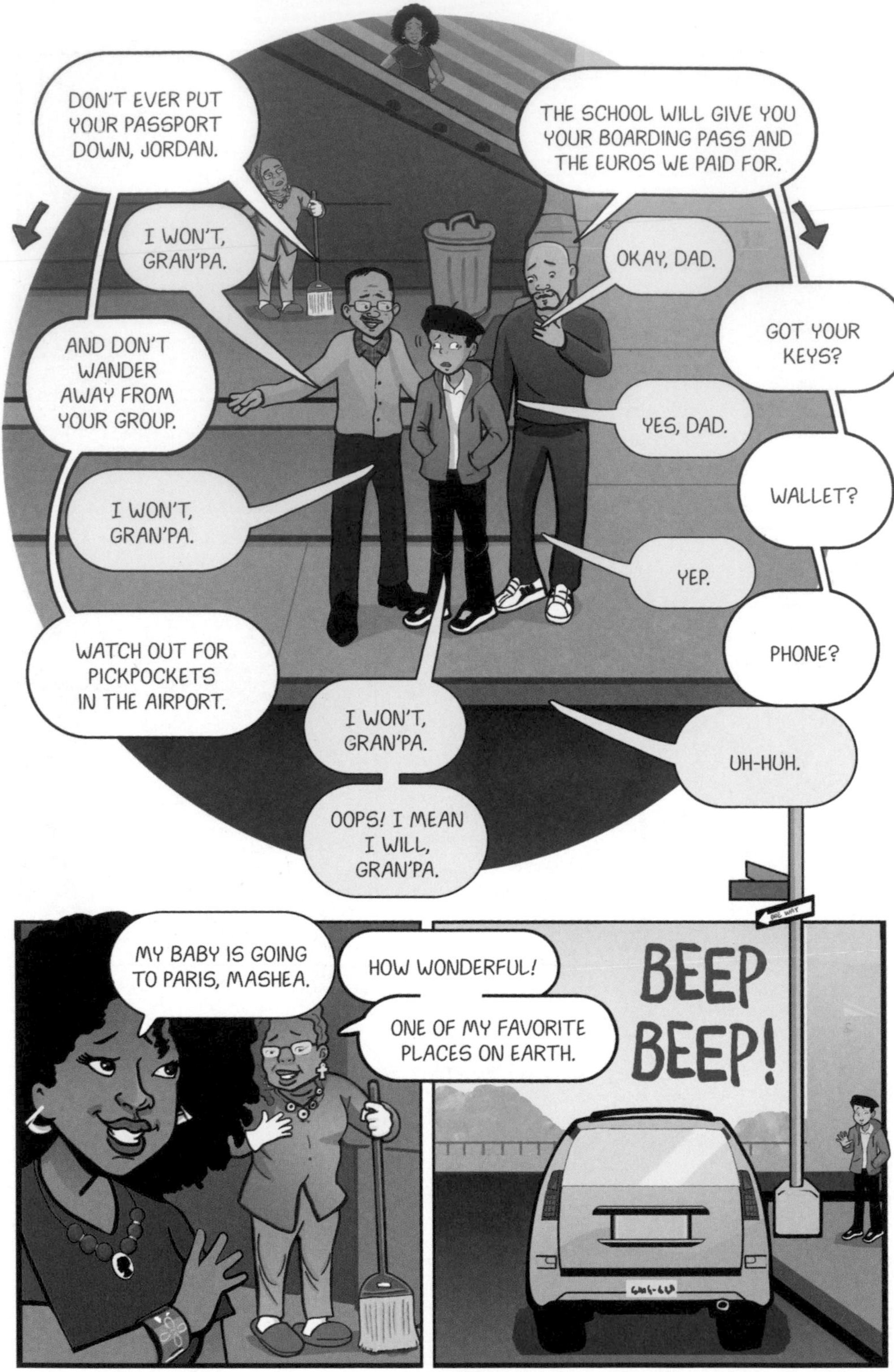
DON'T EVER PUT YOUR PASSPORT DOWN, JORDAN.
I WON'T, GRAN'PA.
AND DON'T WANDER AWAY FROM YOUR GROUP.
I WON'T, GRAN'PA.
WATCH OUT FOR PICKPOCKETS IN THE AIRPORT.
I WON'T, GRAN'PA.
OOPS! I MEAN I WILL, GRAN'PA.
THE SCHOOL WILL GIVE YOU YOUR BOARDING PASS AND THE EUROS WE PAID FOR.
OKAY, DAD.
GOT YOUR KEYS?
YES, DAD.
WALLET?
YEP.
PHONE?
UH-HUH.
MY BABY IS GOING TO PARIS, MASHEA.
HOW WONDERFUL!
ONE OF MY FAVORITE PLACES ON EARTH.
BEEP BEEP!

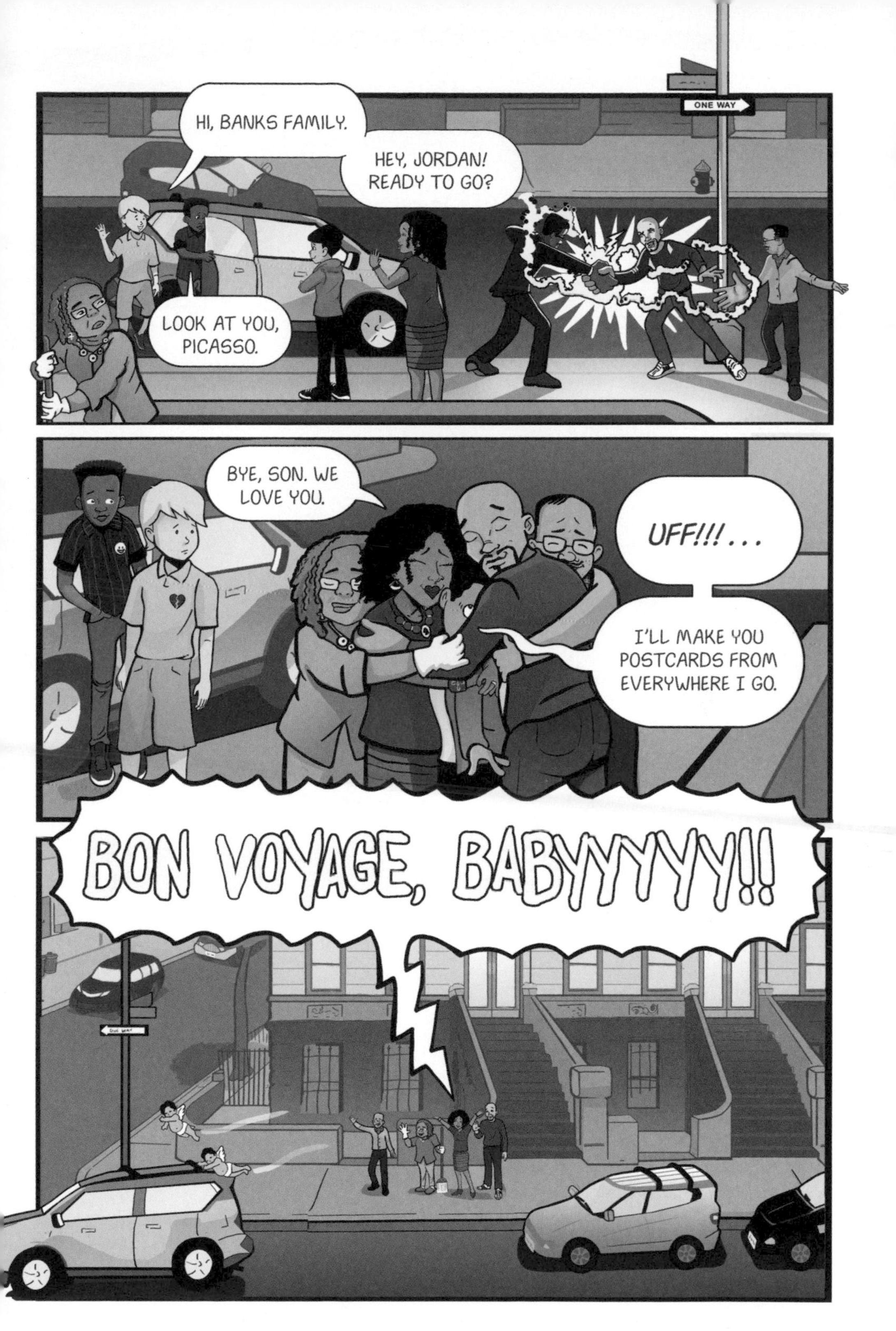
ONE WAY
HI, BANKS FAMILY.
HEY, JORDAN! READY TO GO?
LOOK AT YOU, PICASSO.
BYE, SON. WE LOVE YOU.
UFF!!!...
I'LL MAKE YOU POSTCARDS FROM EVERYWHERE I GO.
BON VOYAGE, BABYYYYY!!

3

A Butterfly With Butterflies!

(In My Stomach!)

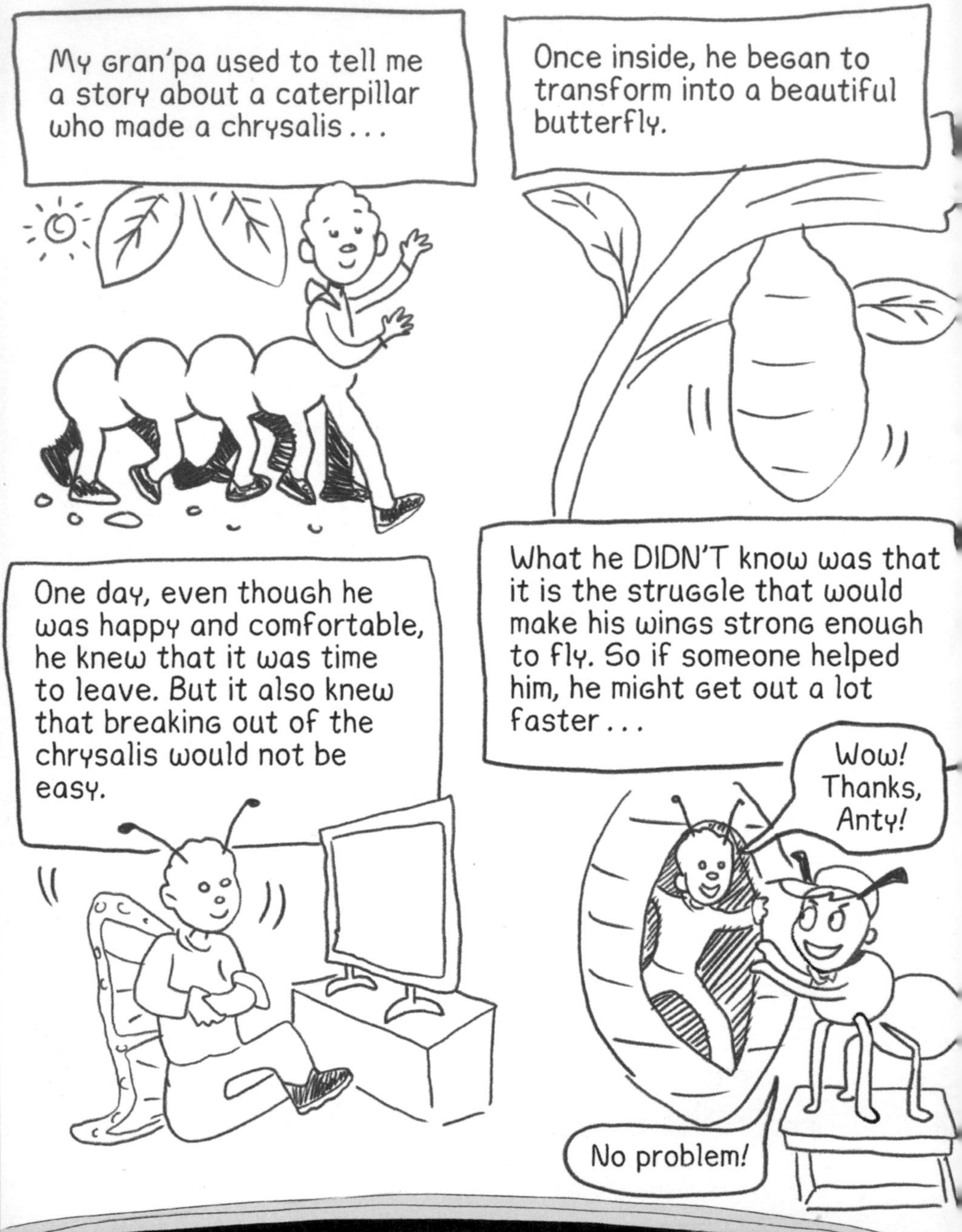

My gran'pa used to tell me a story about a caterpillar who made a chrysalis . . .
Once inside, he began to transform into a beautiful butterfly.
One day, even though he was happy and comfortable, he knew that it was time to leave. But it also knew that breaking out of the chrysalis would not be easy.
What he DIDN'T know was that it is the struggle that would make his wings strong enough to fly. So if someone helped him, he might get out a lot faster . . .
Wow! Thanks, Anty!
No problem!

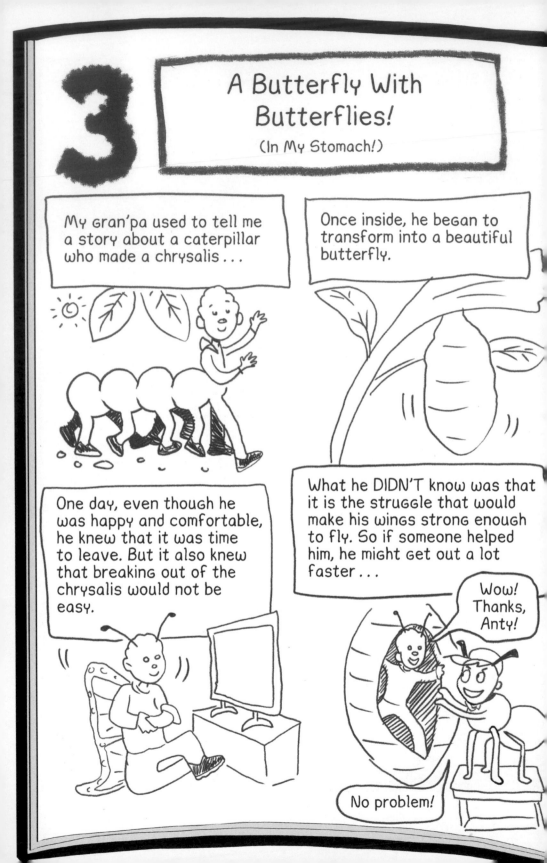

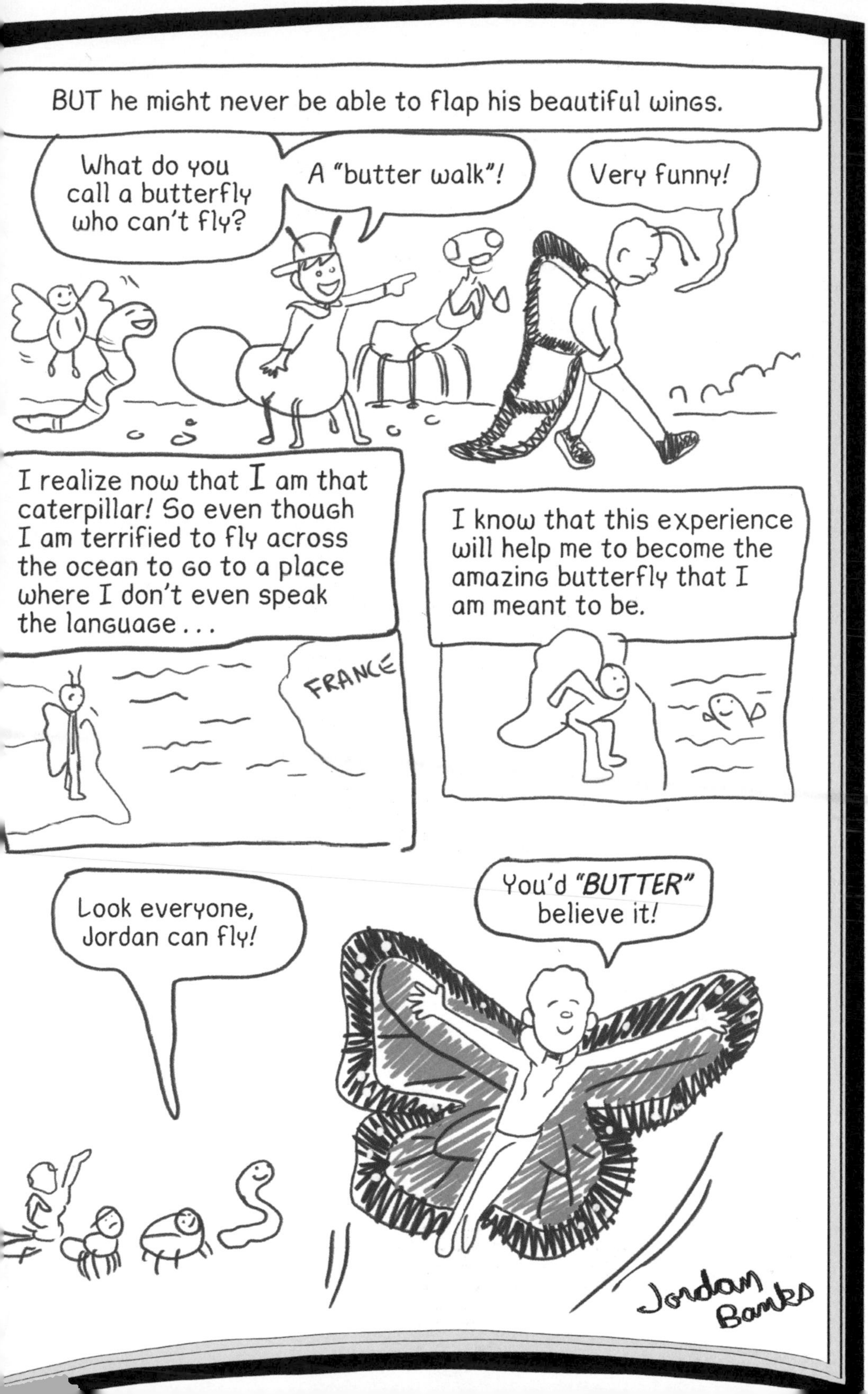
BUT he might never be able to flap his beautiful wings.
What do you call a butterfly who can't fly?
A "butter walk"!
Very funny!
I realize now that I am that caterpillar! So even though I am terrified to fly across the ocean to go to a place where I don't even speak the language . . .
FRANCE
I know that this experience will help me to become the amazing butterfly that I am meant to be.
Look everyone, Jordan can fly!
You'd "BUTTER" believe it!
Jordan Banks

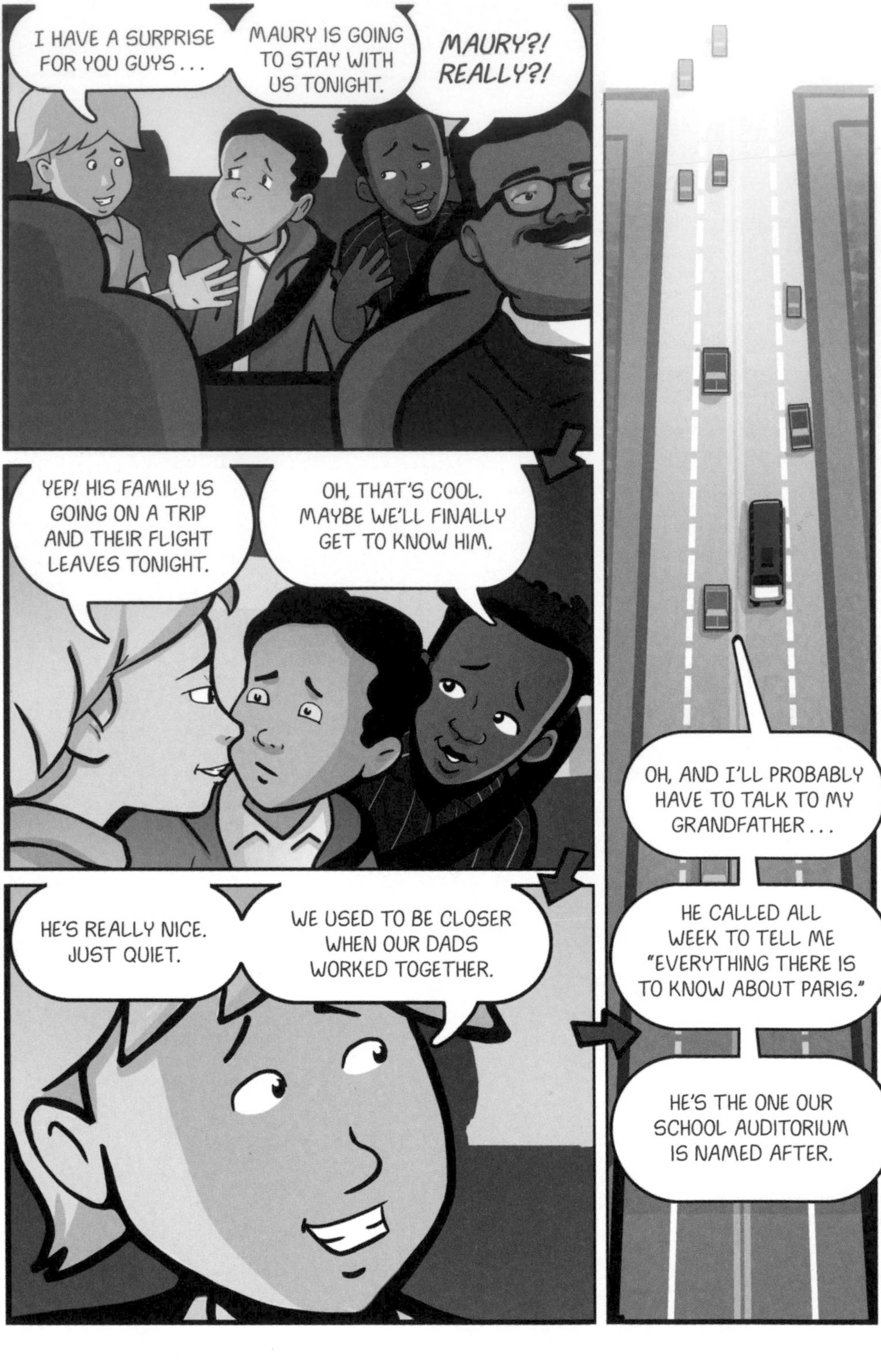
I HAVE A SURPRISE FOR YOU GUYS . . .
MAURY IS GOING TO STAY WITH US TONIGHT.
MAURY?! REALLY?!
YEP! HIS FAMILY IS GOING ON A TRIP AND THEIR FLIGHT LEAVES TONIGHT.
OH, THAT'S COOL. MAYBE WE'LL FINALLY GET TO KNOW HIM.
HE'S REALLY NICE. JUST QUIET.
WE USED TO BE CLOSER WHEN OUR DADS WORKED TOGETHER.
OH, AND I'LL PROBABLY HAVE TO TALK TO MY GRANDFATHER . . .
HE CALLED ALL WEEK TO TELL ME "EVERYTHING THERE IS TO KNOW ABOUT PARIS."
HE'S THE ONE OUR SCHOOL AUDITORIUM IS NAMED AFTER.

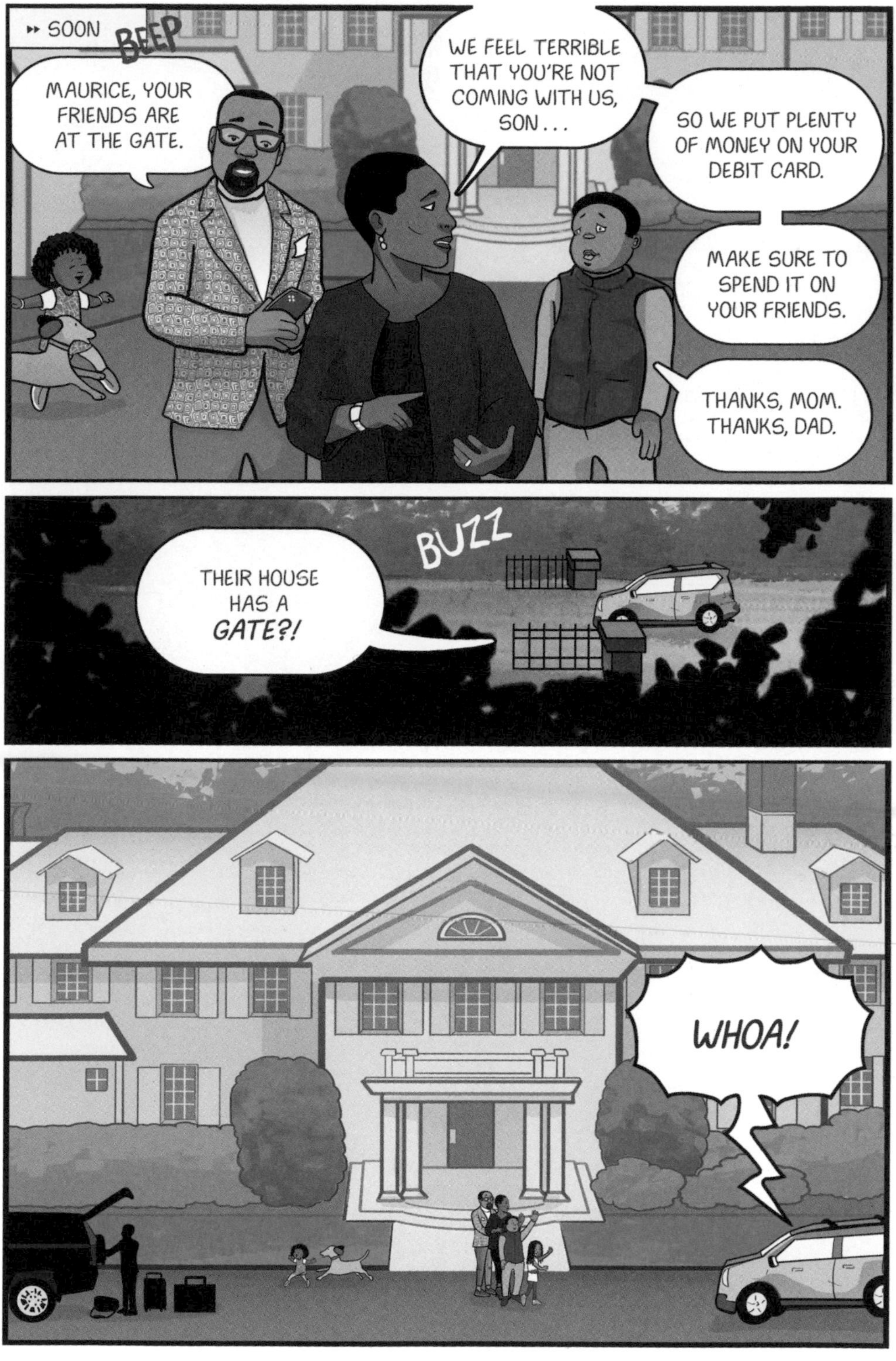
▸▸ SOON
BEEP
MAURICE, YOUR FRIENDS ARE AT THE GATE.
WE FEEL TERRIBLE THAT YOU'RE NOT COMING WITH US, SON . . .
SO WE PUT PLENTY OF MONEY ON YOUR DEBIT CARD.
MAKE SURE TO SPEND IT ON YOUR FRIENDS.
THANKS, MOM. THANKS, DAD.
BUZZ
THEIR HOUSE HAS A *GATE?!*
WHOA!

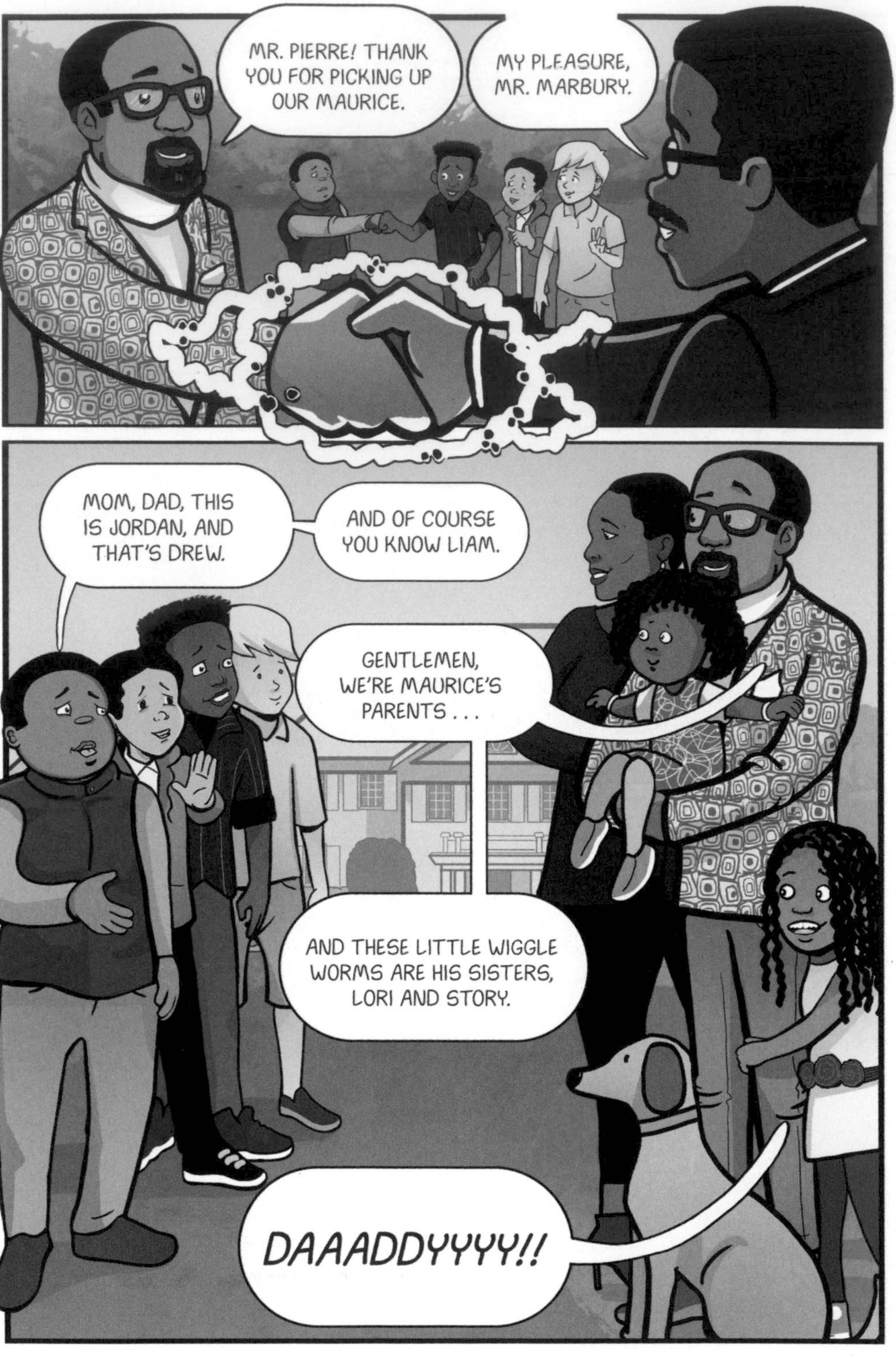
MR. PIERRE! THANK YOU FOR PICKING UP OUR MAURICE.
MY PLEASURE, MR. MARBURY.
MOM, DAD, THIS IS JORDAN, AND THAT'S DREW.
AND OF COURSE YOU KNOW LIAM.
GENTLEMEN, WE'RE MAURICE'S PARENTS . . .
AND THESE LITTLE WIGGLE WORMS ARE HIS SISTERS, LORI AND STORY.
DAAADDYYYY!!

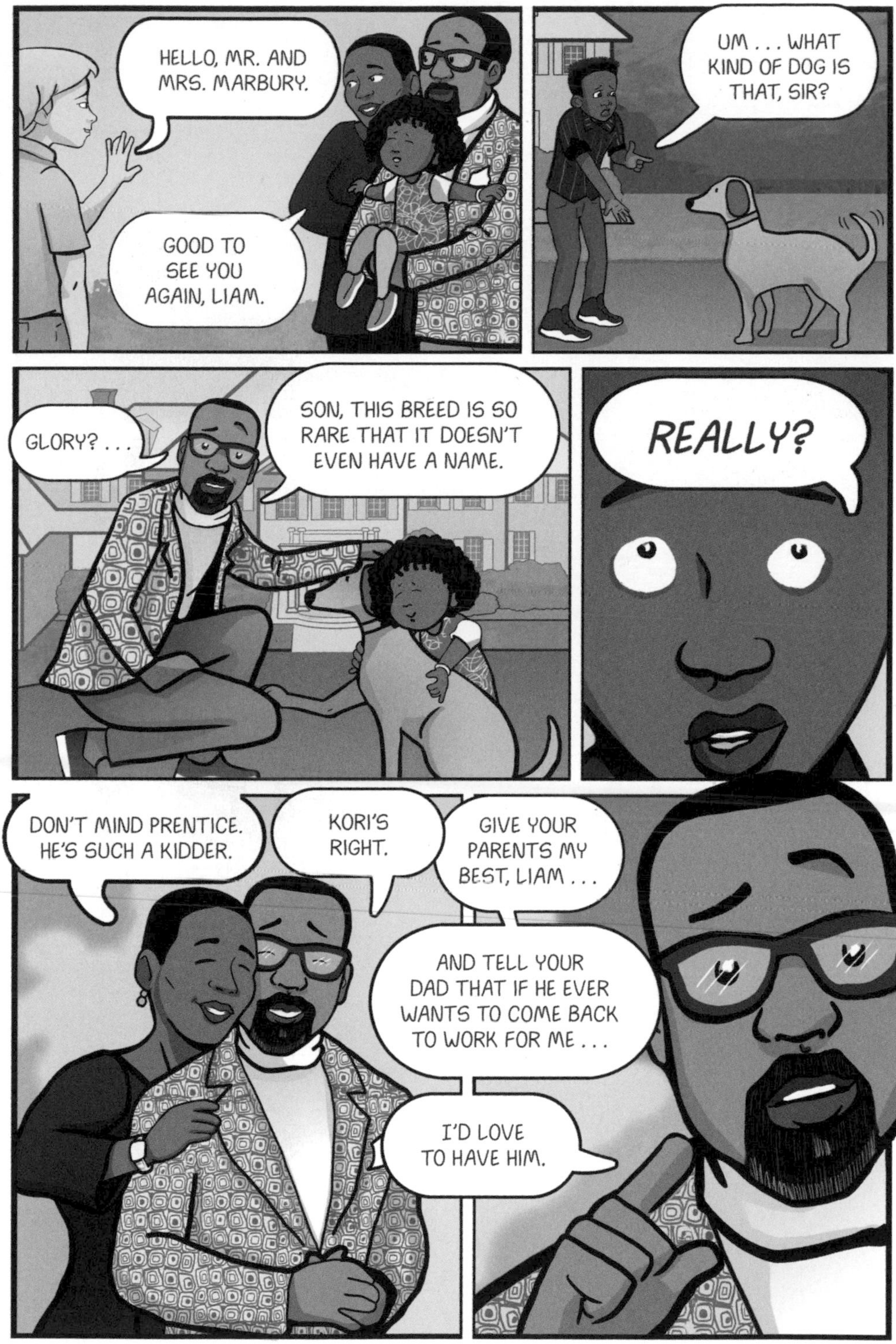
HELLO, MR. AND MRS. MARBURY.
GOOD TO SEE YOU AGAIN, LIAM.
UM . . . WHAT KIND OF DOG IS THAT, SIR?
GLORY? . . .
SON, THIS BREED IS SO RARE THAT IT DOESN'T EVEN HAVE A NAME.
REALLY?
DON'T MIND PRENTICE. HE'S SUCH A KIDDER.
KORI'S RIGHT.
GIVE YOUR PARENTS MY BEST, LIAM . . .
AND TELL YOUR DAD THAT IF HE EVER WANTS TO COME BACK TO WORK FOR ME . . .
I'D LOVE TO HAVE HIM.

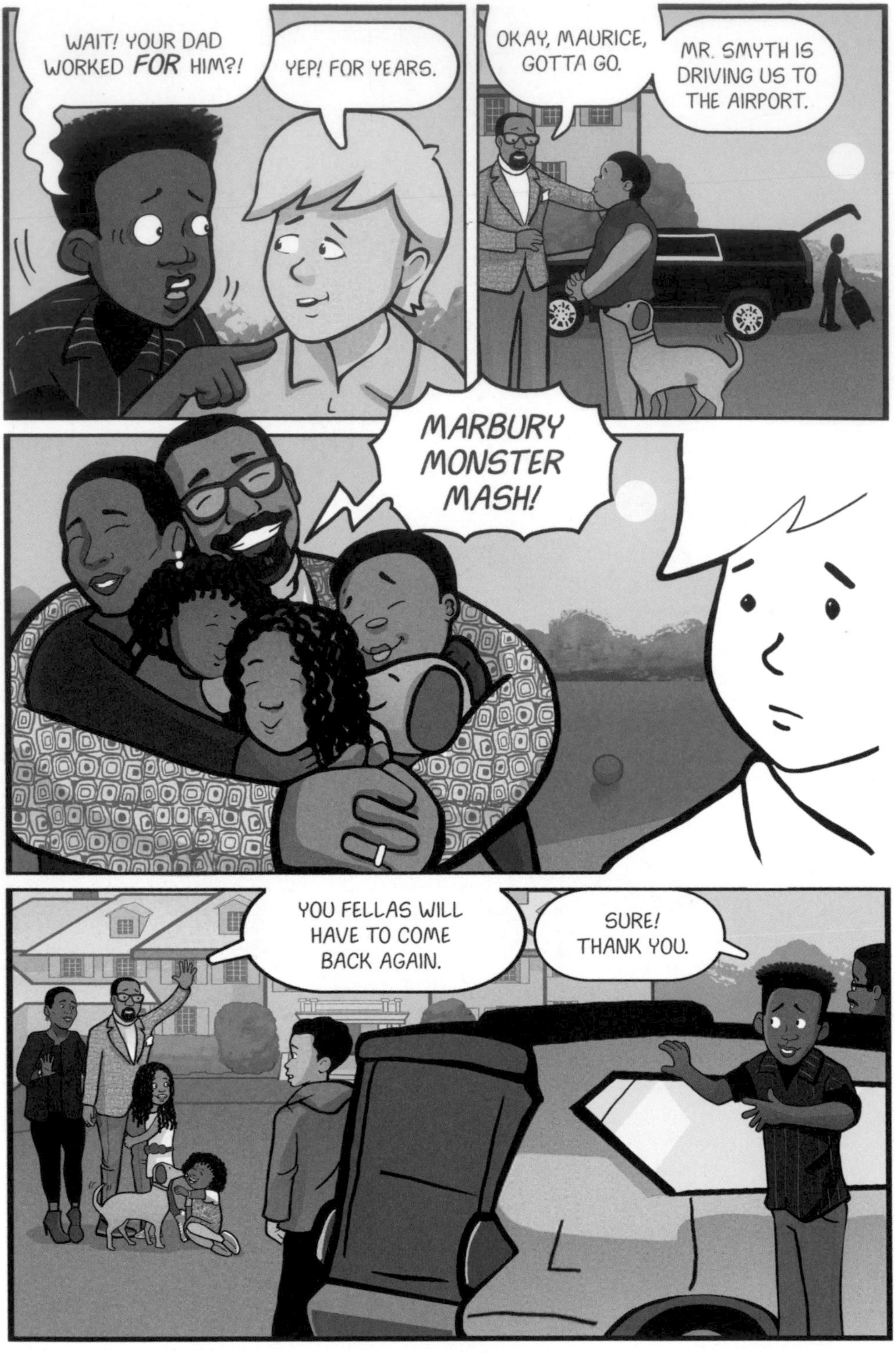

WAIT! YOUR DAD WORKED FOR HIM?!
YEP! FOR YEARS.
OKAY, MAURICE, GOTTA GO.
MR. SMYTH IS DRIVING US TO THE AIRPORT.
MARBURY MONSTER MASH!
YOU FELLAS WILL HAVE TO COME BACK AGAIN.
SURE! THANK YOU.

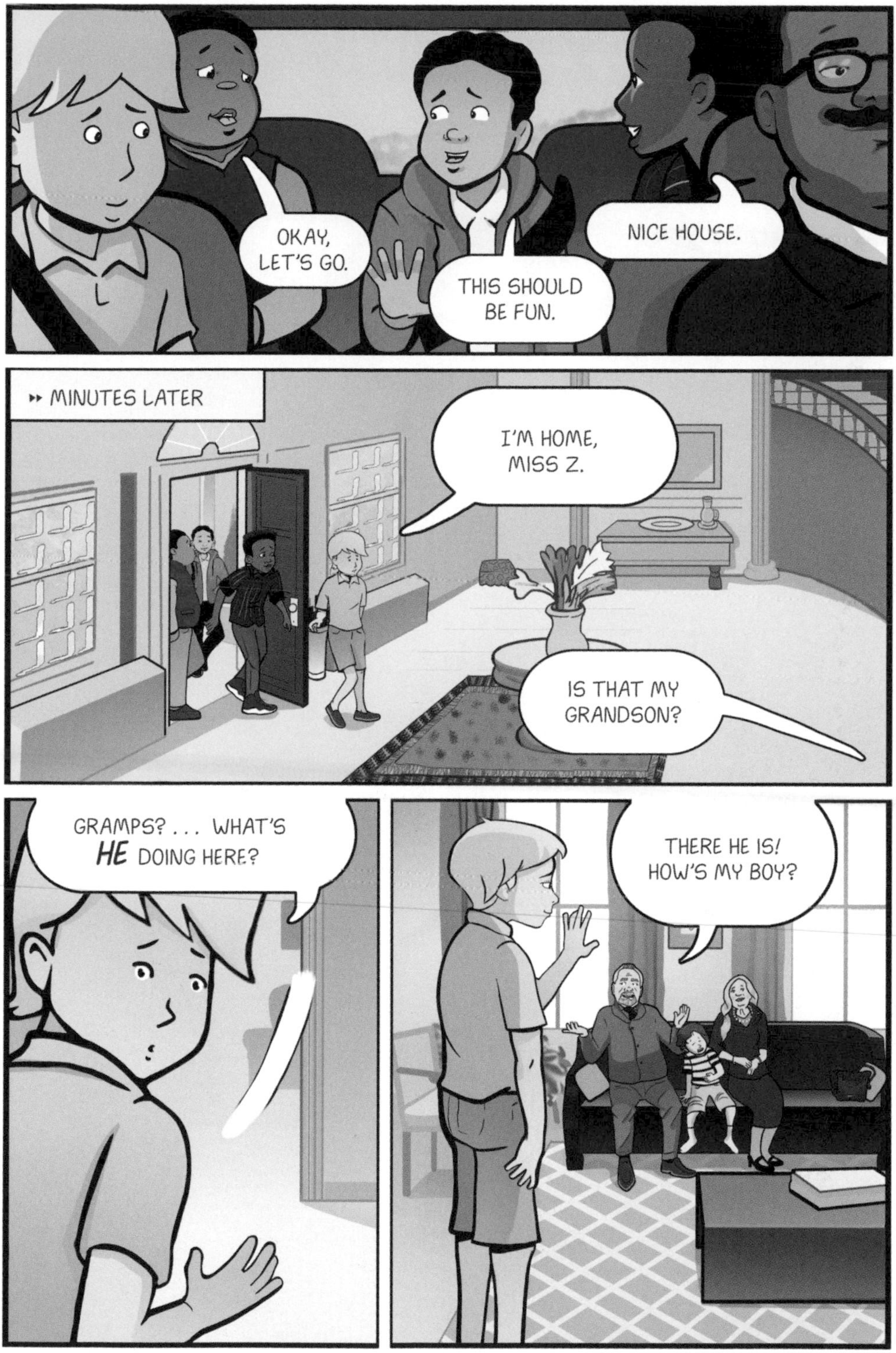
OKAY, LET'S GO.
THIS SHOULD BE FUN.
NICE HOUSE.
MINUTES LATER
I'M HOME, MISS Z.
IS THAT MY GRANDSON?
GRAMPS? . . . WHAT'S HE DOING HERE?
THERE HE IS! HOW'S MY BOY?

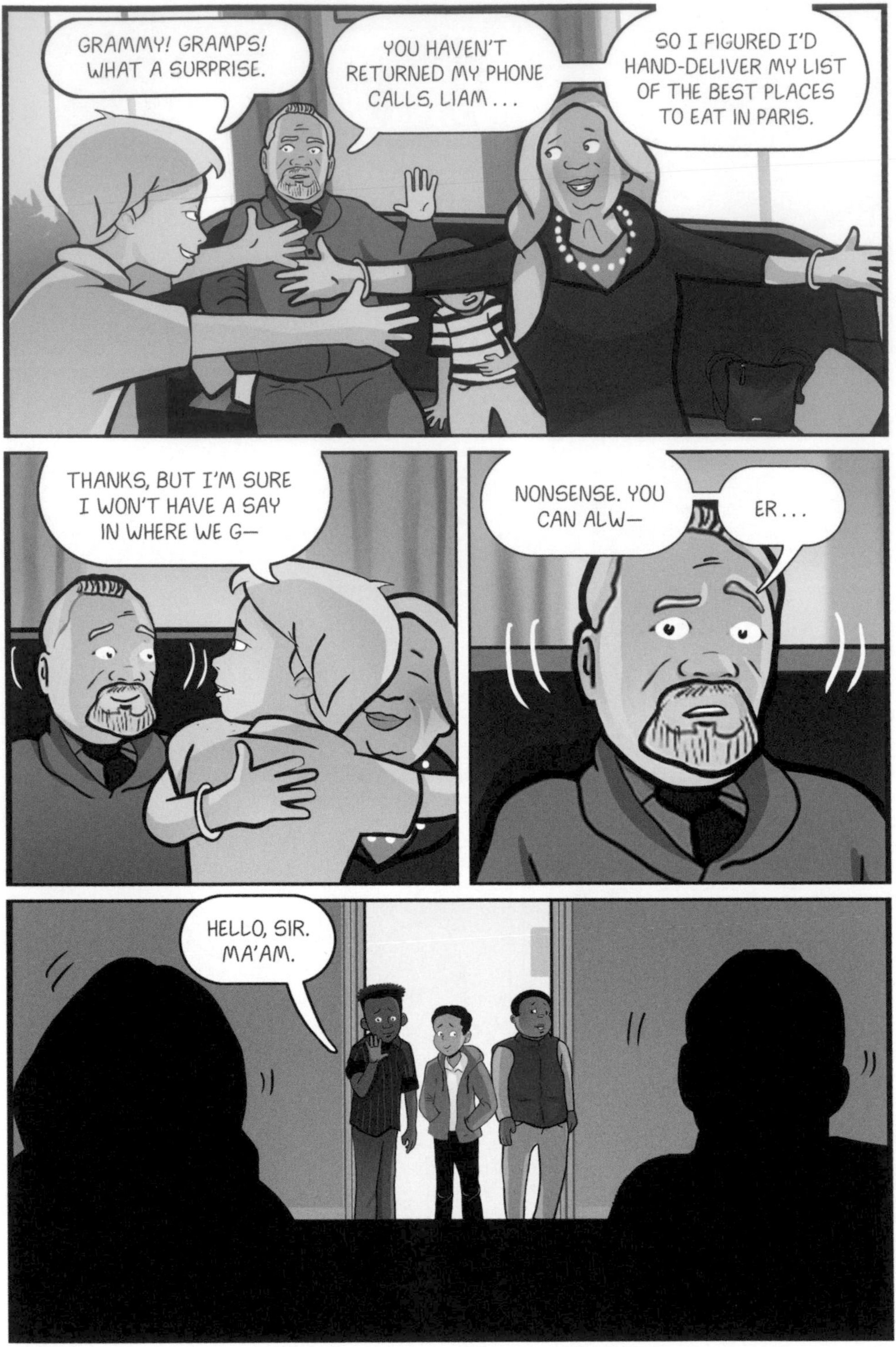
GRAMMY! GRAMPS! WHAT A SURPRISE.
YOU HAVEN'T RETURNED MY PHONE CALLS, LIAM . . .
SO I FIGURED I'D HAND-DELIVER MY LIST OF THE BEST PLACES TO EAT IN PARIS.
THANKS, BUT I'M SURE I WON'T HAVE A SAY IN WHERE WE G—
NONSENSE. YOU CAN ALW—
ER . . .
HELLO, SIR. MA'AM.

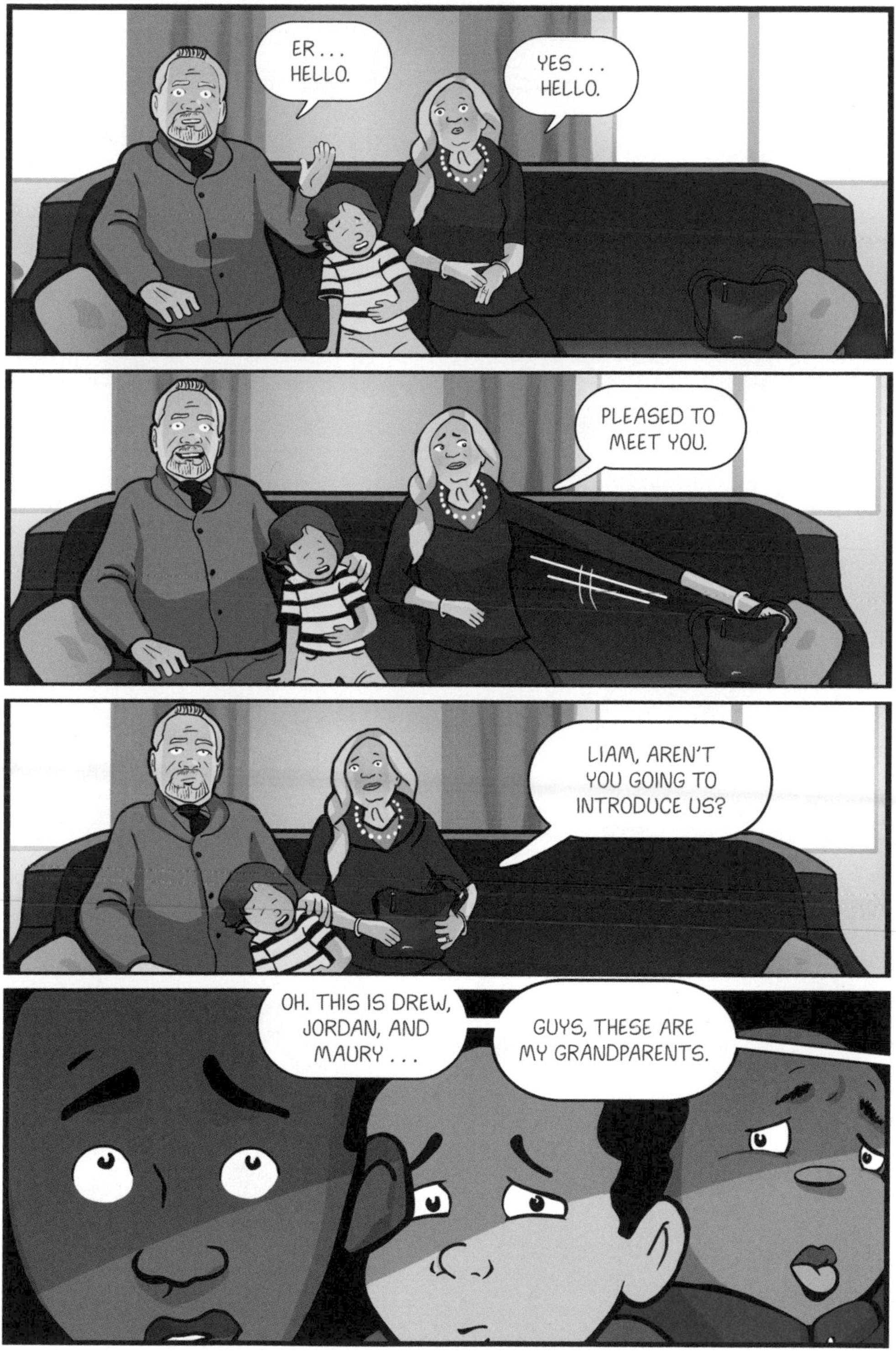
ER . . . HELLO.
YES . . . HELLO.
PLEASED TO MEET YOU.
LIAM, AREN'T YOU GOING TO INTRODUCE US?
OH. THIS IS DREW, JORDAN, AND MAURY . . .
GUYS, THESE ARE MY GRANDPARENTS.

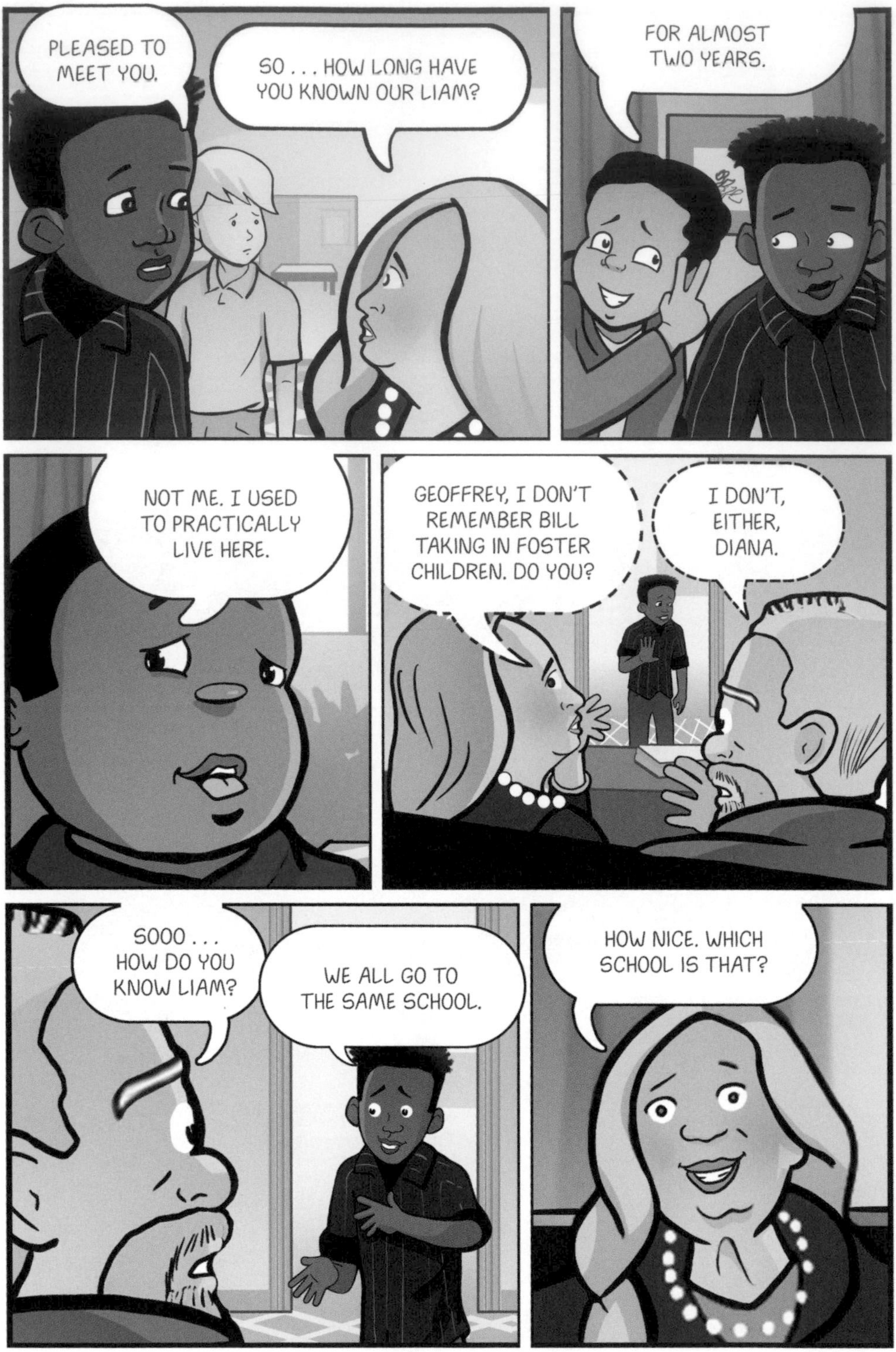
PLEASED TO MEET YOU.
SO . . . HOW LONG HAVE YOU KNOWN OUR LIAM?
FOR ALMOST TWO YEARS.
NOT ME. I USED TO PRACTICALLY LIVE HERE.
GEOFFREY, I DON'T REMEMBER BILL TAKING IN FOSTER CHILDREN. DO YOU?
I DON'T, EITHER, DIANA.
SOOO . . . HOW DO YOU KNOW LIAM?
WE ALL GO TO THE SAME SCHOOL.
HOW NICE. WHICH SCHOOL IS THAT?

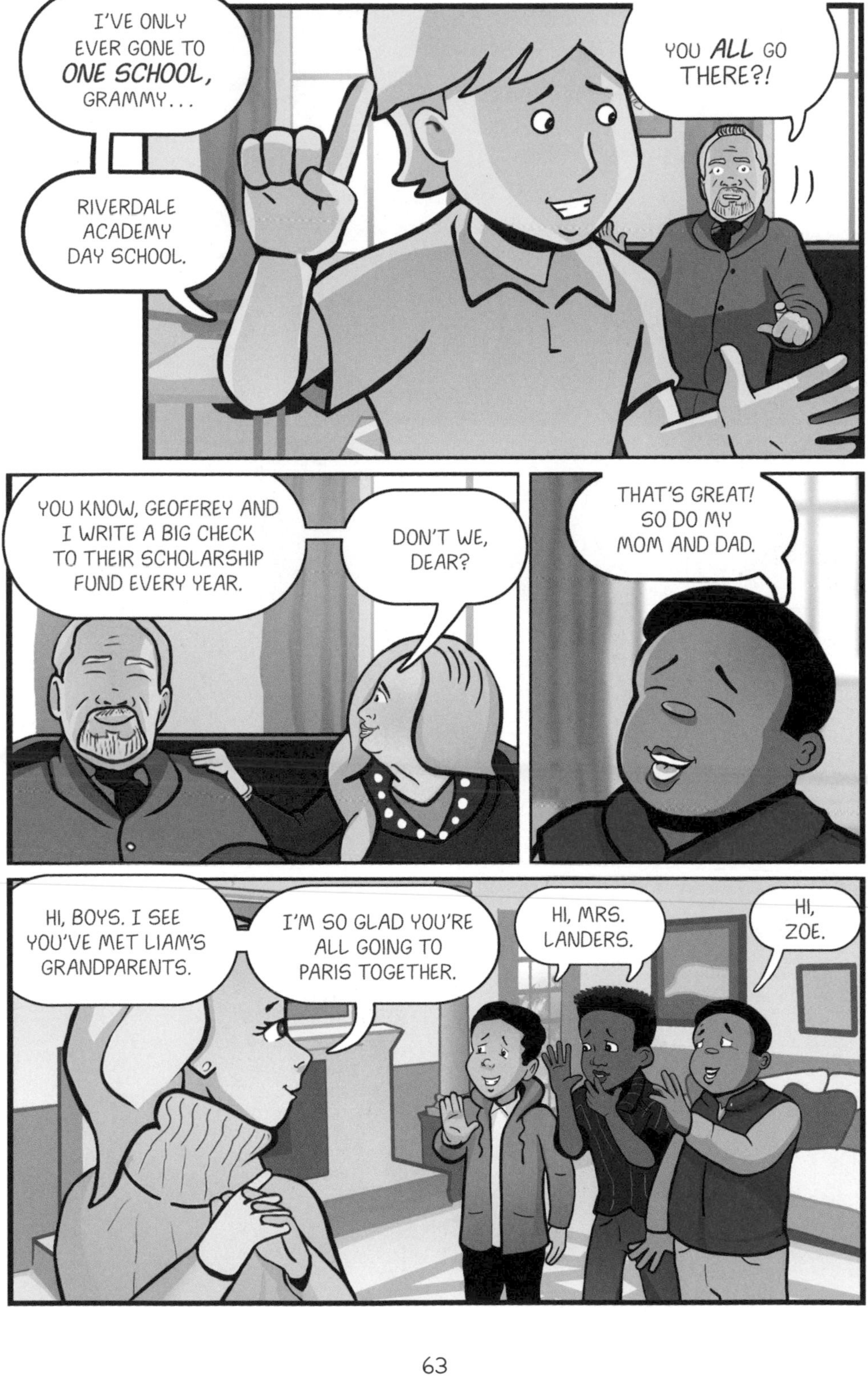
I'VE ONLY EVER GONE TO **ONE SCHOOL,** GRAMMY...
RIVERDALE ACADEMY DAY SCHOOL.
YOU ***ALL*** GO THERE?!
YOU KNOW, GEOFFREY AND I WRITE A BIG CHECK TO THEIR SCHOLARSHIP FUND EVERY YEAR.
DON'T WE, DEAR?
THAT'S GREAT! SO DO MY MOM AND DAD.
HI, BOYS. I SEE YOU'VE MET LIAM'S GRANDPARENTS.
I'M SO GLAD YOU'RE ALL GOING TO PARIS TOGETHER.
HI, MRS. LANDERS.
HI, ZOE.

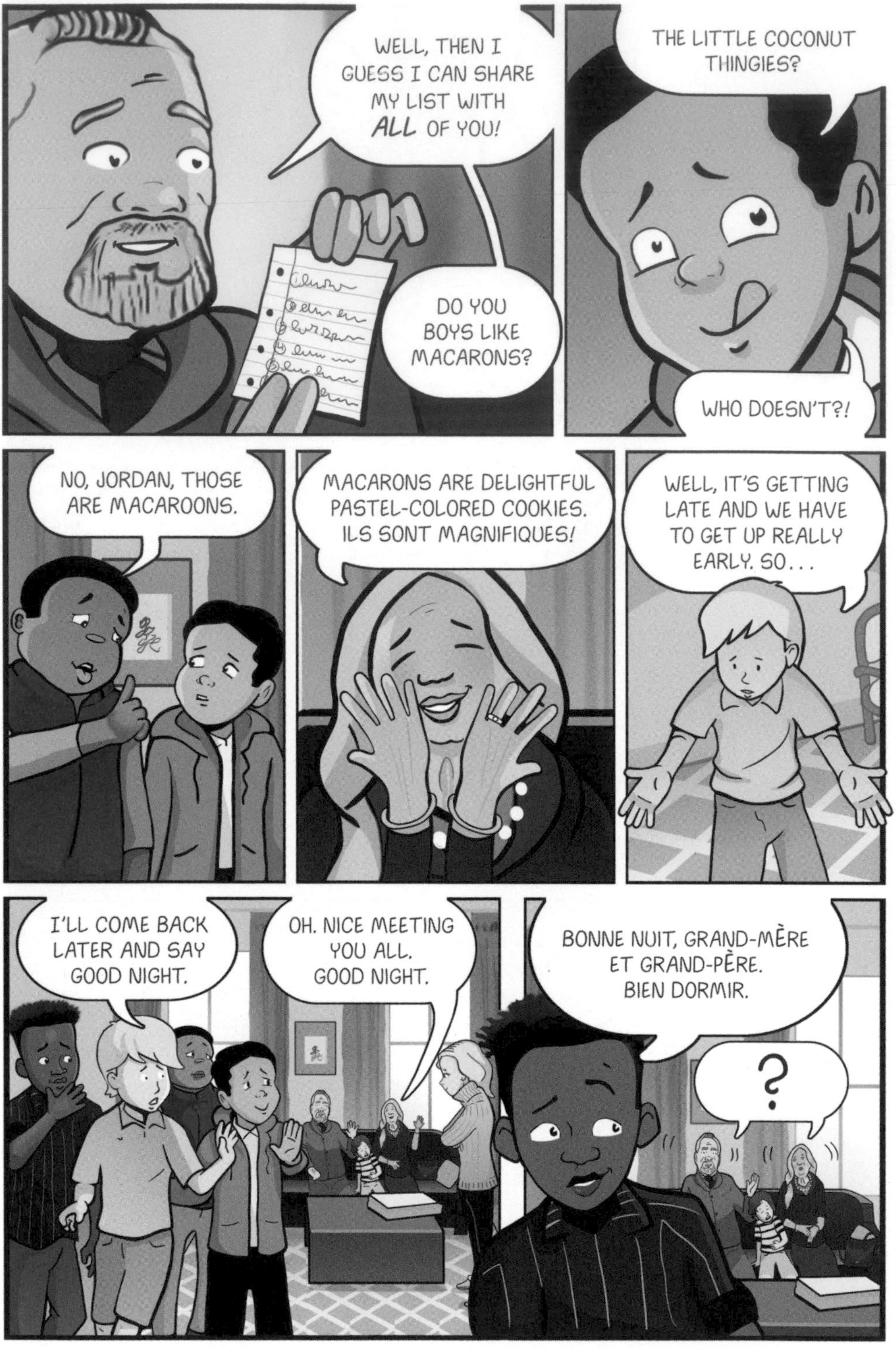
WELL, THEN I GUESS I CAN SHARE MY LIST WITH ALL OF YOU!
DO YOU BOYS LIKE MACARONS?
THE LITTLE COCONUT THINGIES?
WHO DOESN'T?!
NO, JORDAN, THOSE ARE MACAROONS.
MACARONS ARE DELIGHTFUL PASTEL-COLORED COOKIES. ILS SONT MAGNIFIQUES!
WELL, IT'S GETTING LATE AND WE HAVE TO GET UP REALLY EARLY. SO...
I'LL COME BACK LATER AND SAY GOOD NIGHT.
OH. NICE MEETING YOU ALL. GOOD NIGHT.
BONNE NUIT, GRAND-MÈRE ET GRAND-PÈRE. BIEN DORMIR.
?

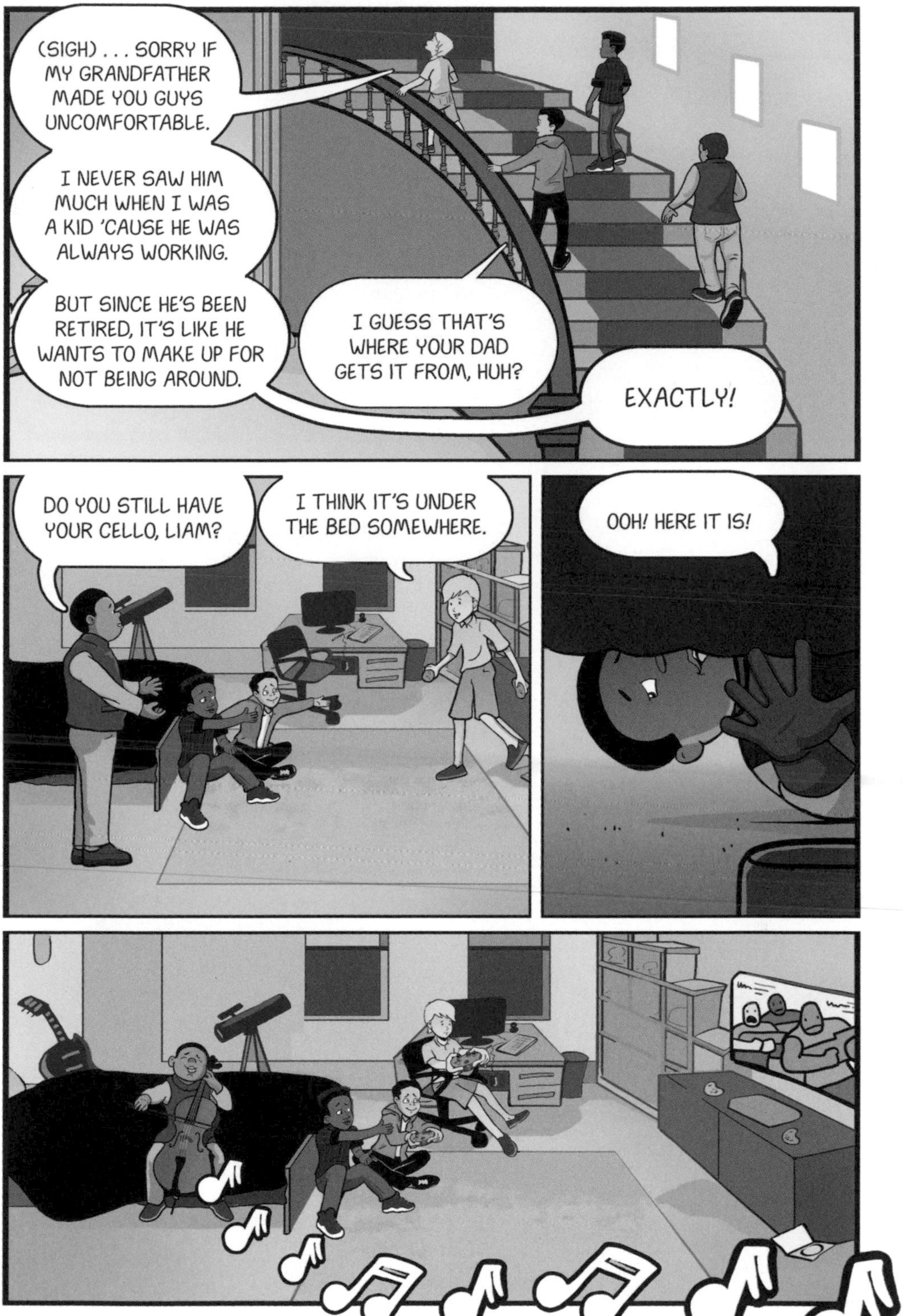
(SIGH) . . . SORRY IF MY GRANDFATHER MADE YOU GUYS UNCOMFORTABLE.
I NEVER SAW HIM MUCH WHEN I WAS A KID 'CAUSE HE WAS ALWAYS WORKING.
BUT SINCE HE'S BEEN RETIRED, IT'S LIKE HE WANTS TO MAKE UP FOR NOT BEING AROUND.
I GUESS THAT'S WHERE YOUR DAD GETS IT FROM, HUH?
EXACTLY!
DO YOU STILL HAVE YOUR CELLO, LIAM?
I THINK IT'S UNDER THE BED SOMEWHERE.
OOH! HERE IT IS!

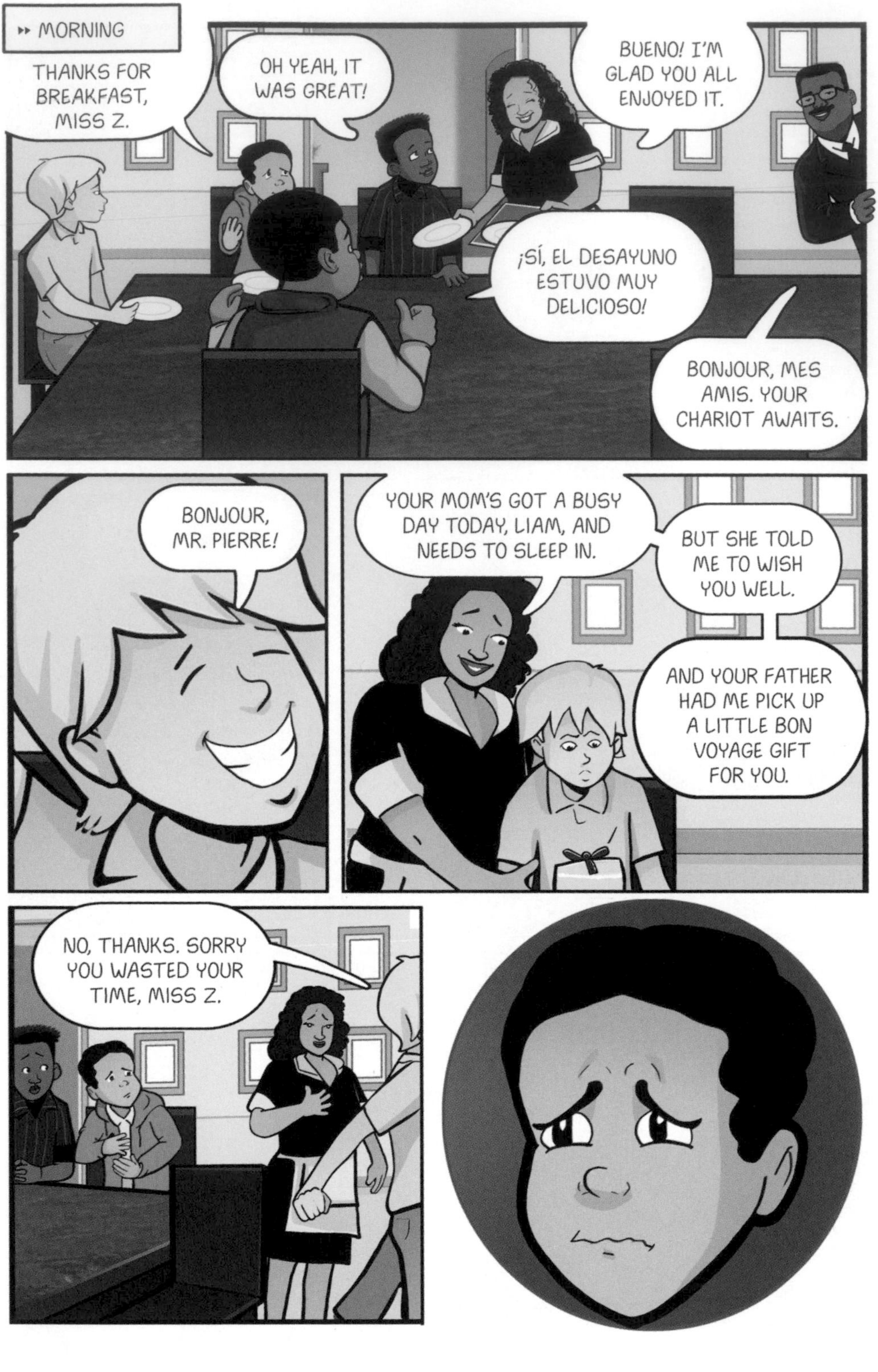
MORNING
THANKS FOR BREAKFAST, MISS Z.
OH YEAH, IT WAS GREAT!
BUENO! I'M GLAD YOU ALL ENJOYED IT.
¡SÍ, EL DESAYUNO ESTUVO MUY DELICIOSO!
BONJOUR, MES AMIS. YOUR CHARIOT AWAITS.
BONJOUR, MR. PIERRE!
YOUR MOM'S GOT A BUSY DAY TODAY, LIAM, AND NEEDS TO SLEEP IN.
BUT SHE TOLD ME TO WISH YOU WELL.
AND YOUR FATHER HAD ME PICK UP A LITTLE BON VOYAGE GIFT FOR YOU.
NO, THANKS. SORRY YOU WASTED YOUR TIME, MISS Z.

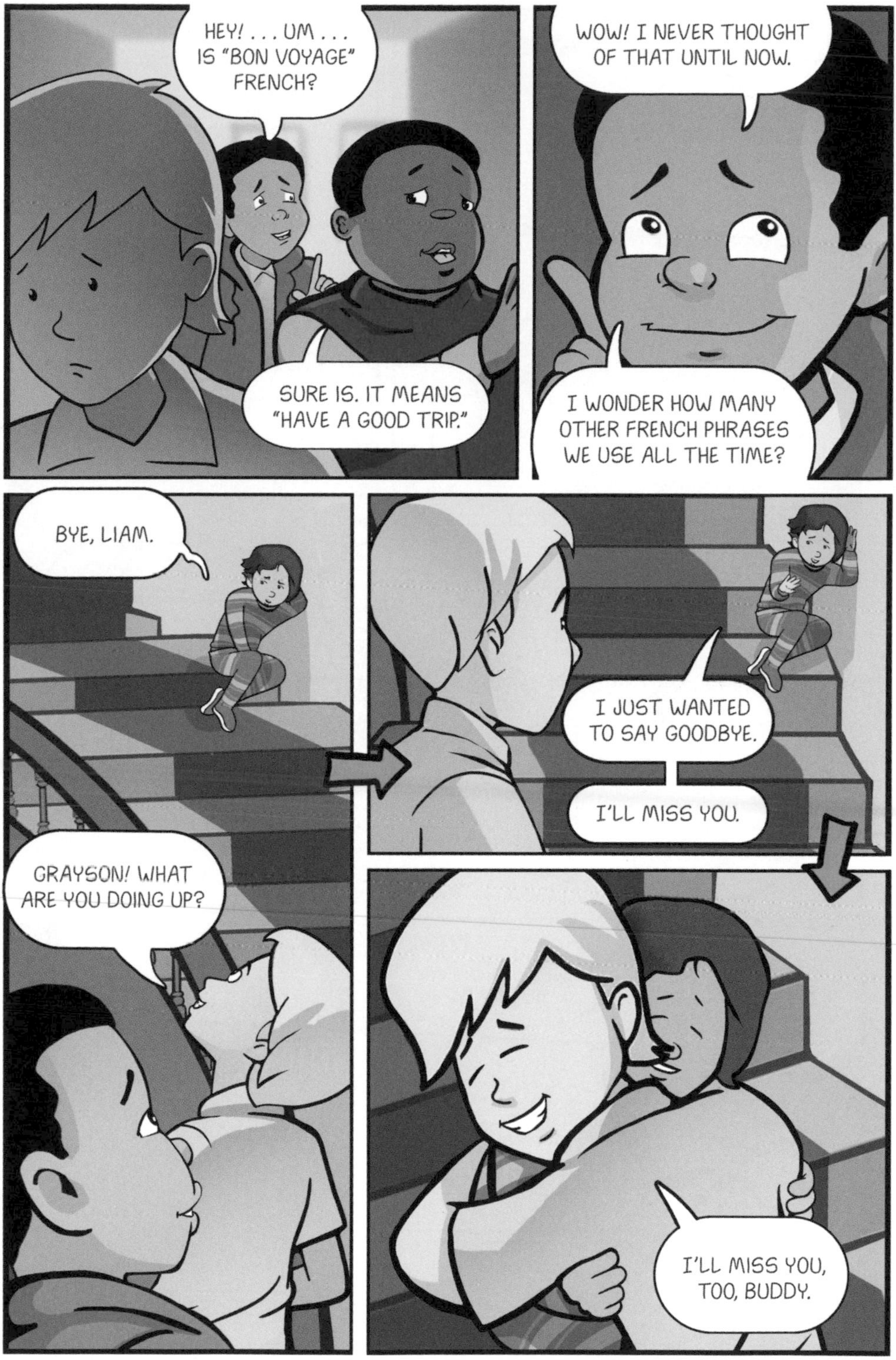
HEY! . . . UM . . . IS "BON VOYAGE" FRENCH?
SURE IS. IT MEANS "HAVE A GOOD TRIP."
WOW! I NEVER THOUGHT OF THAT UNTIL NOW.
I WONDER HOW MANY OTHER FRENCH PHRASES WE USE ALL THE TIME?
BYE, LIAM.
I JUST WANTED TO SAY GOODBYE.
I'LL MISS YOU.
GRAYSON! WHAT ARE YOU DOING UP?
I'LL MISS YOU, TOO, BUDDY.

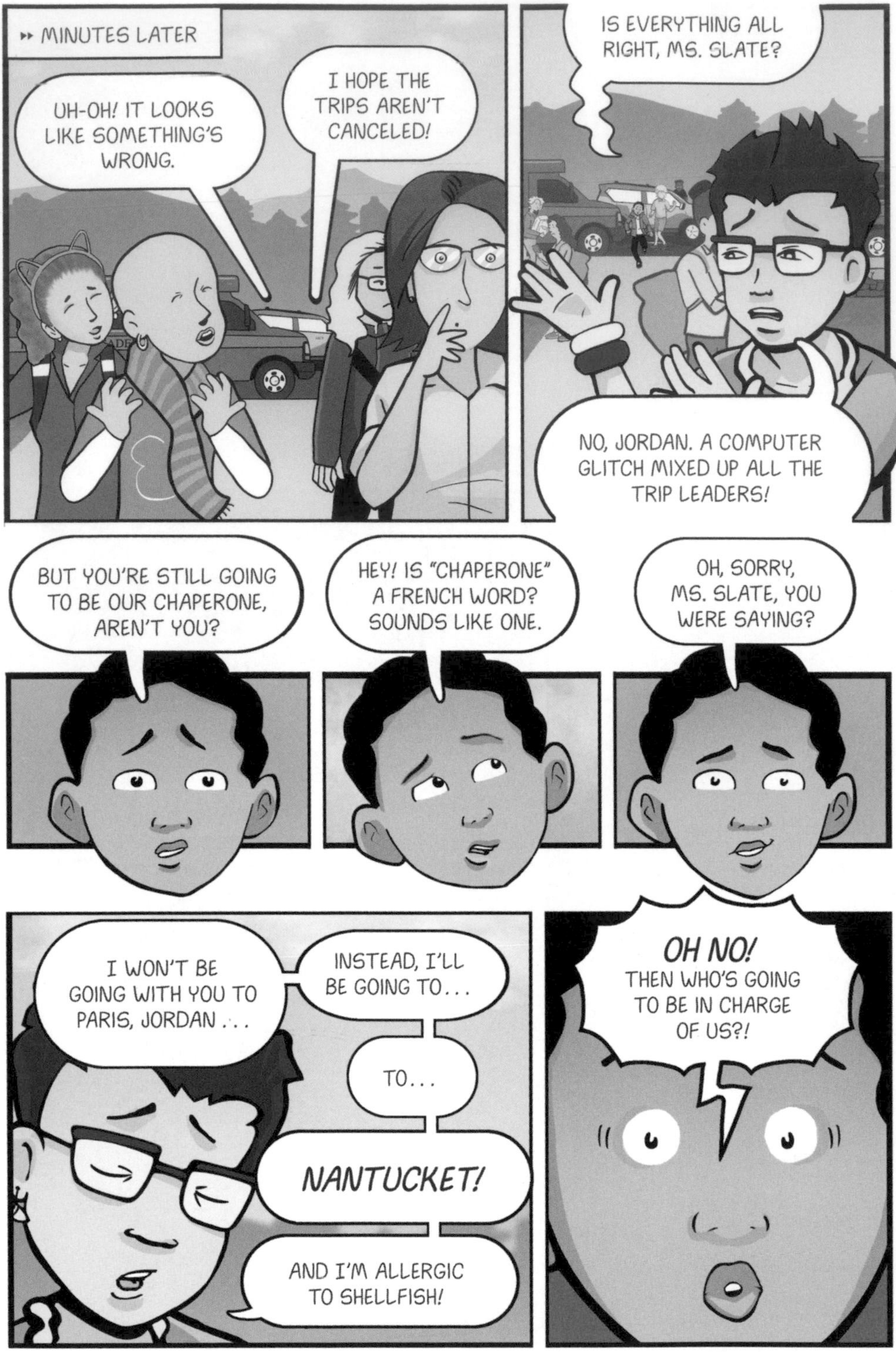
MINUTES LATER
UH-OH! IT LOOKS LIKE SOMETHING'S WRONG.
I HOPE THE TRIPS AREN'T CANCELED!
IS EVERYTHING ALL RIGHT, MS. SLATE?
NO, JORDAN. A COMPUTER GLITCH MIXED UP ALL THE TRIP LEADERS!
BUT YOU'RE STILL GOING TO BE OUR CHAPERONE, AREN'T YOU?
HEY! IS "CHAPERONE" A FRENCH WORD? SOUNDS LIKE ONE.
OH, SORRY, MS. SLATE, YOU WERE SAYING?
I WON'T BE GOING WITH YOU TO PARIS, JORDAN . . .
INSTEAD, I'LL BE GOING TO . . .
TO . . .
NANTUCKET!
AND I'M ALLERGIC TO SHELLFISH!
OH NO!
THEN WHO'S GOING TO BE IN CHARGE OF US?!

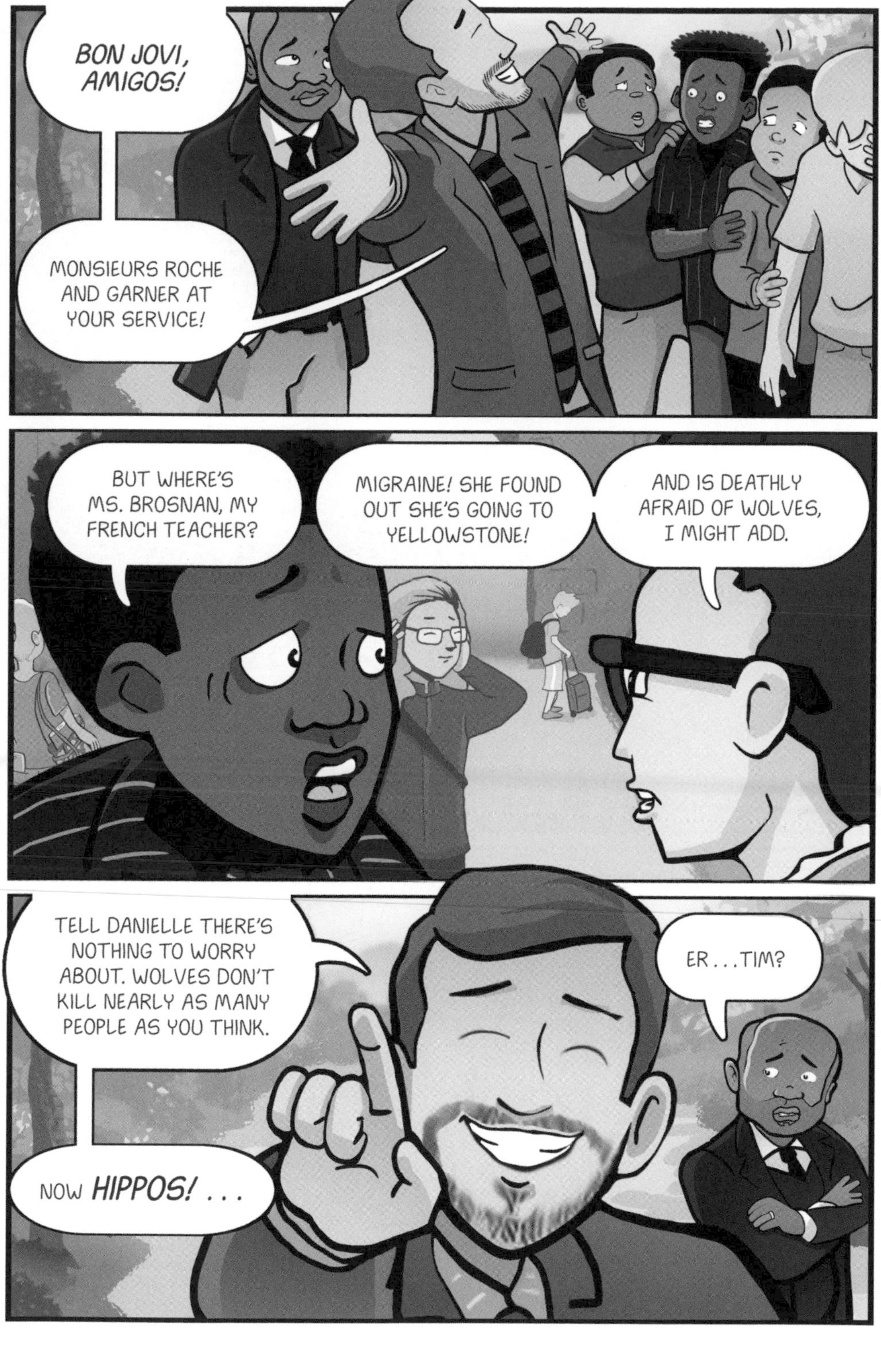
BON JOVI, AMIGOS!
MONSIEURS ROCHE AND GARNER AT YOUR SERVICE!
BUT WHERE'S MS. BROSNAN, MY FRENCH TEACHER?
MIGRAINE! SHE FOUND OUT SHE'S GOING TO YELLOWSTONE!
AND IS DEATHLY AFRAID OF WOLVES, I MIGHT ADD.
TELL DANIELLE THERE'S NOTHING TO WORRY ABOUT. WOLVES DON'T KILL NEARLY AS MANY PEOPLE AS YOU THINK.
NOW HIPPOS! . . .
ER . . . TIM?

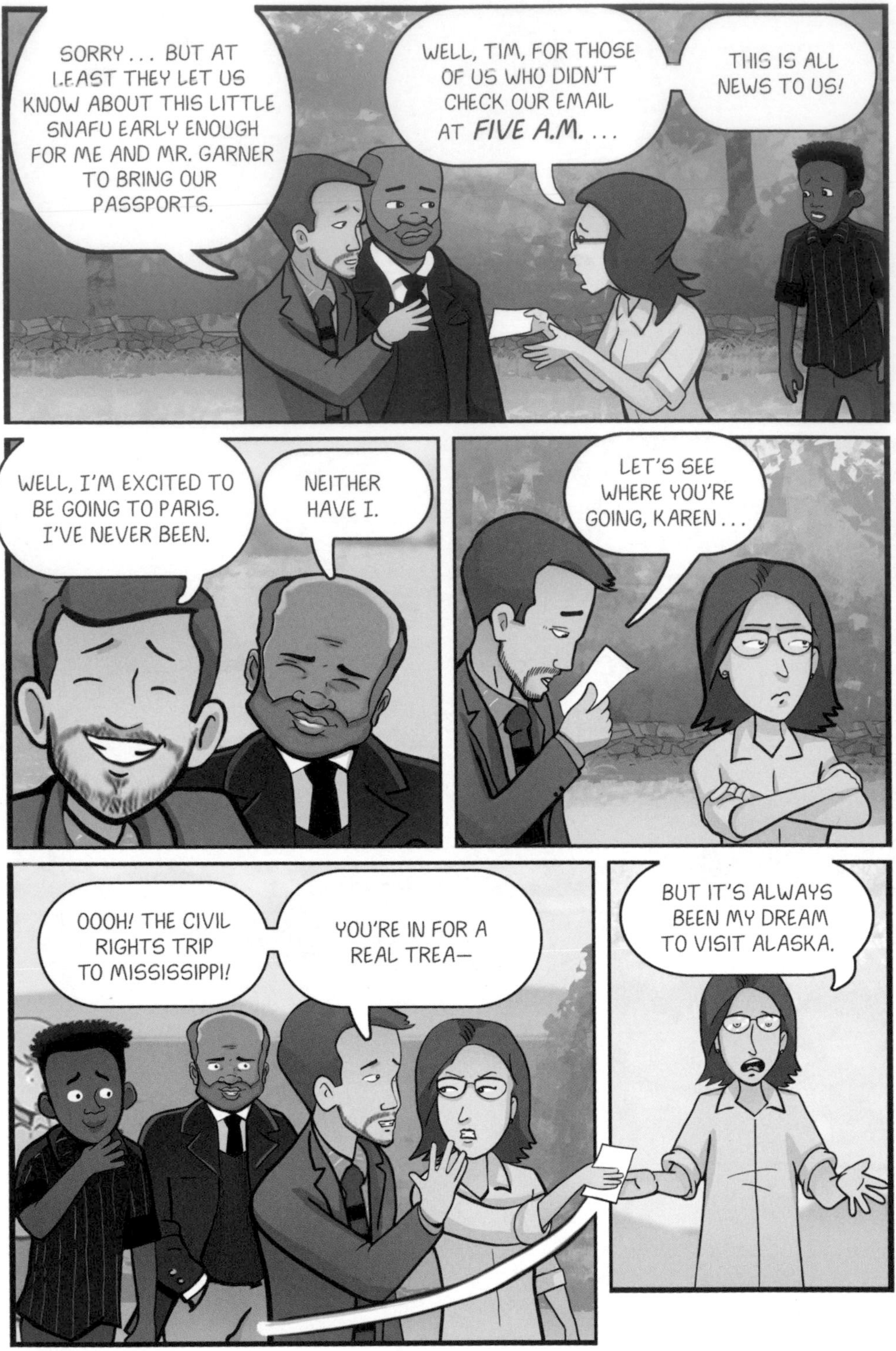
SORRY . . . BUT AT LEAST THEY LET US KNOW ABOUT THIS LITTLE SNAFU EARLY ENOUGH FOR ME AND MR. GARNER TO BRING OUR PASSPORTS.
WELL, TIM, FOR THOSE OF US WHO DIDN'T CHECK OUR EMAIL AT *FIVE A.M.* . . .
THIS IS ALL NEWS TO US!
WELL, I'M EXCITED TO BE GOING TO PARIS. I'VE NEVER BEEN.
NEITHER HAVE I.
LET'S SEE WHERE YOU'RE GOING, KAREN . . .
OOOH! THE CIVIL RIGHTS TRIP TO MISSISSIPPI!
YOU'RE IN FOR A REAL TREA—
BUT IT'S ALWAYS BEEN MY DREAM TO VISIT ALASKA.

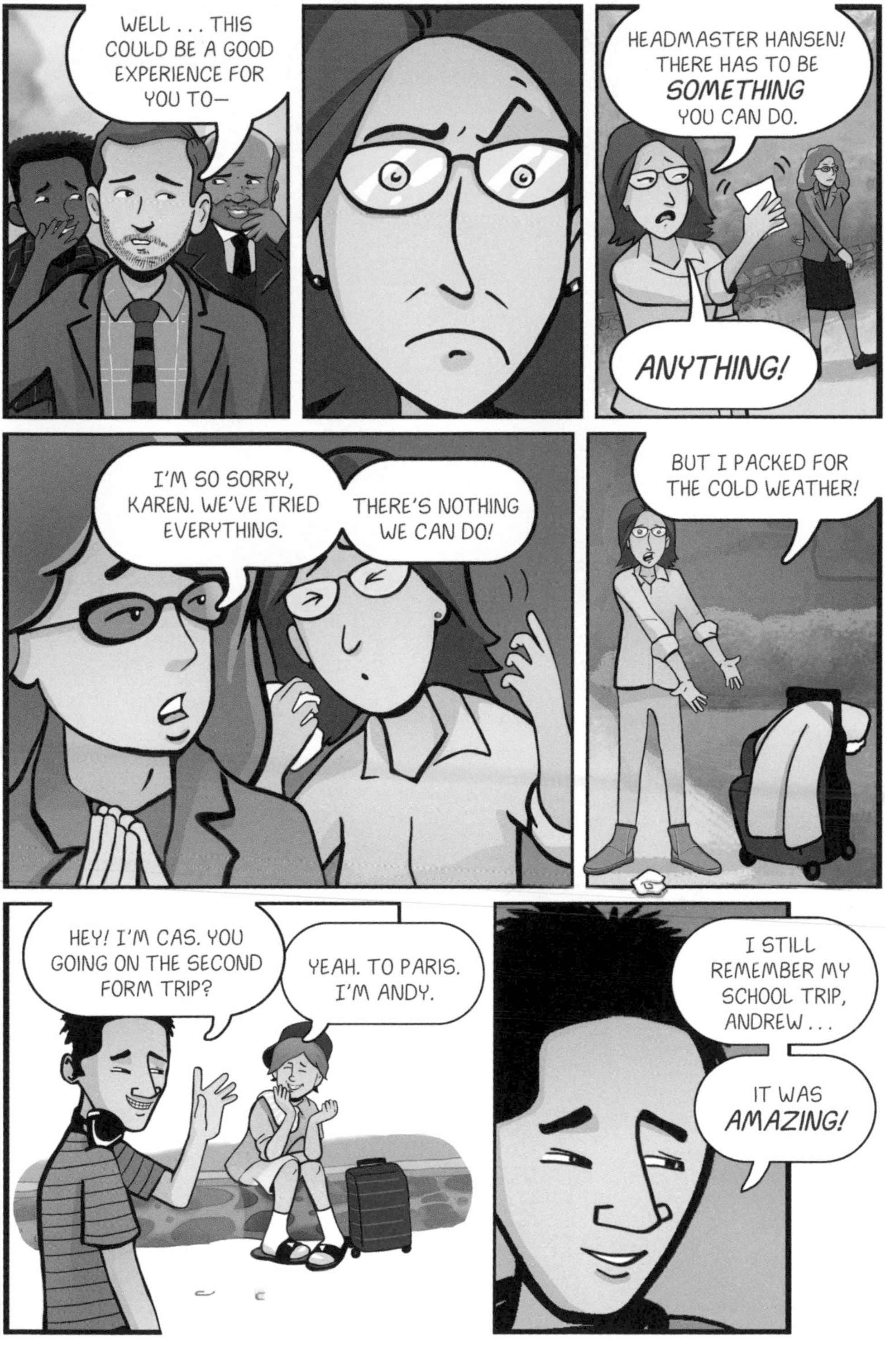
WELL . . . THIS COULD BE A GOOD EXPERIENCE FOR YOU TO—
HEADMASTER HANSEN! THERE HAS TO BE SOMETHING YOU CAN DO.
ANYTHING!
I'M SO SORRY, KAREN. WE'VE TRIED EVERYTHING.
THERE'S NOTHING WE CAN DO!
BUT I PACKED FOR THE COLD WEATHER!
HEY! I'M CAS. YOU GOING ON THE SECOND FORM TRIP?
YEAH. TO PARIS. I'M ANDY.
I STILL REMEMBER MY SCHOOL TRIP, ANDREW . . .
IT WAS AMAZING!

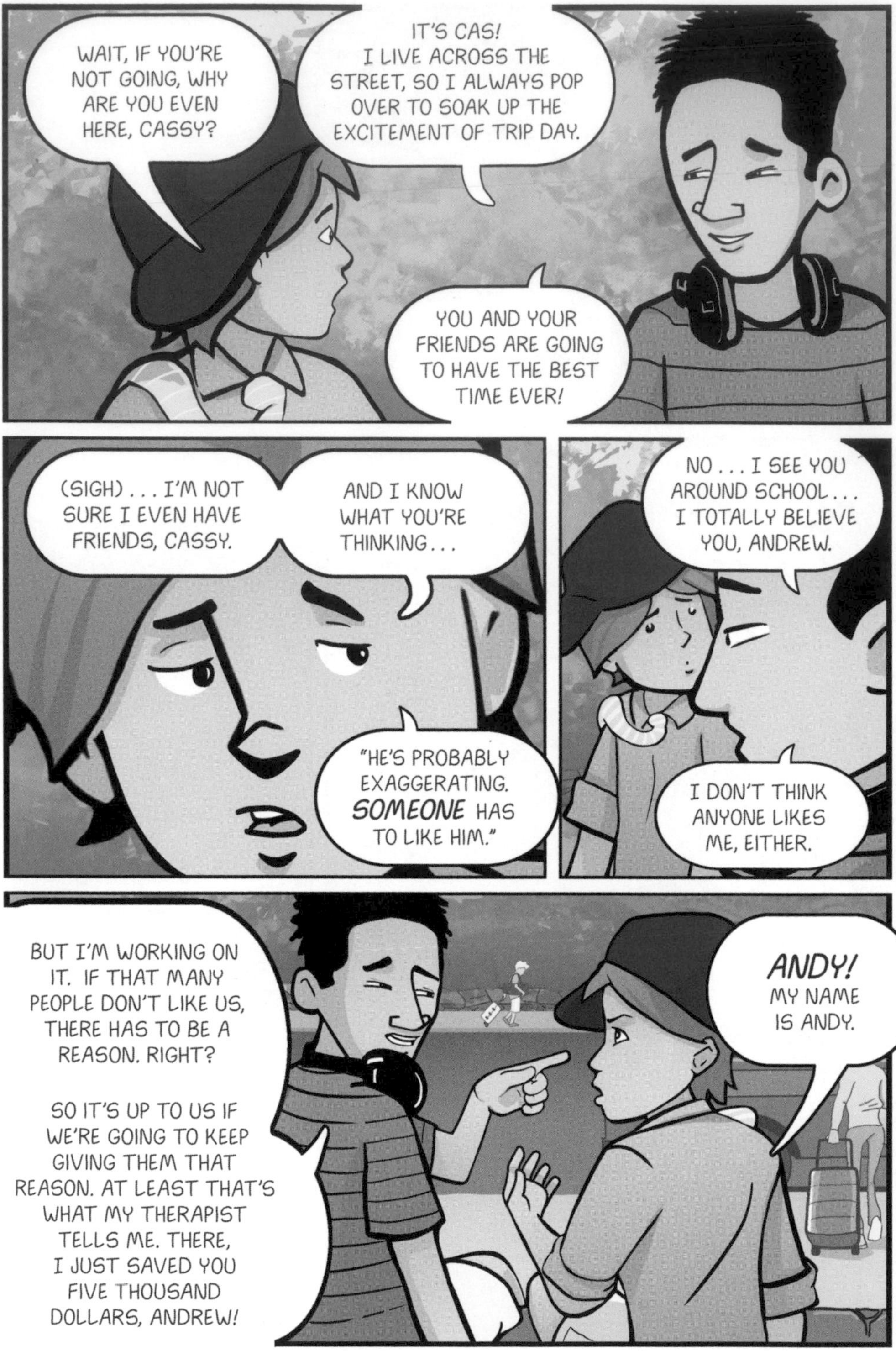
WAIT, IF YOU'RE NOT GOING, WHY ARE YOU EVEN HERE, CASSY?
IT'S CAS! I LIVE ACROSS THE STREET, SO I ALWAYS POP OVER TO SOAK UP THE EXCITEMENT OF TRIP DAY.
YOU AND YOUR FRIENDS ARE GOING TO HAVE THE BEST TIME EVER!
(SIGH) . . . I'M NOT SURE I EVEN HAVE FRIENDS, CASSY.
AND I KNOW WHAT YOU'RE THINKING . . .
"HE'S PROBABLY EXAGGERATING. ***SOMEONE*** HAS TO LIKE HIM."
NO . . . I SEE YOU AROUND SCHOOL . . . I TOTALLY BELIEVE YOU, ANDREW.
I DON'T THINK ANYONE LIKES ME, EITHER.
BUT I'M WORKING ON IT. IF THAT MANY PEOPLE DON'T LIKE US, THERE HAS TO BE A REASON. RIGHT?
SO IT'S UP TO US IF WE'RE GOING TO KEEP GIVING THEM THAT REASON. AT LEAST THAT'S WHAT MY THERAPIST TELLS ME. THERE, I JUST SAVED YOU FIVE THOUSAND DOLLARS, ANDREW!
ANDY! MY NAME IS ANDY.

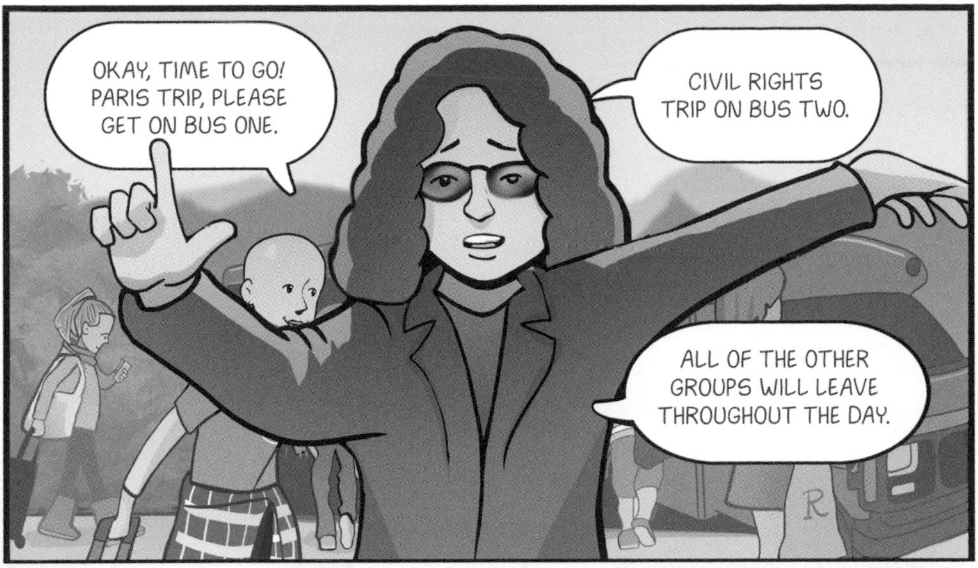
OKAY, TIME TO GO! PARIS TRIP, PLEASE GET ON BUS ONE.
CIVIL RIGHTS TRIP ON BUS TWO.
ALL OF THE OTHER GROUPS WILL LEAVE THROUGHOUT THE DAY.
R

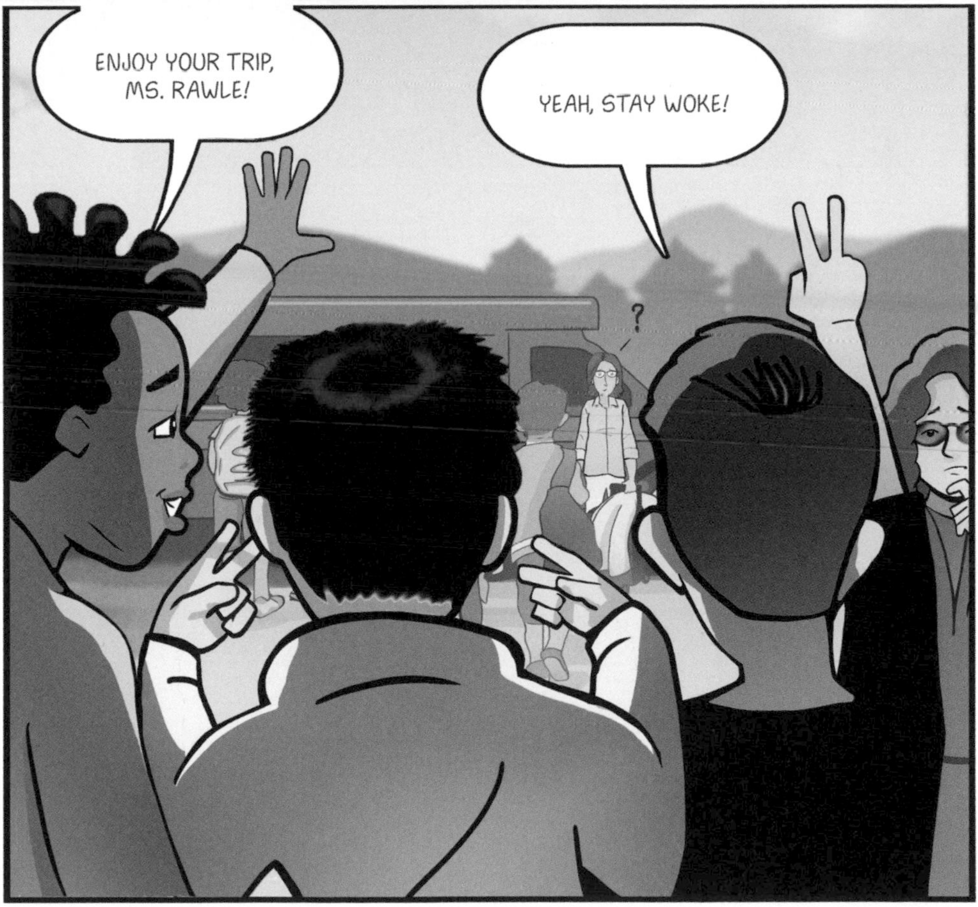
ENJOY YOUR TRIP, MS. RAWLE!
YEAH, STAY WOKE!
?

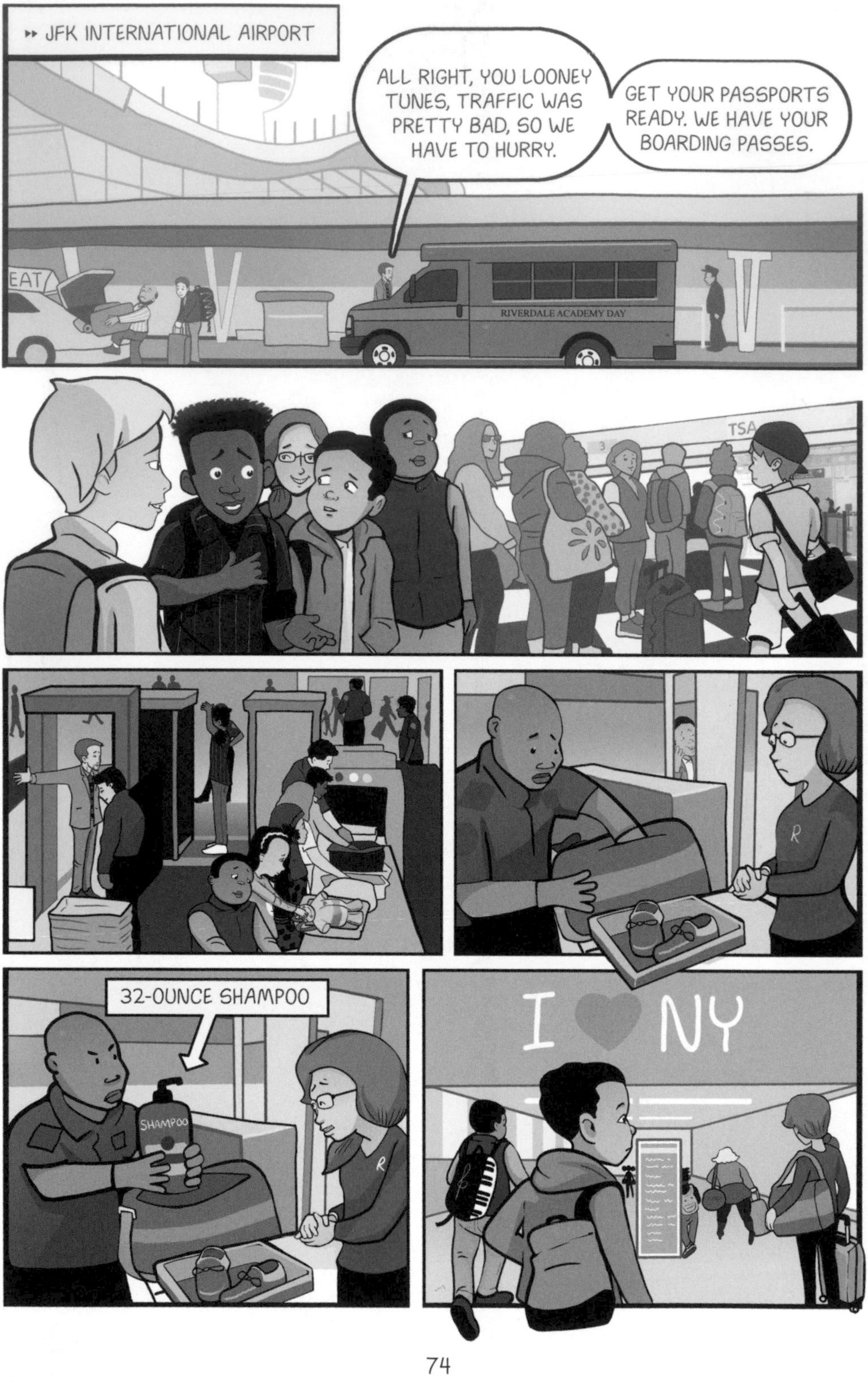
JFK INTERNATIONAL AIRPORT
ALL RIGHT, YOU LOONEY TUNES, TRAFFIC WAS PRETTY BAD, SO WE HAVE TO HURRY.
GET YOUR PASSPORTS READY. WE HAVE YOUR BOARDING PASSES.
EAT
RIVERDALE ACADEMY DAY
TSA
32-OUNCE SHAMPOO
SHAMPOO
I ♥ NY

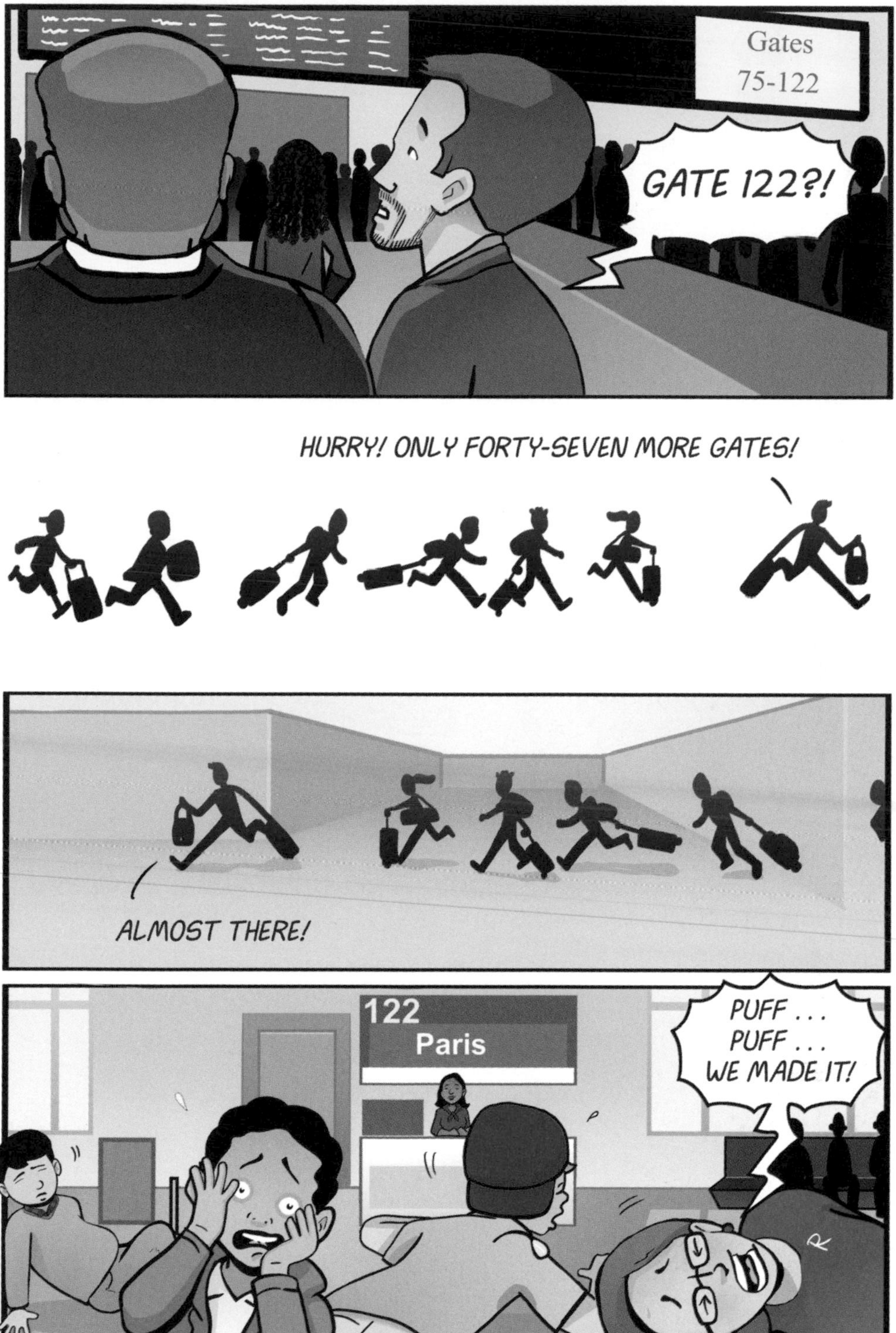
Gates
75-122
GATE 122?!
HURRY! ONLY FORTY-SEVEN MORE GATES!
ALMOST THERE!
122
Paris
PUFF . . .
PUFF . . .
WE MADE IT!

4

Airplane Etiquette

(ET-AH-KIT) The Customary Manner of Polite Behavior

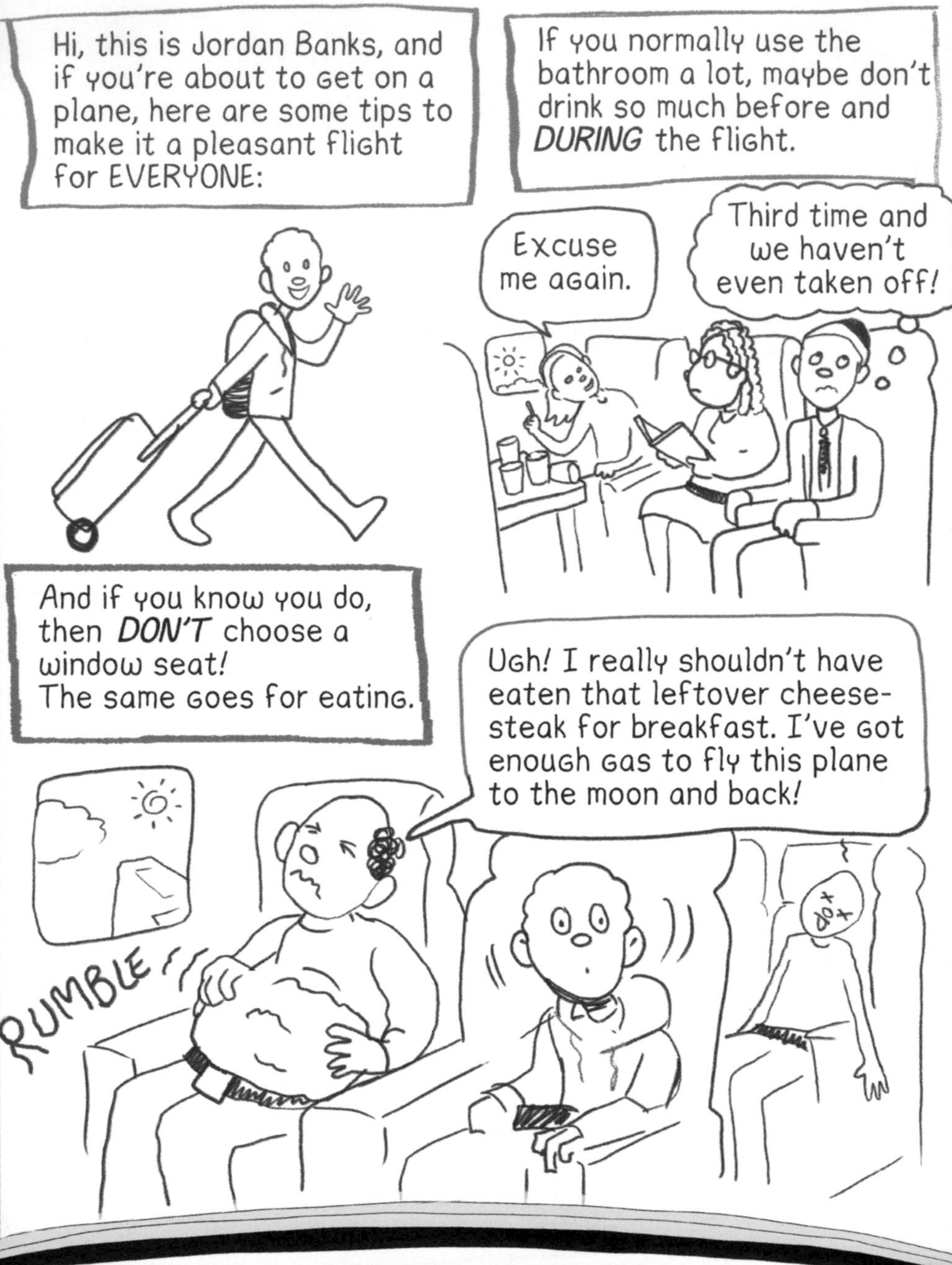

Hi, this is Jordan Banks, and if you're about to get on a plane, here are some tips to make it a pleasant flight for EVERYONE:
If you normally use the bathroom a lot, maybe don't drink so much before and *DURING* the flight.
Excuse me again.
Third time and we haven't even taken off!
And if you know you do, then *DON'T* choose a window seat! The same goes for eating.
Ugh! I really shouldn't have eaten that leftover cheese-steak for breakfast. I've got enough gas to fly this plane to the moon and back!
RUMBLE

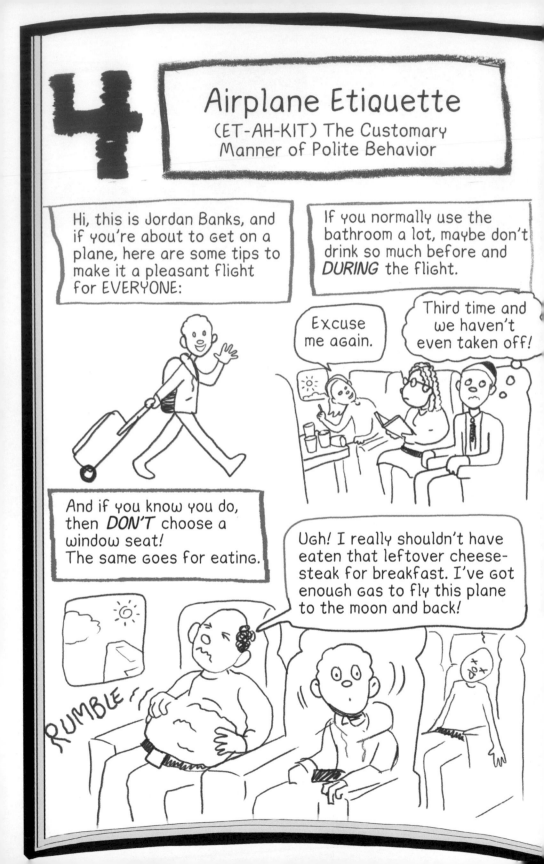

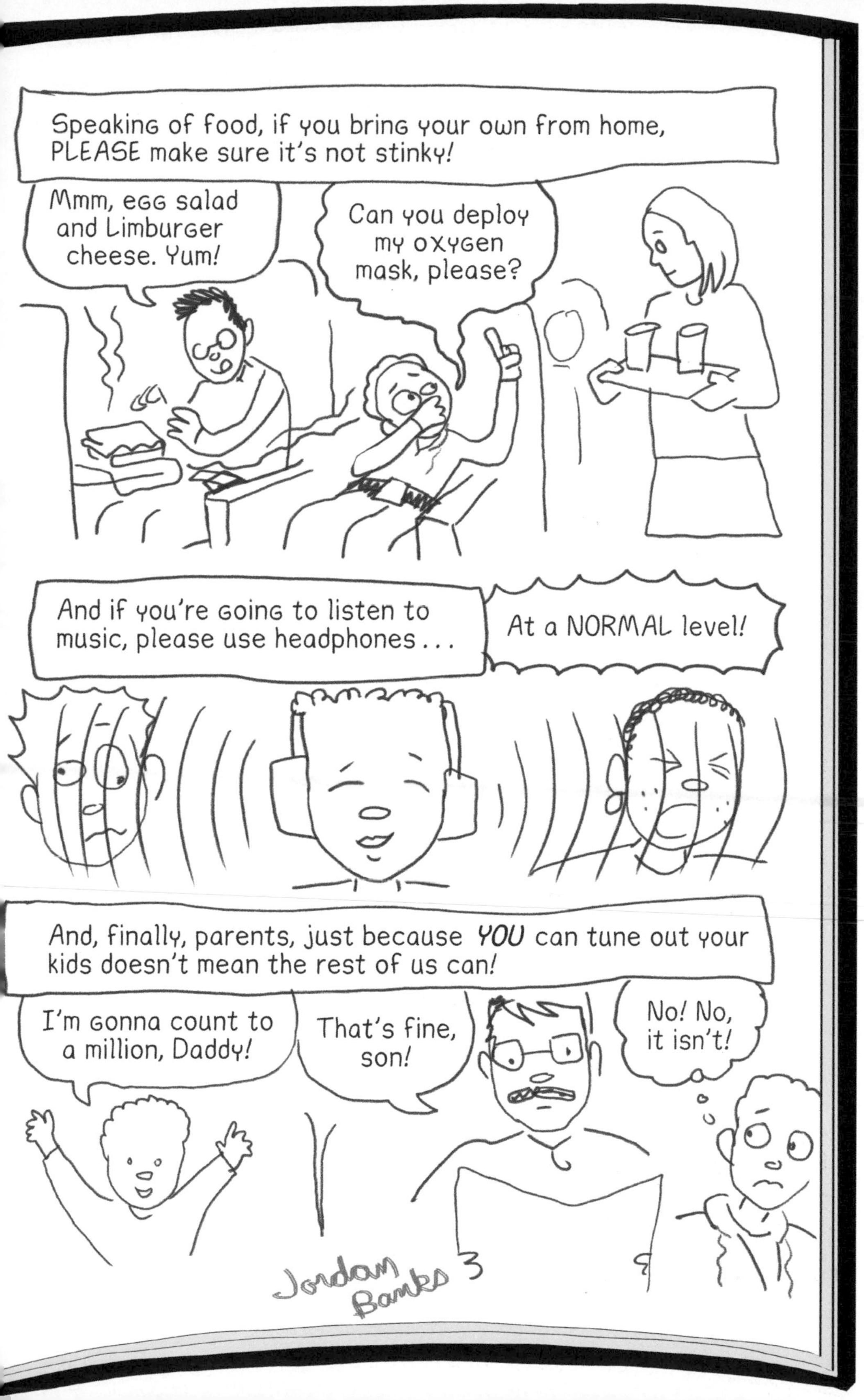
Speaking of food, if you bring your own from home, PLEASE make sure it's not stinky!
Mmm, egg salad and Limburger cheese. Yum!
Can you deploy my oxygen mask, please?
And if you're going to listen to music, please use headphones . . .
At a NORMAL level!
And, finally, parents, just because *YOU* can tune out your kids doesn't mean the rest of us can!
I'm gonna count to a million, Daddy!
That's fine, son!
No! No, it isn't!
Jordan Banks
3

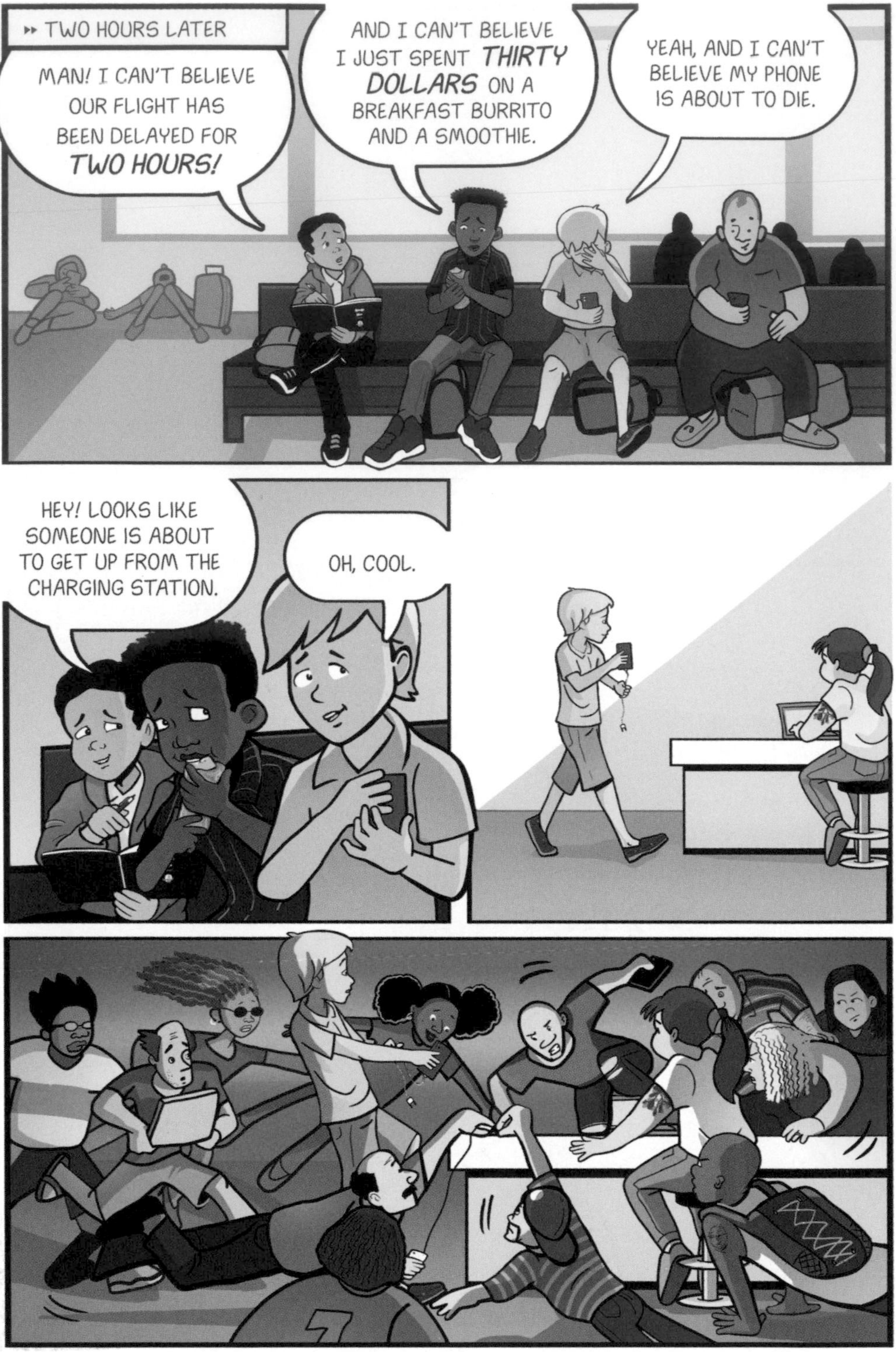

TWO HOURS LATER
MAN! I CAN'T BELIEVE OUR FLIGHT HAS BEEN DELAYED FOR TWO HOURS!
AND I CAN'T BELIEVE I JUST SPENT THIRTY DOLLARS ON A BREAKFAST BURRITO AND A SMOOTHIE.
YEAH, AND I CAN'T BELIEVE MY PHONE IS ABOUT TO DIE.
HEY! LOOKS LIKE SOMEONE IS ABOUT TO GET UP FROM THE CHARGING STATION.
OH, COOL.

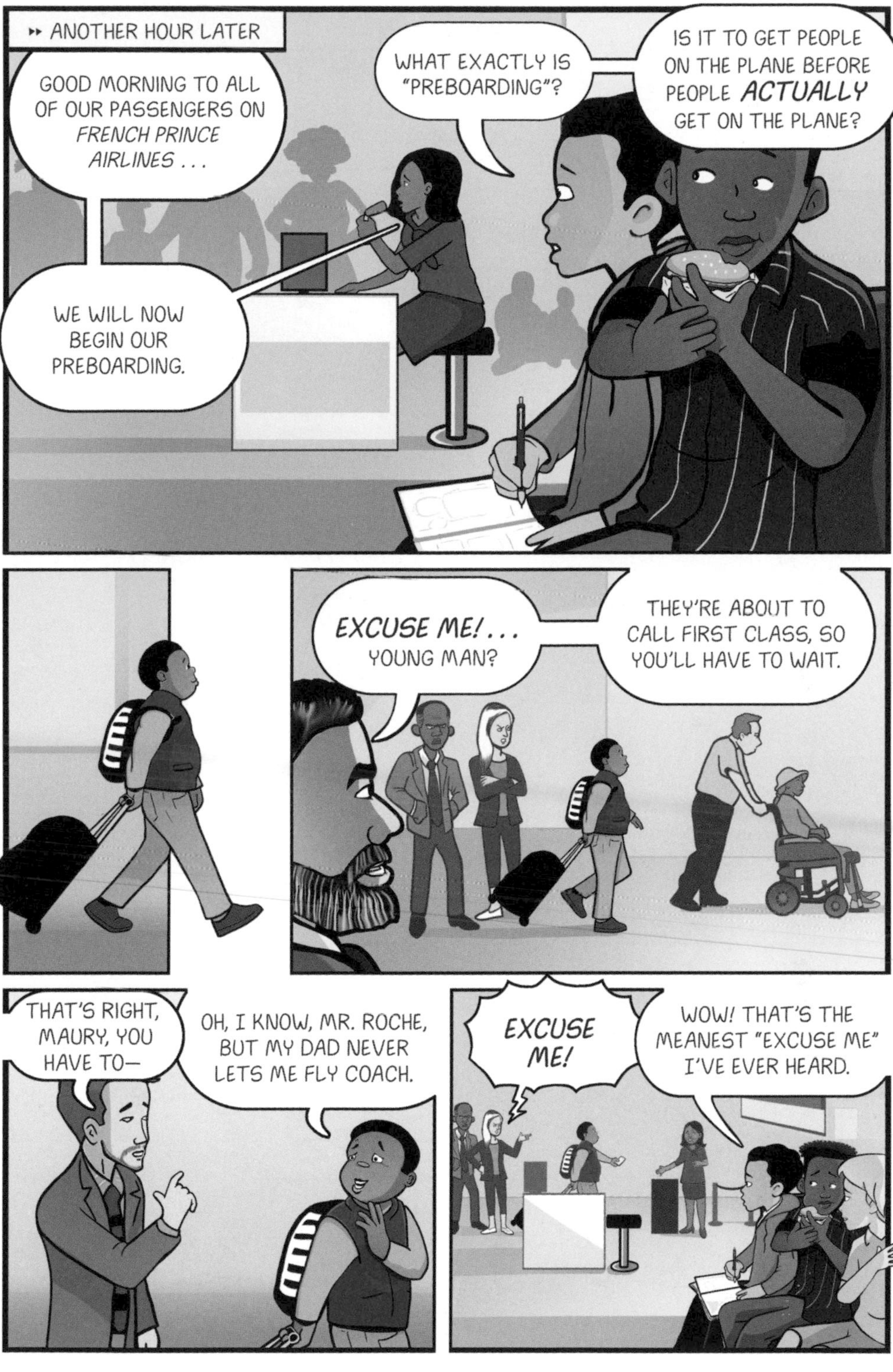
ANOTHER HOUR LATER
GOOD MORNING TO ALL OF OUR PASSENGERS ON *FRENCH PRINCE AIRLINES* . . .
WE WILL NOW BEGIN OUR PREBOARDING.
WHAT EXACTLY IS "PREBOARDING"?
IS IT TO GET PEOPLE ON THE PLANE BEFORE PEOPLE **ACTUALLY** GET ON THE PLANE?
EXCUSE ME! . . . YOUNG MAN?
THEY'RE ABOUT TO CALL FIRST CLASS, SO YOU'LL HAVE TO WAIT.
THAT'S RIGHT, MAURY, YOU HAVE TO—
OH, I KNOW, MR. ROCHE, BUT MY DAD NEVER LETS ME FLY COACH.
EXCUSE ME!
WOW! THAT'S THE MEANEST "EXCUSE ME" I'VE EVER HEARD.

That's Not What I Mean!
(Emphasis on the Word "Mean")

Just because people use nice phrases doesn't mean they're being nice. Here are some common phrases along with what they really mean, depending on the situation.

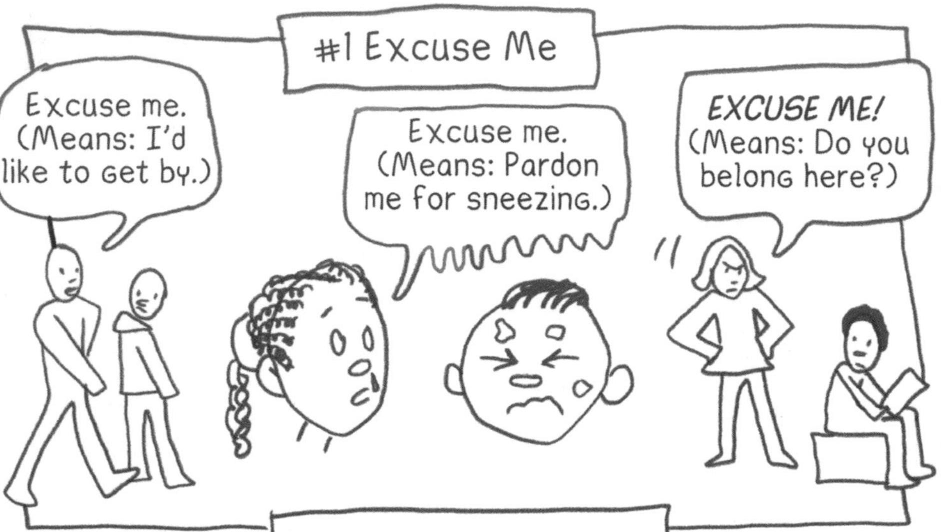
#1 Excuse Me
Excuse me. (Means: I'd like to get by.)
Excuse me. (Means: Pardon me for sneezing.)
EXCUSE ME! (Means: Do you belong here?)

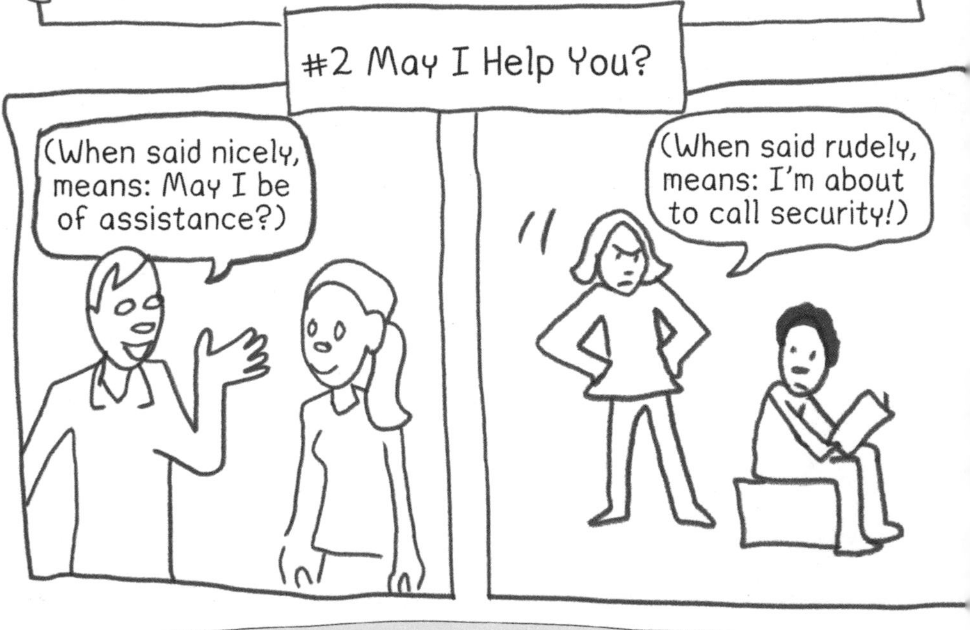
#2 May I Help You?
(When said nicely, means: May I be of assistance?)
(When said rudely, means: I'm about to call security!)

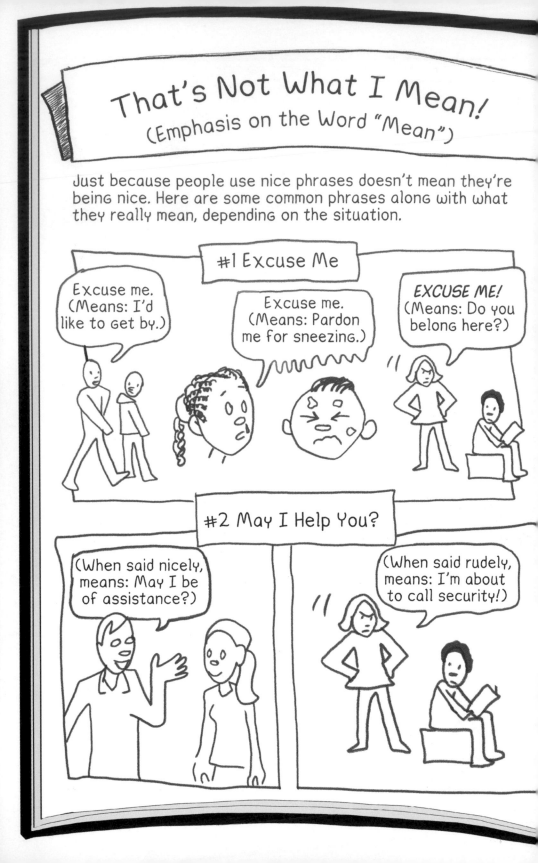

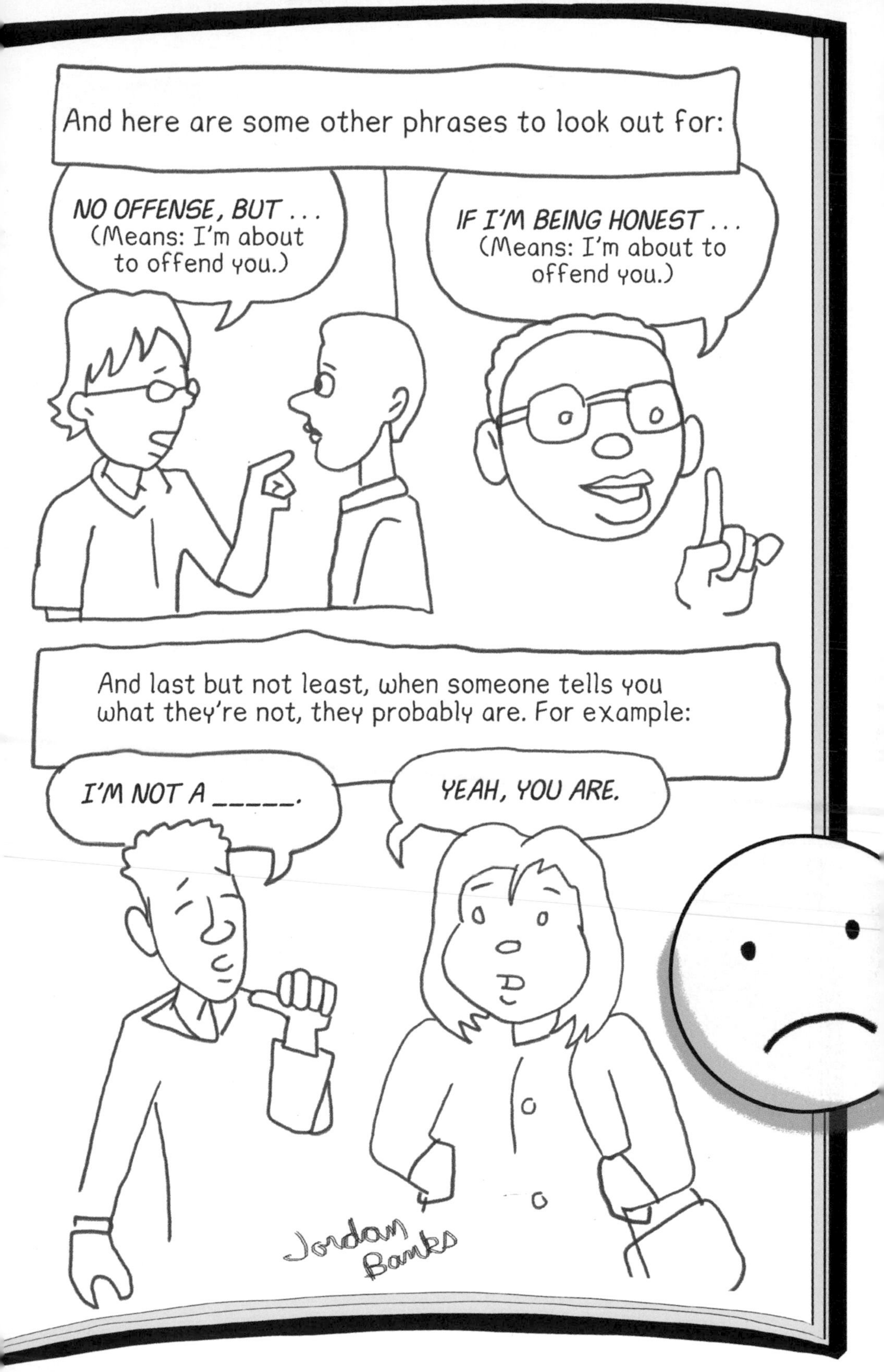
And here are some other phrases to look out for:
NO OFFENSE, BUT . . . (Means: I'm about to offend you.)
IF I'M BEING HONEST . . . (Means: I'm about to offend you.)
And last but not least, when someone tells you what they're not, they probably are. For example:
I'M NOT A _____.
YEAH, YOU ARE.
Jordan Banks

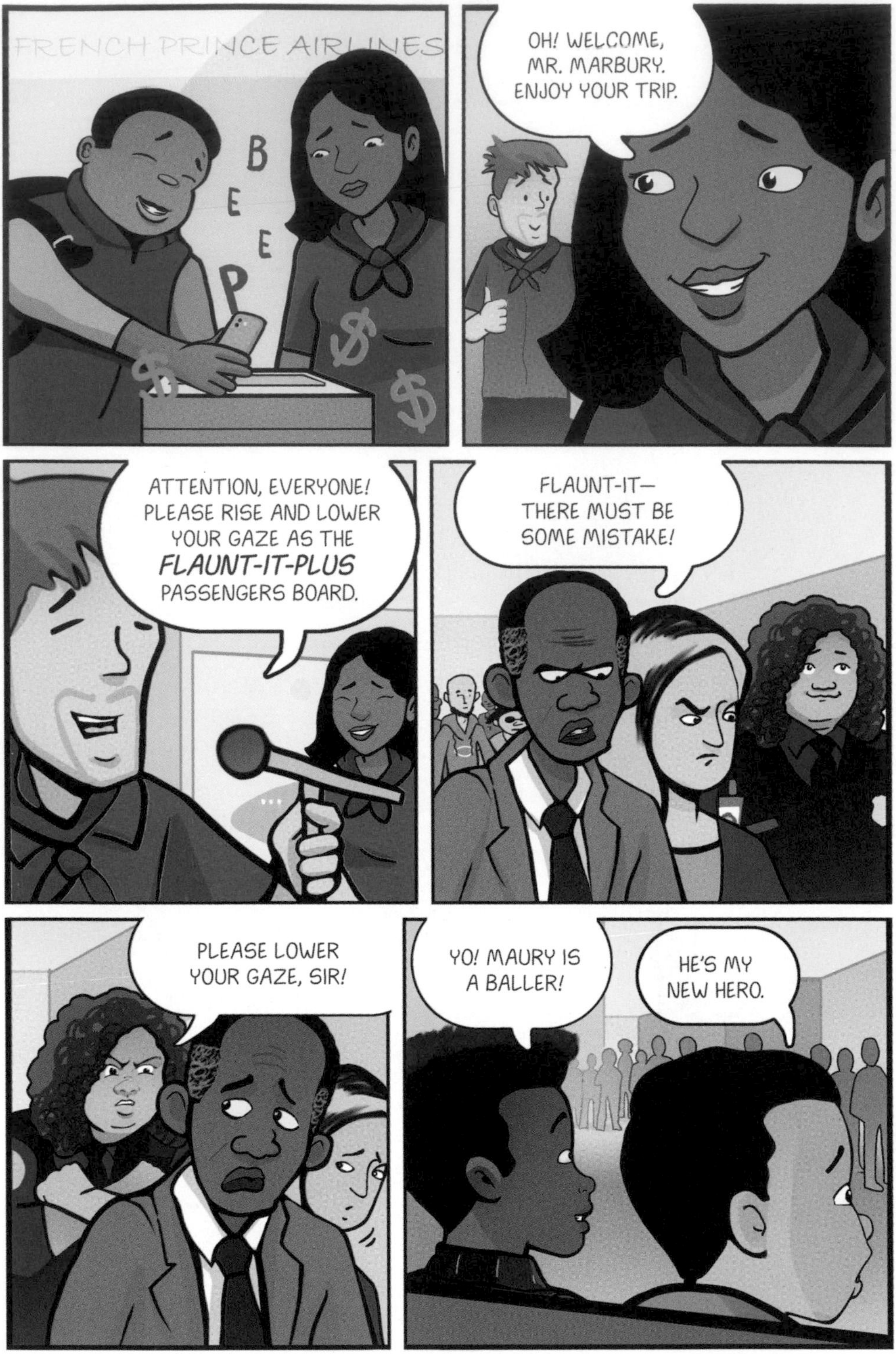
FRENCH PRINCE AIRLINES
BEEP
OH! WELCOME, MR. MARBURY. ENJOY YOUR TRIP.
ATTENTION, EVERYONE! PLEASE RISE AND LOWER YOUR GAZE AS THE *FLAUNT-IT-PLUS* PASSENGERS BOARD.
FLAUNT-IT— THERE MUST BE SOME MISTAKE!
PLEASE LOWER YOUR GAZE, SIR!
YO! MAURY IS A BALLER!
HE'S MY NEW HERO.

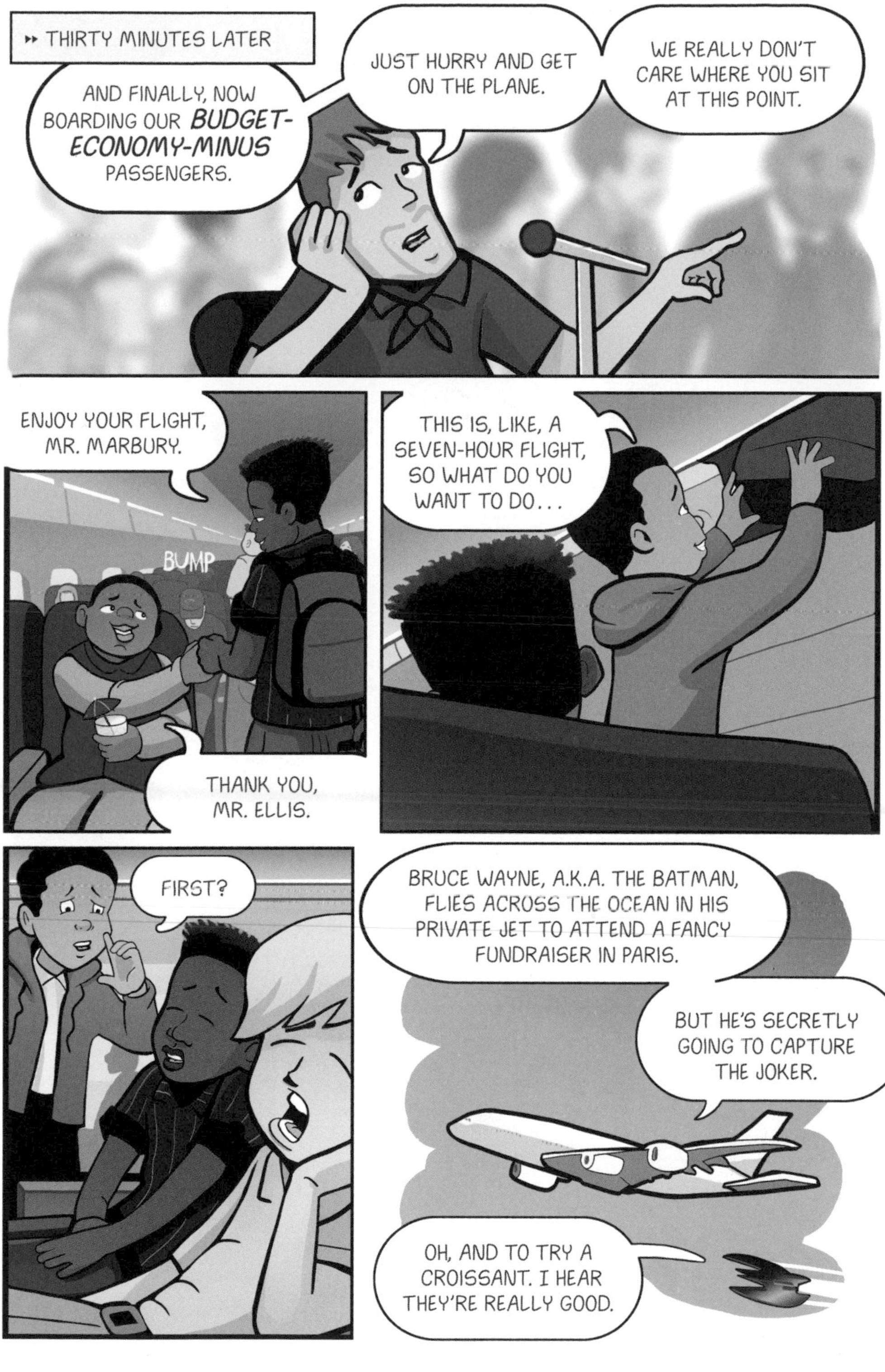
THIRTY MINUTES LATER
AND FINALLY, NOW BOARDING OUR BUDGET-ECONOMY-MINUS PASSENGERS.
JUST HURRY AND GET ON THE PLANE.
WE REALLY DON'T CARE WHERE YOU SIT AT THIS POINT.
ENJOY YOUR FLIGHT, MR. MARBURY.
BUMP
THANK YOU, MR. ELLIS.
THIS IS, LIKE, A SEVEN-HOUR FLIGHT, SO WHAT DO YOU WANT TO DO...
FIRST?
BRUCE WAYNE, A.K.A. THE BATMAN, FLIES ACROSS THE OCEAN IN HIS PRIVATE JET TO ATTEND A FANCY FUNDRAISER IN PARIS.
BUT HE'S SECRETLY GOING TO CAPTURE THE JOKER.
OH, AND TO TRY A CROISSANT. I HEAR THEY'RE REALLY GOOD.

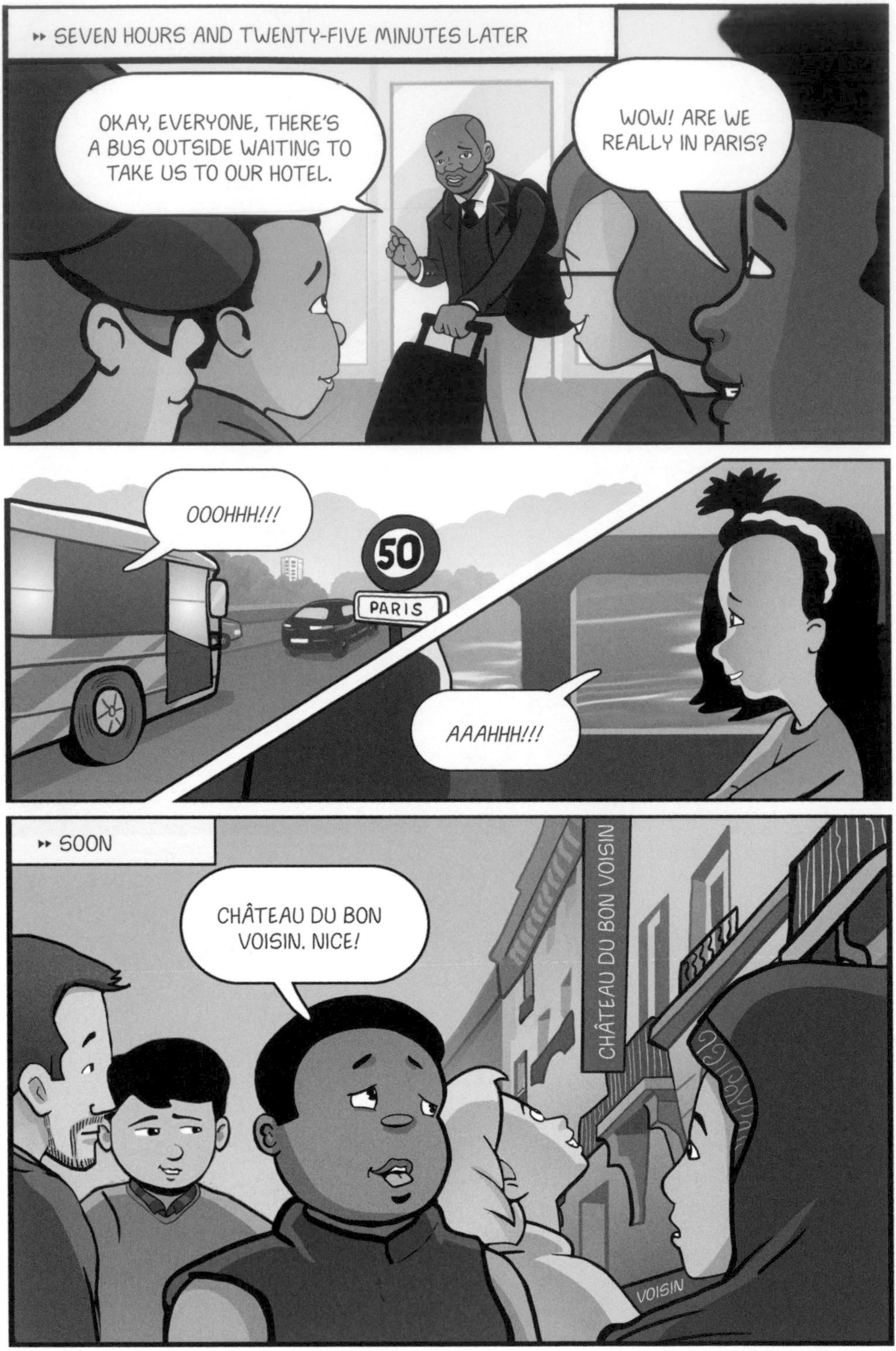
SEVEN HOURS AND TWENTY-FIVE MINUTES LATER
OKAY, EVERYONE, THERE'S A BUS OUTSIDE WAITING TO TAKE US TO OUR HOTEL.
WOW! ARE WE REALLY IN PARIS?
OOOHHH!!!
50
PARIS
AAAHHH!!!
SOON
CHÂTEAU DU BON VOISIN. NICE!
CHÂTEAU DU BON VOISIN
VOISIN

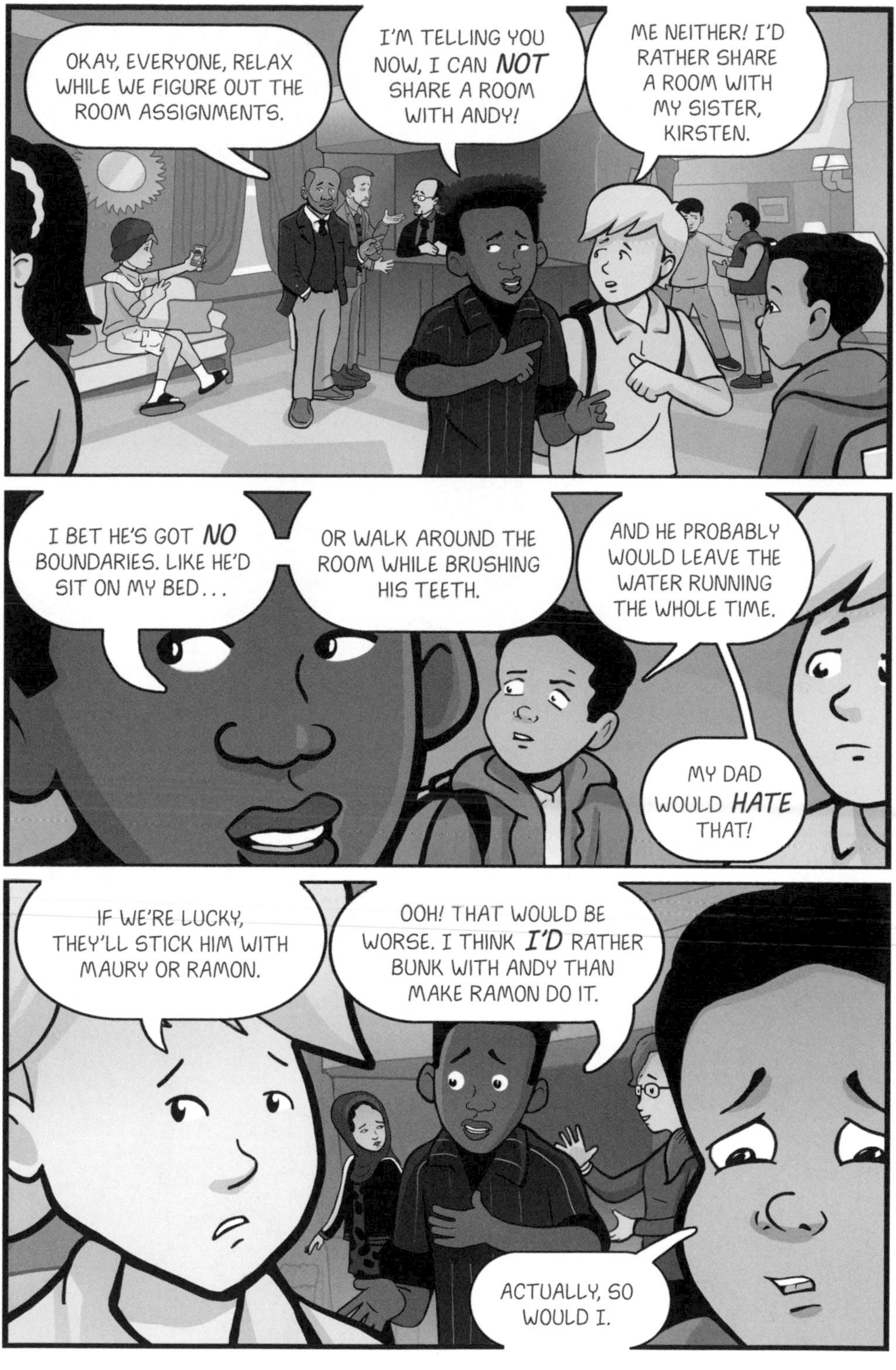
OKAY, EVERYONE, RELAX WHILE WE FIGURE OUT THE ROOM ASSIGNMENTS.
I'M TELLING YOU NOW, I CAN ***NOT*** SHARE A ROOM WITH ANDY!
ME NEITHER! I'D RATHER SHARE A ROOM WITH MY SISTER, KIRSTEN.
I BET HE'S GOT ***NO*** BOUNDARIES. LIKE HE'D SIT ON MY BED . . .
OR WALK AROUND THE ROOM WHILE BRUSHING HIS TEETH.
AND HE PROBABLY WOULD LEAVE THE WATER RUNNING THE WHOLE TIME.
MY DAD WOULD ***HATE*** THAT!
IF WE'RE LUCKY, THEY'LL STICK HIM WITH MAURY OR RAMON.
OOH! THAT WOULD BE WORSE. I THINK ***I'D*** RATHER BUNK WITH ANDY THAN MAKE RAMON DO IT.
ACTUALLY, SO WOULD I.

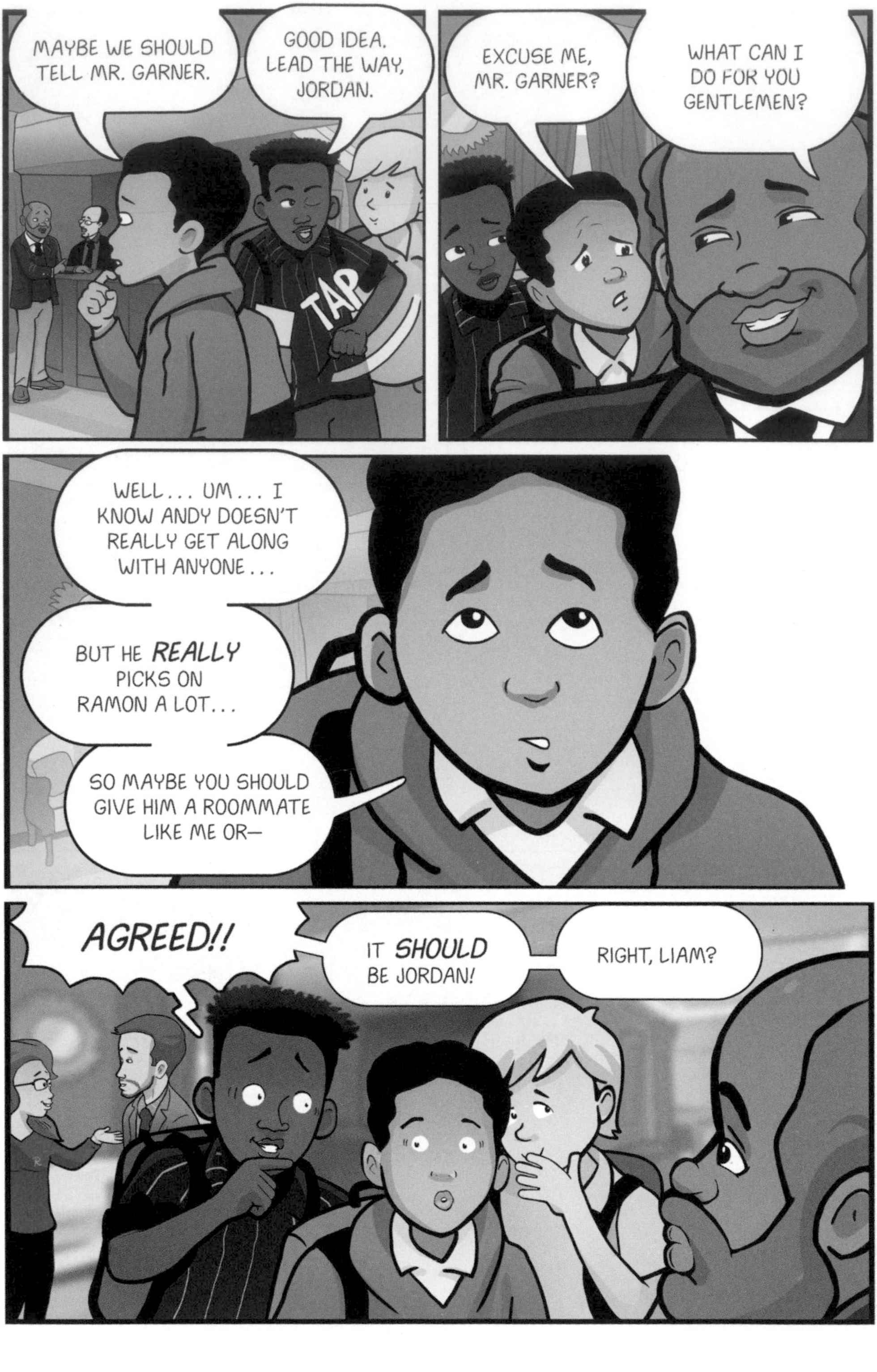
MAYBE WE SHOULD TELL MR. GARNER.
GOOD IDEA. LEAD THE WAY, JORDAN.
TAP
EXCUSE ME, MR. GARNER?
WHAT CAN I DO FOR YOU GENTLEMEN?
WELL . . . UM . . . I KNOW ANDY DOESN'T REALLY GET ALONG WITH ANYONE . . .
BUT HE *REALLY* PICKS ON RAMON A LOT . . .
SO MAYBE YOU SHOULD GIVE HIM A ROOMMATE LIKE ME OR—
AGREED!!
IT *SHOULD* BE JORDAN!
RIGHT, LIAM?

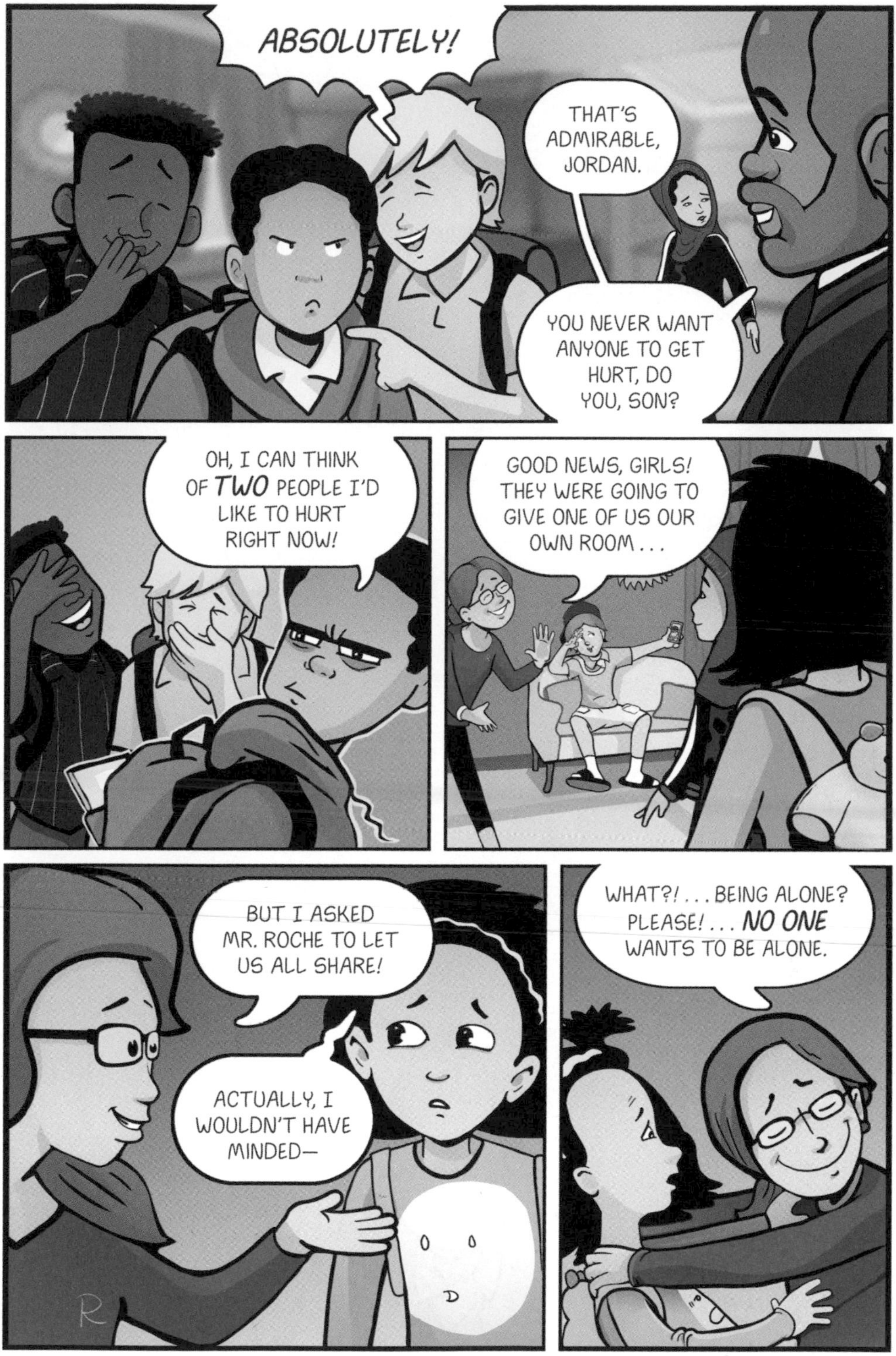
ABSOLUTELY!
THAT'S ADMIRABLE, JORDAN.
YOU NEVER WANT ANYONE TO GET HURT, DO YOU, SON?
OH, I CAN THINK OF TWO PEOPLE I'D LIKE TO HURT RIGHT NOW!
GOOD NEWS, GIRLS! THEY WERE GOING TO GIVE ONE OF US OUR OWN ROOM . . .
BUT I ASKED MR. ROCHE TO LET US ALL SHARE!
ACTUALLY, I WOULDN'T HAVE MINDED—
WHAT?! . . . BEING ALONE? PLEASE! . . . NO ONE WANTS TO BE ALONE.

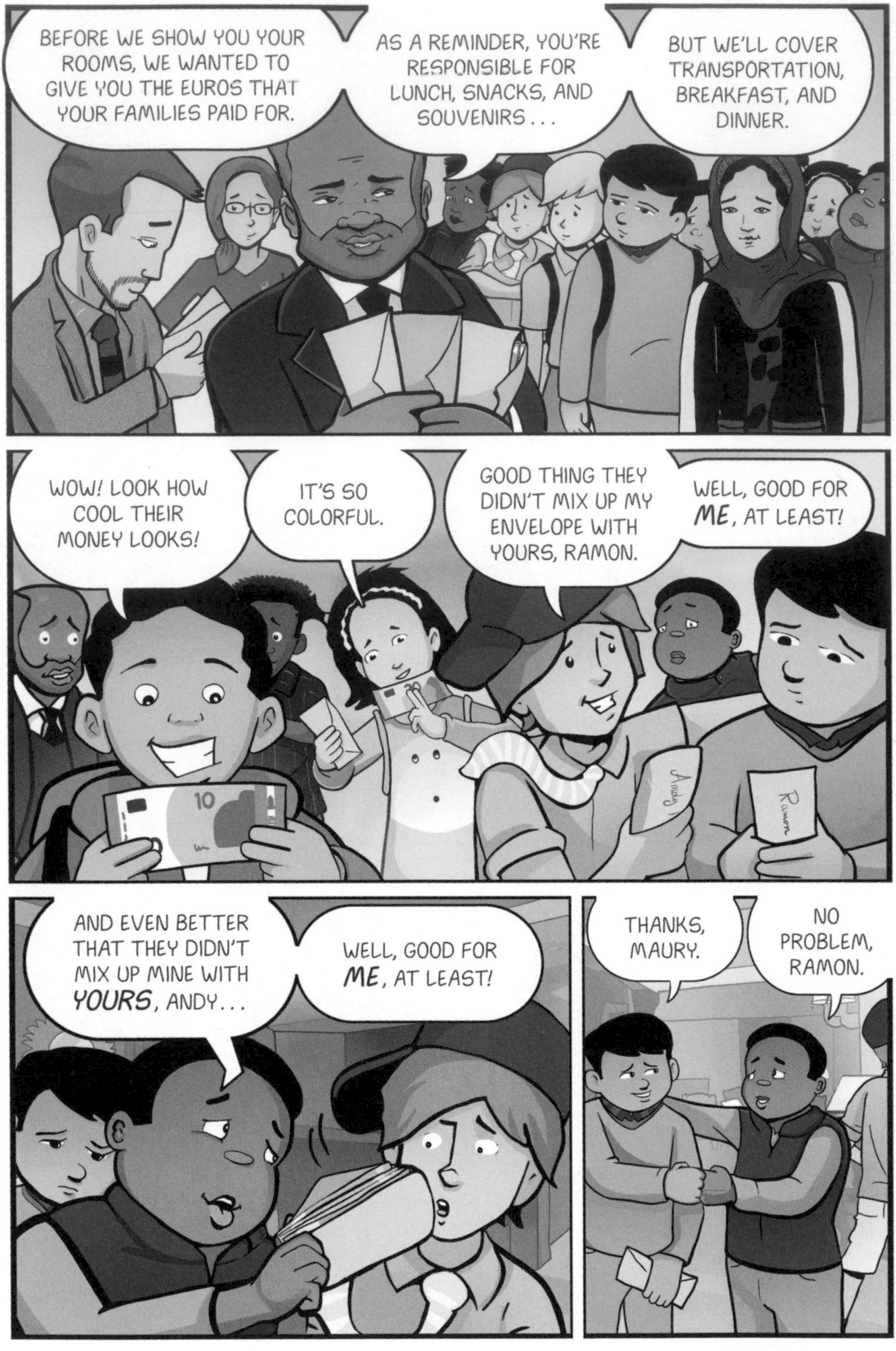

BEFORE WE SHOW YOU YOUR ROOMS, WE WANTED TO GIVE YOU THE EUROS THAT YOUR FAMILIES PAID FOR.
AS A REMINDER, YOU'RE RESPONSIBLE FOR LUNCH, SNACKS, AND SOUVENIRS . . .
BUT WE'LL COVER TRANSPORTATION, BREAKFAST, AND DINNER.
WOW! LOOK HOW COOL THEIR MONEY LOOKS!
IT'S SO COLORFUL.
GOOD THING THEY DIDN'T MIX UP MY ENVELOPE WITH YOURS, RAMON.
WELL, GOOD FOR **ME**, AT LEAST!
Andy
Ramon
AND EVEN BETTER THAT THEY DIDN'T MIX UP MINE WITH **YOURS**, ANDY . . .
WELL, GOOD FOR **ME**, AT LEAST!
THANKS, MAURY.
NO PROBLEM, RAMON.

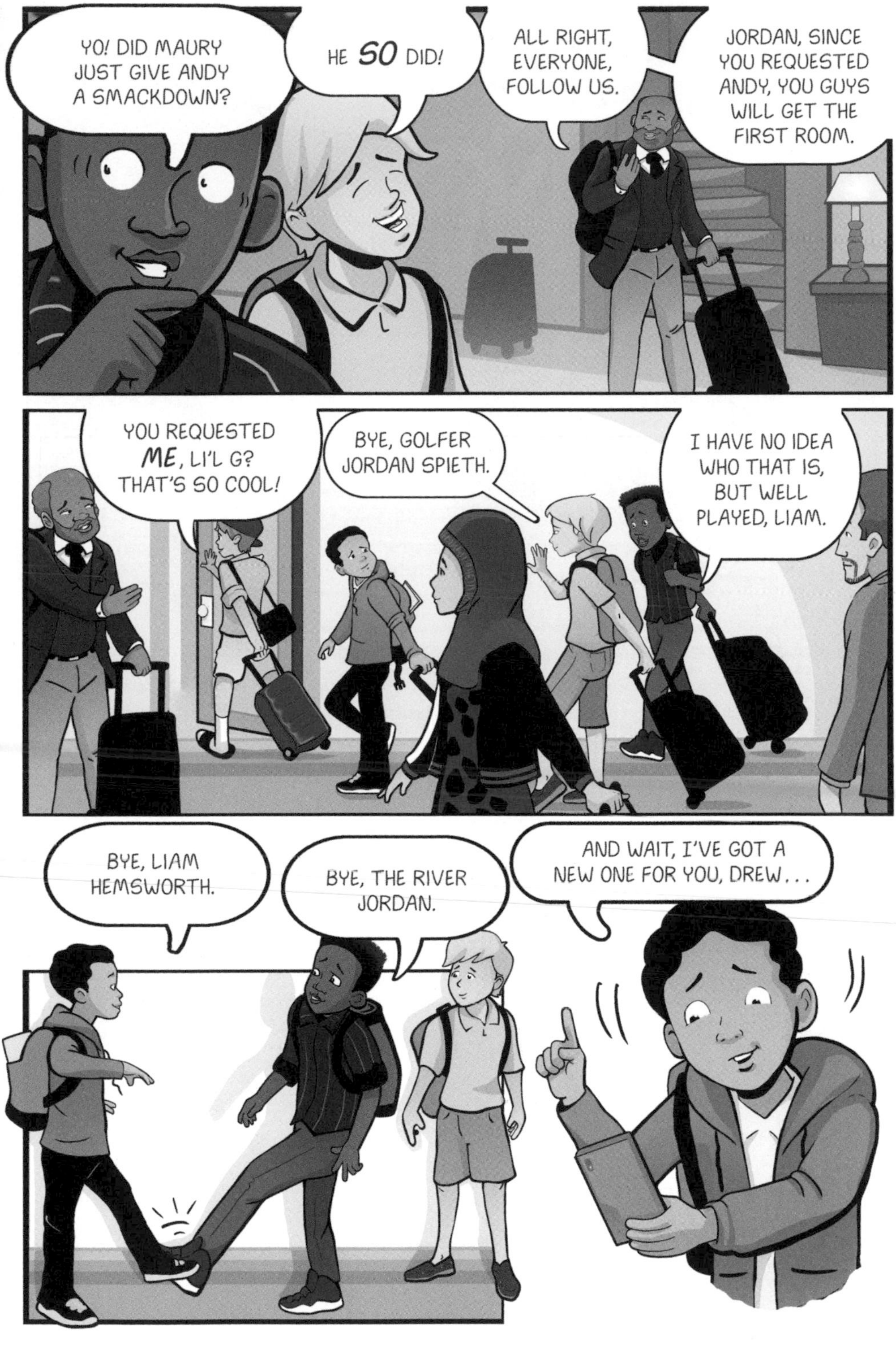
YO! DID MAURY JUST GIVE ANDY A SMACKDOWN?
HE **SO** DID!
ALL RIGHT, EVERYONE, FOLLOW US.
JORDAN, SINCE YOU REQUESTED ANDY, YOU GUYS WILL GET THE FIRST ROOM.
YOU REQUESTED **ME**, LI'L G? THAT'S SO COOL!
BYE, GOLFER JORDAN SPIETH.
I HAVE NO IDEA WHO THAT IS, BUT WELL PLAYED, LIAM.
BYE, LIAM HEMSWORTH.
BYE, THE RIVER JORDAN.
AND WAIT, I'VE GOT A NEW ONE FOR YOU, DREW...

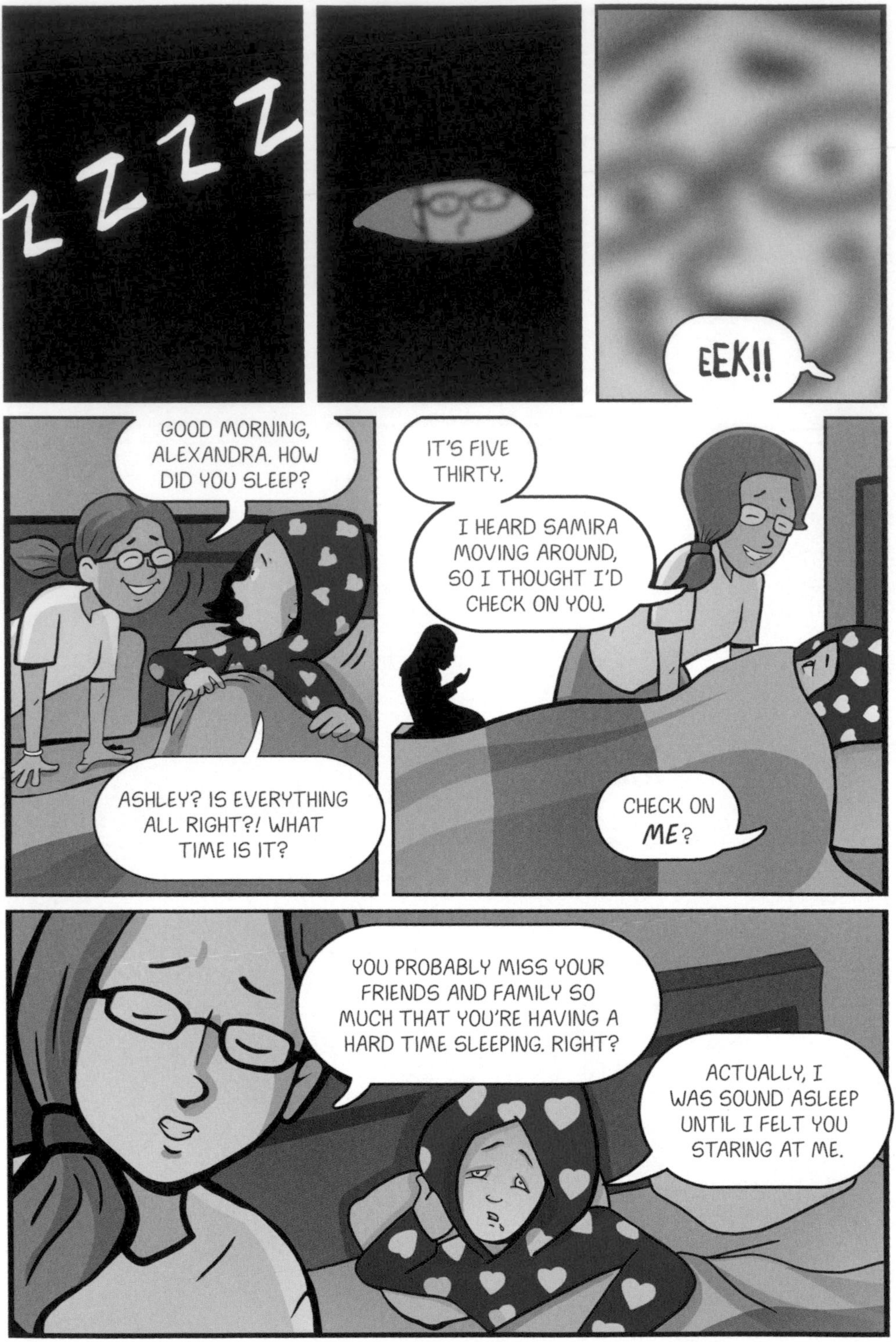
ZZZZ
EEK!!
GOOD MORNING, ALEXANDRA. HOW DID YOU SLEEP?
ASHLEY? IS EVERYTHING ALL RIGHT?! WHAT TIME IS IT?
IT'S FIVE THIRTY.
I HEARD SAMIRA MOVING AROUND, SO I THOUGHT I'D CHECK ON YOU.
CHECK ON ME?
YOU PROBABLY MISS YOUR FRIENDS AND FAMILY SO MUCH THAT YOU'RE HAVING A HARD TIME SLEEPING. RIGHT?
ACTUALLY, I WAS SOUND ASLEEP UNTIL I FELT YOU STARING AT ME.

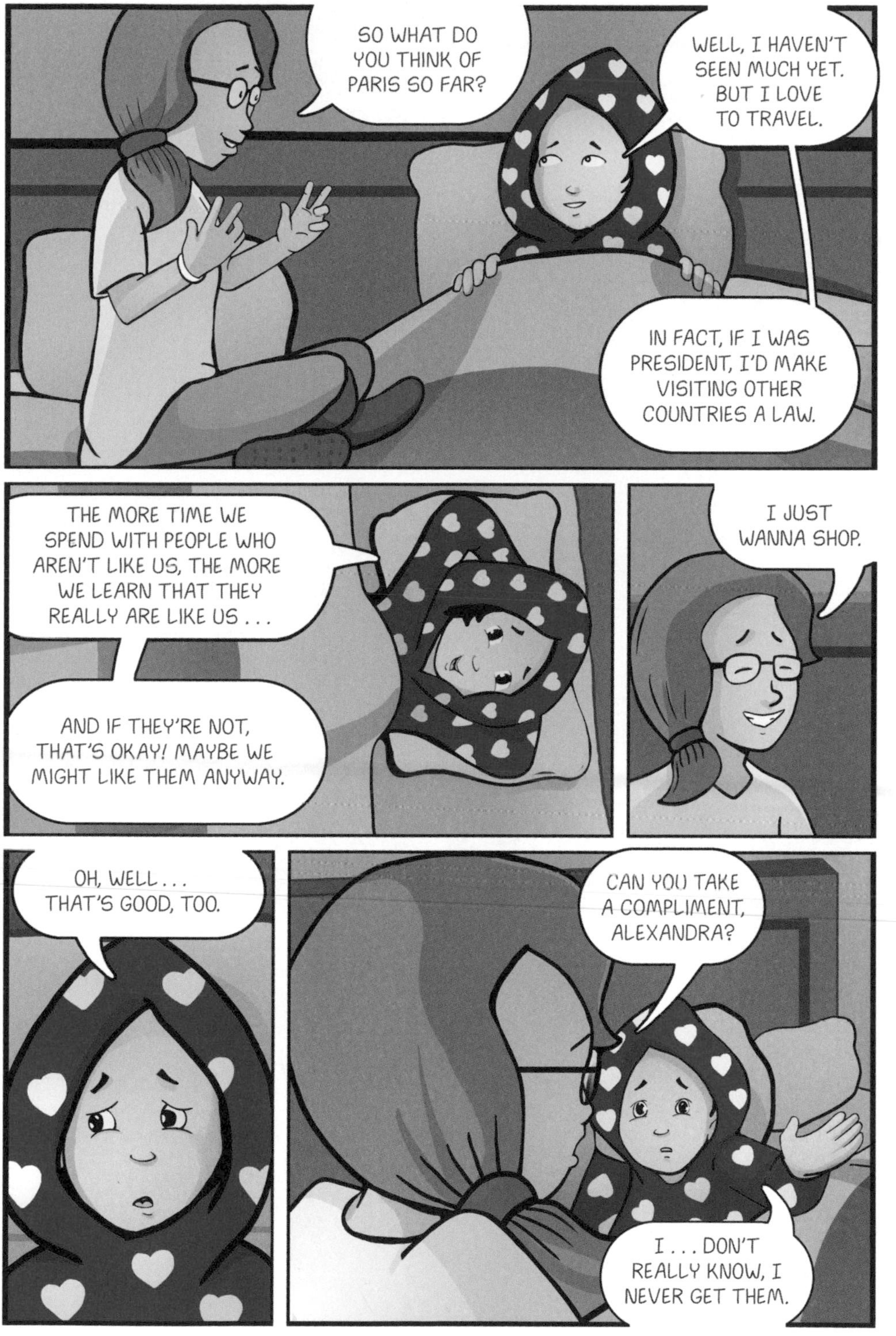
SO WHAT DO YOU THINK OF PARIS SO FAR?
WELL, I HAVEN'T SEEN MUCH YET. BUT I LOVE TO TRAVEL.
IN FACT, IF I WAS PRESIDENT, I'D MAKE VISITING OTHER COUNTRIES A LAW.
THE MORE TIME WE SPEND WITH PEOPLE WHO AREN'T LIKE US, THE MORE WE LEARN THAT THEY REALLY ARE LIKE US . . .
AND IF THEY'RE NOT, THAT'S OKAY! MAYBE WE MIGHT LIKE THEM ANYWAY.
I JUST WANNA SHOP.
OH, WELL . . . THAT'S GOOD, TOO.
CAN YOU TAKE A COMPLIMENT, ALEXANDRA?
I . . . DON'T REALLY KNOW, I NEVER GET THEM.

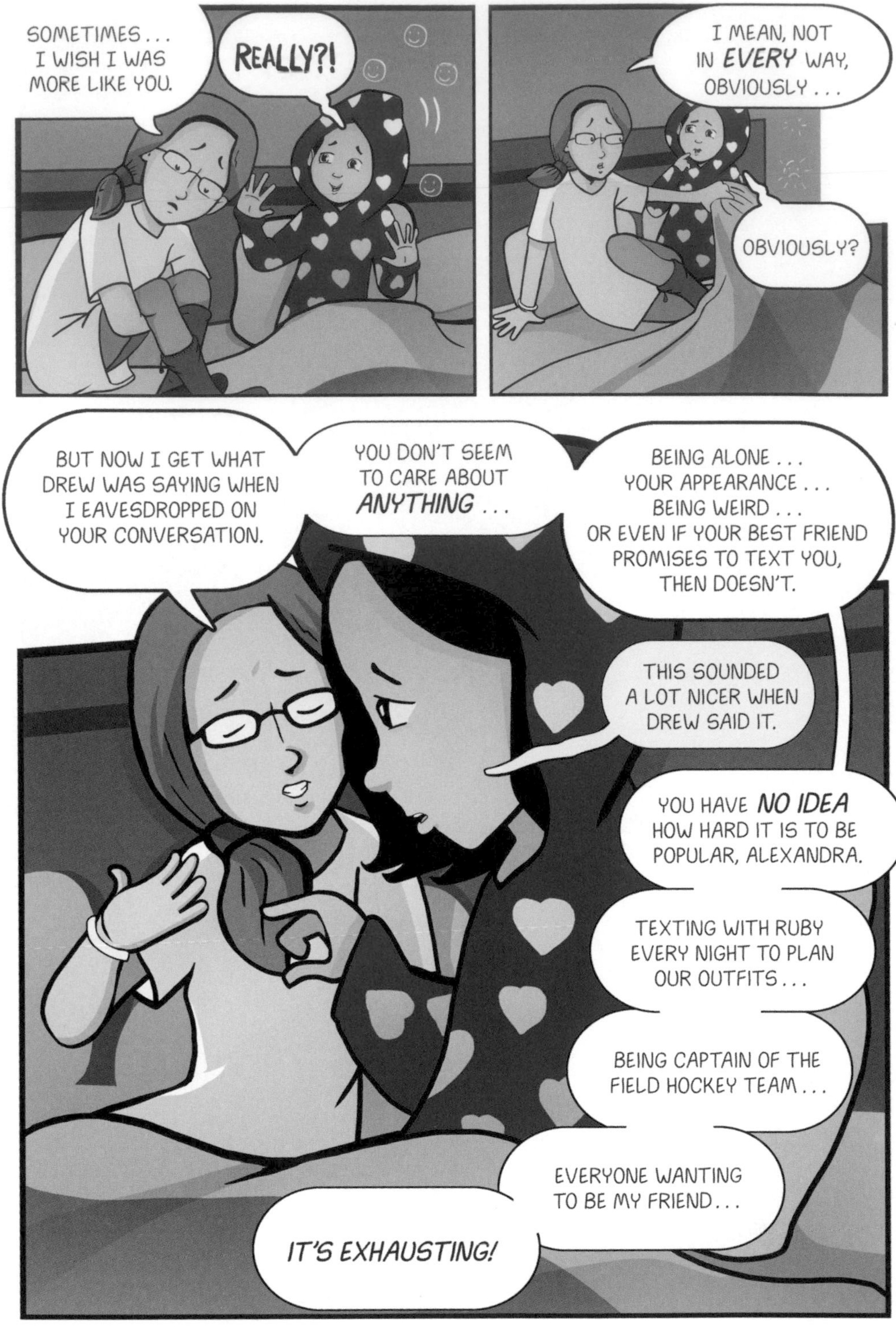
SOMETIMES . . . I WISH I WAS MORE LIKE YOU.
REALLY?!
I MEAN, NOT IN EVERY WAY, OBVIOUSLY . . .
OBVIOUSLY?
BUT NOW I GET WHAT DREW WAS SAYING WHEN I EAVESDROPPED ON YOUR CONVERSATION.
YOU DON'T SEEM TO CARE ABOUT ANYTHING . . .
BEING ALONE . . . YOUR APPEARANCE . . . BEING WEIRD . . . OR EVEN IF YOUR BEST FRIEND PROMISES TO TEXT YOU, THEN DOESN'T.
THIS SOUNDED A LOT NICER WHEN DREW SAID IT.
YOU HAVE NO IDEA HOW HARD IT IS TO BE POPULAR, ALEXANDRA.
TEXTING WITH RUBY EVERY NIGHT TO PLAN OUR OUTFITS . . .
BEING CAPTAIN OF THE FIELD HOCKEY TEAM . . .
EVERYONE WANTING TO BE MY FRIEND . . .
IT'S EXHAUSTING!

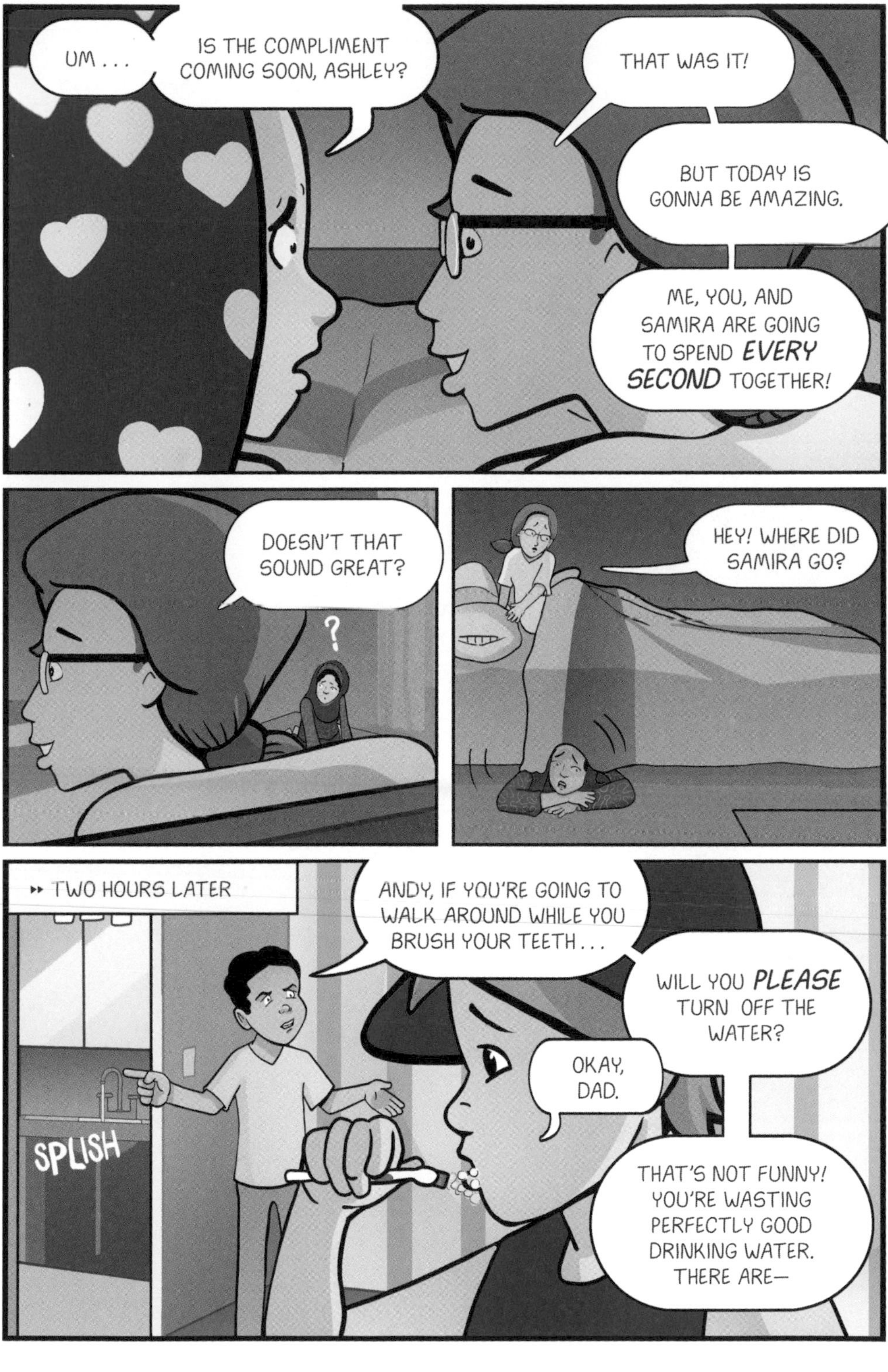
UM . . .
IS THE COMPLIMENT COMING SOON, ASHLEY?
THAT WAS IT!
BUT TODAY IS GONNA BE AMAZING.
ME, YOU, AND SAMIRA ARE GOING TO SPEND **EVERY SECOND** TOGETHER!
DOESN'T THAT SOUND GREAT?
?
HEY! WHERE DID SAMIRA GO?
▸▸ TWO HOURS LATER
ANDY, IF YOU'RE GOING TO WALK AROUND WHILE YOU BRUSH YOUR TEETH . . .
WILL YOU **PLEASE** TURN OFF THE WATER?
OKAY, DAD.
THAT'S NOT FUNNY! YOU'RE WASTING PERFECTLY GOOD DRINKING WATER. THERE ARE—
SPLISH

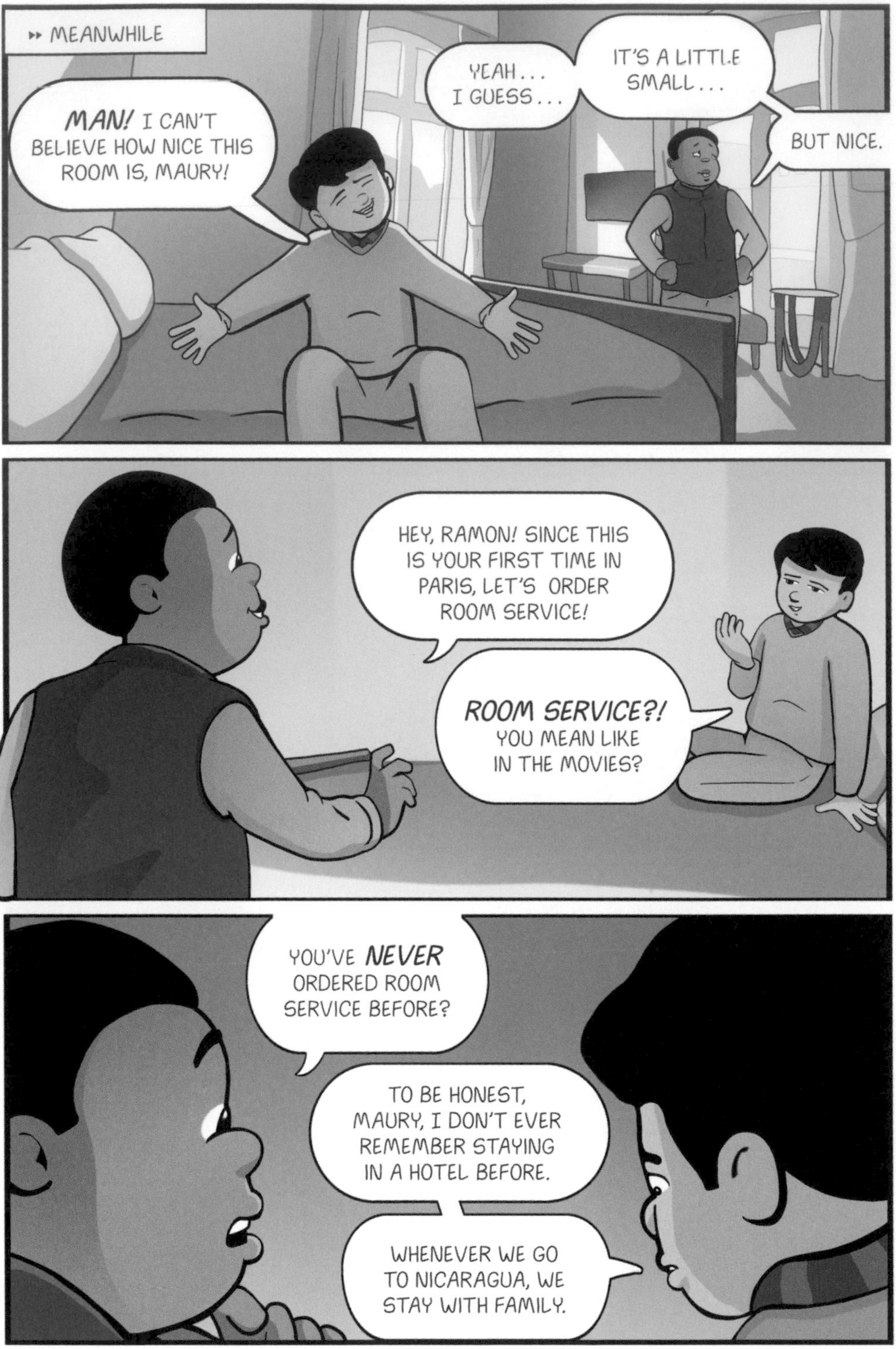

MEANWHILE
MAN! I CAN'T BELIEVE HOW NICE THIS ROOM IS, MAURY!
YEAH... I GUESS...
IT'S A LITTLE SMALL...
BUT NICE.
HEY, RAMON! SINCE THIS IS YOUR FIRST TIME IN PARIS, LET'S ORDER ROOM SERVICE!
ROOM SERVICE?! YOU MEAN LIKE IN THE MOVIES?
YOU'VE NEVER ORDERED ROOM SERVICE BEFORE?
TO BE HONEST, MAURY, I DON'T EVER REMEMBER STAYING IN A HOTEL BEFORE.
WHENEVER WE GO TO NICARAGUA, WE STAY WITH FAMILY.

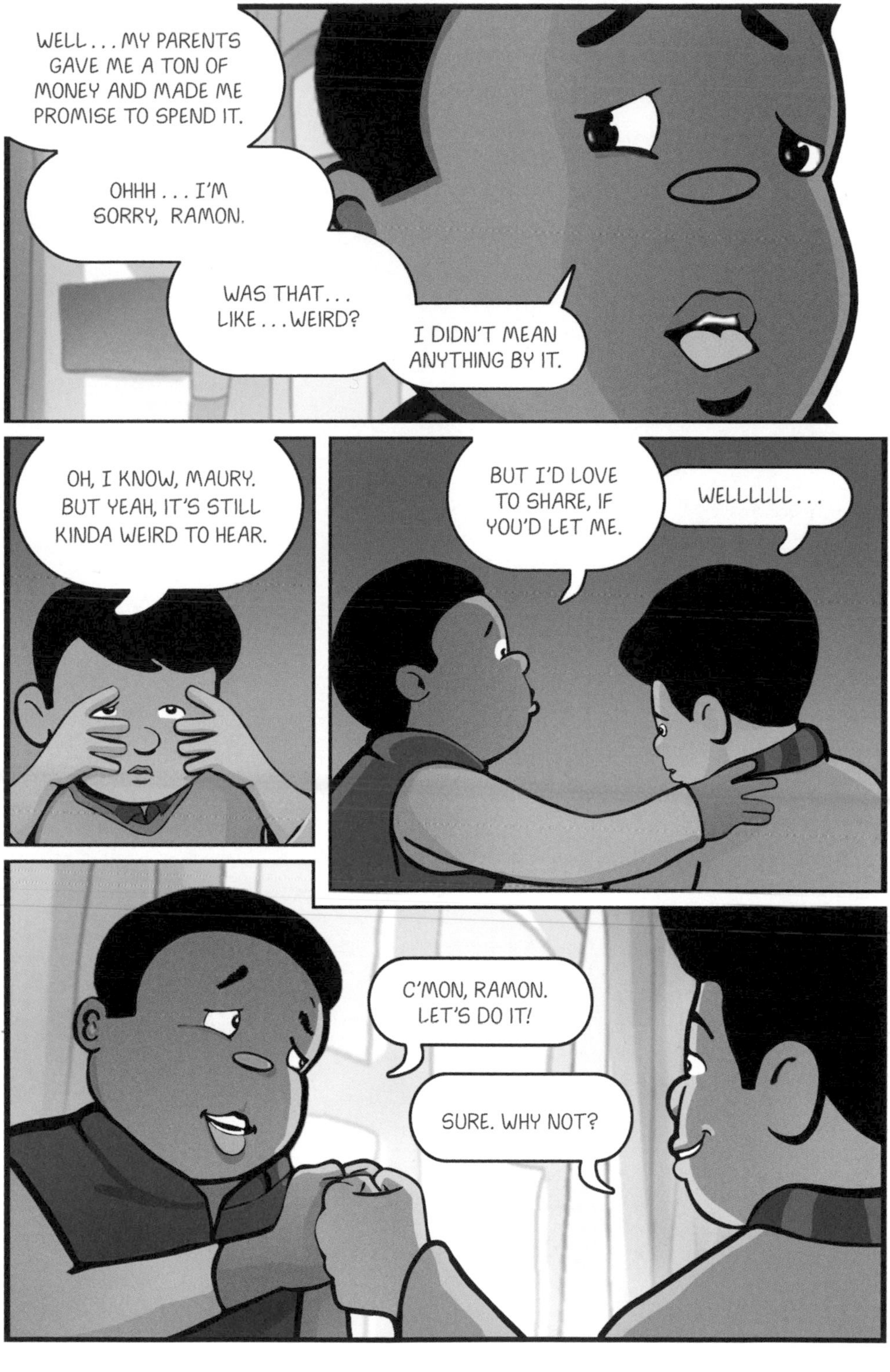
WELL . . . MY PARENTS GAVE ME A TON OF MONEY AND MADE ME PROMISE TO SPEND IT.
OHHH . . . I'M SORRY, RAMON.
WAS THAT . . . LIKE . . . WEIRD?
I DIDN'T MEAN ANYTHING BY IT.
OH, I KNOW, MAURY. BUT YEAH, IT'S STILL KINDA WEIRD TO HEAR.
BUT I'D LOVE TO SHARE, IF YOU'D LET ME.
WELLLLLL . . .
C'MON, RAMON. LET'S DO IT!
SURE. WHY NOT?

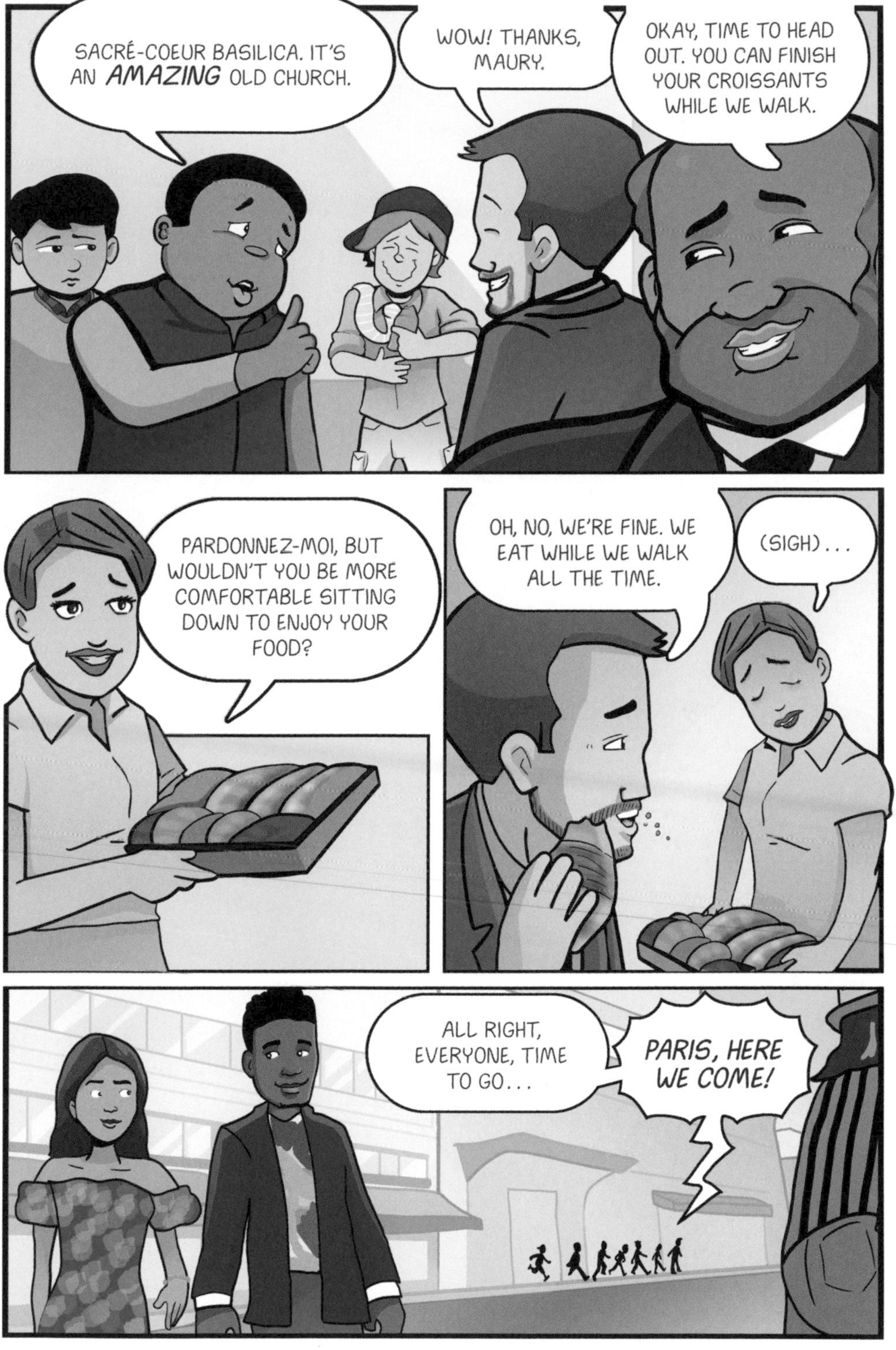
SACRÉ-COEUR BASILICA. IT'S AN AMAZING OLD CHURCH.
WOW! THANKS, MAURY.
OKAY, TIME TO HEAD OUT. YOU CAN FINISH YOUR CROISSANTS WHILE WE WALK.
PARDONNEZ-MOI, BUT WOULDN'T YOU BE MORE COMFORTABLE SITTING DOWN TO ENJOY YOUR FOOD?
OH, NO, WE'RE FINE. WE EAT WHILE WE WALK ALL THE TIME.
(SIGH) . . .
ALL RIGHT, EVERYONE, TIME TO GO . . .
PARIS, HERE WE COME!

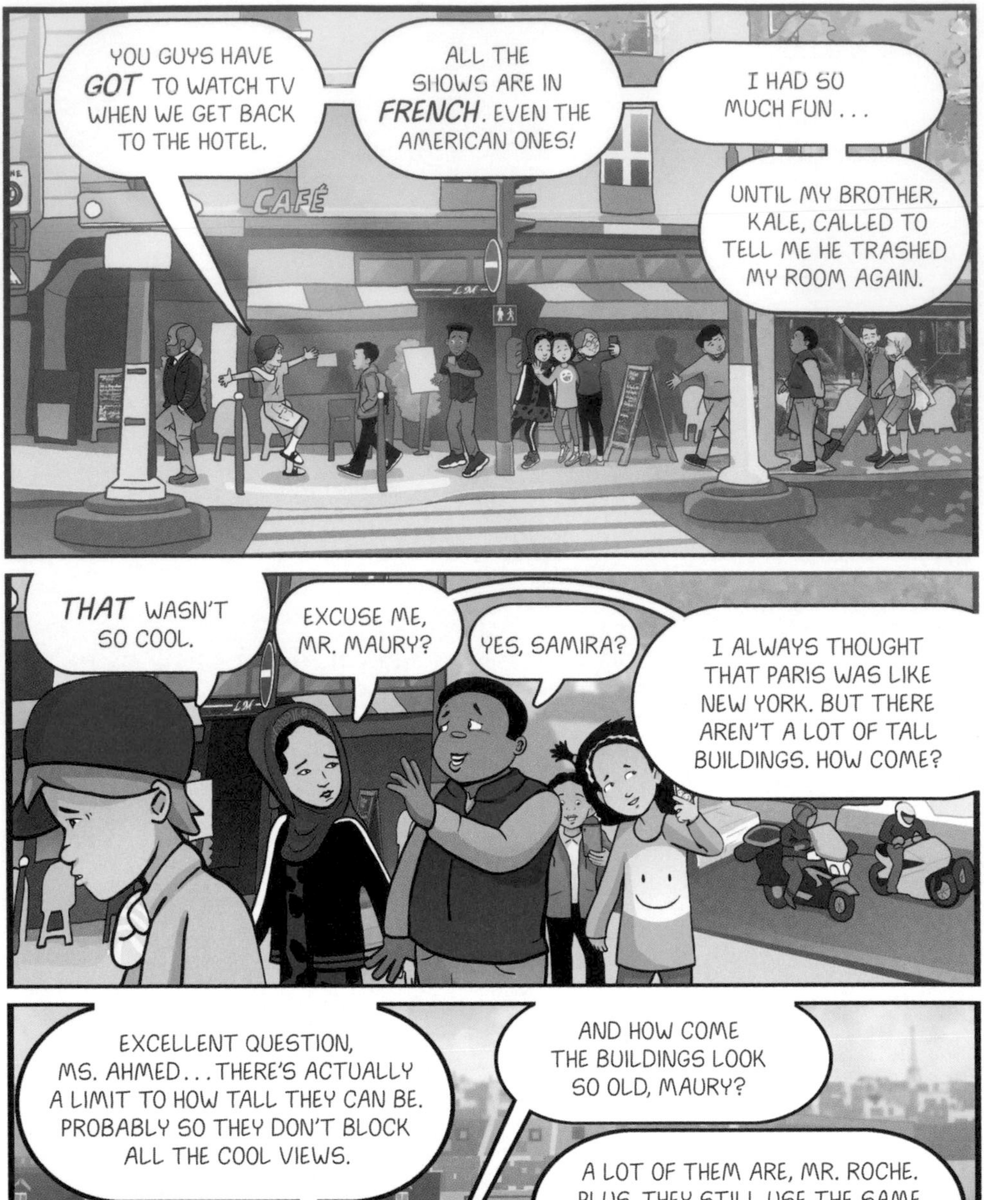
YOU GUYS HAVE GOT TO WATCH TV WHEN WE GET BACK TO THE HOTEL.
ALL THE SHOWS ARE IN FRENCH. EVEN THE AMERICAN ONES!
I HAD SO MUCH FUN . . .
UNTIL MY BROTHER, KALE, CALLED TO TELL ME HE TRASHED MY ROOM AGAIN.
CAFÉ
THAT WASN'T SO COOL.
EXCUSE ME, MR. MAURY?
YES, SAMIRA?
I ALWAYS THOUGHT THAT PARIS WAS LIKE NEW YORK. BUT THERE AREN'T A LOT OF TALL BUILDINGS. HOW COME?
EXCELLENT QUESTION, MS. AHMED . . . THERE'S ACTUALLY A LIMIT TO HOW TALL THEY CAN BE. PROBABLY SO THEY DON'T BLOCK ALL THE COOL VIEWS.
AND HOW COME THE BUILDINGS LOOK SO OLD, MAURY?
A LOT OF THEM ARE, MR. ROCHE. PLUS, THEY STILL USE THE SAME MATERIALS AND DESIGNS FOR NEW BUILDINGS . . .
ALL THOSE GUIDELINES GIVE THE CITY OF PARIS A NICE UNIFORM LOOK. PRETTY COOL, HUH?

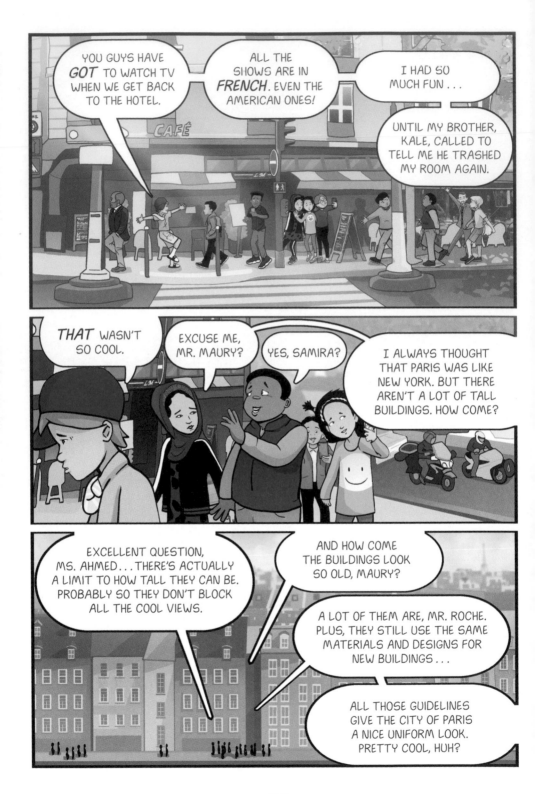

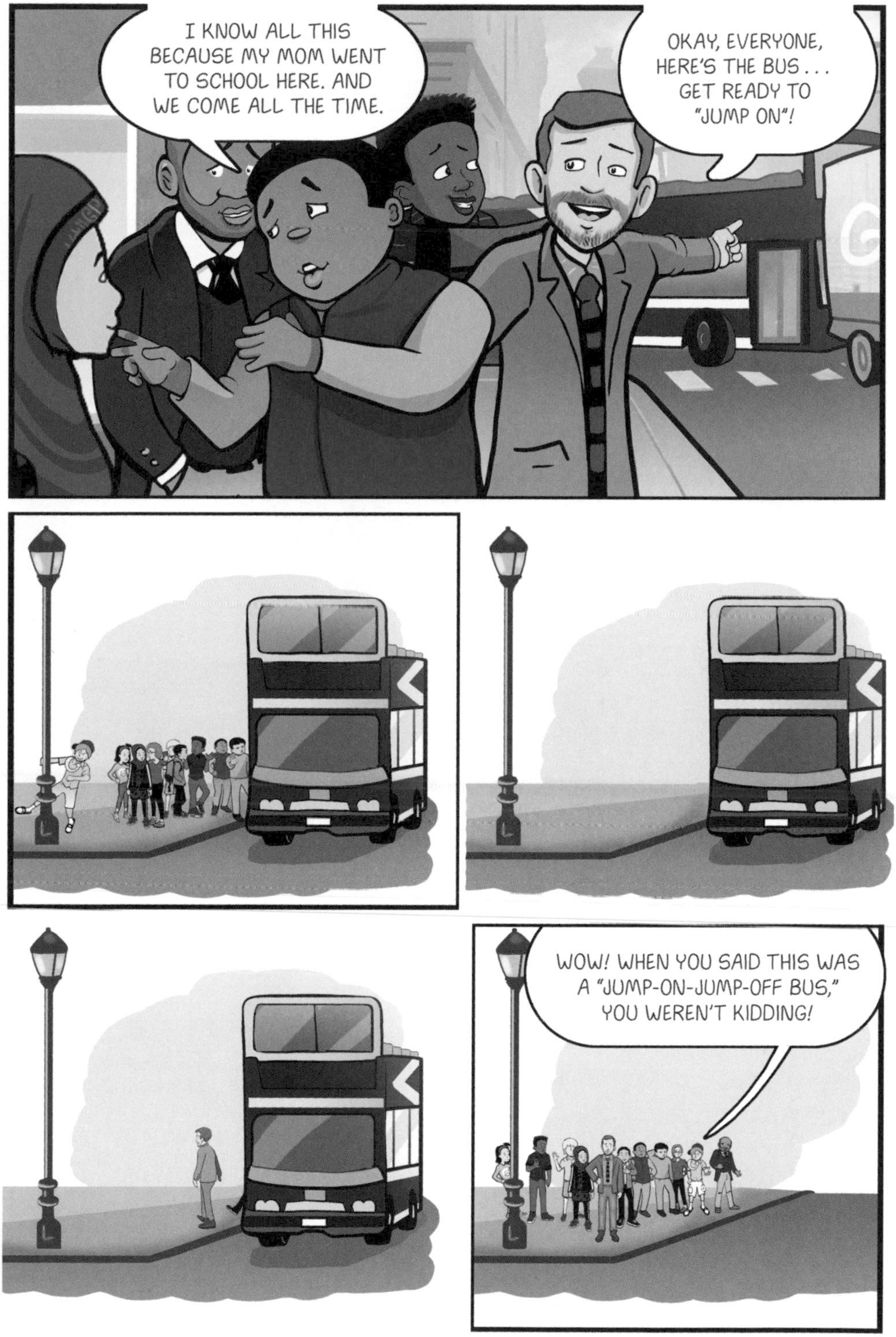
I KNOW ALL THIS BECAUSE MY MOM WENT TO SCHOOL HERE. AND WE COME ALL THE TIME.
OKAY, EVERYONE, HERE'S THE BUS . . . GET READY TO "JUMP ON"!
WOW! WHEN YOU SAID THIS WAS A "JUMP-ON-JUMP-OFF BUS," YOU WEREN'T KIDDING!

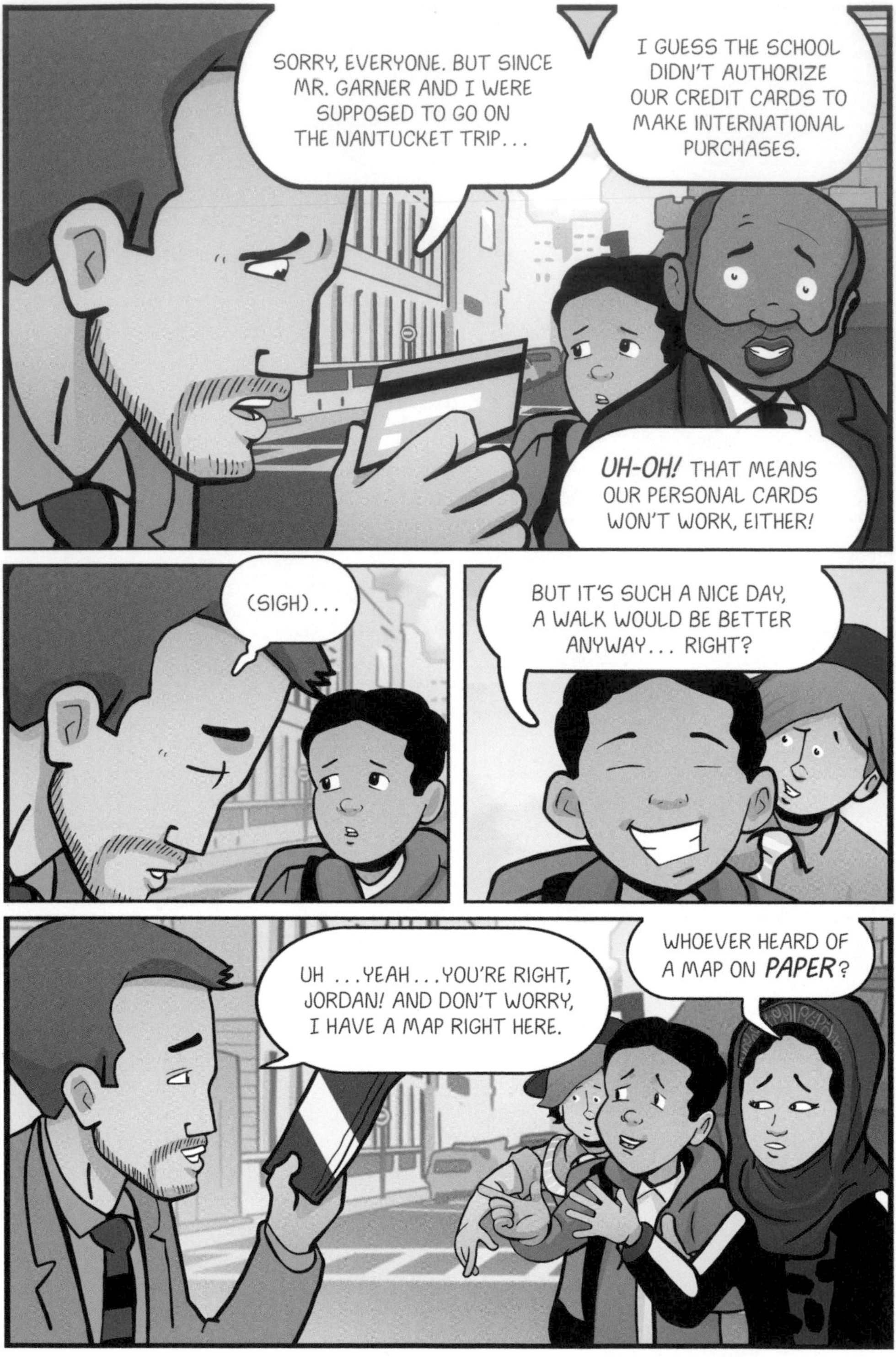
SORRY, EVERYONE. BUT SINCE MR. GARNER AND I WERE SUPPOSED TO GO ON THE NANTUCKET TRIP. . .
I GUESS THE SCHOOL DIDN'T AUTHORIZE OUR CREDIT CARDS TO MAKE INTERNATIONAL PURCHASES.
UH-OH! THAT MEANS OUR PERSONAL CARDS WON'T WORK, EITHER!
(SIGH). . .
BUT IT'S SUCH A NICE DAY, A WALK WOULD BE BETTER ANYWAY. . . RIGHT?
UH . . .YEAH. . .YOU'RE RIGHT, JORDAN! AND DON'T WORRY, I HAVE A MAP RIGHT HERE.
WHOEVER HEARD OF A MAP ON *PAPER*?

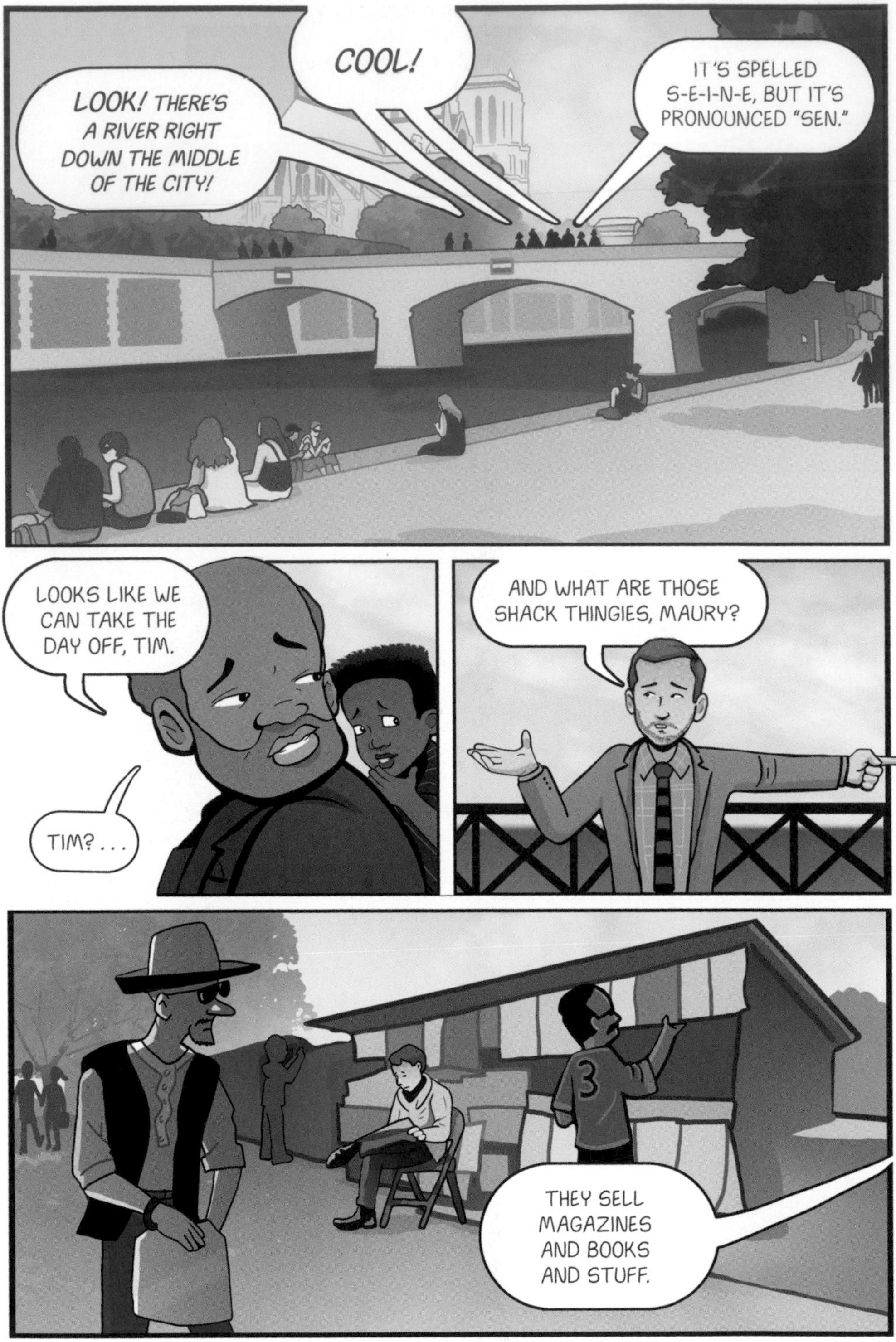
LOOK! THERE'S A RIVER RIGHT DOWN THE MIDDLE OF THE CITY!
COOL!
IT'S SPELLED S-E-I-N-E, BUT IT'S PRONOUNCED "SEN."
LOOKS LIKE WE CAN TAKE THE DAY OFF, TIM.
TIM? . . .
AND WHAT ARE THOSE SHACK THINGIES, MAURY?
THEY SELL MAGAZINES AND BOOKS AND STUFF.

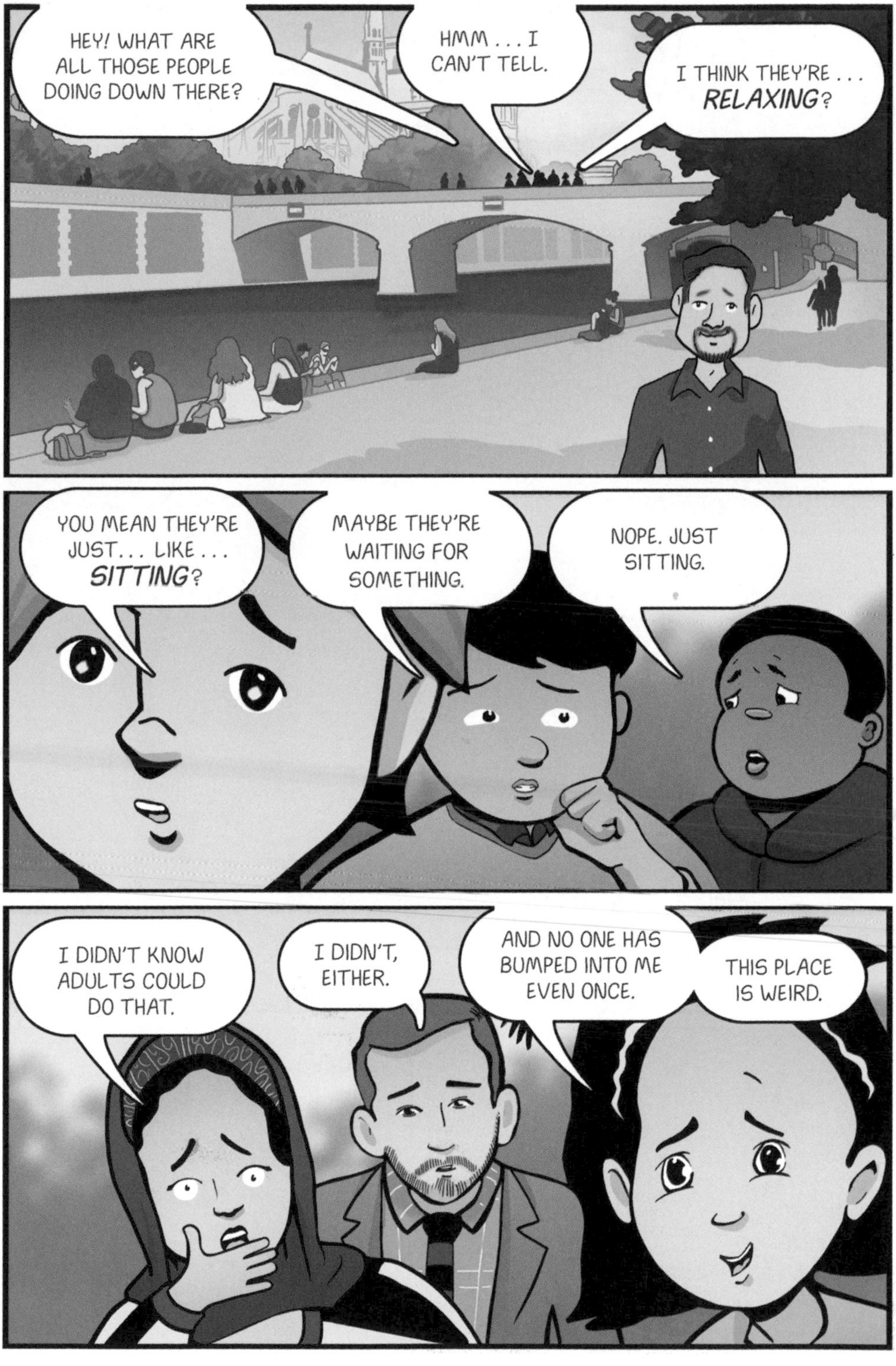
HEY! WHAT ARE ALL THOSE PEOPLE DOING DOWN THERE?
HMM . . . I CAN'T TELL.
I THINK THEY'RE . . . *RELAXING*?
YOU MEAN THEY'RE JUST. . . LIKE . . . *SITTING*?
MAYBE THEY'RE WAITING FOR SOMETHING.
NOPE. JUST SITTING.
I DIDN'T KNOW ADULTS COULD DO THAT.
I DIDN'T, EITHER.
AND NO ONE HAS BUMPED INTO ME EVEN ONCE.
THIS PLACE IS WEIRD.

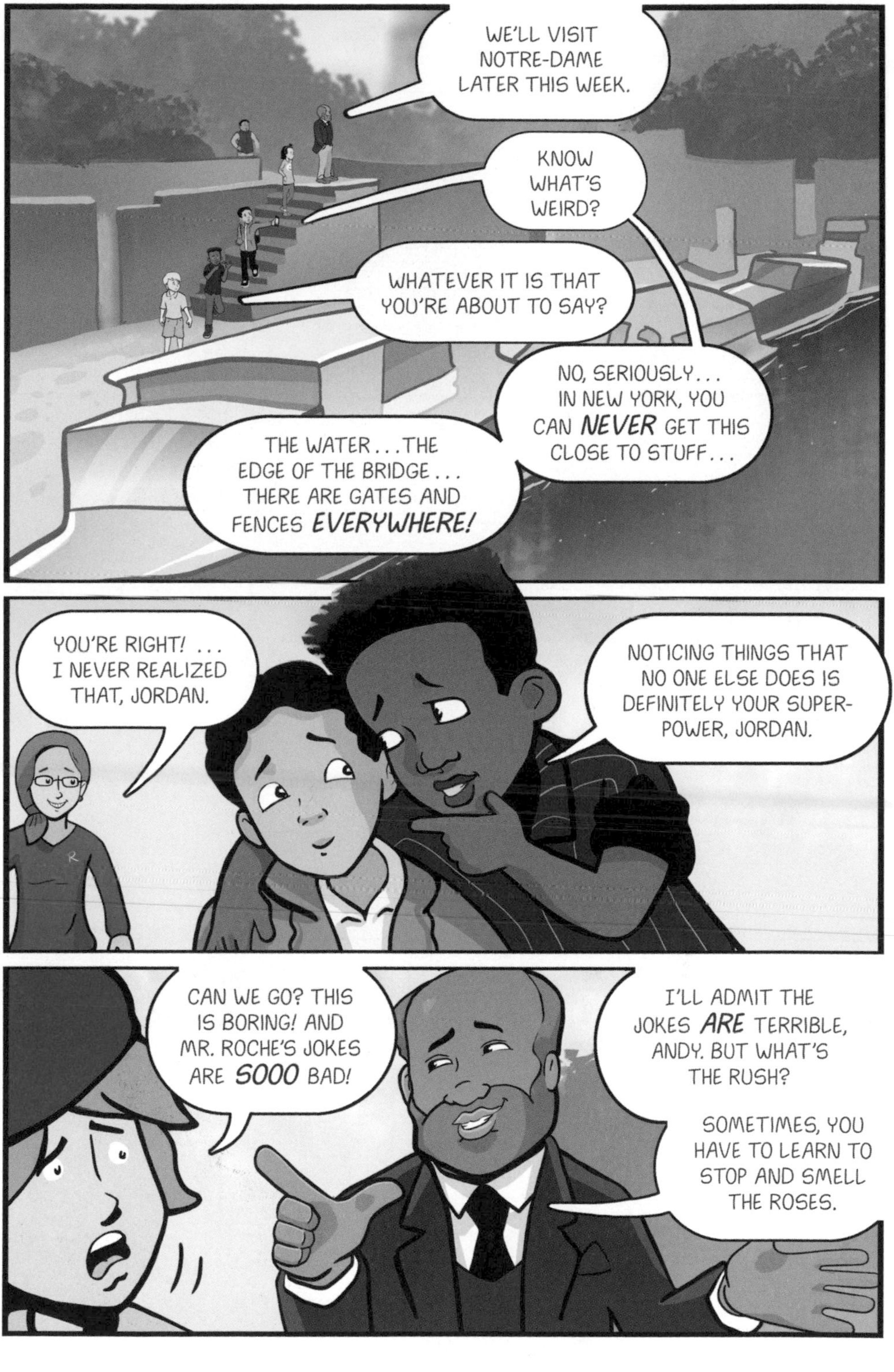
WE'LL VISIT NOTRE-DAME LATER THIS WEEK.
KNOW WHAT'S WEIRD?
WHATEVER IT IS THAT YOU'RE ABOUT TO SAY?
NO, SERIOUSLY... IN NEW YORK, YOU CAN **NEVER** GET THIS CLOSE TO STUFF...
THE WATER...THE EDGE OF THE BRIDGE... THERE ARE GATES AND FENCES **EVERYWHERE!**
YOU'RE RIGHT! ... I NEVER REALIZED THAT, JORDAN.
NOTICING THINGS THAT NO ONE ELSE DOES IS DEFINITELY YOUR SUPER-POWER, JORDAN.
CAN WE GO? THIS IS BORING! AND MR. ROCHE'S JOKES ARE **SOOO** BAD!
I'LL ADMIT THE JOKES **ARE** TERRIBLE, ANDY. BUT WHAT'S THE RUSH?
SOMETIMES, YOU HAVE TO LEARN TO STOP AND SMELL THE ROSES.

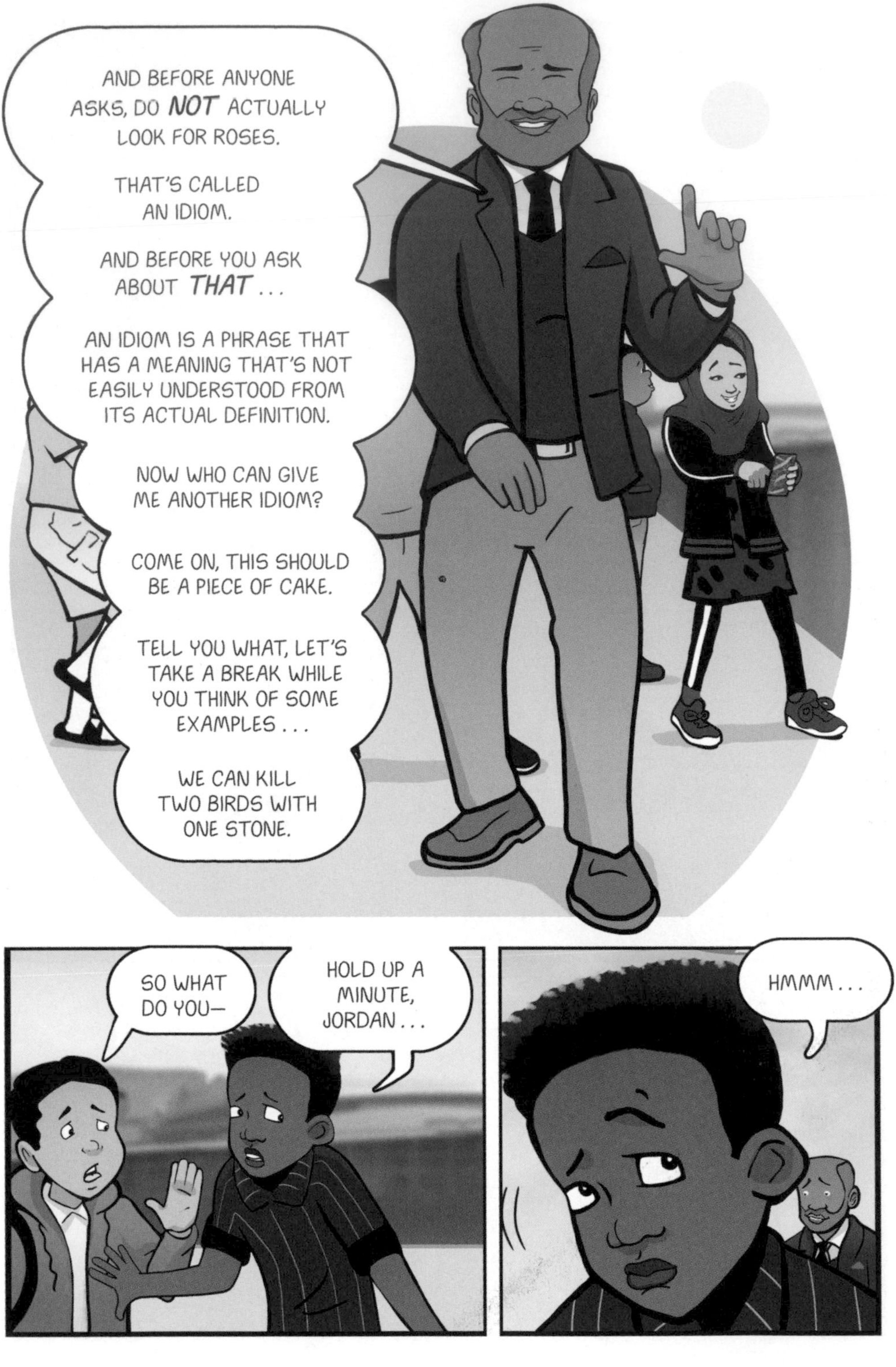
AND BEFORE ANYONE ASKS, DO **NOT** ACTUALLY LOOK FOR ROSES.
THAT'S CALLED AN IDIOM.
AND BEFORE YOU ASK ABOUT **THAT** . . .
AN IDIOM IS A PHRASE THAT HAS A MEANING THAT'S NOT EASILY UNDERSTOOD FROM ITS ACTUAL DEFINITION.
NOW WHO CAN GIVE ME ANOTHER IDIOM?
COME ON, THIS SHOULD BE A PIECE OF CAKE.
TELL YOU WHAT, LET'S TAKE A BREAK WHILE YOU THINK OF SOME EXAMPLES . . .
WE CAN KILL TWO BIRDS WITH ONE STONE.
SO WHAT DO YOU—
HOLD UP A MINUTE, JORDAN . . .
HMMM . . .

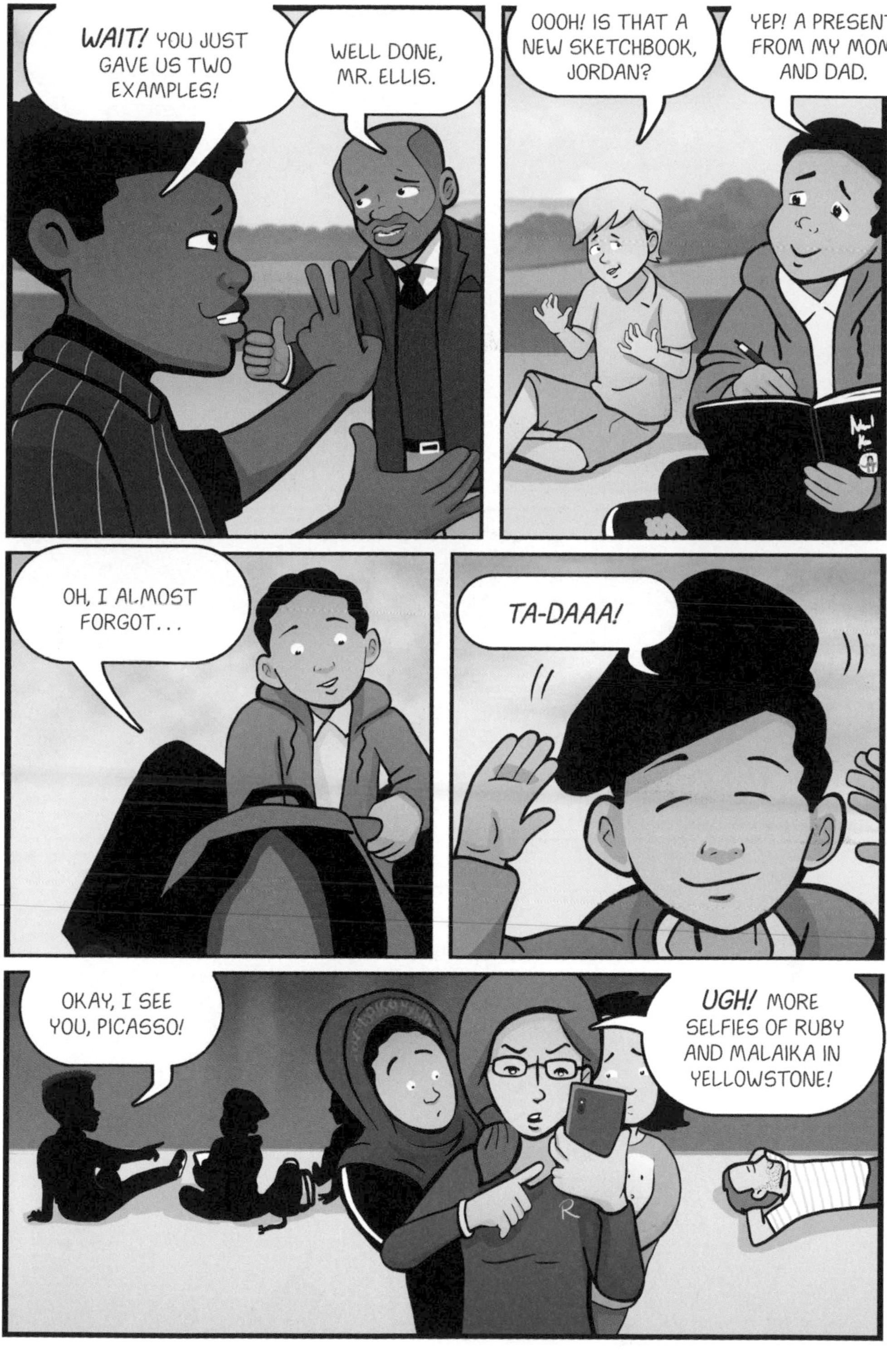
WAIT! YOU JUST GAVE US TWO EXAMPLES!
WELL DONE, MR. ELLIS.
OOOH! IS THAT A NEW SKETCHBOOK, JORDAN?
YEP! A PRESENT FROM MY MOM AND DAD.
OH, I ALMOST FORGOT...
TA-DAAA!
OKAY, I SEE YOU, PICASSO!
UGH! MORE SELFIES OF RUBY AND MALAIKA IN YELLOWSTONE!

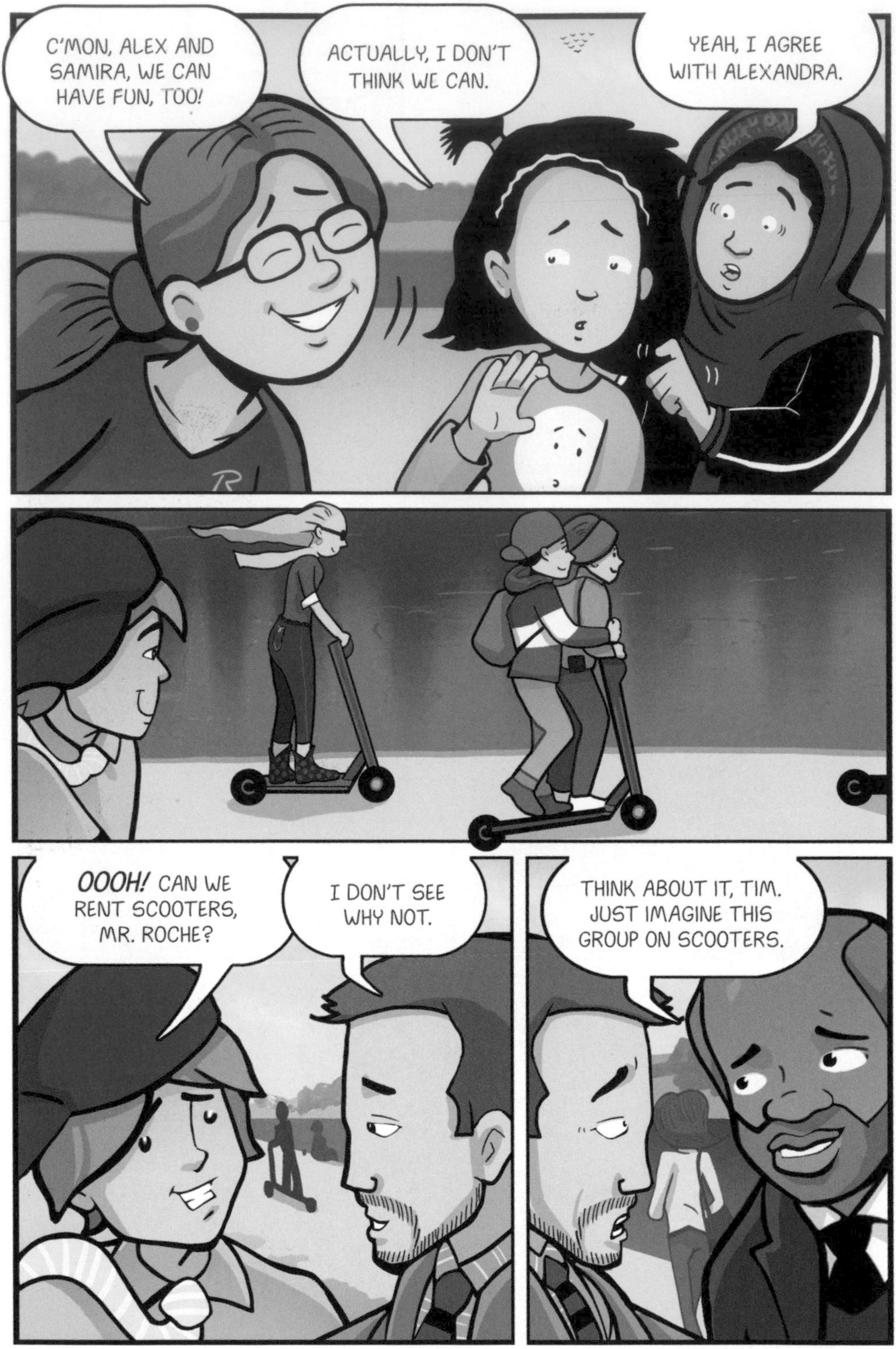
C'MON, ALEX AND SAMIRA, WE CAN HAVE FUN, TOO!
ACTUALLY, I DON'T THINK WE CAN.
YEAH, I AGREE WITH ALEXANDRA.
OOOH! CAN WE RENT SCOOTERS, MR. ROCHE?
I DON'T SEE WHY NOT.
THINK ABOUT IT, TIM. JUST IMAGINE THIS GROUP ON SCOOTERS.

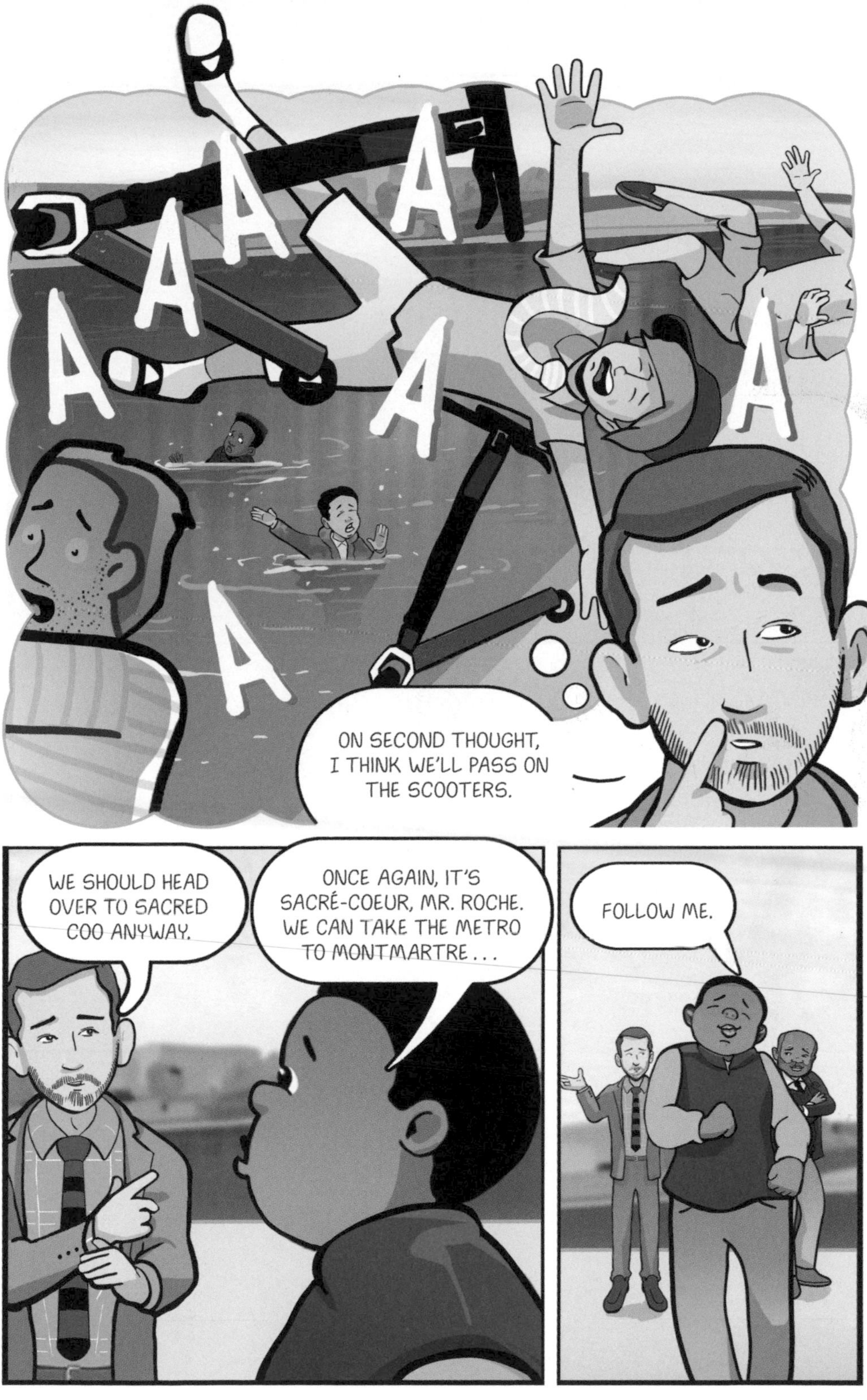
AAAAAAAA
ON SECOND THOUGHT, I THINK WE'LL PASS ON THE SCOOTERS.
WE SHOULD HEAD OVER TO SACRED COO ANYWAY.
ONCE AGAIN, IT'S SACRÉ-COEUR, MR. ROCHE. WE CAN TAKE THE METRO TO MONTMARTRE . . .
FOLLOW ME.

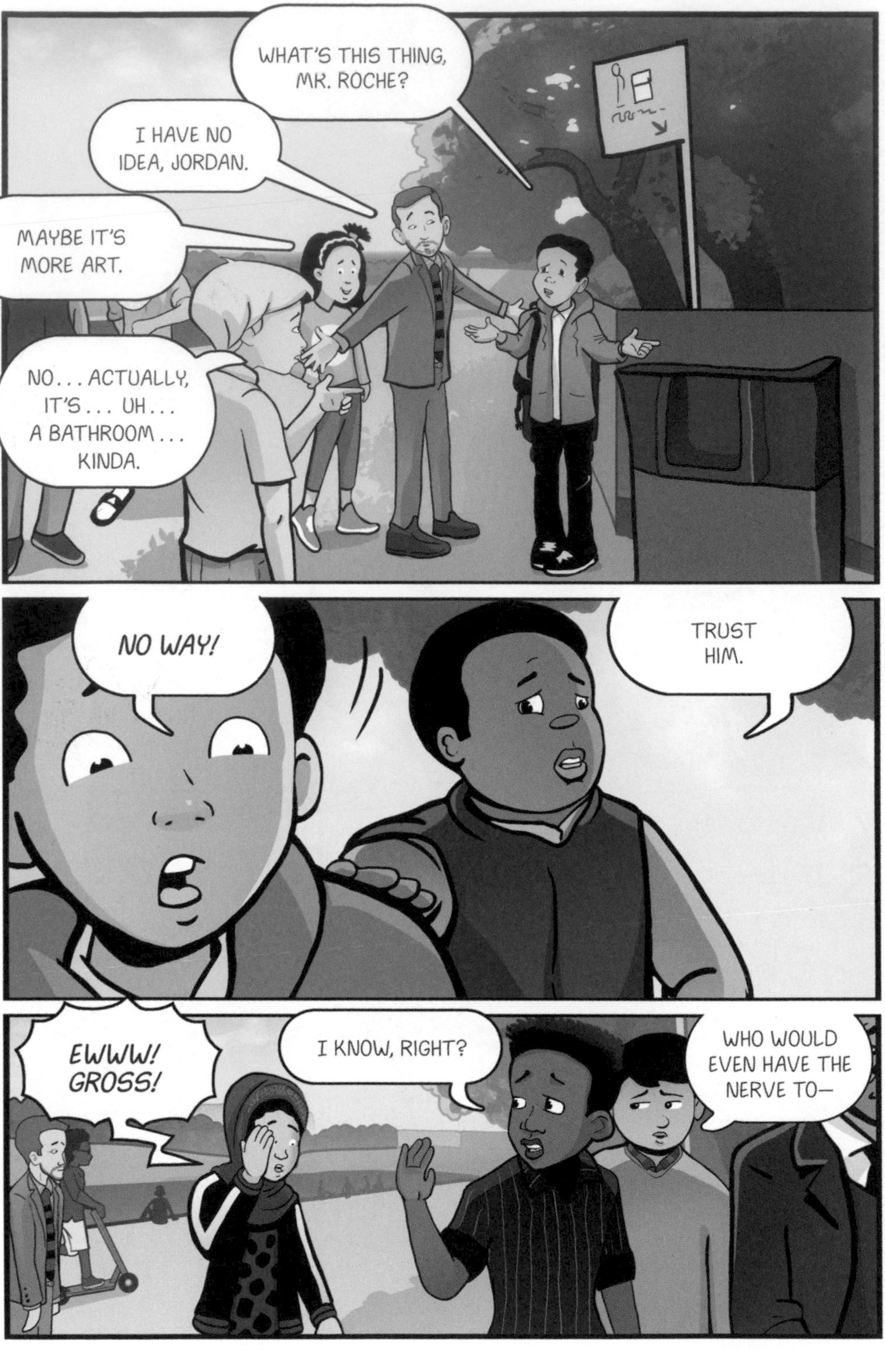
WHAT'S THIS THING, MR. ROCHE?
I HAVE NO IDEA, JORDAN.
MAYBE IT'S MORE ART.
NO... ACTUALLY, IT'S... UH... A BATHROOM... KINDA.
NO WAY!
TRUST HIM.
EWWW! GROSS!
I KNOW, RIGHT?
WHO WOULD EVEN HAVE THE NERVE TO—

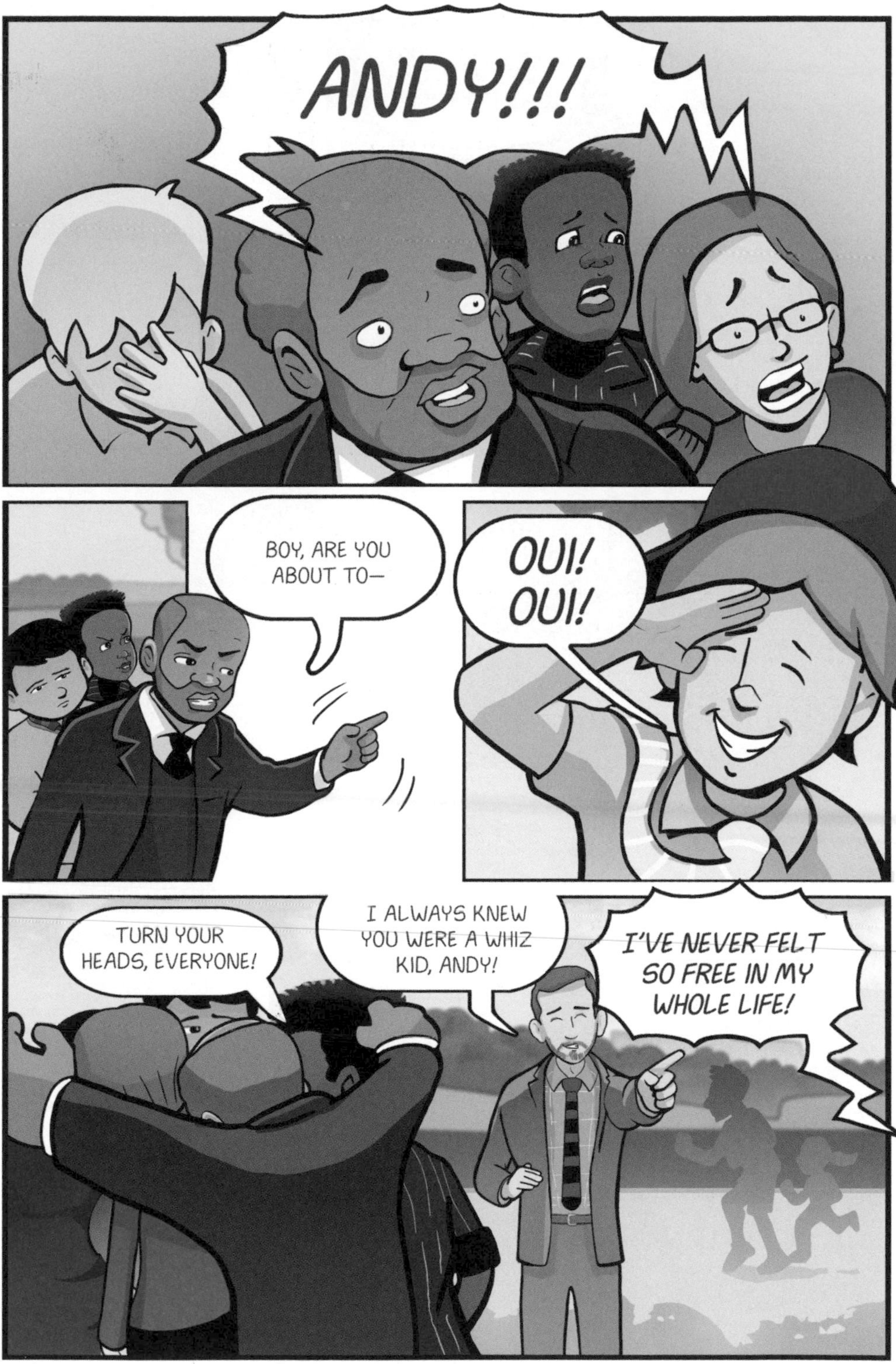
ANDY!!!
BOY, ARE YOU ABOUT TO—
OUI! OUI!
TURN YOUR HEADS, EVERYONE!
I ALWAYS KNEW YOU WERE A WHIZ KID, ANDY!
I'VE NEVER FELT SO FREE IN MY WHOLE LIFE!

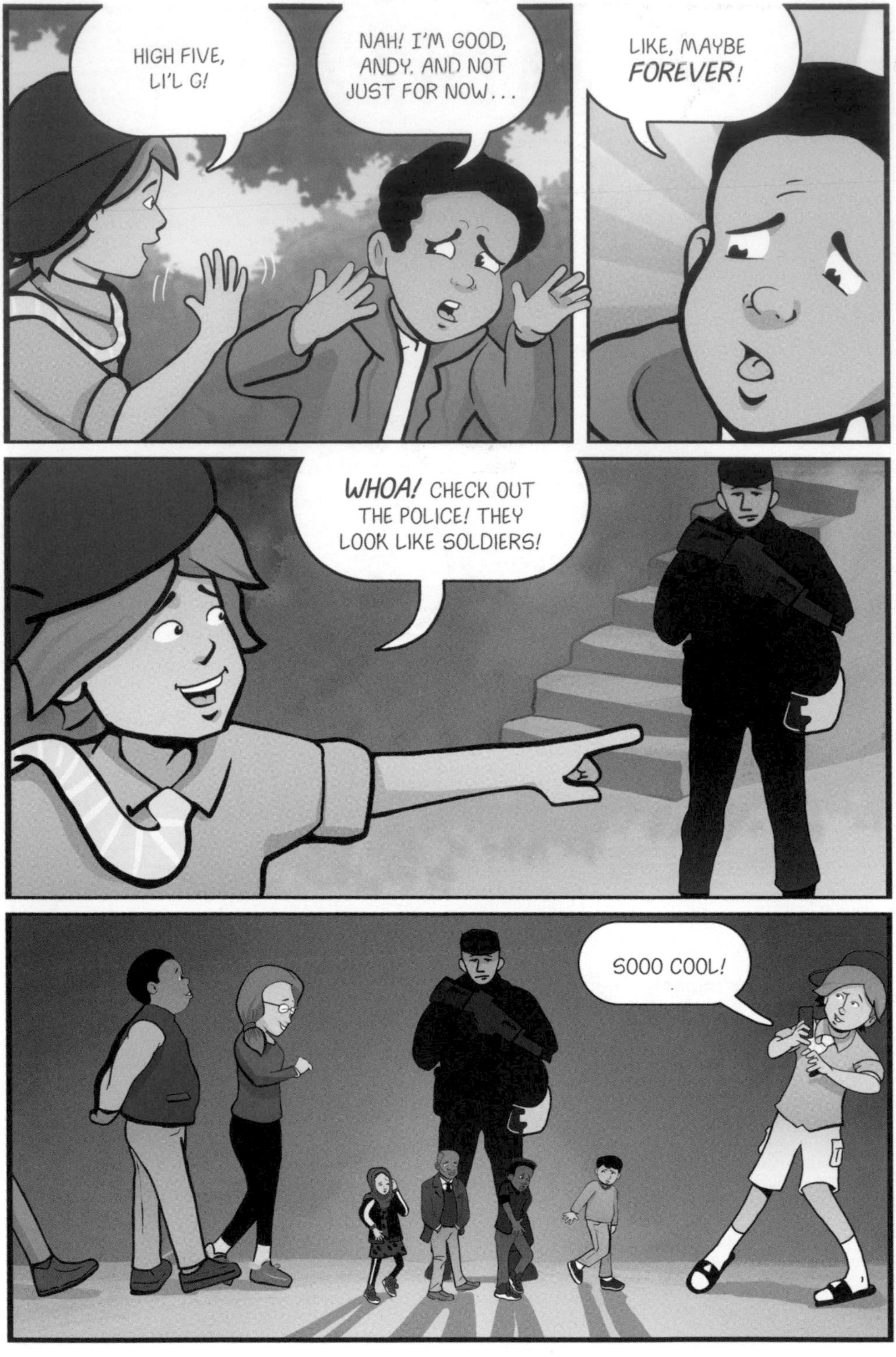
HIGH FIVE, LI'L G!
NAH! I'M GOOD, ANDY. AND NOT JUST FOR NOW . . .
LIKE, MAYBE *FOREVER*!
WHOA! CHECK OUT THE POLICE! THEY LOOK LIKE SOLDIERS!
SOOO COOL!

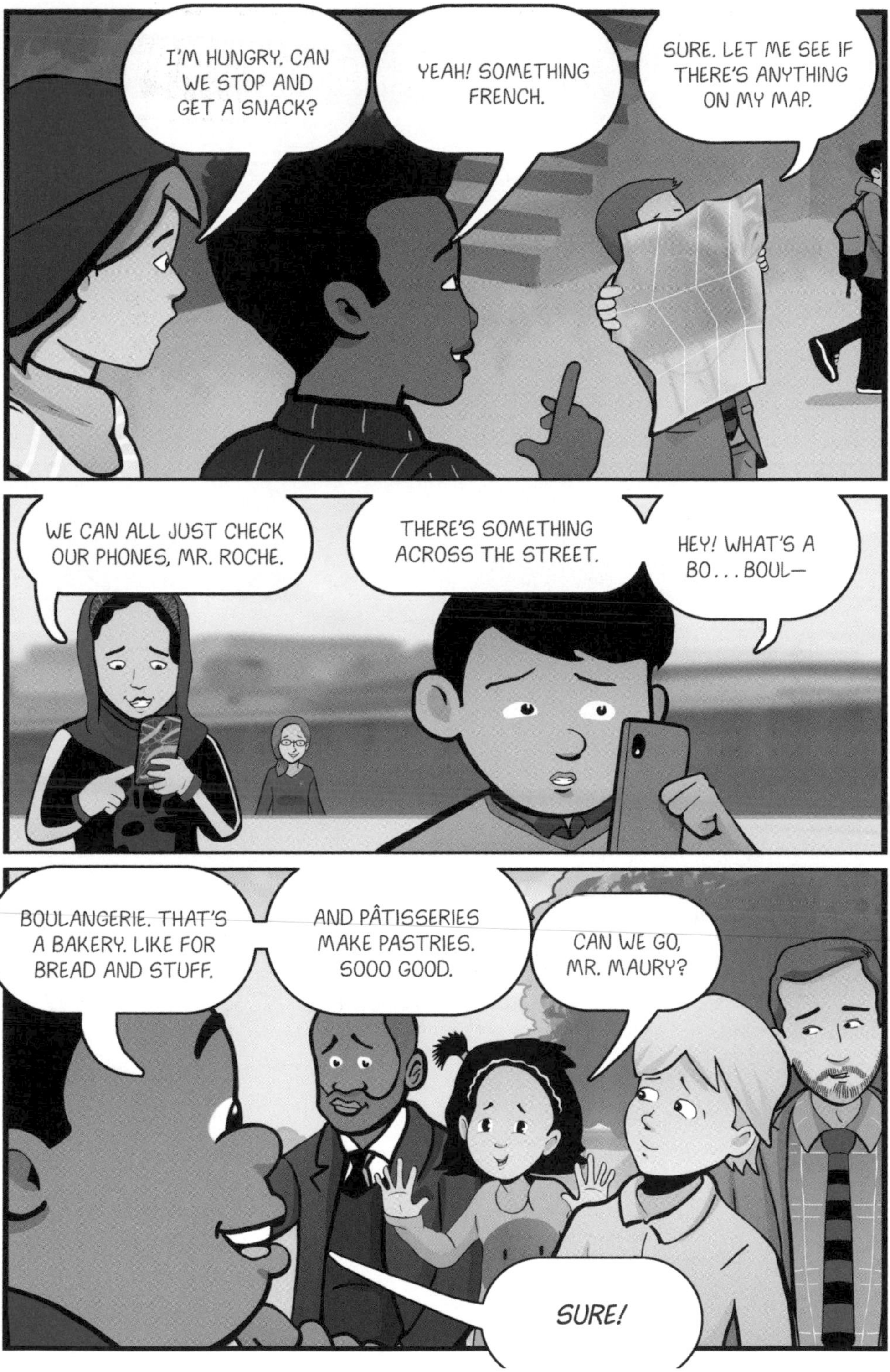
I'M HUNGRY. CAN WE STOP AND GET A SNACK?
YEAH! SOMETHING FRENCH.
SURE. LET ME SEE IF THERE'S ANYTHING ON MY MAP.
WE CAN ALL JUST CHECK OUR PHONES, MR. ROCHE.
THERE'S SOMETHING ACROSS THE STREET.
HEY! WHAT'S A BO. . . BOUL—
BOULANGERIE. THAT'S A BAKERY. LIKE FOR BREAD AND STUFF.
AND PÂTISSERIES MAKE PASTRIES. SOOO GOOD.
CAN WE GO, MR. MAURY?
SURE!

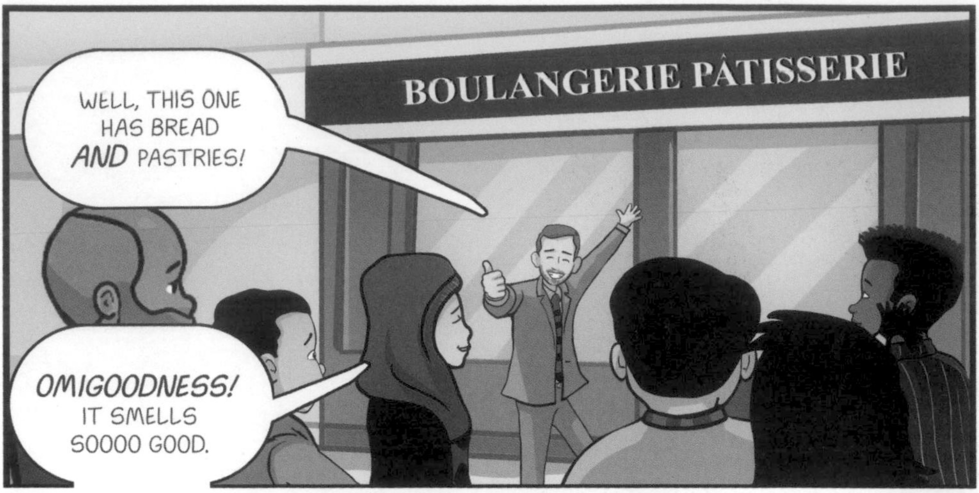
BOULANGERIE PÂTISSERIE
WELL, THIS ONE HAS BREAD AND PASTRIES!
OMIGOODNESS! IT SMELLS SOOOO GOOD.
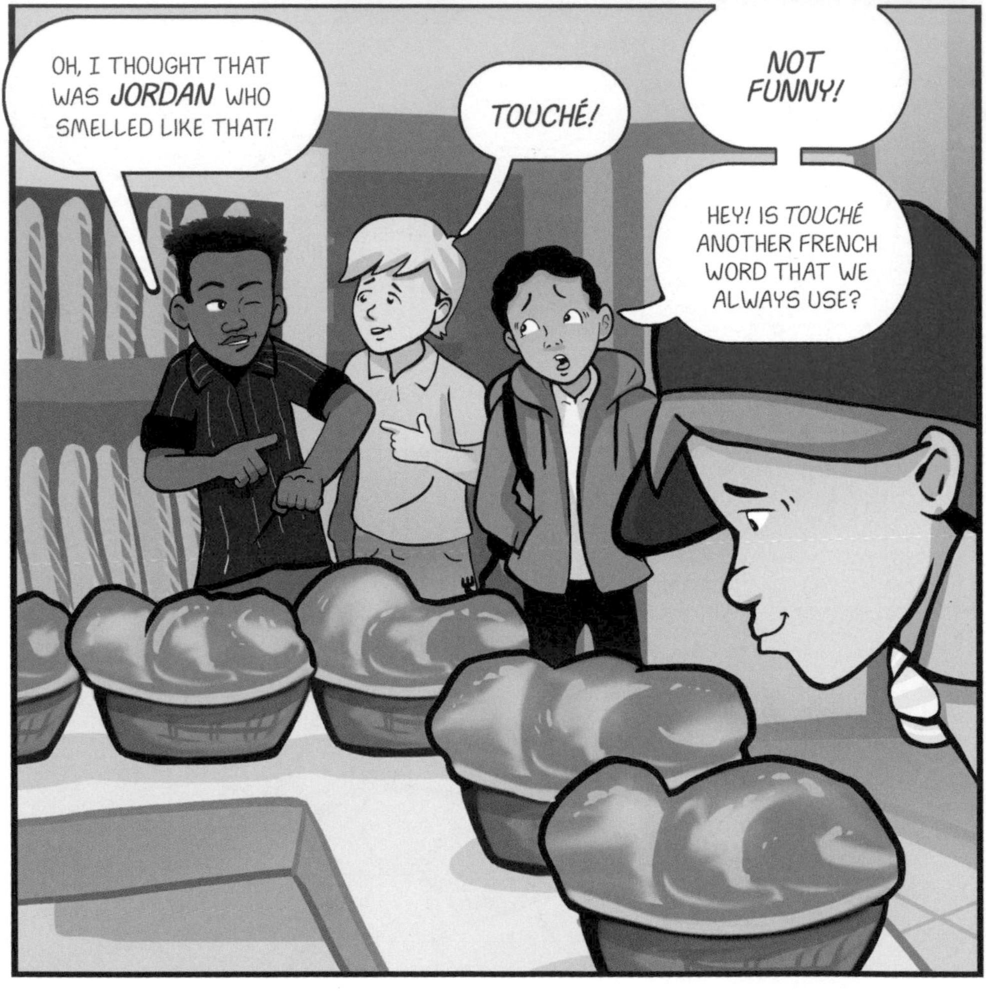
OH, I THOUGHT THAT WAS JORDAN WHO SMELLED LIKE THAT!
TOUCHÉ!
NOT FUNNY!
HEY! IS TOUCHÉ ANOTHER FRENCH WORD THAT WE ALWAYS USE?

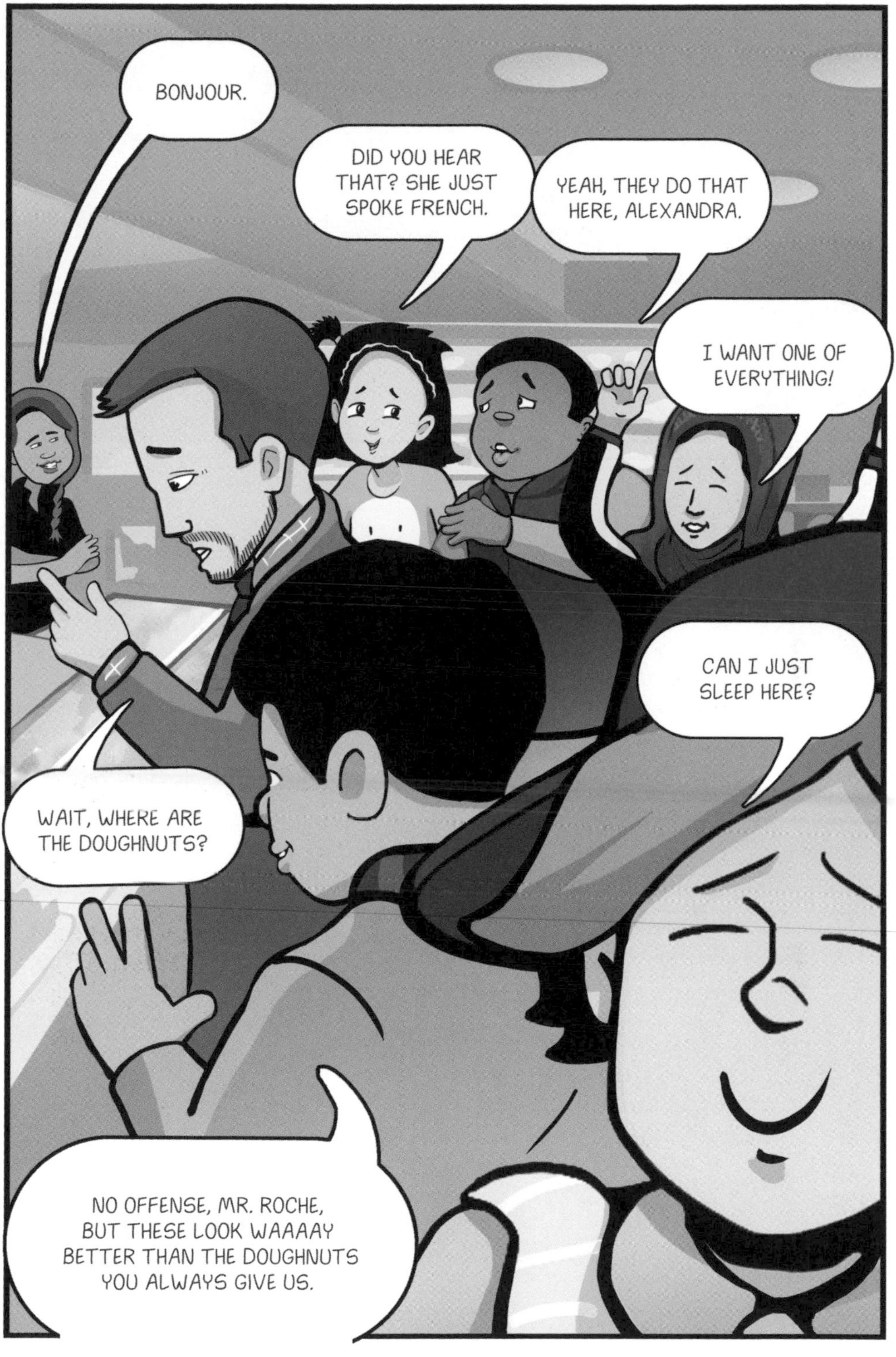
BONJOUR.
DID YOU HEAR THAT? SHE JUST SPOKE FRENCH.
YEAH, THEY DO THAT HERE, ALEXANDRA.
I WANT ONE OF EVERYTHING!
CAN I JUST SLEEP HERE?
WAIT, WHERE ARE THE DOUGHNUTS?
NO OFFENSE, MR. ROCHE, BUT THESE LOOK WAAAAY BETTER THAN THE DOUGHNUTS YOU ALWAYS GIVE US.

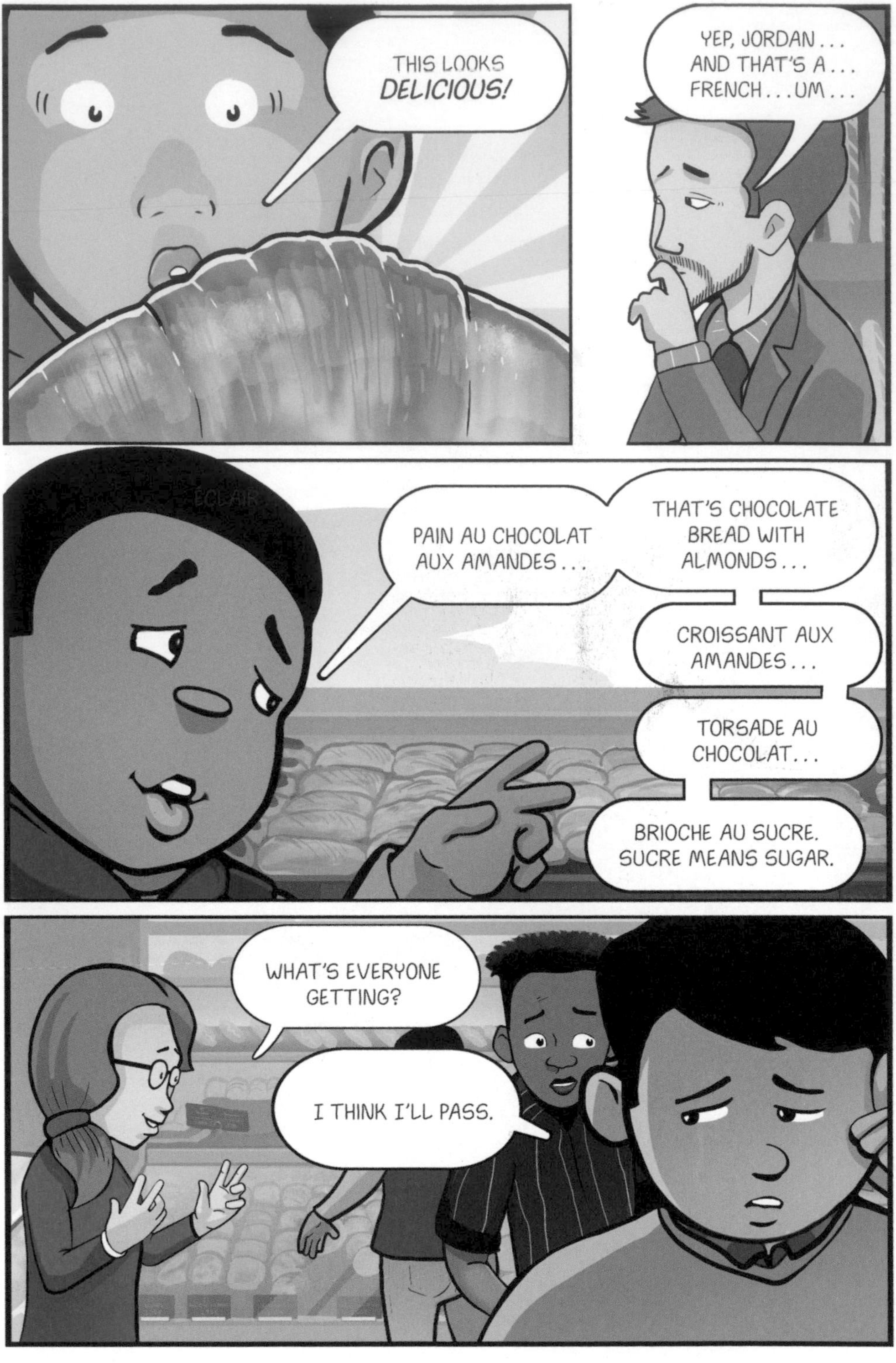
THIS LOOKS *DELICIOUS!*
YEP, JORDAN . . . AND THAT'S A . . . FRENCH . . . UM . . .
ECLAIR
PAIN AU CHOCOLAT AUX AMANDES . . .
THAT'S CHOCOLATE BREAD WITH ALMONDS . . .
CROISSANT AUX AMANDES . . .
TORSADE AU CHOCOLAT . . .
BRIOCHE AU SUCRE. SUCRE MEANS SUGAR.
WHAT'S EVERYONE GETTING?
I THINK I'LL PASS.

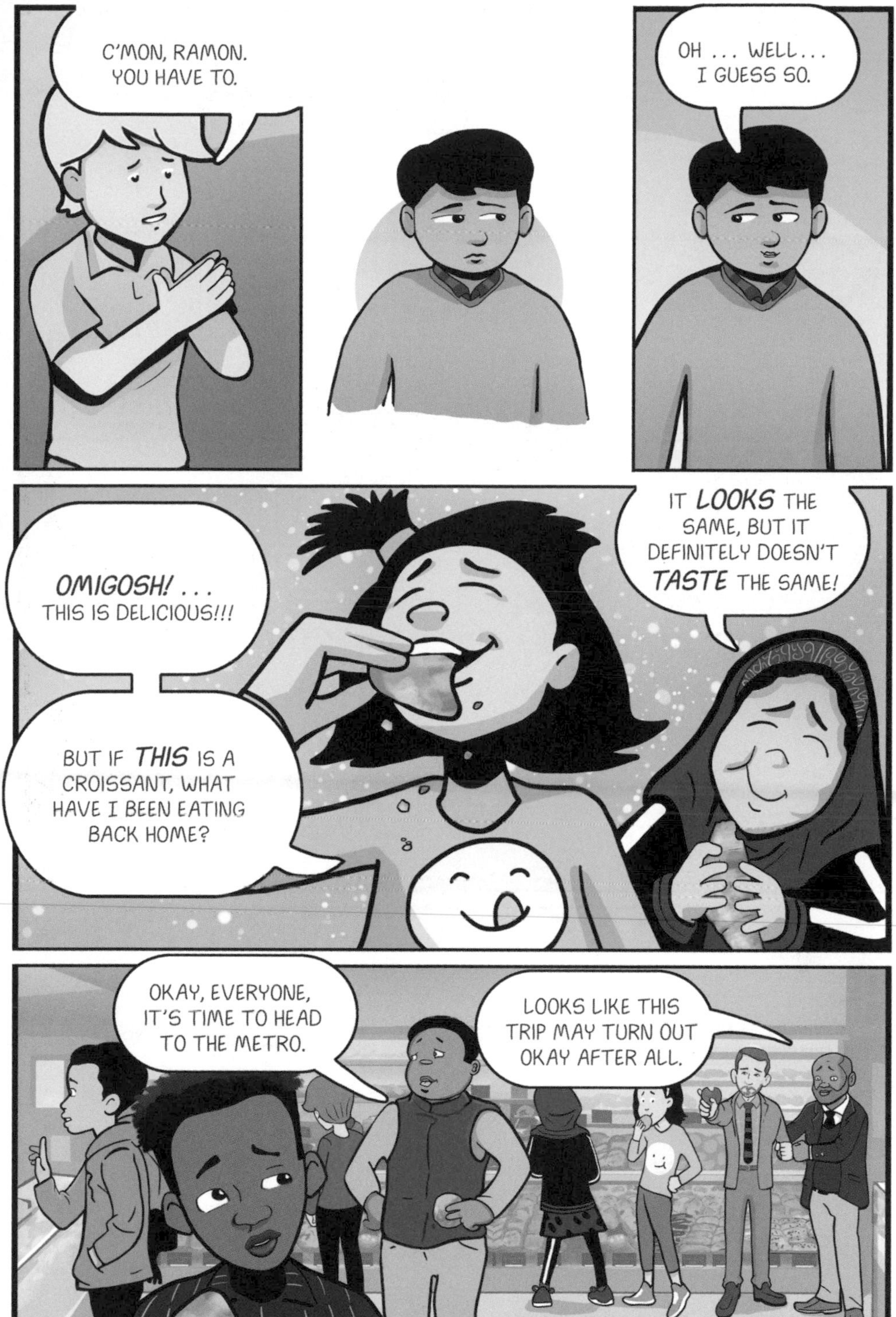

C'MON, RAMON. YOU HAVE TO.
OH . . . WELL . . . I GUESS SO.
OMIGOSH! . . . THIS IS DELICIOUS!!!
BUT IF *THIS* IS A CROISSANT, WHAT HAVE I BEEN EATING BACK HOME?
IT *LOOKS* THE SAME, BUT IT DEFINITELY DOESN'T *TASTE* THE SAME!
OKAY, EVERYONE, IT'S TIME TO HEAD TO THE METRO.
LOOKS LIKE THIS TRIP MAY TURN OUT OKAY AFTER ALL.

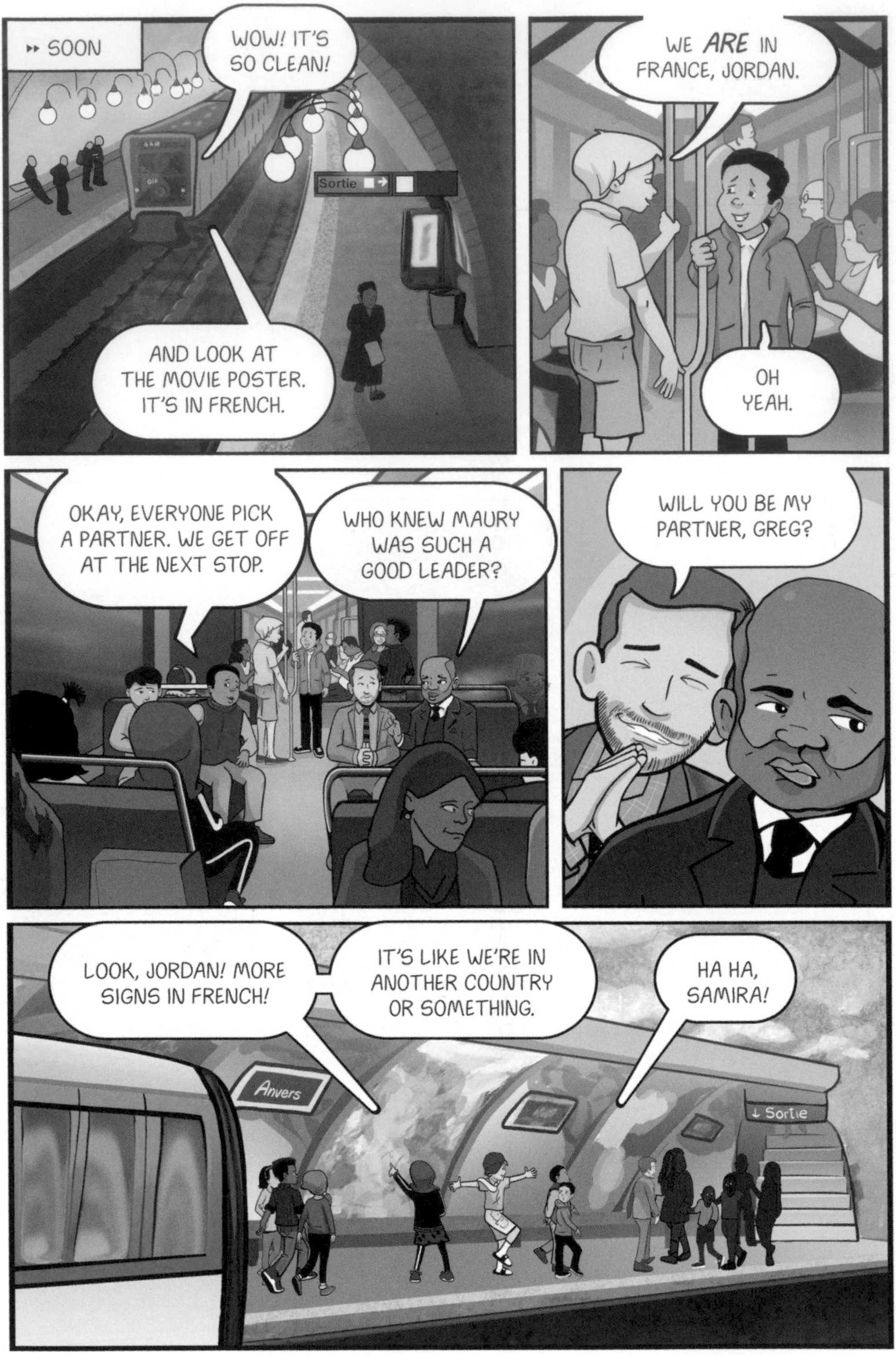
▸▸ SOON
WOW! IT'S SO CLEAN!
Sortie
AND LOOK AT THE MOVIE POSTER. IT'S IN FRENCH.
WE ARE IN FRANCE, JORDAN.
OH YEAH.
OKAY, EVERYONE PICK A PARTNER. WE GET OFF AT THE NEXT STOP.
WHO KNEW MAURY WAS SUCH A GOOD LEADER?
WILL YOU BE MY PARTNER, GREG?
LOOK, JORDAN! MORE SIGNS IN FRENCH!
IT'S LIKE WE'RE IN ANOTHER COUNTRY OR SOMETHING.
HA HA, SAMIRA!
Anvers
↓ Sortie

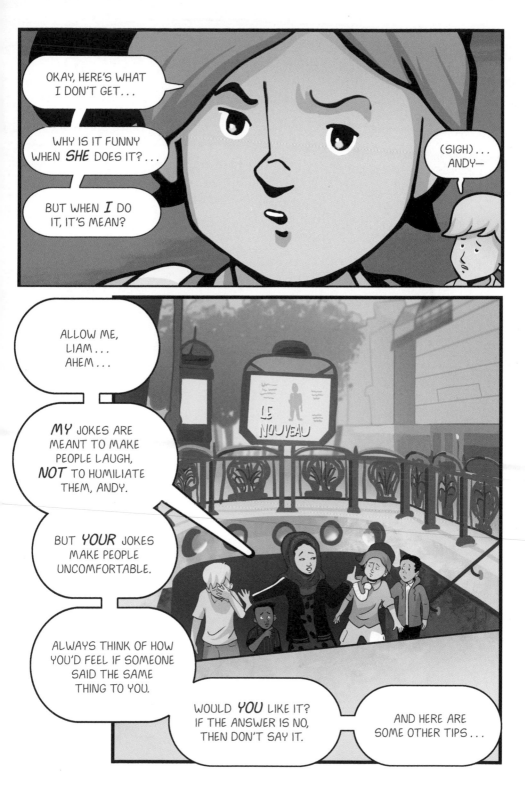

Samira's Guide to Insulting People (And Having Them Stay Your Friend)

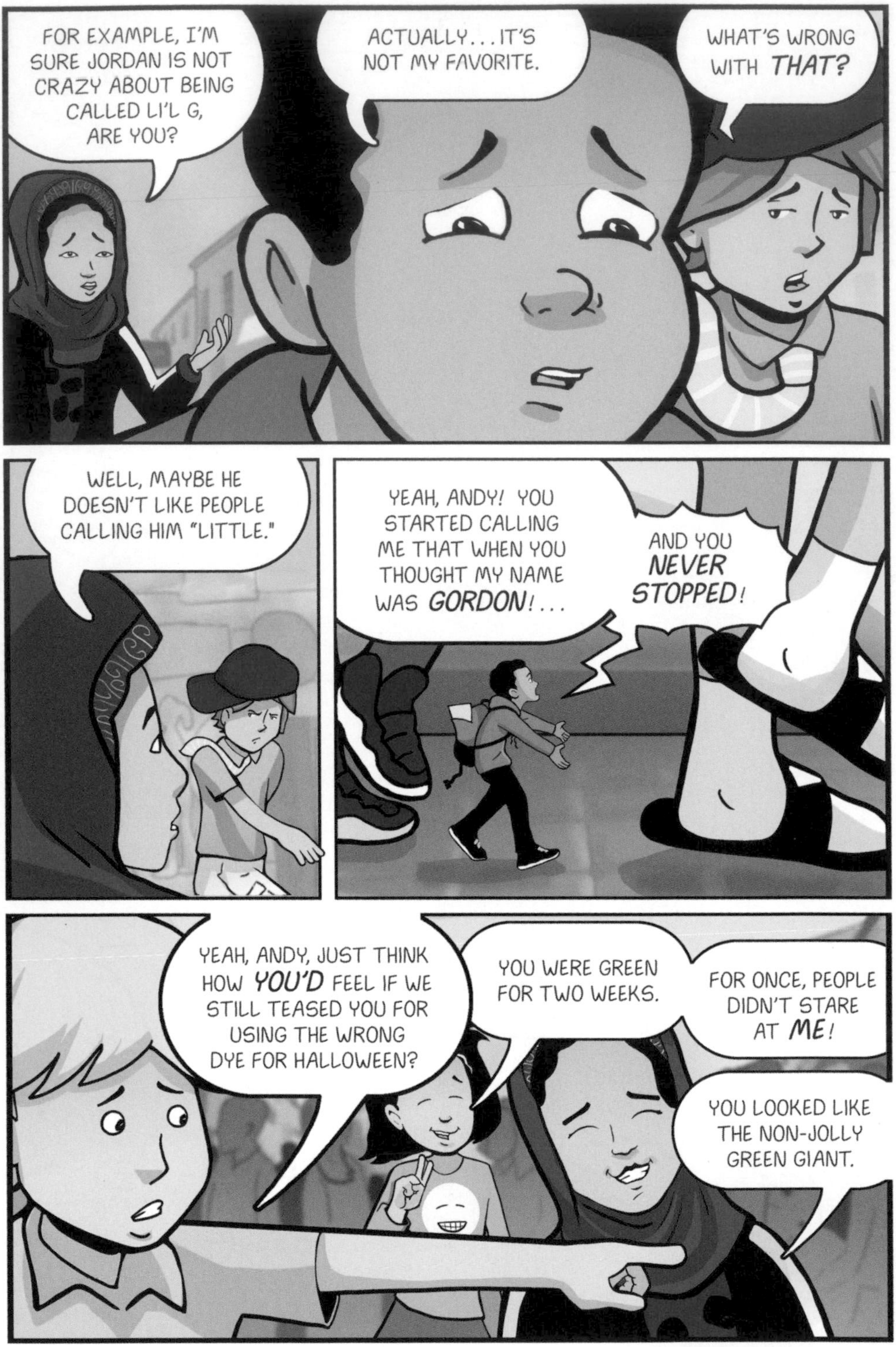
FOR EXAMPLE, I'M SURE JORDAN IS NOT CRAZY ABOUT BEING CALLED LI'L G, ARE YOU?
ACTUALLY... IT'S NOT MY FAVORITE.
WHAT'S WRONG WITH *THAT?*
WELL, MAYBE HE DOESN'T LIKE PEOPLE CALLING HIM "LITTLE."
YEAH, ANDY! YOU STARTED CALLING ME THAT WHEN YOU THOUGHT MY NAME WAS ***GORDON***!...
AND YOU ***NEVER STOPPED***!
YEAH, ANDY, JUST THINK HOW ***YOU'D*** FEEL IF WE STILL TEASED YOU FOR USING THE WRONG DYE FOR HALLOWEEN?
YOU WERE GREEN FOR TWO WEEKS.
FOR ONCE, PEOPLE DIDN'T STARE AT ***ME***!
YOU LOOKED LIKE THE NON-JOLLY GREEN GIANT.

128

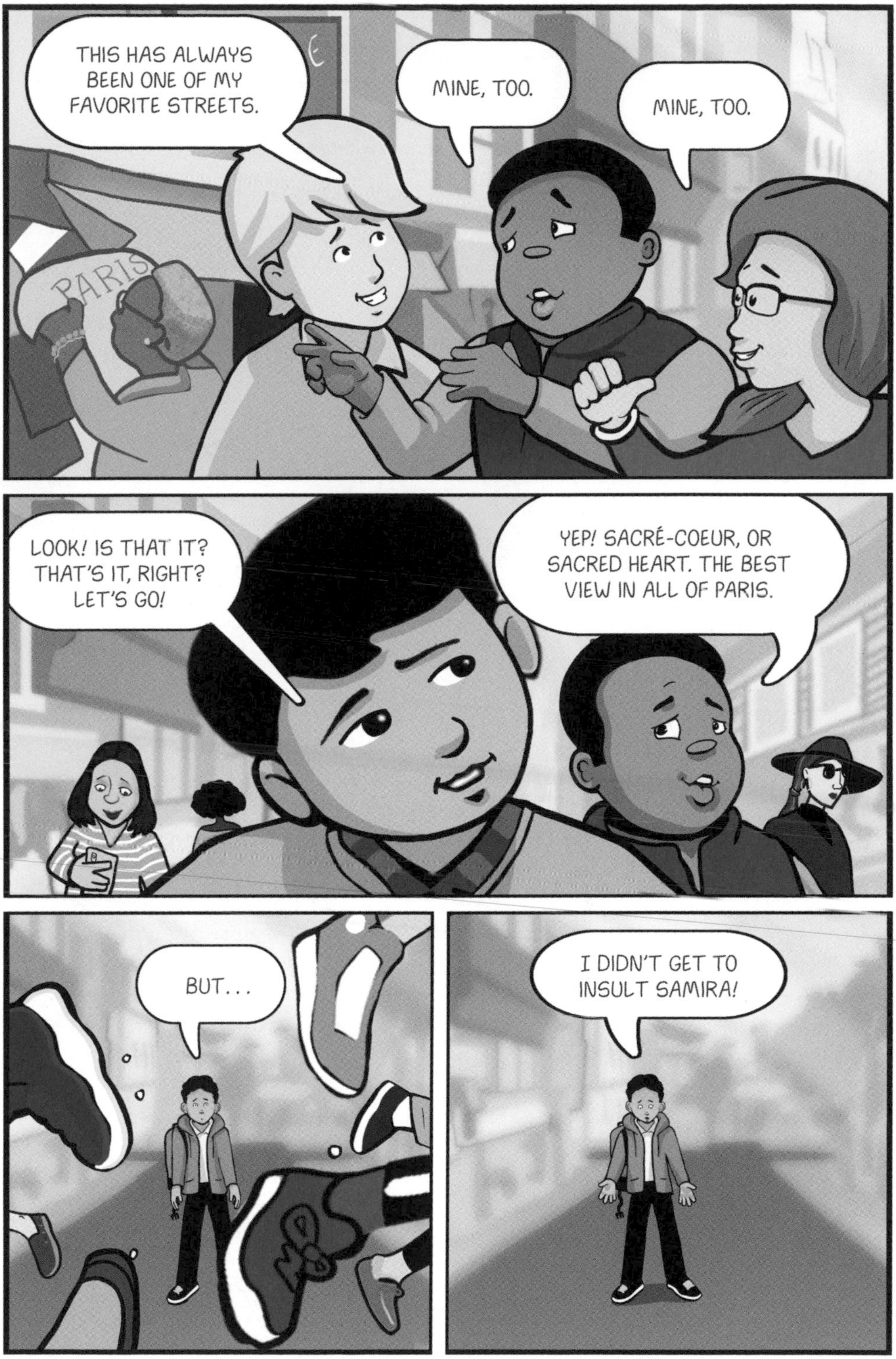
THIS HAS ALWAYS BEEN ONE OF MY FAVORITE STREETS.
MINE, TOO.
MINE, TOO.
PARIS
LOOK! IS THAT IT? THAT'S IT, RIGHT? LET'S GO!
YEP! SACRÉ-COEUR, OR SACRED HEART. THE BEST VIEW IN ALL OF PARIS.
BUT...
I DIDN'T GET TO INSULT SAMIRA!

6 Gooooooals!!!

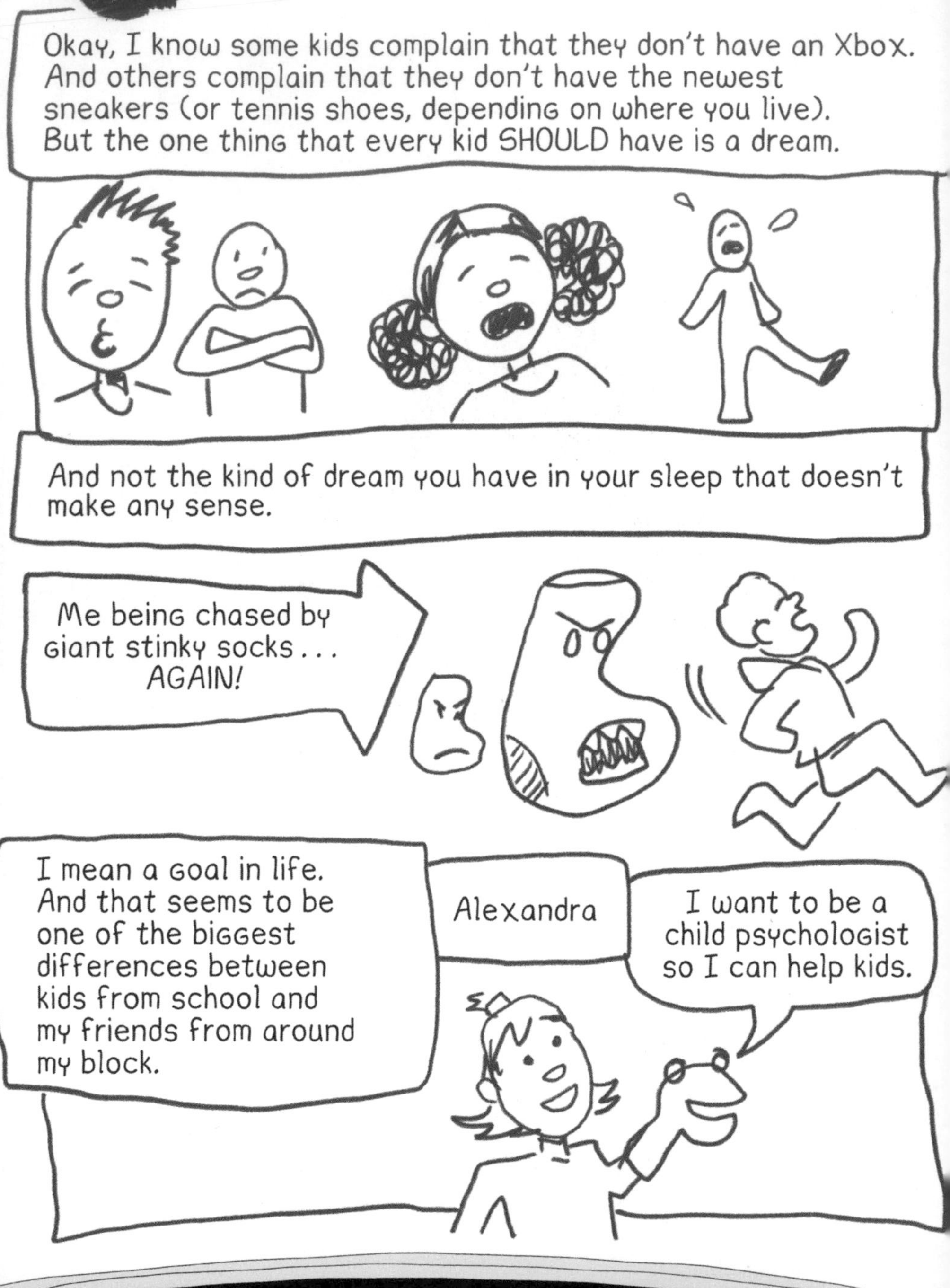
Okay, I know some kids complain that they don't have an Xbox. And others complain that they don't have the newest sneakers (or tennis shoes, depending on where you live). But the one thing that every kid SHOULD have is a dream.
And not the kind of dream you have in your sleep that doesn't make any sense.
Me being chased by giant stinky socks . . . AGAIN!
I mean a goal in life. And that seems to be one of the biggest differences between kids from school and my friends from around my block.
Alexandra
I want to be a child psychologist so I can help kids.

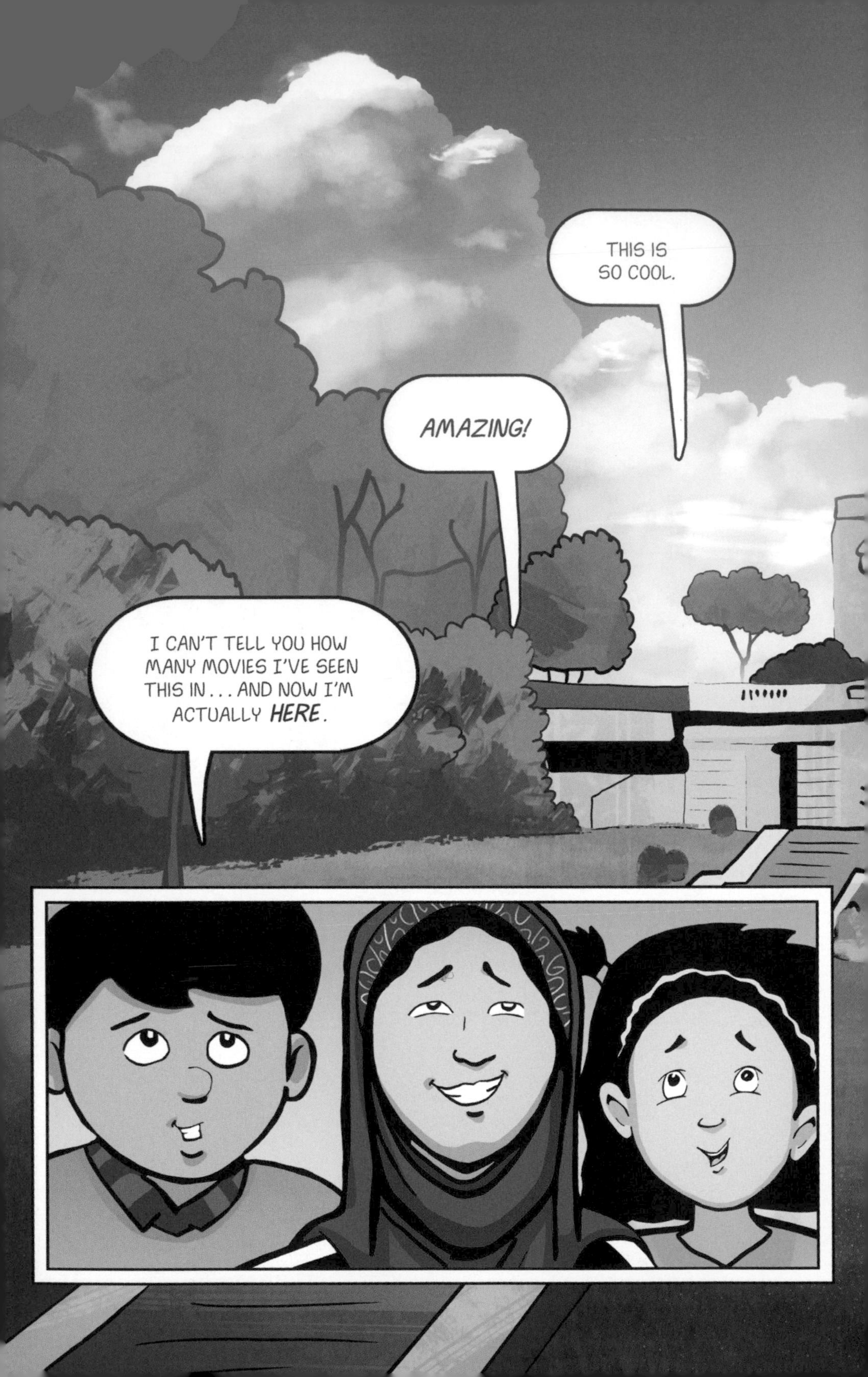
THIS IS SO COOL.
AMAZING!
I CAN'T TELL YOU HOW MANY MOVIES I'VE SEEN THIS IN... AND NOW I'M ACTUALLY HERE.

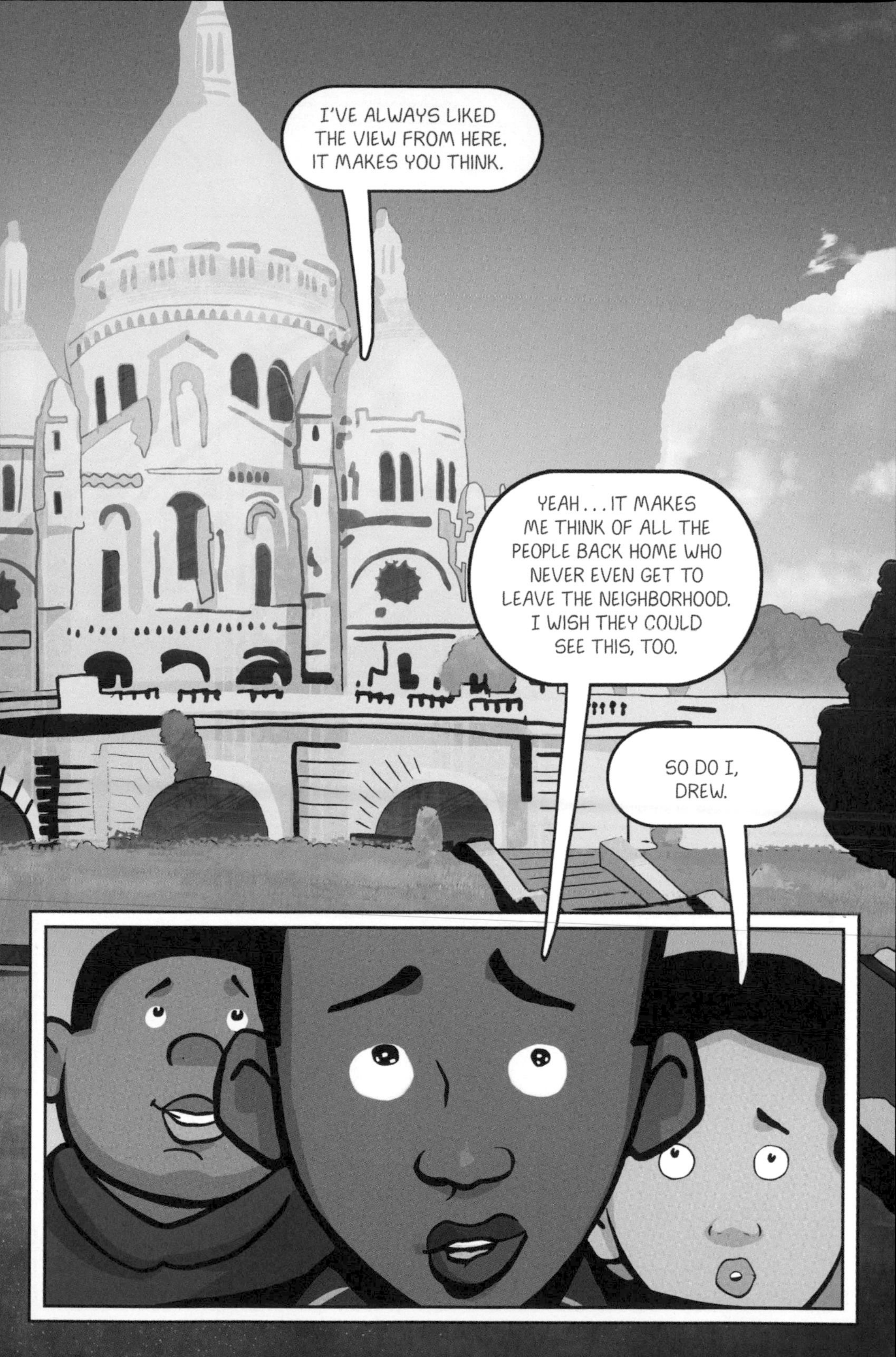
I'VE ALWAYS LIKED THE VIEW FROM HERE. IT MAKES YOU THINK.
YEAH . . . IT MAKES ME THINK OF ALL THE PEOPLE BACK HOME WHO NEVER EVEN GET TO LEAVE THE NEIGHBORHOOD. I WISH THEY COULD SEE THIS, TOO.
SO DO I, DREW.

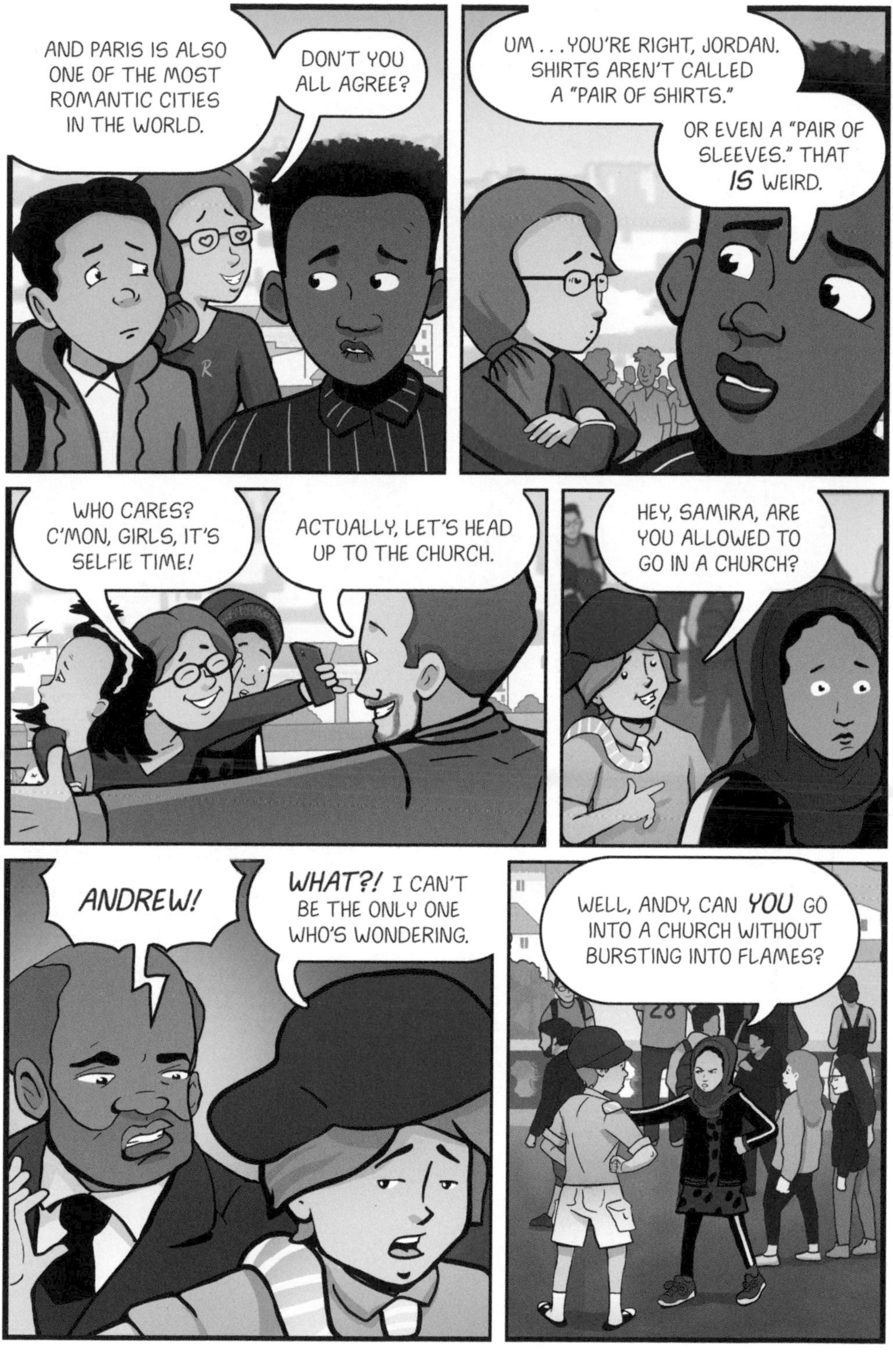
AND PARIS IS ALSO ONE OF THE MOST ROMANTIC CITIES IN THE WORLD.
DON'T YOU ALL AGREE?
UM . . . YOU'RE RIGHT, JORDAN. SHIRTS AREN'T CALLED A "PAIR OF SHIRTS."
OR EVEN A "PAIR OF SLEEVES." THAT *IS* WEIRD.
WHO CARES? C'MON, GIRLS, IT'S SELFIE TIME!
ACTUALLY, LET'S HEAD UP TO THE CHURCH.
HEY, SAMIRA, ARE YOU ALLOWED TO GO IN A CHURCH?
ANDREW!
WHAT?! I CAN'T BE THE ONLY ONE WHO'S WONDERING.
WELL, ANDY, CAN *YOU* GO INTO A CHURCH WITHOUT BURSTING INTO FLAMES?

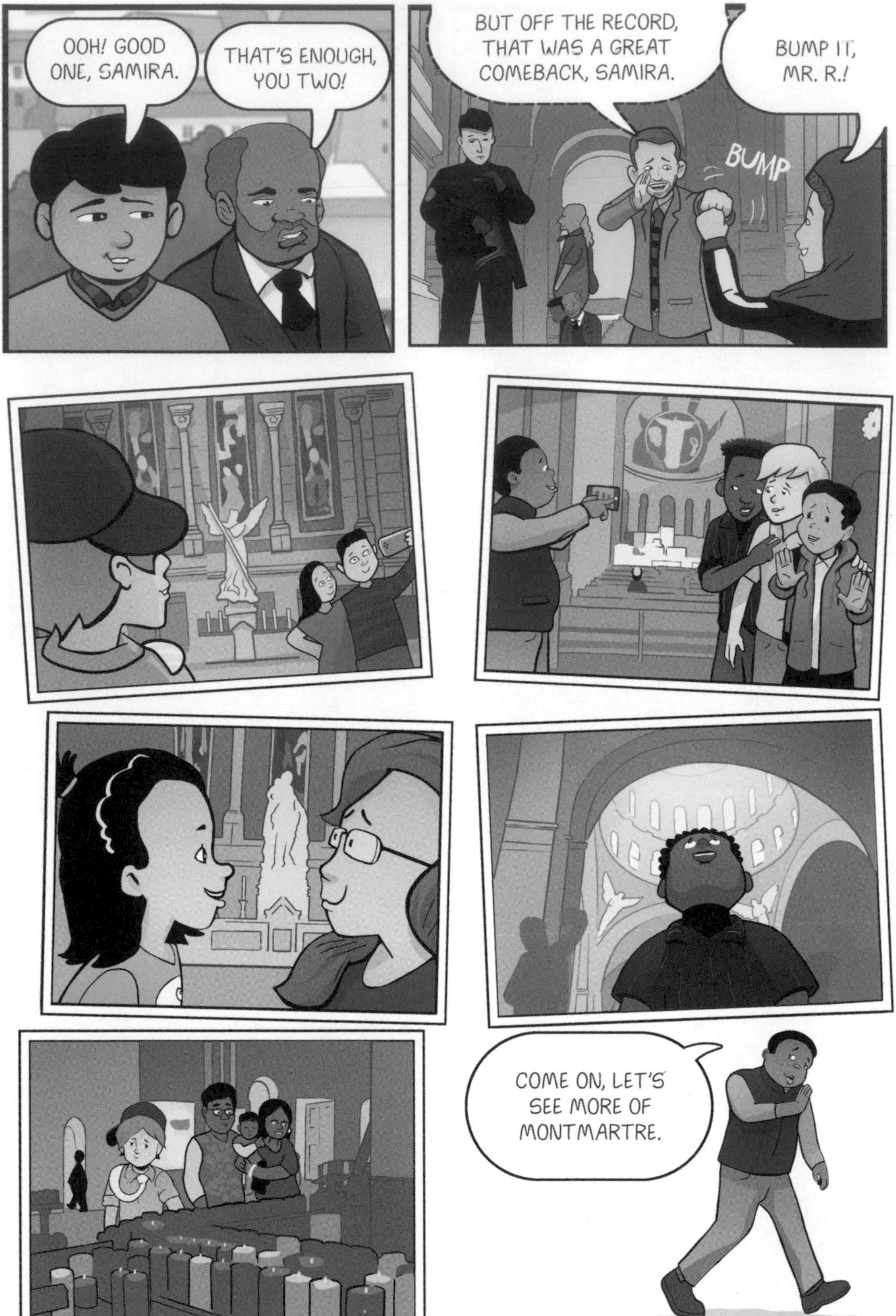
OOH! GOOD ONE, SAMIRA.
THAT'S ENOUGH, YOU TWO!
BUT OFF THE RECORD, THAT WAS A GREAT COMEBACK, SAMIRA.
BUMP IT, MR. R.!
BUMP
COME ON, LET'S SEE MORE OF MONTMARTRE.

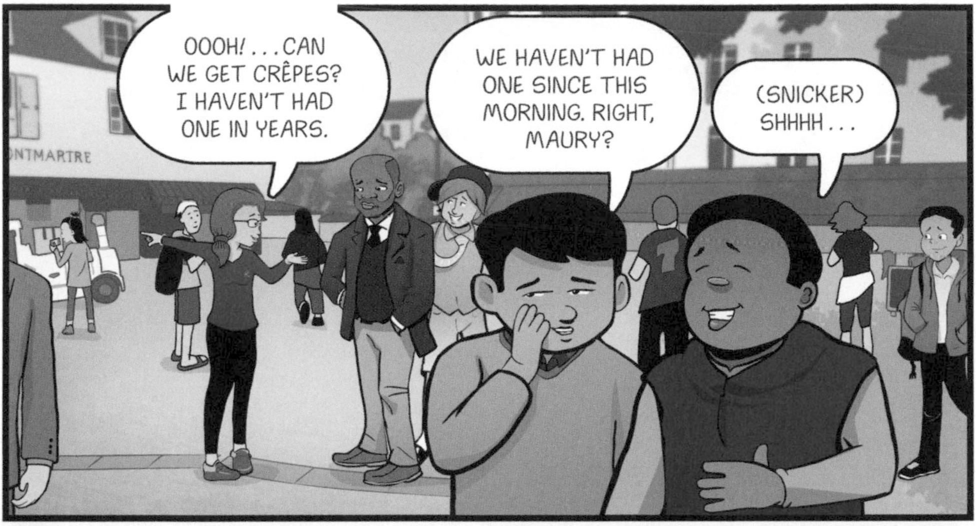
OOOH! . . . CAN WE GET CRÊPES? I HAVEN'T HAD ONE IN YEARS.
WE HAVEN'T HAD ONE SINCE THIS MORNING. RIGHT, MAURY?
(SNICKER) SHHHH . . .

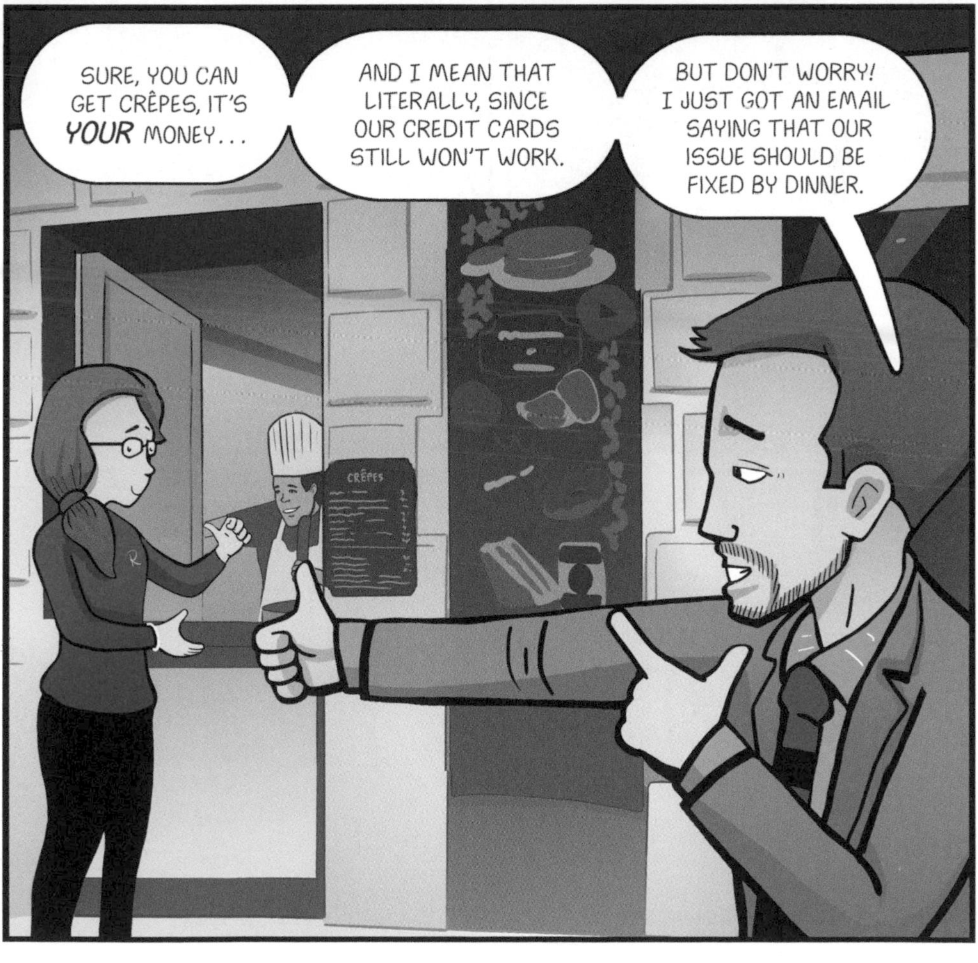
SURE, YOU CAN GET CRÊPES, IT'S YOUR MONEY . . .
AND I MEAN THAT LITERALLY, SINCE OUR CREDIT CARDS STILL WON'T WORK.
BUT DON'T WORRY! I JUST GOT AN EMAIL SAYING THAT OUR ISSUE SHOULD BE FIXED BY DINNER.

141

147

157

160

163

165

171

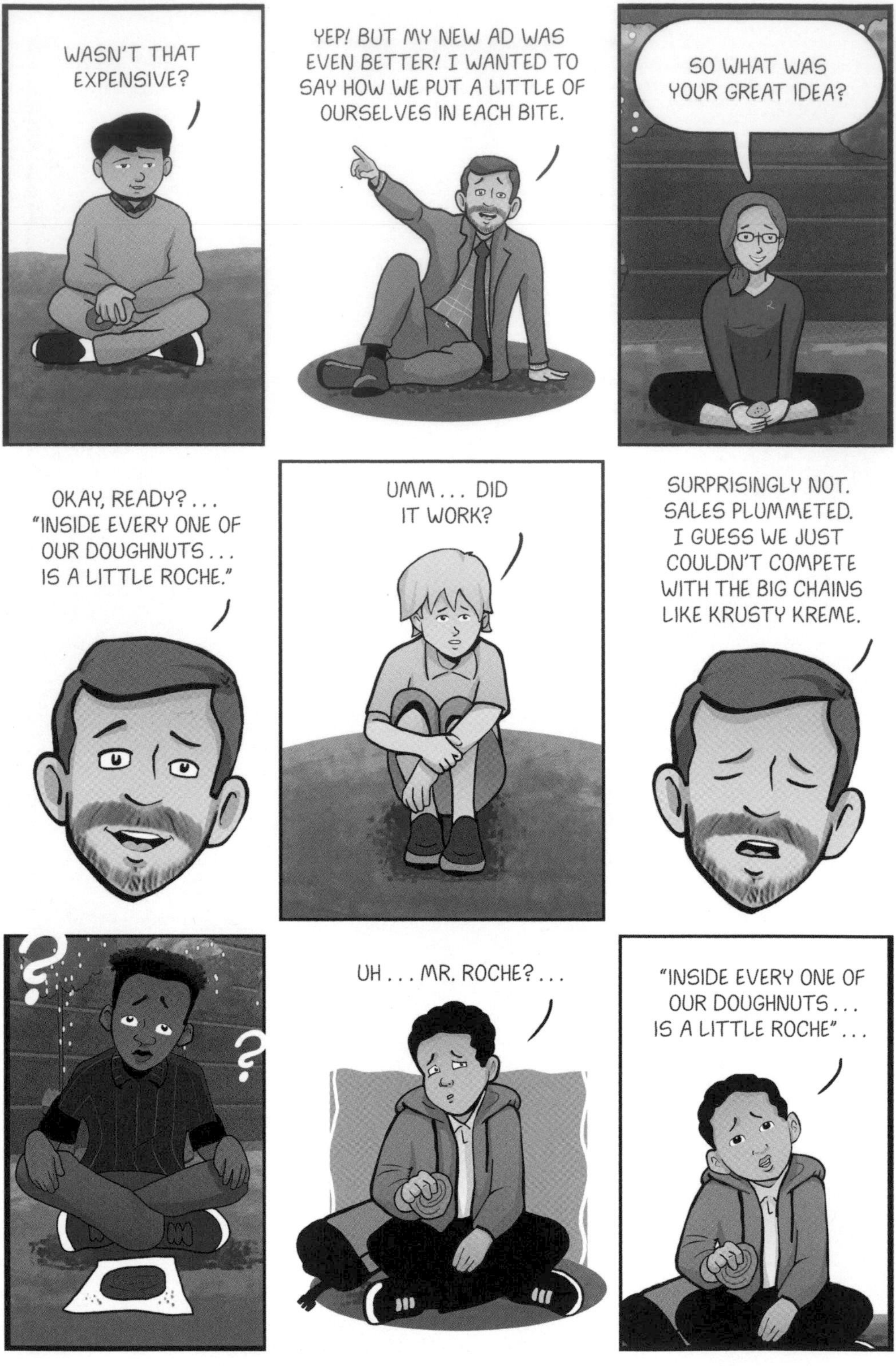
WASN'T THAT EXPENSIVE?
YEP! BUT MY NEW AD WAS EVEN BETTER! I WANTED TO SAY HOW WE PUT A LITTLE OF OURSELVES IN EACH BITE.
SO WHAT WAS YOUR GREAT IDEA?
OKAY, READY? . . . "INSIDE EVERY ONE OF OUR DOUGHNUTS . . . IS A LITTLE ROCHE."
UMM . . . DID IT WORK?
SURPRISINGLY NOT. SALES PLUMMETED. I GUESS WE JUST COULDN'T COMPETE WITH THE BIG CHAINS LIKE KRUSTY KREME.
UH . . . MR. ROCHE? . . .
"INSIDE EVERY ONE OF OUR DOUGHNUTS . . . IS A LITTLE ROCHE" . . .

175

177

178

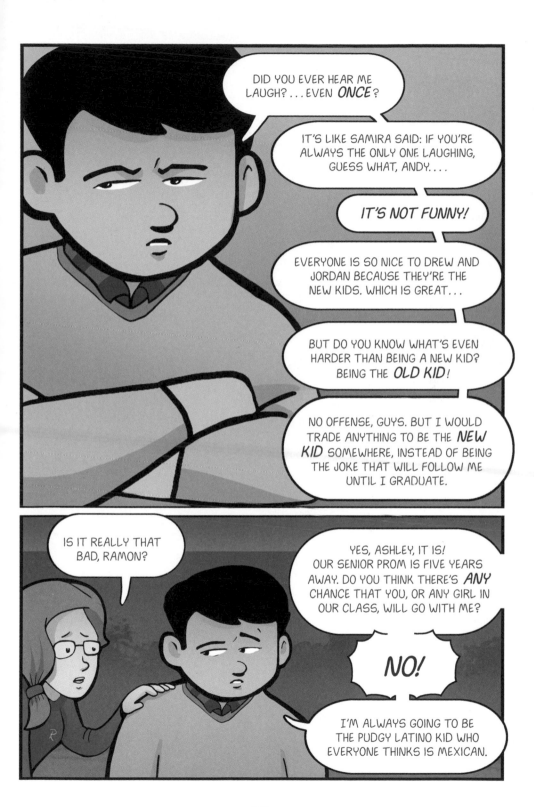

179

181

185

▸▸ IN HONOR OF YET ANOTHER FRENCH WORD THAT WE USE ALL THE TIME (WELL, MAYBE NOT ***ALL*** THE TIME) WE BRING YOU A "MONTAGE" OF THE REST OF OUR DAY.

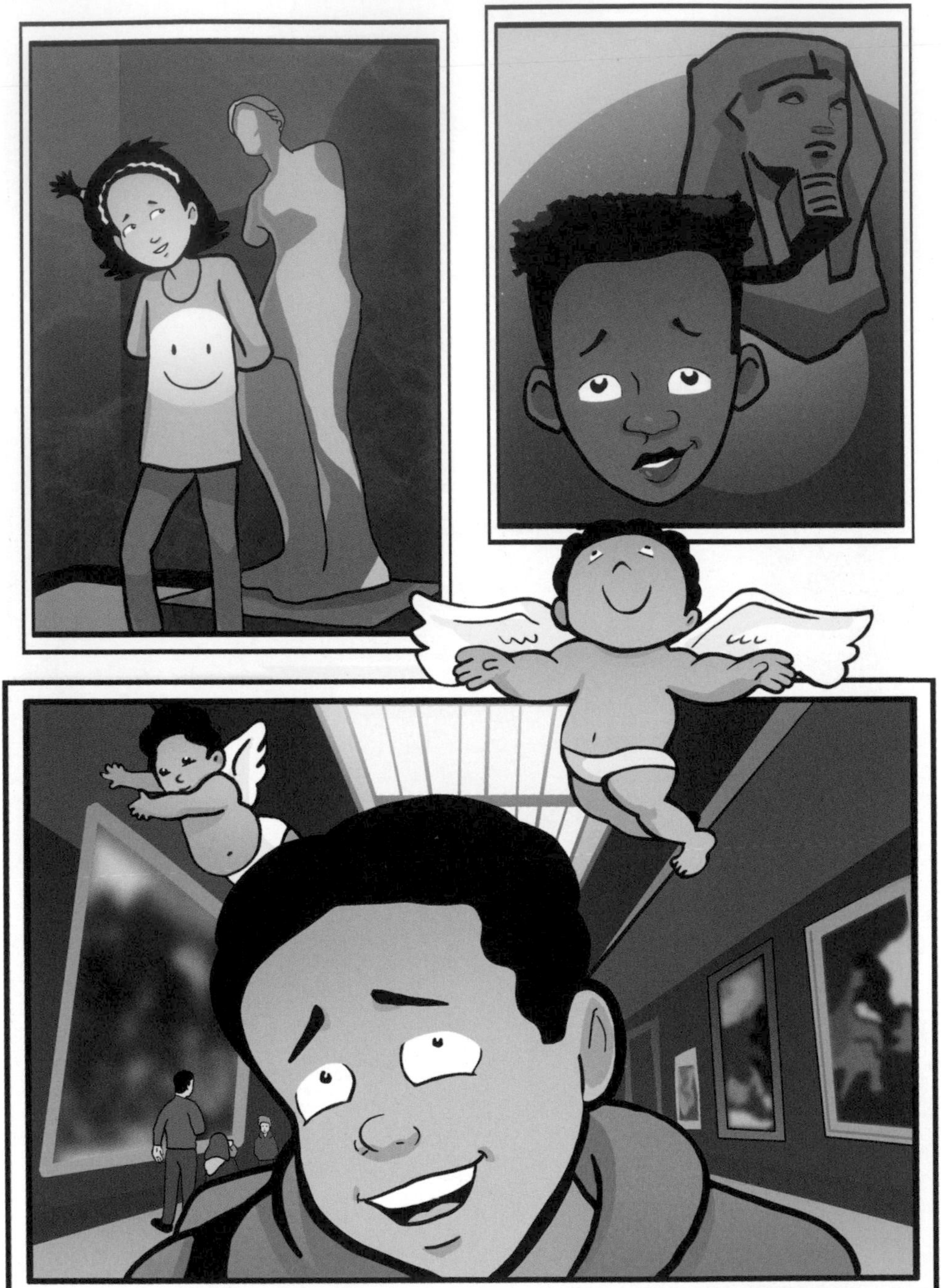

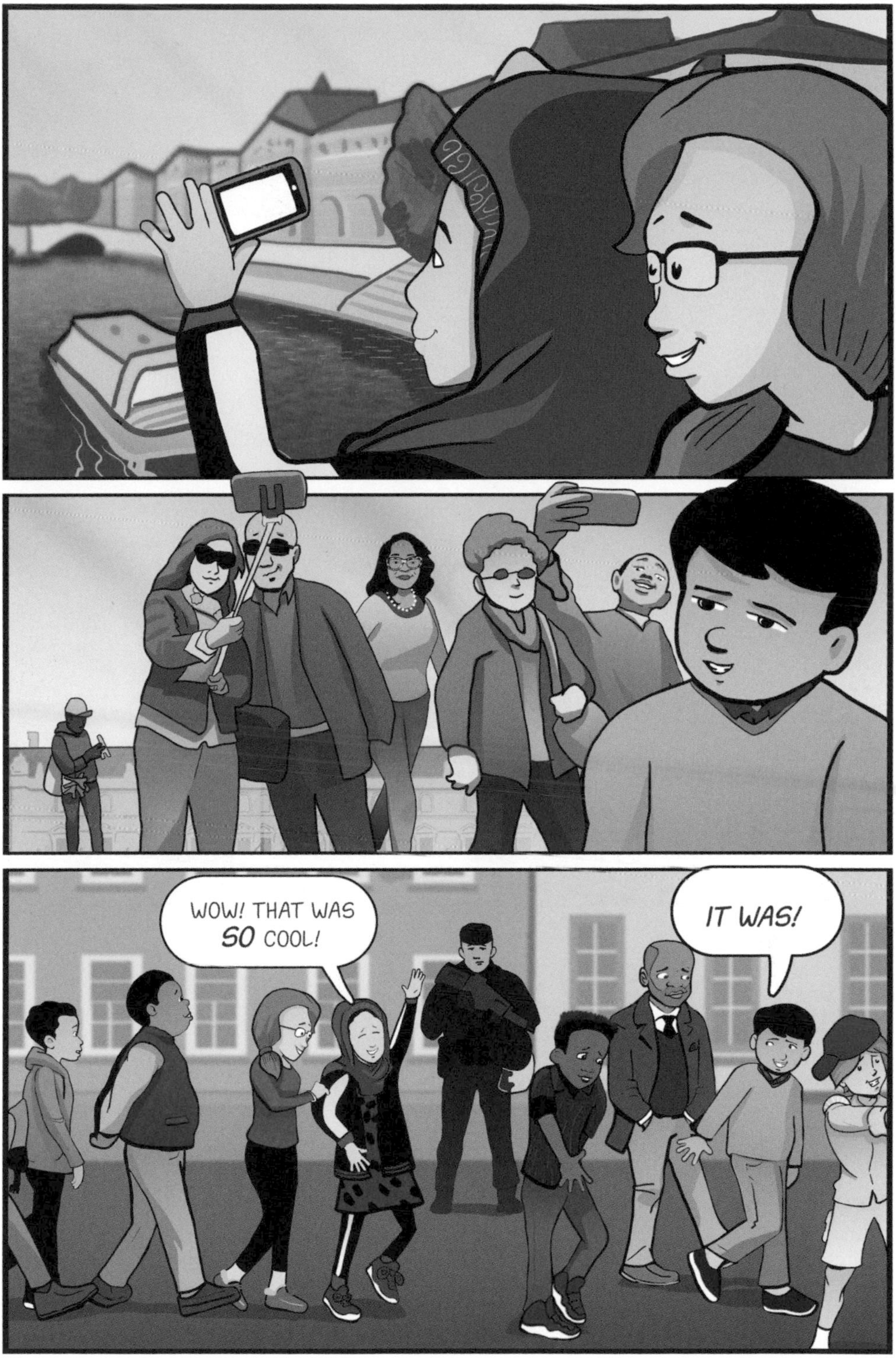
WOW! THAT WAS **SO** COOL!
IT WAS!

198

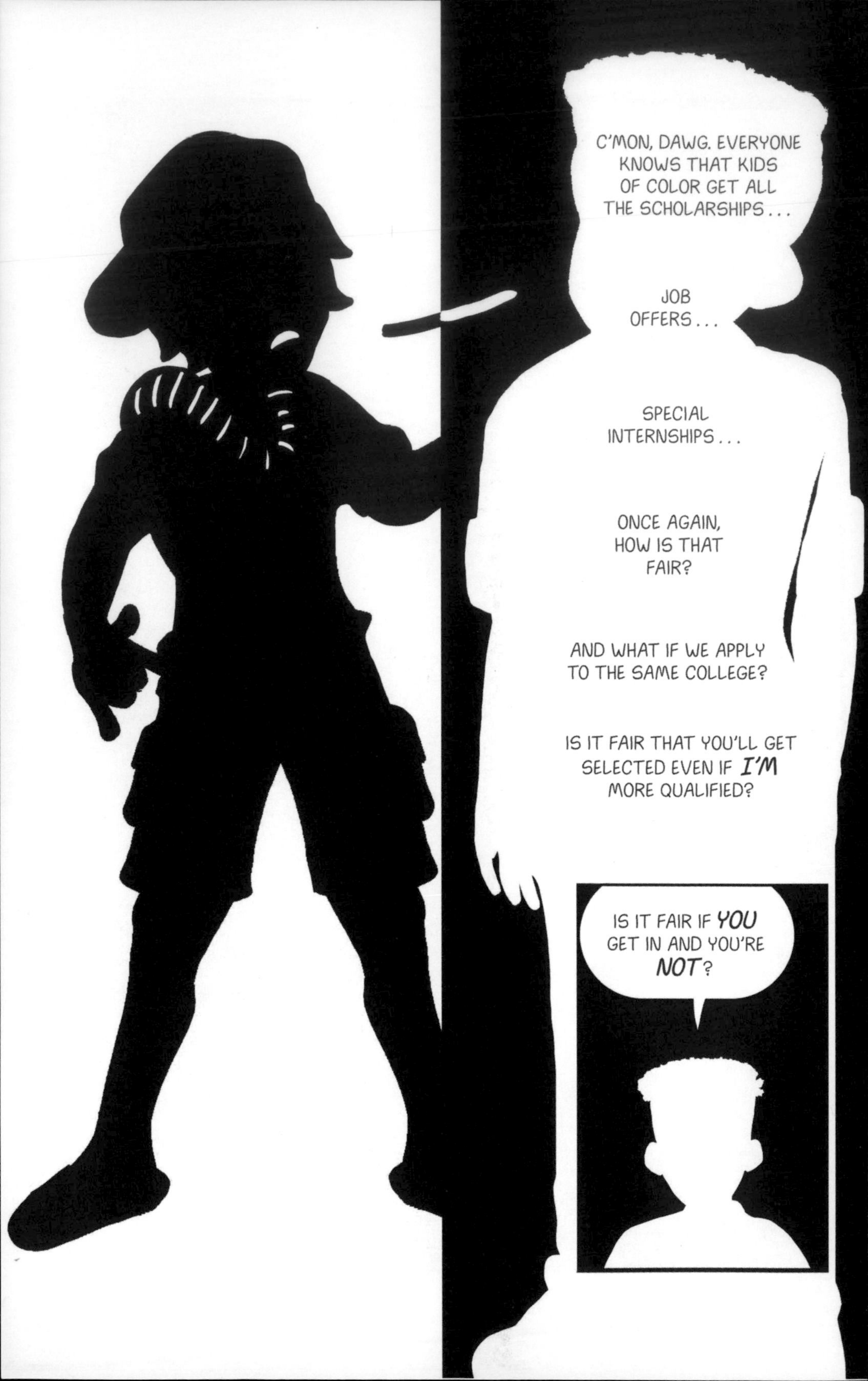

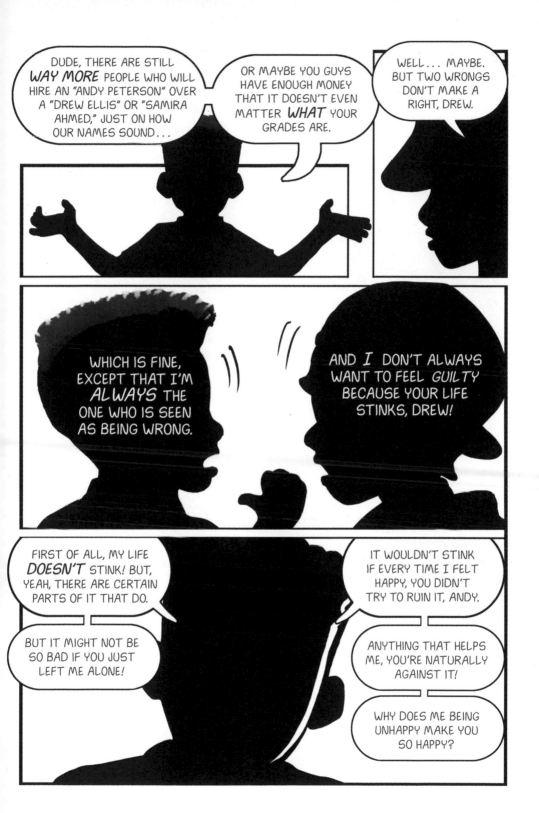

205

206

207

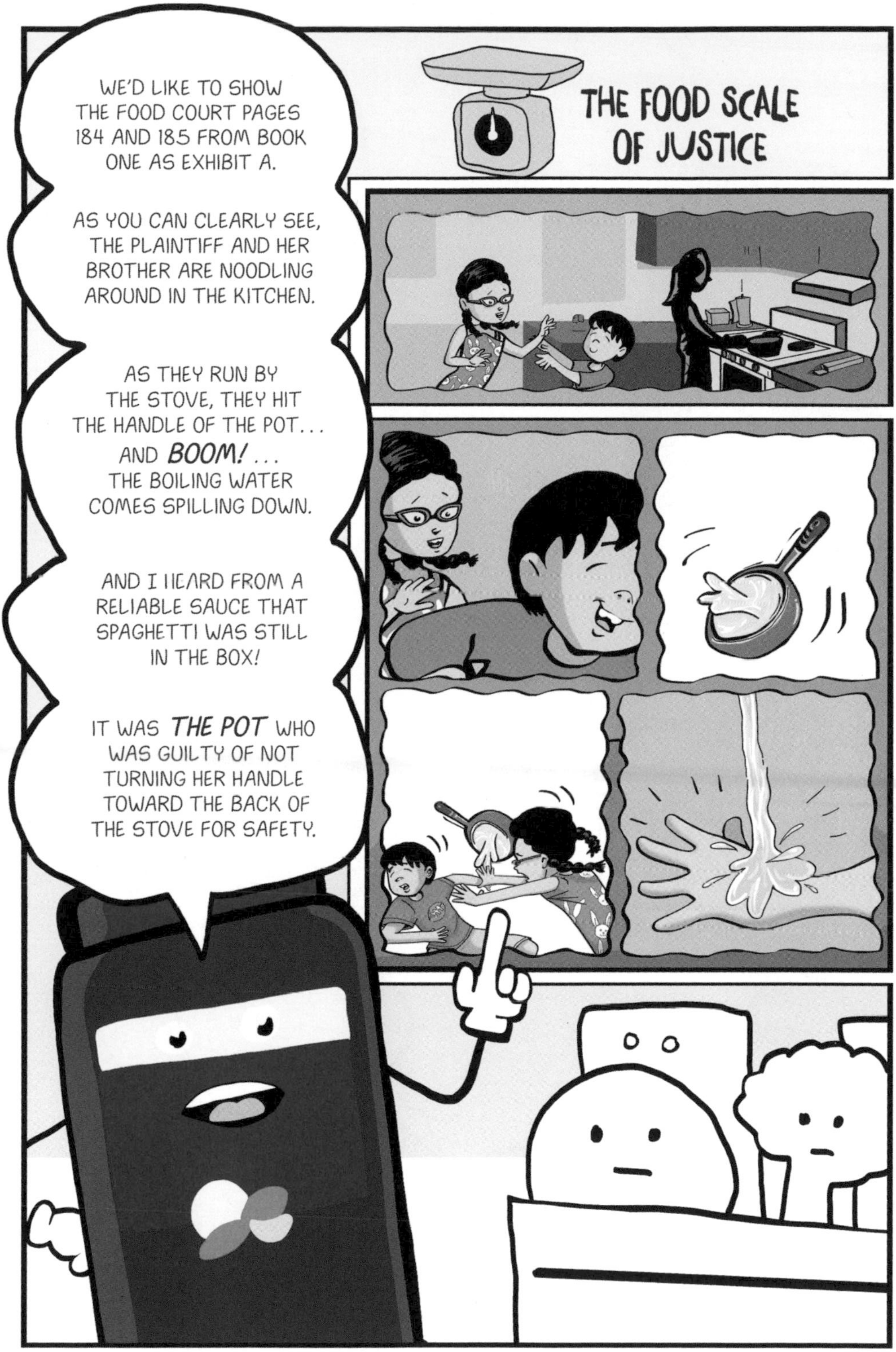
WE'D LIKE TO SHOW THE FOOD COURT PAGES 184 AND 185 FROM BOOK ONE AS EXHIBIT A.
AS YOU CAN CLEARLY SEE, THE PLAINTIFF AND HER BROTHER ARE NOODLING AROUND IN THE KITCHEN.
AS THEY RUN BY THE STOVE, THEY HIT THE HANDLE OF THE POT... AND BOOM!... THE BOILING WATER COMES SPILLING DOWN.
AND I HEARD FROM A RELIABLE SAUCE THAT SPAGHETTI WAS STILL IN THE BOX!
IT WAS THE POT WHO WAS GUILTY OF NOT TURNING HER HANDLE TOWARD THE BACK OF THE STOVE FOR SAFETY.
THE FOOD SCALE OF JUSTICE

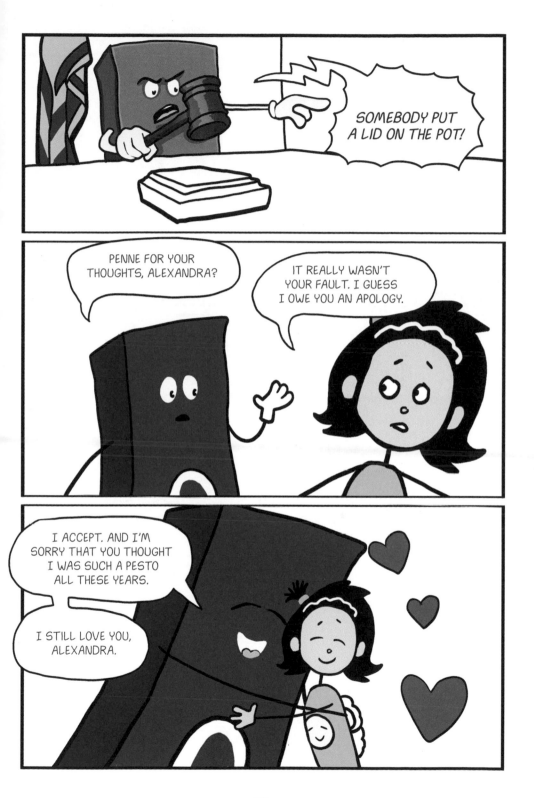

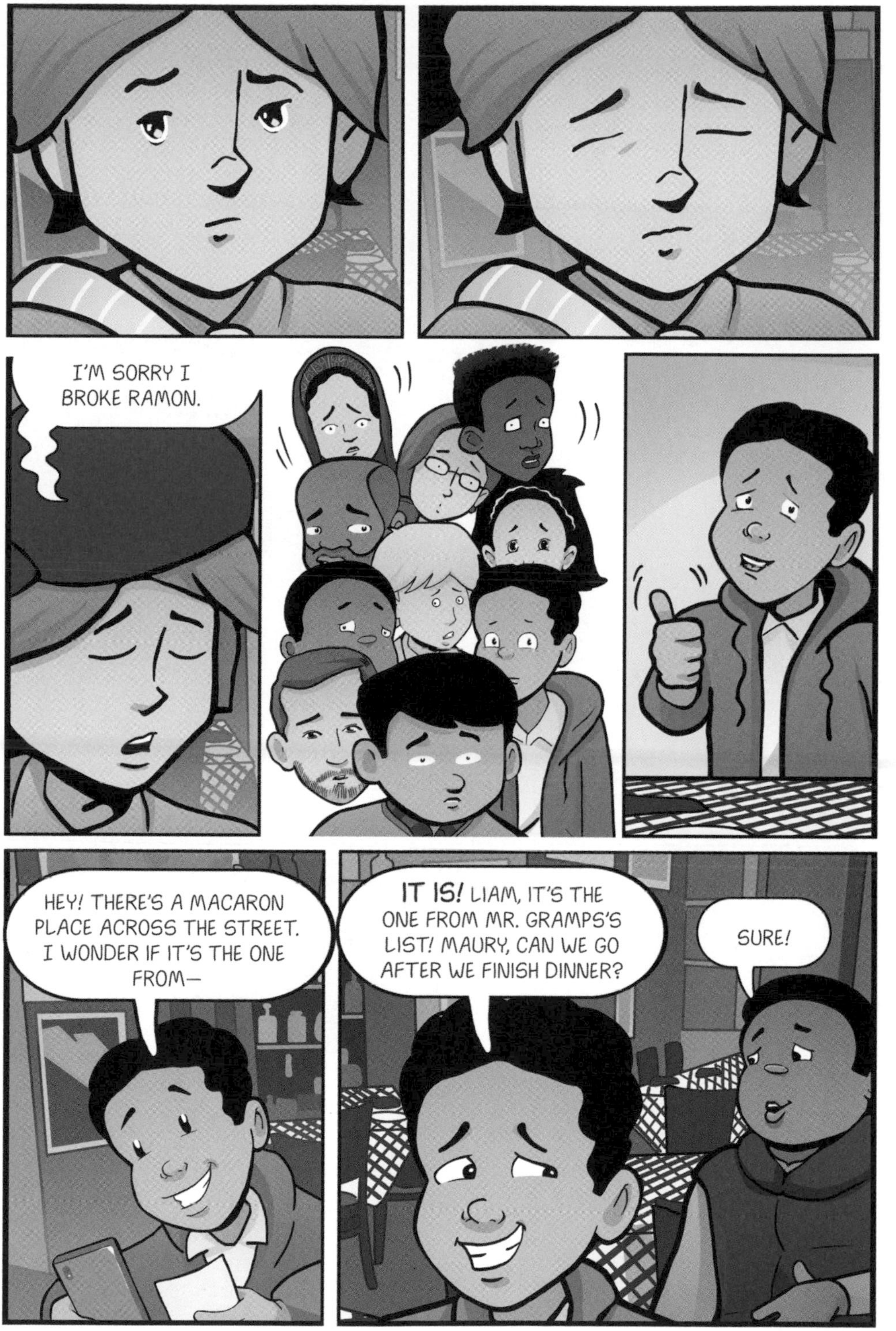
I'M SORRY I BROKE RAMON.
HEY! THERE'S A MACARON PLACE ACROSS THE STREET. I WONDER IF IT'S THE ONE FROM—
IT IS! LIAM, IT'S THE ONE FROM MR. GRAMPS'S LIST! MAURY, CAN WE GO AFTER WE FINISH DINNER?
SURE!

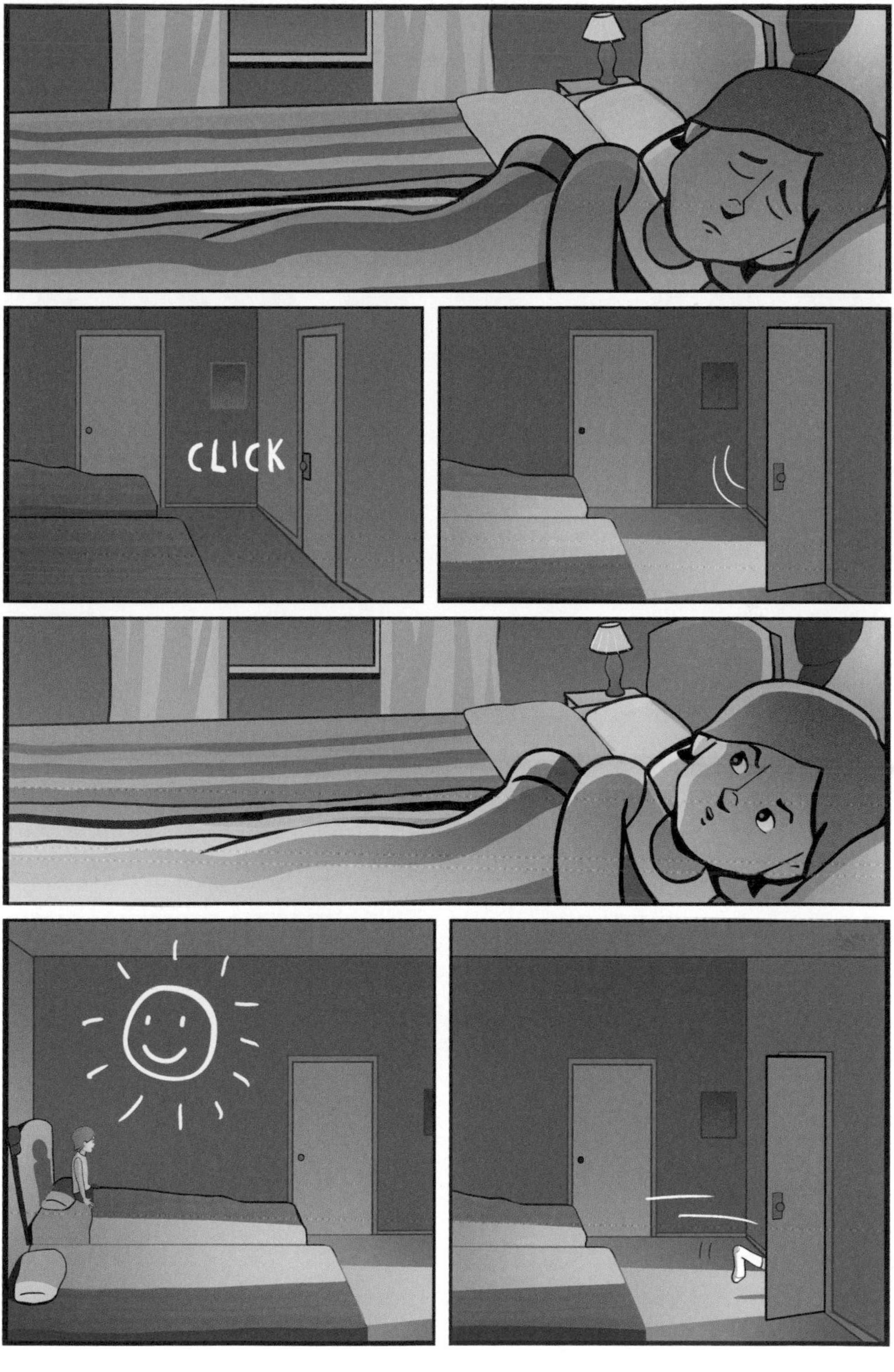
CLICK

219

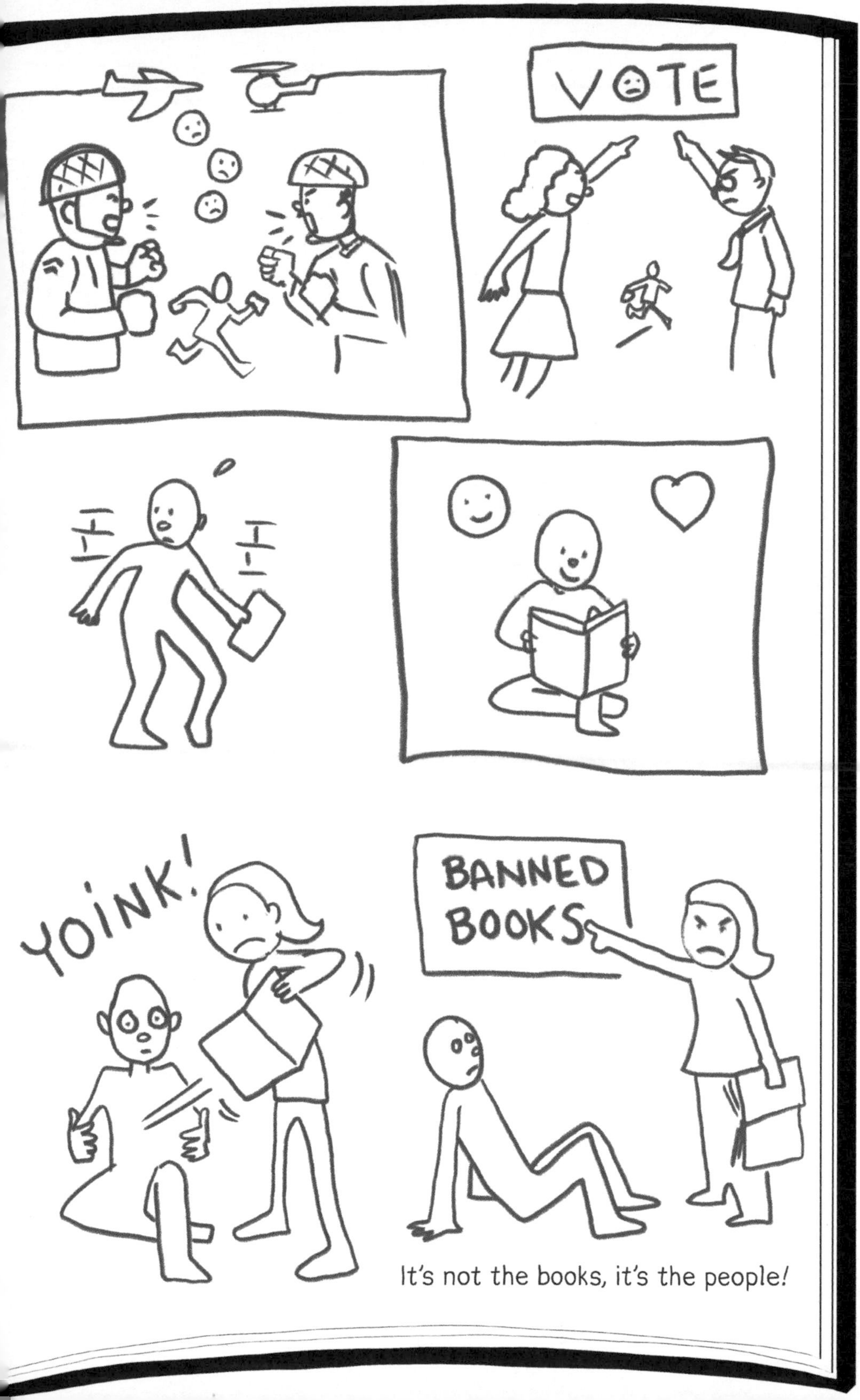
VOTE
YOINK!
BANNED BOOKS
It's not the books, it's the people!

223

224

227

PROMISE ME ONE DAY YOU'LL GO TO PARIS AND SPEND IT.
HUH?
KIRK, YOU'RE MY OLDEST FRIEND. I JUST WANT TO MAKE SURE THAT YOU GET TO STOP AND SMELL THE ROSES, TOO. PROMISE.
IS THAT ANOTHER ONE OF YOUR FAMOUS METAPHORS?
NO, IT'S AN IDIOM. BUT PROMISE.
I NEVER THOUGHT OF IT. BUT, OKAY, JORDAN, I PROMISE ONE DAY TO GO TO PARIS AND SPEND THIS EURO.
GOOD! NOW I GOTTA FINISH TELLING MY FOLKS ABOUT MY TRIP. BUT LET'S CATCH UP SOON.
COOL! LATER, DUDE. AND THANKS.

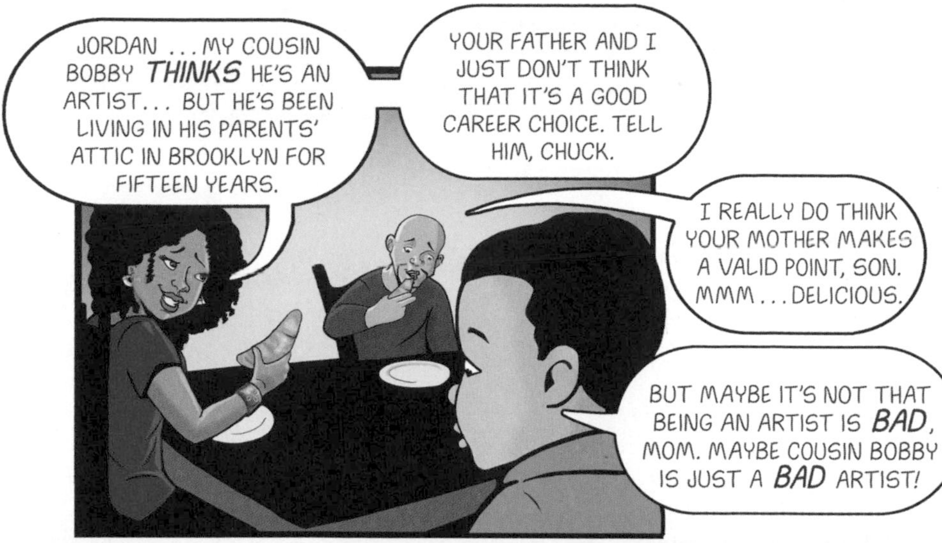
JORDAN ... MY COUSIN BOBBY THINKS HE'S AN ARTIST... BUT HE'S BEEN LIVING IN HIS PARENTS' ATTIC IN BROOKLYN FOR FIFTEEN YEARS.
YOUR FATHER AND I JUST DON'T THINK THAT IT'S A GOOD CAREER CHOICE. TELL HIM, CHUCK.
I REALLY DO THINK YOUR MOTHER MAKES A VALID POINT, SON. MMM... DELICIOUS.
BUT MAYBE IT'S NOT THAT BEING AN ARTIST IS BAD, MOM. MAYBE COUSIN BOBBY IS JUST A BAD ARTIST!

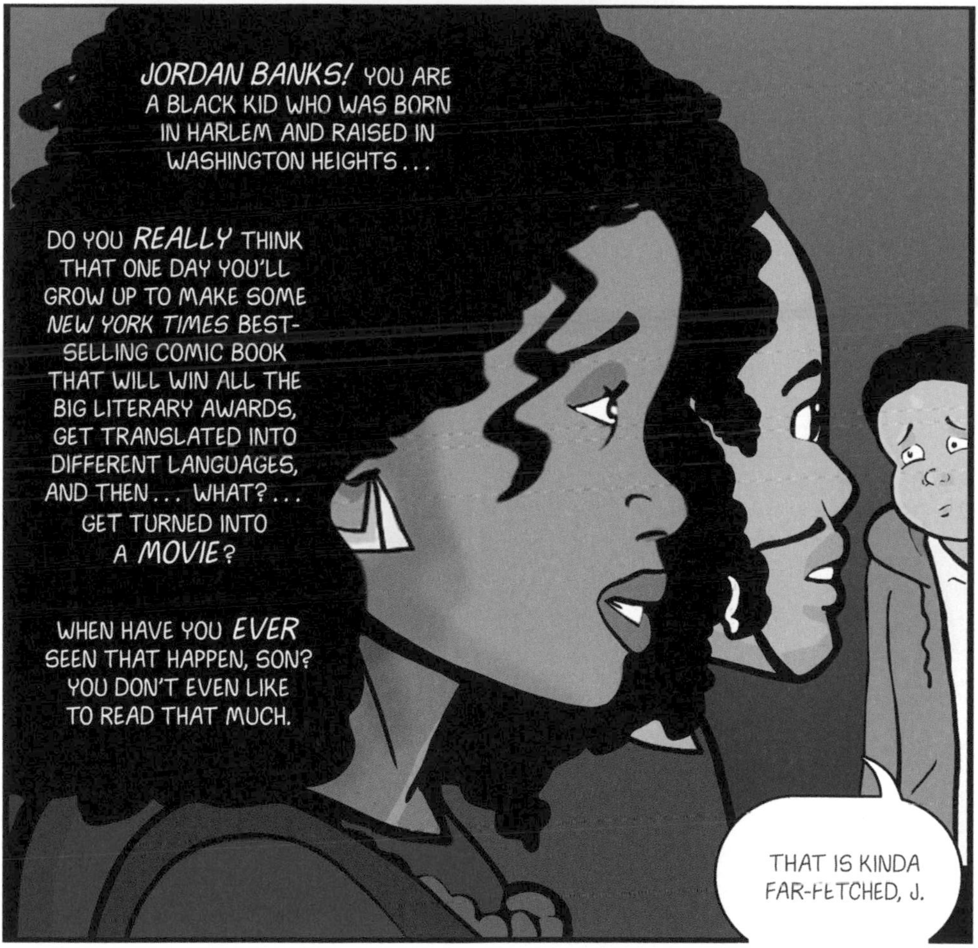
JORDAN BANKS! YOU ARE A BLACK KID WHO WAS BORN IN HARLEM AND RAISED IN WASHINGTON HEIGHTS...
DO YOU REALLY THINK THAT ONE DAY YOU'LL GROW UP TO MAKE SOME NEW YORK TIMES BEST-SELLING COMIC BOOK THAT WILL WIN ALL THE BIG LITERARY AWARDS, GET TRANSLATED INTO DIFFERENT LANGUAGES, AND THEN... WHAT?... GET TURNED INTO A MOVIE?
WHEN HAVE YOU EVER SEEN THAT HAPPEN, SON? YOU DON'T EVEN LIKE TO READ THAT MUCH.
THAT IS KINDA FAR-FETCHED, J.

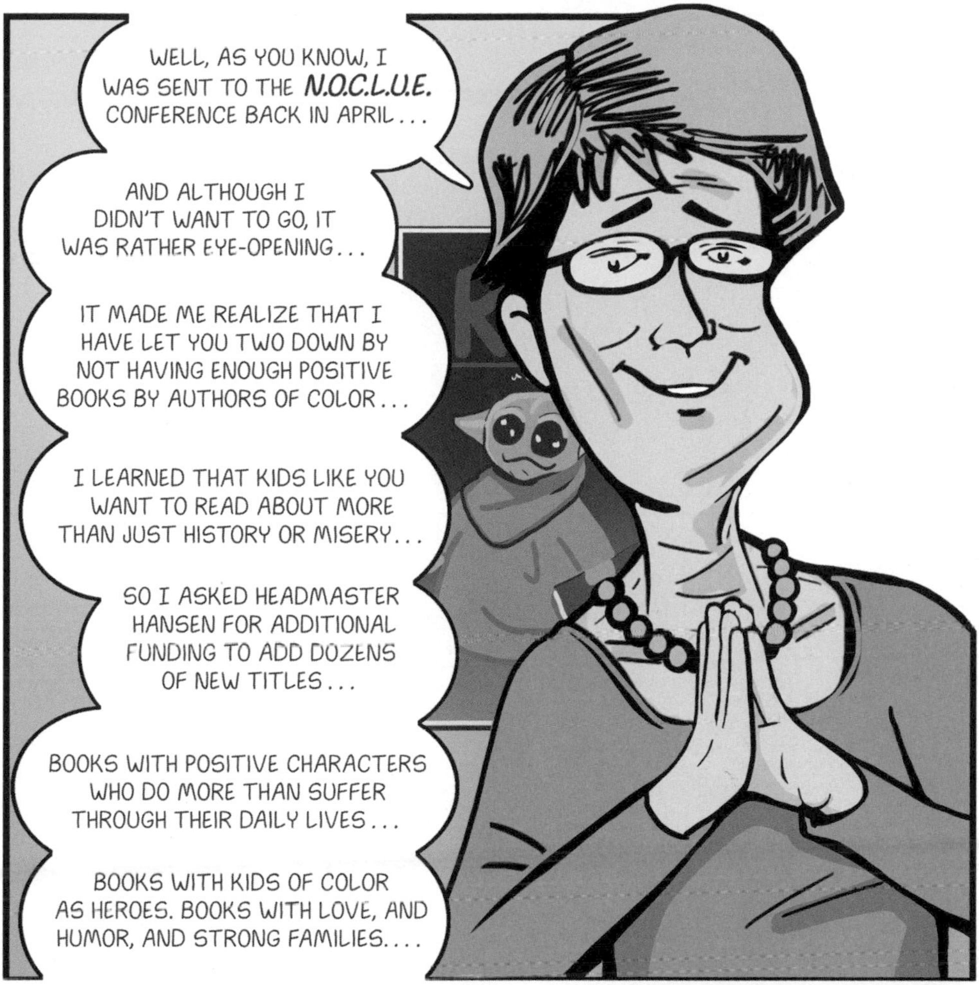
WELL, AS YOU KNOW, I WAS SENT TO THE N.O.C.L.U.E. CONFERENCE BACK IN APRIL...
AND ALTHOUGH I DIDN'T WANT TO GO, IT WAS RATHER EYE-OPENING...
IT MADE ME REALIZE THAT I HAVE LET YOU TWO DOWN BY NOT HAVING ENOUGH POSITIVE BOOKS BY AUTHORS OF COLOR...
I LEARNED THAT KIDS LIKE YOU WANT TO READ ABOUT MORE THAN JUST HISTORY OR MISERY...
SO I ASKED HEADMASTER HANSEN FOR ADDITIONAL FUNDING TO ADD DOZENS OF NEW TITLES...
BOOKS WITH POSITIVE CHARACTERS WHO DO MORE THAN SUFFER THROUGH THEIR DAILY LIVES...
BOOKS WITH KIDS OF COLOR AS HEROES. BOOKS WITH LOVE, AND HUMOR, AND STRONG FAMILIES....

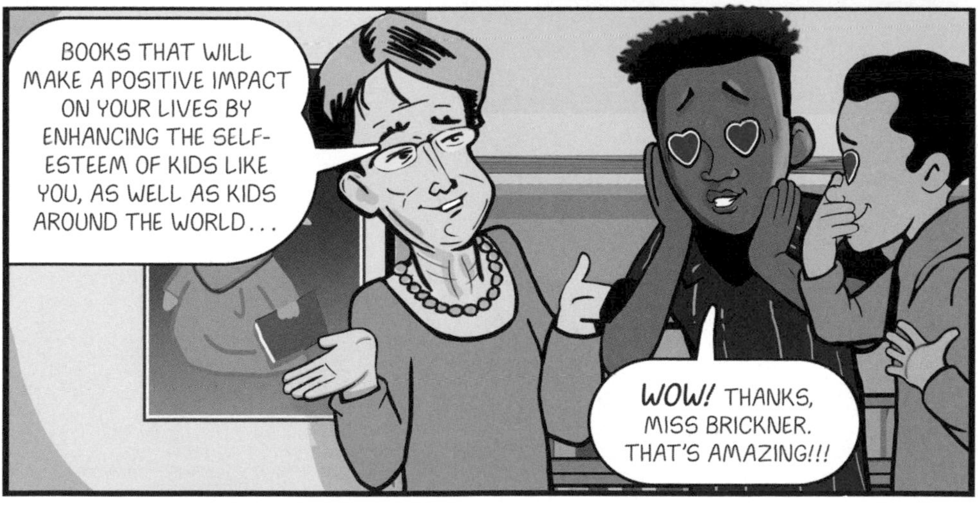
BOOKS THAT WILL MAKE A POSITIVE IMPACT ON YOUR LIVES BY ENHANCING THE SELF-ESTEEM OF KIDS LIKE YOU, AS WELL AS KIDS AROUND THE WORLD...
WOW! THANKS, MISS BRICKNER. THAT'S AMAZING!!!

237

239

240

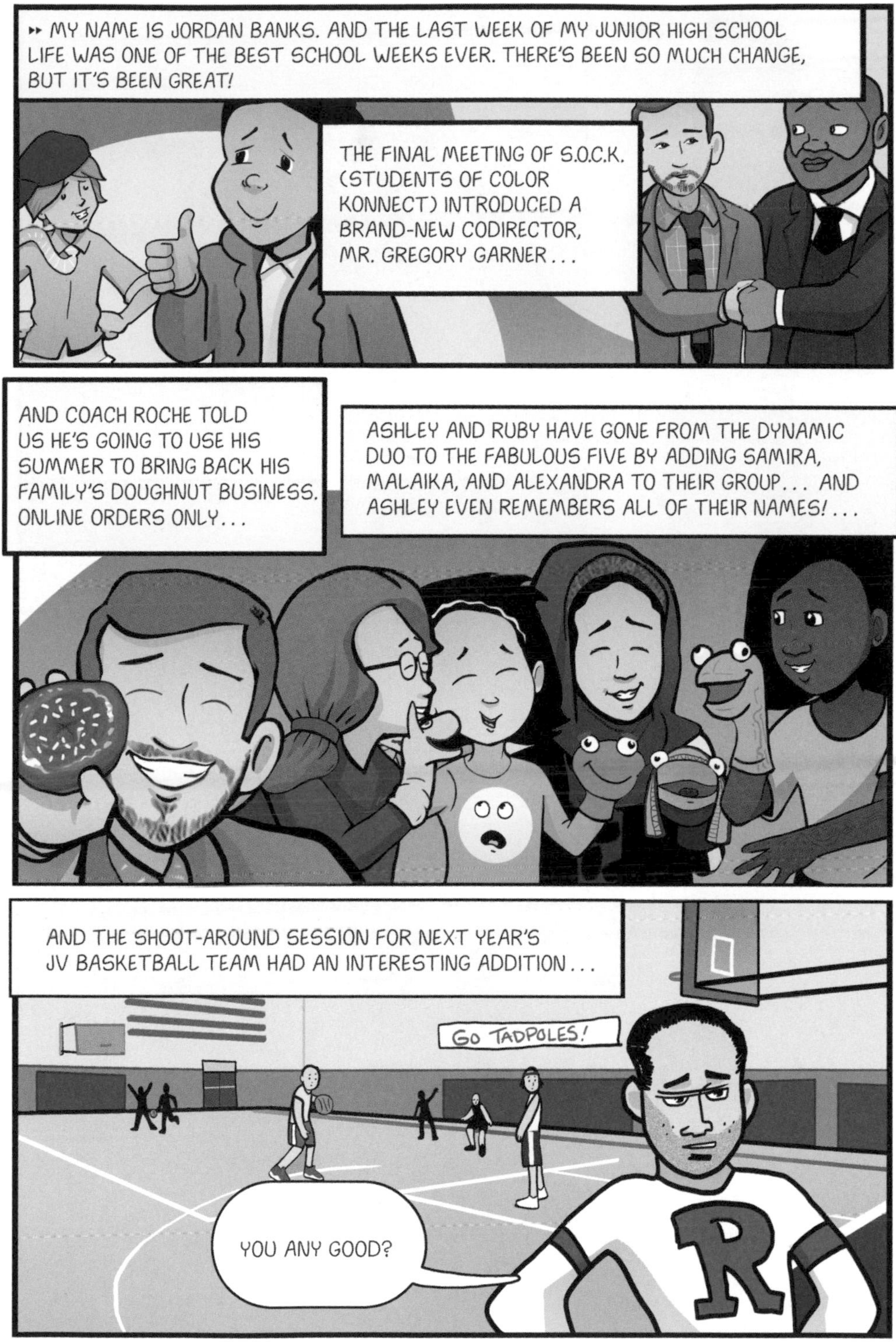
▸▸ MY NAME IS JORDAN BANKS. AND THE LAST WEEK OF MY JUNIOR HIGH SCHOOL LIFE WAS ONE OF THE BEST SCHOOL WEEKS EVER. THERE'S BEEN SO MUCH CHANGE, BUT IT'S BEEN GREAT!
THE FINAL MEETING OF S.O.C.K. (STUDENTS OF COLOR KONNECT) INTRODUCED A BRAND-NEW CODIRECTOR, MR. GREGORY GARNER . . .
AND COACH ROCHE TOLD US HE'S GOING TO USE HIS SUMMER TO BRING BACK HIS FAMILY'S DOUGHNUT BUSINESS. ONLINE ORDERS ONLY . . .
ASHLEY AND RUBY HAVE GONE FROM THE DYNAMIC DUO TO THE FABULOUS FIVE BY ADDING SAMIRA, MALAIKA, AND ALEXANDRA TO THEIR GROUP . . . AND ASHLEY EVEN REMEMBERS ALL OF THEIR NAMES! . . .
AND THE SHOOT-AROUND SESSION FOR NEXT YEAR'S JV BASKETBALL TEAM HAD AN INTERESTING ADDITION . . .
GO TADPOLES!
YOU ANY GOOD?
R

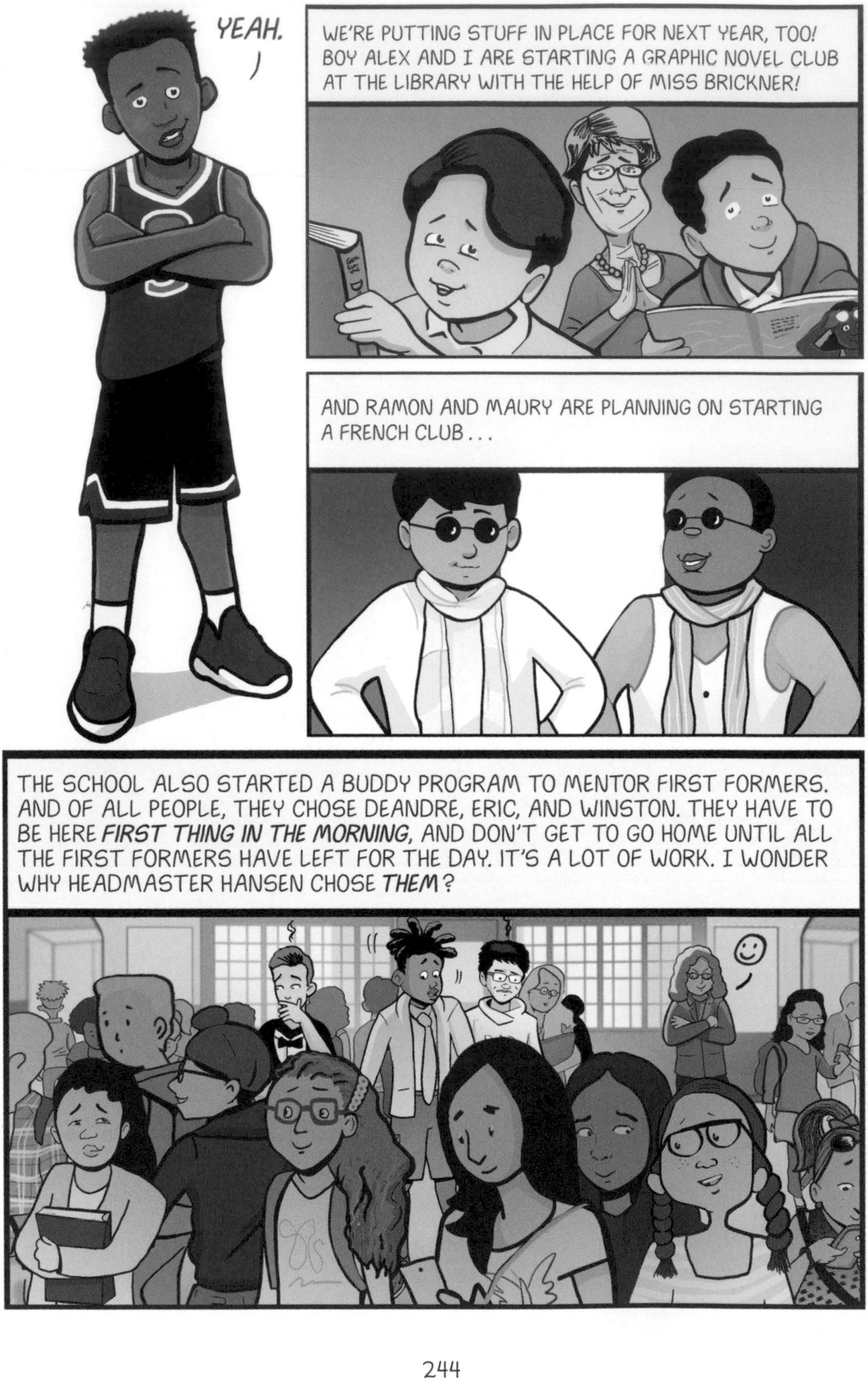
YEAH.
WE'RE PUTTING STUFF IN PLACE FOR NEXT YEAR, TOO! BOY ALEX AND I ARE STARTING A GRAPHIC NOVEL CLUB AT THE LIBRARY WITH THE HELP OF MISS BRICKNER!
AND RAMON AND MAURY ARE PLANNING ON STARTING A FRENCH CLUB . . .
THE SCHOOL ALSO STARTED A BUDDY PROGRAM TO MENTOR FIRST FORMERS. AND OF ALL PEOPLE, THEY CHOSE DEANDRE, ERIC, AND WINSTON. THEY HAVE TO BE HERE ***FIRST THING IN THE MORNING***, AND DON'T GET TO GO HOME UNTIL ALL THE FIRST FORMERS HAVE LEFT FOR THE DAY. IT'S A LOT OF WORK. I WONDER WHY HEADMASTER HANSEN CHOSE ***THEM***?

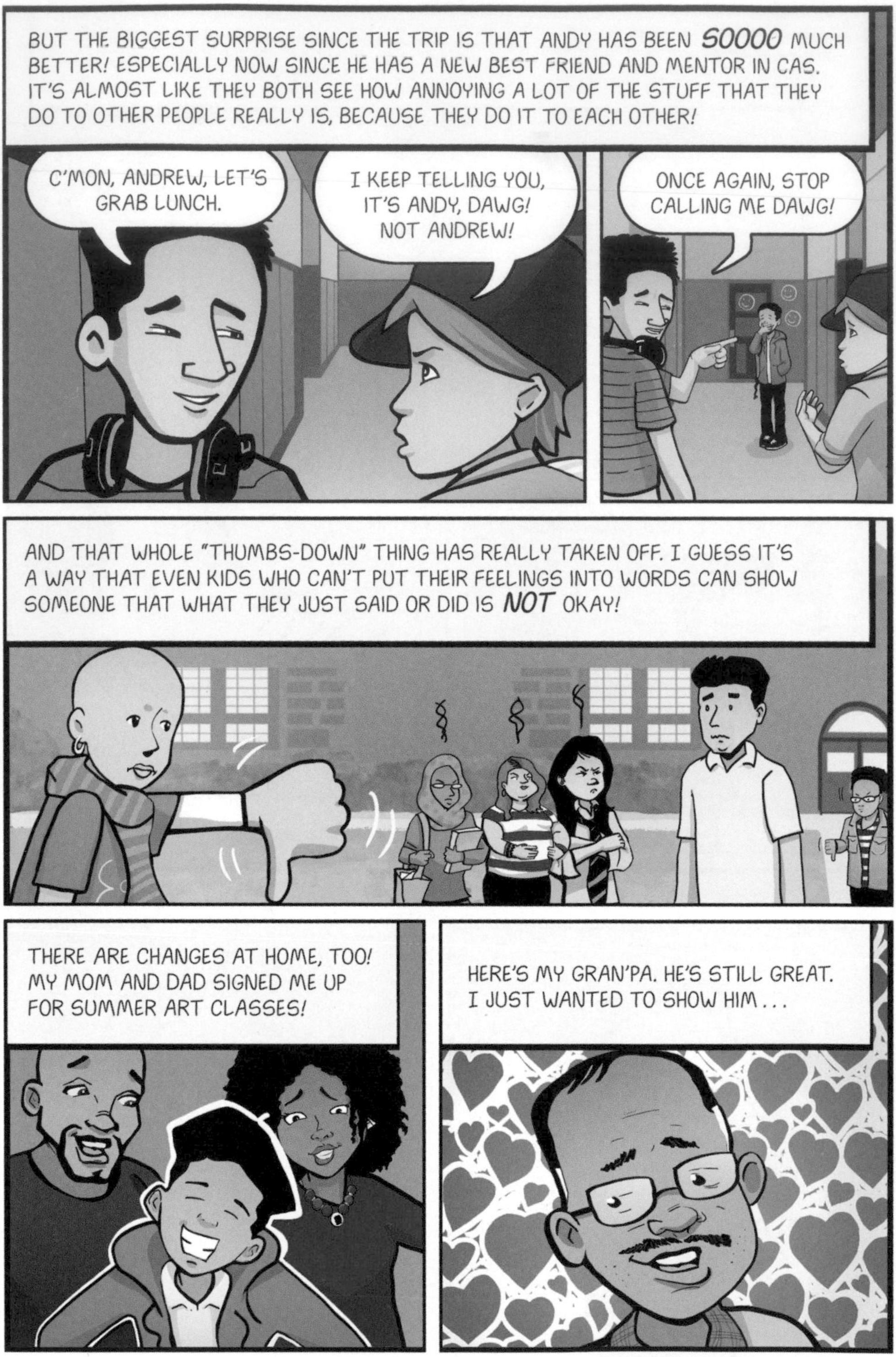

BUT THE BIGGEST SURPRISE SINCE THE TRIP IS THAT ANDY HAS BEEN SOOOO MUCH BETTER! ESPECIALLY NOW SINCE HE HAS A NEW BEST FRIEND AND MENTOR IN CAS. IT'S ALMOST LIKE THEY BOTH SEE HOW ANNOYING A LOT OF THE STUFF THAT THEY DO TO OTHER PEOPLE REALLY IS, BECAUSE THEY DO IT TO EACH OTHER!
C'MON, ANDREW, LET'S GRAB LUNCH.
I KEEP TELLING YOU, IT'S ANDY, DAWG! NOT ANDREW!
ONCE AGAIN, STOP CALLING ME DAWG!
AND THAT WHOLE "THUMBS-DOWN" THING HAS REALLY TAKEN OFF. I GUESS IT'S A WAY THAT EVEN KIDS WHO CAN'T PUT THEIR FEELINGS INTO WORDS CAN SHOW SOMEONE THAT WHAT THEY JUST SAID OR DID IS NOT OKAY!
THERE ARE CHANGES AT HOME, TOO! MY MOM AND DAD SIGNED ME UP FOR SUMMER ART CLASSES!
HERE'S MY GRAN'PA. HE'S STILL GREAT. I JUST WANTED TO SHOW HIM . . .

SPEAKING OF GRANDFATHERS, LIAM DECIDED TO GIVE HIS GRANDPARENTS A CHANCE...

AND KIRK AND THE REST OF MY FRIENDS FROM AROUND MY BLOCK ARE STILL THE BEST...

SO THERE YOU HAVE IT. I MAY HAVE STARTED AS THE "NEW KID," BUT WITH A LITTLE TALKING AND A LOT OF LISTENING, WE'RE ALL THE "NEW AND IMPROVED KIDS."

HERE, CAS...

OUR GOAL IS TO MAKE RIVERDALE ACADEMY DAY SCHOOL NOT JUST A PLACE *I* WANT TO COME BACK TO, BUT A PLACE WHERE EVERYONE WANTS TO COME BACK TO...

DON'T GET ME WRONG. IT'S NOT EASY. BUT NOW, WHENEVER THERE'S *DRAMA*, INSTEAD OF BEING *GHOSTS* WHO DISAPPEAR, WE TRY TO WORK IT OUT...

IT TAKES A LITTLE *GUTS* TO MAKE CHANGES. BUT WHEN WE ALL THINK ABOUT HOW MUCH BETTER OUR SCHOOL CAN BE...

THAT JUST MAKES US ALL...

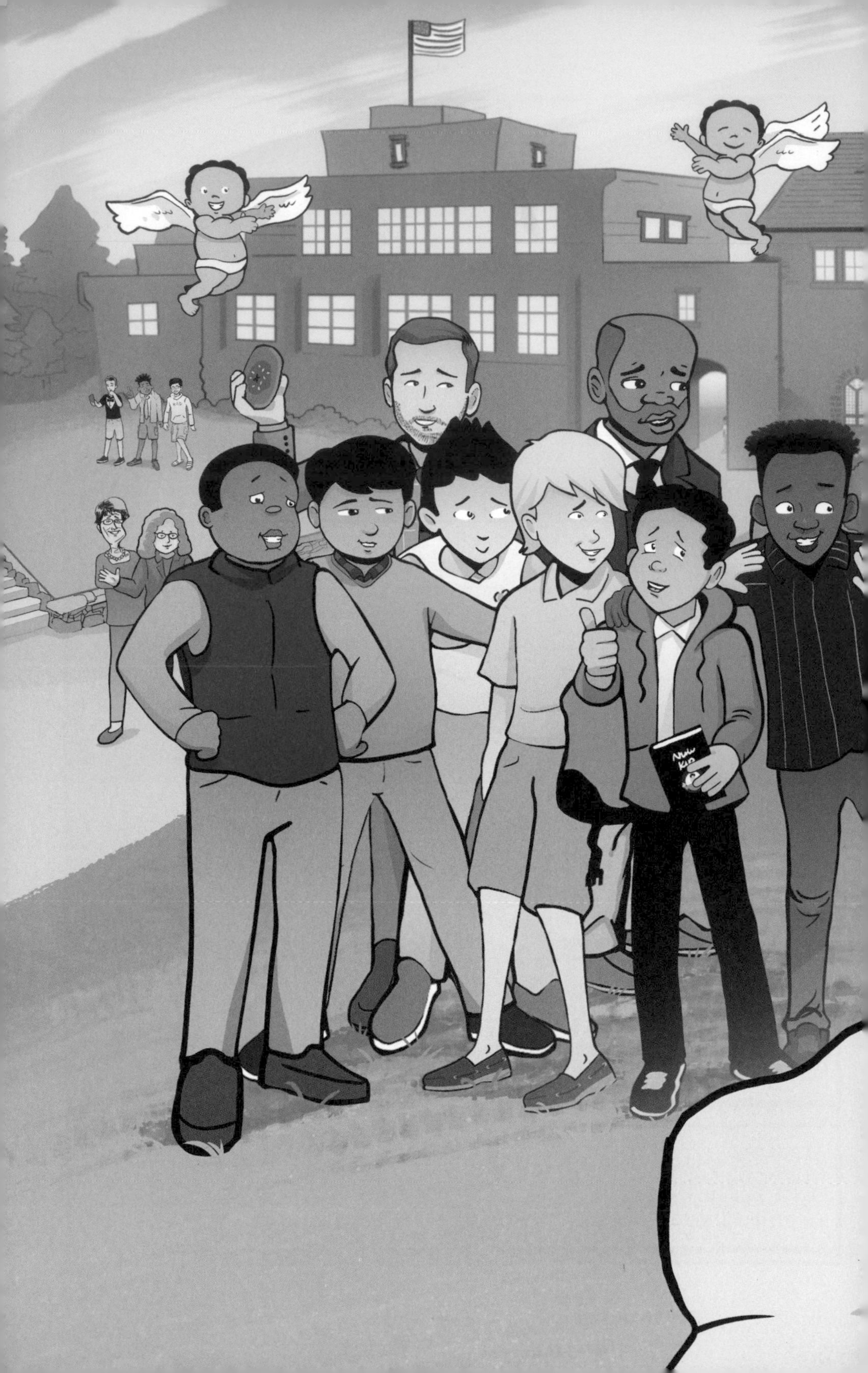

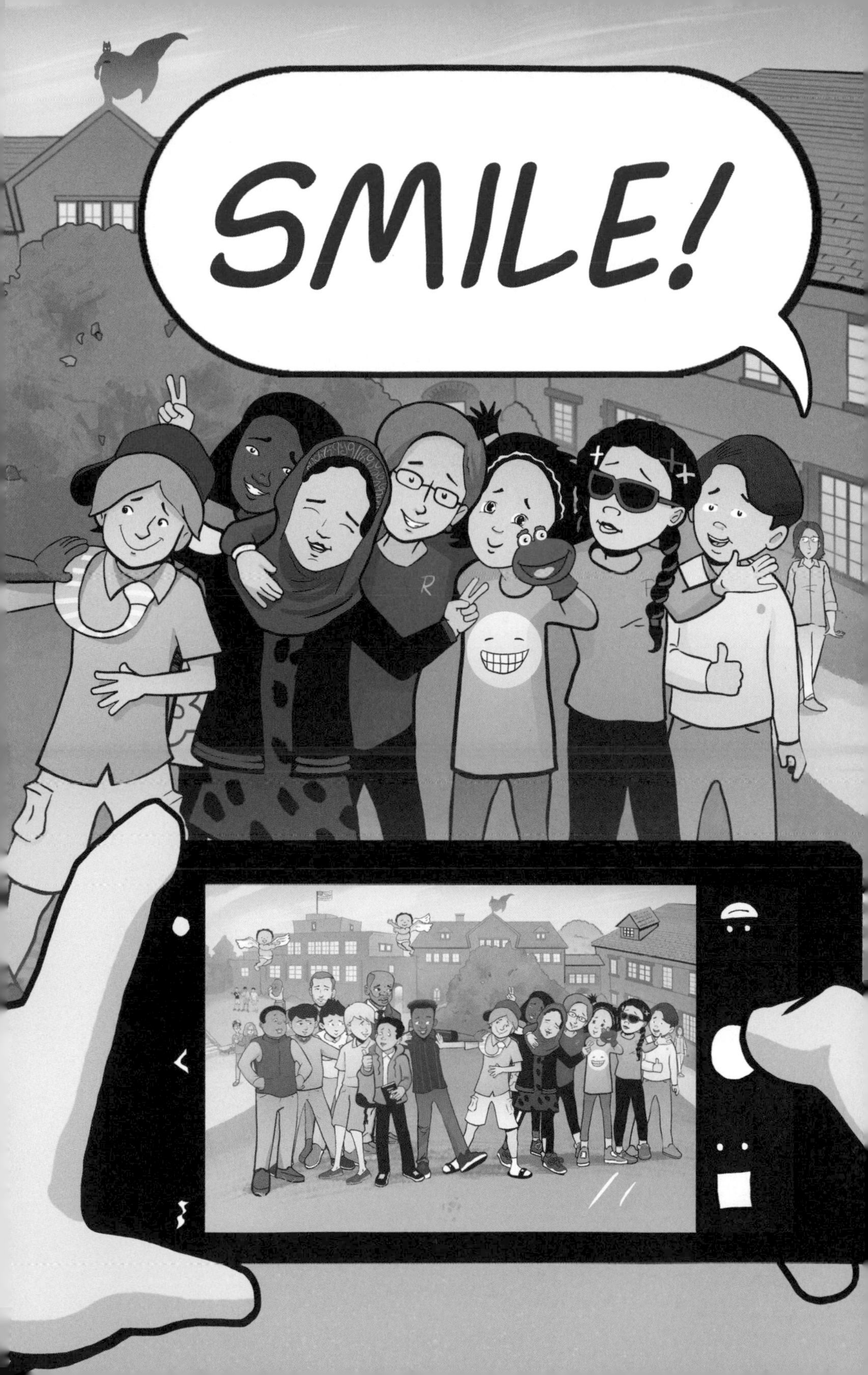
SMILE!

All I have ever wanted to do was to make the books that I wish I had when I was a kid. To show kids of color in new and positive ways. Like traveling to Paris! And that is why this book is so important to me. But there would be no *School Trip* without my first two books.

In January 2017, I signed with HarperCollins to do a graphic novel called *New Kid* and my life has never been the same. A mere three years later, it became the first graphic novel ever to win the John Newbery Medal for the most outstanding contribution to children's literature, the Kirkus Prize for Young Readers' Literature, and the Coretta Scott King Author Award for the most outstanding work by an African American writer.

In October 2020, *New Kid* was joined by its companion book, *Class Act*, which was welcomed with six starred reviews and quickly also became a #1 *New York Times* bestseller.
Since then, I have seen *New Kid* listed as one of the most influential children's books of all time, as well as one of the most banned and challenged. I have also seen my books read by fans all over the world as they have been translated into more than a dozen languages.

But I couldn't have done it without the support of some incredible people. Thank you to the supertalented Der-shing Helmer for bringing my colors to life! And to my art assistant, John-Raymond De Bard, for making my workload a little easier.

Thank you to Suzanne Murphy, Rosemary Brosnan, and my amazing team at Quill Tree Books.

A huge thank-you to my agent, Judy Hansen, who has stood with me from the very beginning to help bring *New Kid*, *Class Act*, and *School Trip* to life.

Thank you to my fans: The kids. The teachers. The librarians. The parents. The book groups. The reviewers. The bloggers. The publications. And the award committees who have shown my books so much love.

And last but not least, to my sons, Jay and Aren, for always supporting their dad. And to my wife, Denise, for keeping me company during my eighteen-hour workdays.